THE

HOP

ALSO BY DIANA CLARKE

Thin Girls

THE

HOP

A NOVEL

DIANA CLARKE

HARPER

An Imprint of HarperCollins*Publishers*

THE HOP. Copyright © 2022 by Diana Clarke. All rights reserved. Printed in the United States of America. No part of this book may be used or reproduced in any manner whatsoever without written permission except in the case of brief quotations embodied in critical articles and reviews. For information, address HarperCollins Publishers, 195 Broadway, New York, NY 10007.

HarperCollins books may be purchased for educational, business, or sales promotional use. For information, please email the Special Markets Department at SPsales@harpercollins.com.

FIRST EDITION

Library of Congress Cataloging-in-Publication Data has been applied for.

ISBN 978-0-06-308909-9

22 23 24 25 26   LSC   10 9 8 7 6 5 4 3 2 1

For mothers, mine and yours

ACT I

HOME

Since each of us was several there was already quite a crowd.

—Gilles Deleuze, *A Thousand Plateaus*

Lisa Hamilton

(FEATURES EDITOR, *VOGUE*)

Lady Lane is Marilyn Monroe. She's Brigitte Bardot. Farrah Fawcett. Cindy Crawford. Kim Kardashian. That glowing skin, the hair she can't seem to tame, the way she moves, smooth, like she's used to the world moving round her. Or like she knows exactly how to move around the world—like a liquid. Like she's always wet. Lady Lane *is* sex. It's so easy to erase girlhood from a woman like that; so hard to imagine Lady Lane as a kid, playing with a Barbie doll or cooking on an Easy-Bake oven, but every adult has been a child. Our youth is one of the only things we all have in common. For Lady Lane, though, it's something she's never talked about, not in any interview, feature, story. She talks about her life like it started the day she arrived at the Hop. She was our June 2017 cover, and when I asked her about her childhood, she said *Pass.* She said *Pass.* To *Vogue.* That girl will give you five graphic sex scenes before she tells you a single thing about her parents. It's like she just appeared one day, like she was born into the world beautiful and tall and of legal age.

There's talk of a multimillion-dollar book deal on the table for Lady Lane's biography, but no one can get her to agree to tell the whole story.

Lady Lane

(NÉE KATE BURNS, BUNNY, THE HOP)

I'll start from the beginning: I was named after the baby born just before me at Fenbrook Hospital. That's what Ma always told me. That a nurse had asked what she should write on my papers, and Ma hadn't thought of a name yet. No, she had, but the name she'd decided on was Lancôme, after her best-selling night cream, and now, free from the pregnancy haze, she was rethinking her decision. *What's that baby called?* Ma asked, pointing across the room at the couple whose baby's birth she'd witnessed just minutes before her own. They were crowded over their newborn, smiling down. The father was wearing a suit, and the mother had made it through labor with lipstick intact. They seemed like the kind of parents who would've come up with a sensible name, Ma decided, a name that would keep a kid safe in the world. *They named their little girl Kate,* is what the nurse said.

Kate. Ma tried it out. *I don't mind that.* And so I was Kate. Kate Burns.

. . .

My childhood was happy. I guess people think, because I've never talked about it, that I had a hard life. They imagine years of trauma and violence and abuse or something, but that's what they want to believe.

They were always going to make up their own stories about me, and I let them. I let them believe that I've wiped my childhood from my mind or buried it deep to keep from having to think about it, but that's not the truth. The real truth, the whole truth, is that I was a happy kid. I loved my ma.

I must've been called about that house upward of fifty times over a decade and a half. Teachers, neighbors, strangers, they all called to warn about Kate's mother's ways. I still know her address by heart, and that should tell you a little something about the kind of mother Merrill Burns was. But Kate really loved her. Some kids, you turn up and you just know their parents have bribed them into faking okay, but Kate really did seem okay. She was always smiling, always cheerful. Once I turned up and Kate answered the door and I asked where her mother was—this kid was probably five at the time—and she was clearly covering for Merrill. She took me by the hand and led me inside, into the kitchen, and pulled a seat back from the table. There were roaches in their house, I remember that. Scuttling around, as comfortable as if they were paying rent. Little five-year-old Kate goes, "Ma's just touching up her face, but please, let me get you a snack." She went to the cupboard, opened it, and said, "I'd like you to try my favorite cereal." And that's all that was in there. One single box of cereal. Kate poured some into a bowl and added water, like it was normal to eat cereal with water, and set the bowl in front of me. "Please," she said. "Enjoy." Merrill turned up a couple minutes later, came through the front door cursing like a sailor, and Kate goes, "Here she is! You finished powdering your nose, Ma?" As if this woman had been touching up her makeup outside on the driveway. She was a performer, that girl, could really turn it on, but I don't think her performance was covering any kind of abuse. I think Kate was a genuinely happy kid.

Lady Lane

(NÉE KATE BURNS)

She was doing the best she could, my ma was. If life's a bitch, then Ma was too; she refused to let our situation get us down. She worked three jobs, which gave us enough money to keep cereal in the cupboard, hot water in the shower, and acrylics on her fingers. You barely need anything to survive, and sure, I was always wanting this or that, some toy I saw on TV, but wants are not needs, and I wanted a lot but needed little. That's something Ma taught me when I told her I needed a puppy, an ice cream, a Barbie doll. *No, bunny,* is what she'd say. *You* want *a Barbie doll, you* need *to get the hell out of my face.*

· · ·

I didn't want a Barbie doll; I wanted the company. Ma was gone most of the time, so I raised myself and I did it alone, a solo parent. I spent a lot of time in front of the TV.

The Barbie commercials showed a doll come to life, plastic but person, talking with the child that kept her: *Barbie can walk! She can talk! She can play! Barbie can be your best friend!*

They laughed together, Barbie and girl; they went to school together, ate lunch together. How I wanted a tiny silicone friend to take with me. I dreamed about the day that, doll in hand, I'd never feel alone again.

What the commercial didn't tell was a fact I'd later learn at work:

Barbie is the descendant of a German toy called Lilli, the world's first doll with adult proportions. She was based on a comic strip, and in the story she made her living by seducing wealthy businessmen. The doll wasn't made for children, either, but for men to give one another as gag gifts at bachelor parties. She was also used to solicit sex. A man presented a woman he suspected might be working with a Lilli, and if she was in the industry, the woman would take them both. She's had a long career in curing loneliness, Barbie has.

. . .

We loved commercials, me and Ma did. Could recite hundreds off the cuff, no cues, no mistakes. We talked back to the TV. *Maybe it's Maybelline*, we sang. *L'Oréal, because you're worth it*, we whispered. And, *Da-da-da-da-da, I'm lovin' it.*

Commercials, is what Ma told me, *they invent want out of nothing.*

Not nothing. I wanted the Barbie, the plastic doll, the one who could talk, laugh, sing.

She said, *You don't want it, bunny, you just want to want it.* She had a philosophy: people are going to want no matter how much they have. Give a man a family, a good salary, a home, and he'll be pining after a boat, a lake house, a helicopter. Give a man a helicopter and he'll hope for an island. Give a man an island and he'll want to take over the world. It was better, Ma thought, to let your little wants lie.

So at the grocery store, coupons in hand, we'd stick to what the government subsidized, but when we passed each of our products, we'd exchange a look. A wink. In the soda aisle, we pointed at the red label we knew so well. *Taste the happiness*, I'd tell Ma, before reaching for the knockoff kind. *They're grrrreat!* she'd say in the breakfast aisle before taking the store-brand oats, half price. We didn't want the products, we wanted to want them.

I watched the other kids in the store wrestle with their parents. They tossed boxes into shopping carts, uninstructed. They could grab whatever they wanted. When they opened their refrigerators, it probably looked like a whole commercial break in there. I never tried to coerce Ma into a brand-name cereal boasting a toy at the bottom of the bag. I knew better. A plastic car that could transform into a robot? What use did I have for knickknacks?

Ma wanted things like a boob job, a car that didn't burp and break with every bump in the road, and a burger from the Wendy's down the street. Ma's wants could be bought, and we didn't have any money but, still, it must've been nice to know that *if.*

My wants were always different, more complicated, not easily solved by a lottery win or a payday. I was young. Stupid. When Ma asked me, each January, what I wanted from the year, I told her, *I just want you.* I wanted her to work less, be home more, read to me at night. I wanted my mother.

Me? she said. *Bunny, you've gotta aim higher. We need all the juju we can muster if we're gonna get a new car this year.*

I know, I said. *And I do want you to have a new car, Ma, but that's your want, not mine.*

Well, I want you, said Ma, pausing long enough to take a drag of her cigarette, long enough for me to look up, hopeful, *to wish for a new car.*

Right, I said, *a new car. Sunroof.* The best way to please Ma was to want what she wanted. A car, a new bathroom sink, a spray tan, and a celebrity for a daughter.

A sunroof, said Ma, pleased with my change of heart. *Or maybe one of those convertibles.*

Red. With a black fabric ceiling.

Imagine us, said Ma, smoke almost making thought bubbles above her head. *Driving down the coast, hair wrapped up in scarves.*

And I could see the scene playing out in her pupils, and for a moment, for as long as the scene itself, I *did* want what she wanted, something as simple as a car, a vacation, my hair tucked into a silk scarf. I said, *We'd wear little sepia sunglasses and pack sandwiches for the beach.*

We'd be called Mona and Flora.

We'd say "Oh my!" when a scarf flew off in the wind.

We'd wave to the boys with wiggling fingers.

We'd arrive at the beach windswept, rosy cheeked.
We're friends, aren't we, Ma? I said.
Friends? said Ma. *We're Mona and Flora.*
Are Mona and Flora friends?
Like Thelma and Louise, she said.

. . .

My other friend was Lacey. Lacey and I met at Fenbrook Primary School, five years old and already ousted, outsiders, because I was wearing my mother's lingerie top as a dress, and she wasn't wearing any shoes. All the popular girls were white and rich and called Courtney and Britney and Whitney. Lace was Maori, and she lived in a trailer.

They were cruel with wealth, those *-ney* girls. They wore clothes that fit, that matched, that were clean, that smelled of lavender and love. "Why is your dress see-through?" is what one said when I sat down to eat lunch at their table on the first day. They stood together, controlled by the same higher power, and they moved, like water, to the next table over.

"Hi," said Lacey, shoeless and hair so matted it looked like she had a rug draped over her head. She set her lunch on the table, my table. "I'm Lacey."

"That's a weird name," is what I told her.

"I'm named after my Dad's favorite sex actress."

I choked on my juice box. I hadn't said *sex* yet. "What?"

"My dad's favorite sex actress is Lacey Duvalle, and that's why I'm called Lacey."

"I'm Kate," I said. "Where are your shoes?"

"I don't like shoes," said Lacey.

I lifted my leg, showing her my sandal, pink and made of a cheap jelly plastic that moved with my foot.

"Well, I like *those* shoes," said Lacey. Her knotted black hair, grubby knees, too-big T-shirt with WALT'S PUB across the chest.

We were poor, me and Ma, but Lacey was *poor.* I was wearing my ma's lingerie top, but she'd also bought those new sandals especially for my first day. She packed my lunch box full to the brim with clearance candy, and Lacey didn't even have a backpack. It wasn't ideal for my social situation, befriending Lacey, but as Ma was always saying, you can't play hard to get if you're hard to want.

So I unbuckled a sandal and I said, "One each," and she took the shoe, and I think we both already knew we were forever.

Until I got to the Hop, I hadn't really made a friend since.

Lacey Kahu

(CHILDHOOD FRIEND OF KATE BURNS)

I told her not to go. I want that on record: I told Kate not to go to the Hop. I told her she was running away from her problems, and I told her she belonged back home with me. But she was a runner, Kate was. Always had been. Ran when things were bad, ran when things were good. Once she got an A on a Shakespeare paper. It was so good that our teacher read the first paragraph aloud to the class, but instead of being proud or taking the paper home to show her ma, get it stuck to the fridge or whatever, Kate stood up and told the teacher the paper was plagiarized. Told the class she'd stolen the whole thing from her older sister.

Well, Kate didn't have an older sister, and I'd watched her write the essay by hand that morning before school.

Kate walked up to the front of the room and grabbed her paper from Mr. Gilman, tore it to shreds and dropped it in the trash on her way out. She ditched the rest of the day.

She had a good thing going here, too. A job, boyfriend, house to call her own. But Kate talked herself into catastrophes, and once she felt like her world was falling apart, she crumbled it in her own hands. She didn't have an easy life here—no one's saying that. Her ma put her through some shit, but Kate never blamed her ma for anything.

Lady Lane

(NÉE KATE BURNS)

Yeah, I remember that day. Of course I do. Those things stick with a girl; ask any girl, and she'll tell you a memory just like it. Gilman called me back after class, and I thought he was going to give me a detention, but instead he goes, "It was a great essay, Cat."

"Kate," I said.

He gestured to a desk, and I sat.

"Of course," he said. "Kate. The way you explored the lust at work in *Twelfth Night* was—well, it's just surprising for such a young student to understand desire in that way."

He was too close, him standing, me sitting, his crotch at my eye level, his open fly staring.

"Thanks," I said. "Am I in trouble?"

"In trouble?" he said.

"For leaving?"

He set a hand on my knee.

"Mr. Gilman," I said. "I have to go home."

"You do understand desire, though, don't you?" he said. He had golden fillings. I remember that. They shone from the dark of his mouth like eyes in the night.

"I have to go," I said.

"A girl like you," he said. "You're going to have so many desirers. You're going to be desired by everyone." His slacks bulged at the crotch, and standing up meant pushing against him, feeling him, and he wheezed when I did.

"I really have to go," I said.

"It was a great essay, Kate," he said. I closed the classroom door behind me and cried the whole way home. I went to tell Ma but her door was locked, which meant she was entertaining.

· · ·

Ma's men—manfriends, is what she called them—they liked sports, but that was the only common denominator. She liked fat men, thin men, tall men, short men, trans men, cis men, hairy men, bald men, tattooed men, tidy men, bespectacled men, and men with 20/20 vision. She liked men carrying briefcases and men in construction hats and men with name badges pinned to their chests. Ma liked men called Kyle and men called Christopher and men called Kahurangi and men called Krishna and men called Cletus and men called Kang. She didn't have a type. Or, no, her type was *man*. They were all the same to her. Grout to fill a gap. They came over most nights, after dinner. They knocked a knock that meant I had to disappear.

During their visits, I learned to think. I learned to avoid thinking about one thing by thinking about everything else. *Go to your room, bunny*, is what Ma would say. And: Room. Roomy. Space. Saturn. Satin. Ball gown. Cinderella. How improbable that the glass slipper fit only her. Nearly fifty percent of women wear an 8. Ma and I both wore an 8, but 10s are always on sale, and if you stuff the toes with tissues, you can walk just fine.

· · ·

Go to your room, bunny, is what Ma would say when a manfriend arrived. Some of them would say hi to me, even give me a gift, a piece of candy or a grocery store cupcake, try to make some kind of impression, play daddy for the night, but I was under strict instructions: go to your room and stay there. *The only man you can trust is your manicurist*, Ma would say, tapping the tip of my nose with her acrylic.

She had a sound track, my ma, it followed her everywhere she went. The clackety-clack of plastic fingernails on any surface they could find, the hiss of hair spray escaping an aerosol, the whoosh of a lit match, the soft exhale of smoke.

In my room on manfriend nights, I'd turn on my television, a piece of shit we picked up from the curb that could never get a signal. I'd fiddle with the antenna until it found one of its two stations; a Chinese news show or a religious channel. I liked how the news was constant sound, indecipherable to me; I fell asleep to it each night. I liked the religious station, too, the way a man would pace his stage, palms raised to the ceiling. He'd say things like *Your life is exactly the way it is meant to be* and *Trust him and he will lead* and *God is always watching over you.*

I liked the preacher's words. I liked his confidence. I liked the way his shouting disguised the sound of skin on skin, sex, or violence or, more often than not, a combination of the two, leaking through the gaps in the house's joinery.

Ma, when she was done with the man of the evening, would drum on my door with her nails, clickety-clickety-click, our own little all clear. She'd push the door open and lean on the frame. *What're you watching that load of crap for?*

When I told her I liked it, that I liked hearing what God could do, that he was looking after me, she snorted. *You don't need God to look after you, bunny. You've got me.*

But can God really make sure everything's going to be okay?

No, said Ma, sitting on the foot of my bed, settling into the dip she'd made in the mattress over the years. She was never there to sing me to sleep, but most nights I'd wake to her snoring, her body curled around my feet like a faithful pet. *No, God's just another man we can't trust.*

Is he really a man in the sky?

He's a man and that's for sure, Ma said, lighting her somethingth cigarette of the day, turning away to exhale a cloud of smoke. *Only a man could fuck things up this bad.*

Ma loved men being in her bedroom and hated them being in the world.

. . .

While Ma scrubbed herself clean, I'd sometimes go out to find a man-friend sitting in front of the television, splayed on the couch, drinking one of our beers, watching a game. Sometimes they'd raise a hand in a wave. Sometimes they wanted to explain Bitcoin or the government or how liberal politics were ruining comedy. Most times they barely noticed me.

Once, a manfriend whistled low, and when I asked what was going on, he told me that a player had just been sold for $100 million. Ma and I hadn't been able to afford our $20 gas bill that month.

"Who bought him?" is what I asked, wondering if I, too, could be for sale.

. . .

I was already working. Ma had put me to work from the day I was born, and by the time I was a kid, I was a good earner. She'd take me to five-star hotels. Hiltons. Marriotts. She liked hotel chains' bars because the staff couldn't give a single shit about how much money you didn't spend, and she wanted people to assume she could afford a room in a place where she could barely afford a drink. She sat on a stool and did her best to look lonely, cradled a glass of water until some traveling businessman took the bait. Ma was beautiful—they always took the bait.

Another reason Ma liked hotel bars was because she could send me to the bathroom to pump lotion into palms and dry hands and offer tampons and curtsy for cash. She pinned a badge to my chest that read POLLY, which was my bathroom attendant name. She pinched my cheeks red and told me to smile big.

People were more generous in bathrooms than they were in other places. Panhandle on the footpath and they'd push past, too busy, or on the roadside they'd drive on, eyes averted. In public, it was easy for people to think that the two of us had nothing to do with one another. Or they wanted others to think that. But in the bathroom everyone was more vulnerable. We were confined. I'd just heard them pee. I'd heard the zip of their fly and the rustle of their underwear and, sometimes, if I was lucky, because this increased tips exponentially, the telltale tear of a tampon wrapper. Toilets are the great equalizer.

. . .

I took money from rich ladies in hotel lobby bathrooms, but I never stole. People always expect sex workers to have murky pasts, drugs and guns and a couple nights behind bars up their sleeves, but I never broke the law. I was *good*. I wanted to be good.

Ma didn't break the law either. She didn't like to steal; she liked to steal-adjacent. We couldn't take a pair of stilettos from a shop, but we could take the little stockings they'd given us to try the shoes on with. We couldn't take food from the shelves, but we could use a supermarket's restroom and pump hand soap into our purses. We never dipped on our bill at a restaurant, but we took every ketchup packet from the table. That kind of thing.

Once, we got nabbed by a mall cop for taking all the napkins from a Subway. The guy was on a Segway, and he had a cup of soda in one hand and a walkie-talkie in the other, one of those guys who takes the tiny amount of power he has in the world and lets it turn him into a dictator. He wheeled over to us and held up his hand, *Stop*, and he said, *A Sandwich Artist saw you steal those.*

And Ma goes, *A Sandwich Artist?*

From Subway, said Mall Cop. He sipped from his straw. He had a goatee.

They call those minimum-wage-earning teenagers Sandwich Artists?

Mall Cop rocked on his Segway. You have to keep them moving or you'll fall off. Like a bike. Or a life. *You took all their napkins*, he said.

Ma looked at me, then back at Mall Cop. *Are they not free?*

Mall Cop was sweating despite the building's polar air-conditioning. Condensation dripped from the bottom of his soda cup and onto the dirty tile. People walking past slowed to stare. I stared back.

My mistake, sir, Ma said. *I thought the napkins were free.*

They are free.

Ma looked at me, then back at Mall Cop. *I'm sorry,* she said. *But how do you steal something that's free? Do I steal from my kitchen faucet every time I pour a glass of water? Am I stealing oxygen right now, by breathing?*

Mall Cop hated himself by then. He rocked back and forth, back and forth. There was something in his goatee. Iceberg lettuce, I deduced, maybe from Subway.

You took every single napkin they had, ma'am.

I'm sorry, sir, said Ma. *I didn't see a napkin limit.*

He held out his hand for the napkins. Wavered a little on his Segway. Ma looked at me, then back at Mall Cop, then back at me. She winked. Then she bopped the bottom of the cop's soda cup and he wobbled and lost his footing and a wheel spun out from underneath him and he flung his soda into the air, pouring its contents down the front of his shirt, covering the word SECURITY in the sticky neon of Mountain Dew.

God damnit it to goddamn hell, said Mall Cop.

Oh, honey, said Ma. *Here,* she said, taking a wad of napkins from her purse. *Take these,* she said.

We weren't thieves, is what Ma promised me. We were *opportunists.* We were taking what was offered.

It's strange, thinking back, thinking that we couldn't afford a pack of napkins, and now, I mean, now I can afford . . . but I'm getting ahead of myself.

• • •

We weren't meant to be poor. This is something Ma knew to be true. She knew that girls like us were made to be millionaires and it was just a matter of time until money came our way. She had plans, too: I was going to be famous. This is something Ma truly, truly believed.

She loved the stars. She loved all of them, but she especially loved Billy Bob Thornton. She called him her boyfriend, back when she wasn't dead. *There's my boyfriend*, she'd say as she flipped through channels. It's how she watched television, one show after another, never more than a moment on each. The surfing formed its own station after a while, sentence fragments strung together to make sense. *Get in quick to . . . an accident? Call . . . you never loved me, Reginald . . . if you're having heart problems . . . we won by two . . . shootings in Denver, Colorado . . . 5.99 a month . . . symptoms include death.* Ma would stop switching channels for only a handful of reasons: she'd fallen asleep, an antiaging infomercial, or Billy Bob Thornton. *He's not all looks either, bunny*, she'd tell me every time he showed up in our living room. Then she'd explain his method acting. The way he, for *Sling Blade*, filled his shoes with crushed glass, hoping to perfect his character's limp. Billy Bob Thornton didn't want to perform his character, Ma told me, he wanted to become his character.

He got an Oscar for that, bunny, Ma said, every time. *That's what hard work gets you in the end. Just another too-small man with a too-small dick. You could get you an Oscar if you wanted, bunny*, she said. She always thought I was born to be famous. *And an Oscar's the only kind of man you need. Got it?*

Ma thought of celebrities as compilations of every role they'd ever done. She didn't believe they were human, thought they were bigger than that, bigger than a single life. What Ma loved was narrative, the plots, the hair and makeup, the set, the roles that could've been played by almost anyone, be it Julia Roberts, Julia Stiles, Julie Andrews, see, what Ma really loved was story, fiction, she loved the ideas of people, imaginary characters doing imaginary things. Ma loved performance and rejected reality as if the two were separate things.

Lacey Kahu

Her ma's head was in the sky. Way, way up there. She had this fixation on Kate becoming famous—as if that was a viable dream for a scruffy little white girl from Podunk, New Zealand, with teeth that bucked like a rabbit's and barely a dollar to her name. But Kate's ma talked about fame like it was just a matter of time. She'd say, *We'll get ourselves a housekeeper once you're famous*, and *We won't have to worry about affording utilities once the world knows your name.*

She was always teaching Kate these impressions, and Kate was good, don't get me wrong, but a decent Danny DeVito isn't going to get you noticed, and Kate's ma didn't really do anything to make fame happen. She just *knew* that celebrity would fall into their laps.

Kate never seemed to want fame for herself, though. I'd always ask her what she wanted, what would make *her* happy, and she would shrug. Her ma's dreams were so big, it was like there was no room left for her own.

Lady Lane

(NÉE KATE BURNS)

America was Ma's idea. *America, bunny,* is what she said as she waxed her crotch using an old washcloth torn to shreds. *Ouch, fuck,* she said, tearing away a strip to reveal bare skin, sore and pink as raw meat. *That's where we belong, bunny. That's where the stars live.*

She had big dreams before she got pregnant with me, and she liked to remind me that I was, first and foremost, an interruption. I kept her from getting famous. She was going to be an actress, a star, and then I arrived and, like a tickle in her throat, I just wouldn't leave, kept growing, kept growing her, and she had to stop going to auditions as her body grew and grew and she had to give up what little she had just to keep me alive and then she was too old, she told me, too wrinkled to be in the spotlight, but me? It was my birthright, my responsibility, to live out her fantasies. Just as soon as we could fix my teeth.

We can't afford flights to America, I said.

We'll sell this dump of a house.

We can't sell the house.

Why not? Ouch, fuck.

Where will we live?

In America!

She stood in front of me and gestured to her groin. She'd made a little upturned triangle, an arrow. *Is it even?*

It wasn't. I pointed to where she needed to level out the hairline.

Once we're in America, you'll be famous in no time, she told me. *Ouch, fuck. Once we're in the right place, you'll be a star, bunny.*

All Kate ever wanted was to feel good enough for Ma, but Merrill saw her daughter as a way to climb the rungs of the world's social ladder. Merrill could see what she was working with: this beautiful, talented kid of hers, and that's how she thought of Kate, too, as *hers*, to own, to use, to exploit. Don't get me wrong, Ma loved Kate. She did. But loving someone doesn't mean you're treating them right. I know that better than anyone.

Lady Lane

(NÉE KATE BURNS)

Before she got sick, Ma cleaned on weekends. Put on some manfriend's old T-shirt and latex gloves and tied her hair up in a loop atop her head. It was the only time she went out without makeup on, her cleaning days. When she caught the flu, when she got dumped, when she got a demotion, when we both had the chicken pox, when there was an earthquake that shook the whole country, even when she was diagnosed with cancer, she uncapped her favorite shade, Miss Scarlet, and crayoned her lips in. If Ma's mouth wasn't red, she was either cleaning or she was dead.

She only cleaned for one family: the Hobbes, who owned the department store she worked at on weekdays. They had a twelve-bedroom mansion on the North Shore with an indoor pool and a basketball court and a patio whose lip pouted out over the ocean. Once I asked Ma if it was embarrassing, cleaning her boss's house.

Nothing embarrassing about hard work, bunny, she told me as she struck a match to light her cigarette. She didn't like lighters—something about the drama of a matchstick flickering aflame. *Plus, these people live like there's a plague. It's spotless already. I usually just walk into a room with a vacuum and a duster, count to a hundred, and leave again. Sometimes I think that just by going in there I make it dirtier.*

Some days I asked to go with her. I'd help clean, I insisted, but I mostly wanted to know if the rumors were true. If they really had a life-size replica of Michelangelo's *David* in their foyer. She always shook her head. *The grass is always greener, bunny*, she said. *Sometimes it's better not to know how green someone's grass can get. Sometimes we're better off not knowing just how brown our own grass is.*

On the days she wasn't cleaning, she worked the beauty counter at Hobbes, the biggest department store in Auckland. She had the best sales in the cosmetics department, but she was never rewarded for it. Minimum wage, no benefits, no bonuses, she stuck with the job anyway. She was a high school dropout, and if she asked for a promotion, they'd just hire the next girl in line. And anyway, she got all expired makeup half off, and sometimes she nicked the samples brought in by cosmetic reps and we did makeover nights on Sundays.

Back when I was stupid and young, I asked her why she had to have two jobs while some girls' mothers had no jobs at all.

Gotta save up, bunny, she told me, *gotta save up for your new set of teeth.*

. . .

I was a pretty kid. I knew that. Grandmas told me at bus stops and strangers stopped us in the streets to admire my face and shopkeepers gave me an extra stick of gum with a wink, and they'd say something like *You're going to be a heartbreaker, sweetheart.*

I was pretty until I opened my mouth. In there, though, I had two long front teeth like a rabbit, a beaver, like a freak, and when I smiled, people's eyes changed.

People look at pretty things and feel happier—it's something chemical. They call it being *attractive* because beauty attracts your attention and you can't look away. Looking at a beautiful person makes you feel in love. But ugly people? People prefer not to look at ugly people at all. I was both at once. I felt every onlooker fall in love with me and wish me gone in the same sentence, the hinge being the moment I opened my mouth.

You seen those American movie stars? is what Ma said. *They've got white picket fences in their mouths. They've got piano keys, hold the flats and sharps. They've got teeth straighter and whiter than the whole cast of* Friends. *They're realtor teeth, bunny. Flight attendant teeth. Infomercial teeth. We gotta get rid of those bunny teeth and get you some movie teeth if you're ever gonna be a star.*

The other girls at school, their mothers were boring. They'd stopped wearing makeup, started wearing beige sweaters. They made sandwiches for their kids' lunches and went off to their boring jobs behind boring desks, plugging numbers into computers, shuffling papers and frowning. They wore pants. They wore sensible shoes, which means ugly shoes. They wanted their daughters to grow up to be mothers, to be lawyers, doctors, accountants. My ma only ever wanted me to be a star.

My ma wore skintight pencil skirts and bright blouses unbuttoned to her cleavage. She never left the house without her hyphen of red across her lips and a black frame around each eye. Her hair was platinum blond, and she dyed it herself over the kitchen sink, humming "Billie Jean" and saying, *Smell that, bunny?* She meant the bleach, gestured to the air. *That's the smell of youth. Inhale it, bunny, stay young forever.*

. . .

She died at fifty-five. Breast cancer. We're not there yet, we have a bunch of healthy years to cover before we get there. But it's worth a warning: she died, and it wasn't a quick and painless death. It was long and slow and she was hurting the whole time. When she got her diagnosis, she said, *I'll let it kill me before I'll let you take my girls.* She meant her tits.

Lacey Kahu

Her ma got sick. Breast cancer. And that's when we started the Sugar Club.

Lady Lane

(NÉE KATE BURNS)

No, we'd already started the Sugar Club long before Ma got sick. Lacey and I would sit at the back of our local convenience store, the magazine section, and educate ourselves. We never bought anything, but the owner of the store didn't mind because we stopped the boys from tucking issues of *Brazzers* into their backpacks while he was on the phone shouting at every family member he had. I think he liked our company too. Sometimes he'd call, from one side of the store to the other, "You two doing okay back there?" Sometimes he'd give us his expired sodas and Popsicles scarred with freezer burn. We didn't cause him any trouble, we just wanted to read.

See, at school, teachers rambled on at us about algebra and trigonometry, physics and novels that were written a hundred years ago. Some girls might need to know that stuff: $e = mc^2$, pi, scarcity principles, the conditional tense. Those girls would go to university and major in something that would lead them behind a desk to battle their office patriarchy for eighty thousand bucks a year, but girls like us, like me and Lacey, the daughters of a beauty-counter-salesperson-cum-housecleaner and a couple who'd been on unemployment for a decade, respectively, we needed different skills. We learned from *Cosmo* and *Elle* and sure, even *Brazzers*.

Lacey Kahu

We were poor, sick of being poor, and we found a way to make some cash. Some kids tutored other kids; the ones who were good at history taught the ones who were bad at history for twenty bucks an hour. Some kids, the kids who had the means, sold drugs or crushed up allergy pills they pretended were drugs. Kate and I weren't good at history and we didn't have drugs, but what we did have? Bodies.

Lady Lane

(NÉE KATE BURNS)

Lacey's gonna tell you that we needed the money, but that's not how the Club came about.

There's a specific time in any girl's life when she realizes that she is either being watched or she isn't, but other girls are. The first time you follow a man's gaze to the ass of some passerby in heels, or the time you realize that the object that a man is staring at so intently is yourself. For me, 2009. I was sixteen. The boys had started to watch the girls at school, but they didn't watch Lacey and they didn't watch me. We were poor and we weren't desirable and we got tired of existing in the margins. We sat at the back of every class and saw how boys chased the girls who had curled hair and lip gloss. The way they tugged on those girls' ponytails and screwed up little balls of paper to toss across the room in the hopes of earning a scowl or a middle finger.

Lacey pinched her sides and said, "It's because they're so skinny around the middle."

"It's because they've got nice teeth," I said, running the pad of my thumb over mine.

"It's because they're rich."

"It's because their parents love them."

The loneliest thing in the world might be watching someone else be wanted.

We were yet to learn how to perform for the eye of a man.

. . .

I had a crush on Oliver van Ness. He played rugby and wore checker-board Vans and dyed the tips of his hair white-blond and stuck it up all spiky, and once I'd seen him scoop a spider off the sidewalk outside of school and deliver it safely to a hedge. That was the kind of security I was looking for in a partner.

One day, after physics, he stuck his finger in Whitney Hughes's ear as she put her books in her backpack. Lacey knew about my crush because she knew everything about me and she went, "Why don't you two just make out and get it over with."

Whitney scoffed and zipped her bag.

"Come on, Lace," I said, trying to drag her out of the room.

"Why don't *you* make out with him?" Whitney said to Lacey.

"I wouldn't even do it for twenty bucks," said Lacey.

"No?" said Oliver, then he turned to me. "Would you?"

My face flushed and I swallowed and Lacey held my hand in hers and she said, "It's going to cost you more than twenty bucks."

Oliver took out his wallet.

. . .

Ma and I did Make-Out Mondays. We played famous movie kisses and ranked them out of ten. *Never Been Kissed?* Eight out of ten; points for location, duration, and anticipation, points lost for making Drew Barrymore cry first and having an audience of high school students. *The Notebook?* Six out of ten; points for hotness of both parties, points lost for the bad weather.

I'd never kissed a boy before, and I'd always feared, watching those perfect movie kisses, that my buckteeth would get in the way, but sometimes you just have to get things over with, so I took the fifty from Oliver and I passed it to Lacey to keep my hands free enough to run through his hair. He held my waist.

"God," said Whitney. "Are you two about to fuck or something?"

Oliver's lips were soft, and his breath tasted of oranges, and the whole interaction was gentler than I would've liked, a whisper I couldn't quite make out. My teeth? I barely noticed them. Oliver's mouth fit perfectly with mine. Afterward, he stepped back and blinked and touched his lip, and he looked at me like, *What the hell just happened*, and I won't ever forget the way his eyes shone with something new, something sparkly and dirty, hungry and afraid and excited all at once; that's what desire looks like.

Lacey applauded, and I took the fifty and tucked it into my bra. When I got home, I told Ma about it, my first kiss, but I didn't tell her about the transaction, and I told her he'd asked me to be his girlfriend afterward but I'd said no. She high-fived me and said, *Attagirl, bunny. Ladies like us don't need to be tied down unless it's with leather straps and we asked for it.* I kept the bill, Oliver's fifty, in my pillowcase.

• • •

After that, the Sugar Club's business model was simple: we gave lessons for cash. Kissing lessons, flirting lessons, touching lessons. Our peers could pay an even twenty for a ten-minute make-out tutorial. From the lean-in, to the peck, the opening of the mouth, the slow introduction of the tongue. We offered an idiotproof step-by-step with a money-back guarantee upon complaint.

For the flirting-challenged, we charged twenty-five and spent the evening texting back and forth with the client, correcting missteps, guiding conversation. After the session, clients only had to replicate the conversation with their crush. They'd sometimes ask, *Can't you just send the texts for me?* But we were running a moral business and our ethical code was strict, and we shook our heads with the firm resolution of the kinds of kids who didn't have bills to pay. Teach a man to flirt, and all that.

Touching lessons were our most lucrative endeavor. For a hundred bucks, we'd guide their trembling teenage hands. Deal a smooth, sharp slap of the wrist if they went straight for the chest. *No*, we'd say. *Slower.*

We taught them how to start with the face, the hair, the nape of the neck, *that's it*, now work downward, slowly, *slower!* The arms, waist, lower back, now you can slowly, *I said slowly*, work your way across the butt, squeeze, if that's what you're into, and only then, never before, could they snake their fingers up, under the shirt, *one at a time please*, we'd teach them to brush the pad of their thumb over a nipple to get it to pay attention. We taught them not to chew gum while they kissed. We taught them to keep their teeth to themselves.

Sometimes a guy would get too confident, try the button of our jeans, maybe force our fingers over his crotch or start on his belt buckle, but Lacey and I each kept a can of travel-sized hair spray in our back pockets for this very occasion, and we'd spray their eyes until they screamed a surrender.

Kids called us *slut* and *whore* and *hooker* and *ho*, and the ones who called us those names were usually the ones requesting Sugar Club appointments the very next day.

• • •

Oliver van Ness kept coming back for more, but I stopped charging him and I didn't tell Lacey. He was hot and he didn't have any acne and he looked like a man, tall, shoulders. He had hair on his face. He told me I was pretty in the dark of the janitor's closet. He told me I was smart. I might have loved him, or at least I thought I did. I was a love hypochondriac in those days; I always thought it was the real deal or I wanted to think it was. I'd seen the transaction of desire in the movies: men buying women drinks, buying them houses, buying their hand. The only difference I could see between those movie girls and me was the presence of want; the men were paying for a reciprocated desire. And so I decided to want. I wanted every zit-studded kid who came through the Sugar Club's doors. The kid who held the back of my head as we made out. The one who kissed my knuckles at the end of our appointment. I called it all love and I made myself daydream whole futures with those boys until the next one came along. But Oliver van Ness was the person

I thought about even while someone else's tongue was in my mouth. He was the one in my imagined scenarios deep in the middle of the night.

He was dating Whitney Hughes by now. Whitney Hughes, who used *vacation* as a verb and who vacationed in France and Japan, who wore pearls, real ones, and who kept a tin of scented gel pens on her desk and switched out the color for every word. Whitney Hughes, who had perfect, straight white teeth, not a single digit out of line. Once she'd flung a thong at me, *since you can't seem to keep yours on*. She didn't know that I was kissing her boyfriend in private, and I didn't want her to know. I liked being Oliver's secret. Sometimes he'd catch my eye in class and we'd smile and I knew that was our little code. It meant that even though he couldn't talk to me in the hall, or take me on a date, or ask me to a dance, we were still special to one another. The secret made it even more special, I thought.

. . .

One day, at lunch, I let Oliver van Ness lift my skirt, shift my underwear to the side. I let him press me up against the gardener's shed, and I barely felt the splinters break my skin. He told me he liked me. That he'd always had a crush on me. "You're gorgeous," he said. "You're the most beautiful girl in school." I knew he was lying, and I believed him anyway. This was something I did all the time. When Ma told me that a manfriend was just an old friend she needed some alone time with, to catch up, reminisce. When Santa went to every kid's house but mine. I believed Ma and I believed in Santa and I believed Oliver van Ness when he said I was the most beautiful girl in school.

He still kissed like a wind chime—too light to the touch. But I liked his face, I liked his letterman jacket, and I liked the way I could hear his friends calling for him somewhere out on the rugby field. They wanted him, but I had him. Popularity was a currency more coveted than cash, even for me, and I let him take my virginity behind that tumbledown shed, and afterward, afterward, the way he looked at me, I thought he might ask me to go to the dance with him. He didn't. He asked Whitney Hughes, who wore Calvin Klein and hired a limo. It felt like a tragedy until I felt tragedy.

• • •

This wasn't the story I'd tell guests at the Hop, by the way. When any guest asked, and many of them did, about my virginity, expecting brutality, expecting that, given my line of work, I had to be some sort of fucked-up about sex, I gave them what they wanted. I'd tell them about a stepfather or a teacher or a drink spiked at a high school house party. My tiny teenage trauma wasn't enough to satisfy them, see, they wanted to be right about rape. So when I told them whichever sordid tale of the day, they would nod and nod with a great satisfaction. *I knew it*, their pitying looks said, while their mouths stayed shut tight. Guests at the Hop liked us Bunnies to fit the mold they'd dreamed up for us. Or maybe they liked to know they were treating us better than someone else once had. Or maybe men just like a tortured woman. It doesn't matter, anyway, we're not up to that part of the story, yet. Where was I?

• • •

The next day, the whole school knew that Oliver van Ness had received a different kind of lesson than what Lacey and I usually advertised. My phone blew up. *How much for the van Ness special?* said everyone.

Lacey was furious. She said, "We're not hookers, Kate. Jesus Christ, have some dignity."

"I know."

"The Sugar Club's a classy establishment. You can't go around boning clients. How much did you make him pay?"

"I didn't."

"You what?"

"I didn't make him pay."

"Jesus, Kate," she said. She was walking in tiny circles. "Jesus Christ, Kate. What were you—"

"Can we drop it?"

"You'd better go back there and get some money out of him for it. This is business, Kate. Text him."

"It's not business this time," I said. "He loves me."

"He loves you?"

"We're in love."

"You're not in love. He's dating Whitney Hughes."

"But he's *in love* with *me*."

"He told you that to get out of paying for a session."

"No," I said. "No."

"It's not real," Lacey said. "He played you."

"He wouldn't."

"He did."

"He wouldn't."

"The whole school knows, Kate. Who do you think told them? He played you."

My cheek was sore from the splinters that had stuck there yesterday. My throat was sore from all the hurt welling up inside. "He played me?"

Lacey took my hands in hers. Squeezed them. She said, "He played you. Now you need to get yourself paid."

I couldn't. When the school was alight with the rumor, I checked my phone, kept checking my phone, for the message from Oliver, the apology that would tell me how sorry he was for accidentally letting the secret slip to a friend. I hadn't yet learned not to expect regret from the men who wronged me. The message, of course, never came. "I can't," I told Lacey.

"What?"

"I can't."

"Kate!"

The shame ebbed, and anger swelled in its place. "I said no."

"This is my business too. You're cheating me here too."

I snapped. "I make twice as much as you, and we split profits down the middle. You're welcome. Now can we just drop it?"

Lacey looked hurt. I'd meant it to hurt. But I also immediately wanted to take it back. I wanted to harm her as quick as a stepped-on pin or a bee sting to the palm. But that's not how it works. When a human hurts another human, the pain lasts longer than the pinch.

"Right," said Lacey. "Okay."

"I didn't mean—"

"I mean, you're not wrong," said Lacey. There were tears in her eyes. "You do make more than me."

I did. We both knew it. When kids requested appointments with us via scraps of paper tucked into our lockers, a gross number of them said, in listing their preference of service provider, *The white girl*, or *Not the brown one*. Lacey and I never talked about it. I didn't think she'd want to. After all, what did I know about race? I was white.

"Maybe you *should* be getting a higher cut," she said.

"I don't want a higher—" And I didn't. It was easy to forget that Lacey was poor, since she was always wearing all the crap we bought with our profits. Juicy Couture sweatsuits, designer shoes on clearance, a thousand rings stacked on each finger. She wore a full face of makeup and hung huge golden hoops from her ears. She didn't look poor. But her family didn't have a real house. They didn't have a car. They lived off a weekly visit to the food bank and the half-smoked cigarettes of other smokers who could afford to waste a millimeter of nicotine.

"Why did you bring it up, then?"

"I didn't, I don't. Listen, Lace. I just wanted to get you off my back about Oliver van Ness is all, okay? Just let me have this one. Just this one time."

She frowned.

"I just don't want my virginity to have been paid for," I said. "That's all."

She softened. "This *one* time."

"This one time."

Then, she asked, "So how was it?"

"How was what?"

"You know," she said. "The sex."

I told her everything. How he'd pressed his thumb inside me, how his fingernail had a snag that kept catching, scratching, how he'd spun me around and pressed my cheek to the wall of the woodshop, how I'd heard him spit in his hand before rubbing the saliva on himself for lubrication. How, when he pushed into me, it felt like trying to stuff a sleeping bag into its sack, that it couldn't possibly fit, until it did.

"Did it hurt?"

It had hurt, but not like falling over hurts. Not like scraping a knee or stubbing a toe. Not like the sting of a swift slap across the face from one of Ma's manfriends. It was an ache you could breathe into, I'd told Lacey, like a stretch.

"So sex is yoga," she said. We laughed, and all was forgiven.

Lacey Kahu

Kate had her logic. I got it. She said, "I just don't want my virginity to have been paid for," and what she didn't realize was that because Oliver didn't pay for it, Kate did. She fell for him hard, and he was never going to love her back, because Oliver van Ness's parents had a boat and Kate's ma worked a beauty counter. Getting those boys to pay us was a way to make up for the socioeconomic difference between client and provider. It was a levelling of power. What Kate didn't understand was that the moment she stopped charging Oliver, she started paying for those sessions herself.

Anyway, we agreed that the Oliver thing was a mistake and that we would release a PSA to the students of Fenbrook High. No sex. Kissing, flirting, and touching only, and that was final. We posted a notice on the school's bulletin board. We weren't discreet about our business. The teachers knew exactly what we were doing. Some teachers even came to visit us. We charged them double.

Christopher Maloy
(PRINCIPAL, FENBROOK HIGH SCHOOL)

Of course none of the faculty knew about a scheme like that. What kind of school do you think I'm running? If we'd known about some amateur brothel being run in our supply closet, we would have shut it down and expelled those responsible immediately. Immediately.

Lady Lane

(NÉE KATE BURNS)

Sitting at the back of Clark's Convenience, reading the new issue of *Cosmo* on the first day of every month, we went by our own syllabus. Learned about chlamydia and syphilis and herpes and crabs. We learned about UTIs and birth control. We learned about blow jobs and fetishes and positions that seemed logistically impossible until we tried them, Lacey in a handstand against the back wall of the store, me lifting her by the waist, her wrapping her arms around my legs, we wove our bodies into each position, just to see if we could. We took quizzes, the best sex position for your star sign, which porn star are you most compatible with, what's your hooker name. Here's how you find out: take the name of your first pet and the name of the street you grew up on. Mine: Lady Lane.

• • •

Lady was a standard poodle we'd found on the side of the road. We got a lot of stuff from the side of the road. Our couch, its cushions already smiling from the weight of a generation of asses; Ma made me load it into the trunk and walk beside the car as she drove, holding the back end to make sure it didn't slip out on the slow commute back home. Our TV, which had a crack in the corner that sometimes, if they stood in just the right place, made actors look like they had a stick up their butts. Our table, wobbly but easily corrected with a wadded tissue or a sock folded under the back-left leg. Our neighbors loved putting things outside, and Ma wasted no time picking up their old shit and calling it ours.

Lady was another curb-side find. She was covered in mange, flea-ridden, eyes sealed shut with gunk. She was on the side of the highway, a gravel inlet made for people with cops on their tail to pull off the road, pacing back and forth like she was waiting for someone.

We were on our way home from school, and Ma pulled over so fast I got whiplash.

Look, said Ma.

She'd never been a dog person, never been an animal person, so I didn't know what we were looking at. *What?*

I think that's a poodle, bunny.

Okay?

A French poodle.

Ma crouched, arm outstretched, crept toward the dog. The poodle looked at her like, *What the hell are you doing*, and Ma said *Here, girl, here, girl*. The dog sat down, unimpressed by Ma's little routine, and gave one low growl. *Come with us, girl*, Ma said, and the dog didn't have to be told twice. She jumped into the back seat as if she'd been riding in cars her whole life. She sniffed the upholstery, turned around, settled down, and began to snore.

Why are we picking her up?

Look at her, bunny. She might be a purebred.

She was, too. She was pretty once we got her cleaned up, groomed, her nails clipped down and her feet trimmed into poofs. *This is a rich girl's dog*, is what Ma said. *This is the dog equivalent of a string of pearls, bunny. A dog for a lady.*

The dog, curled beside the hearth, looked up.

You like that, girl? Ma said. *You like the name Lady?*

The dog yawned.

Well then, Ma said. *Lady it is.*

· · ·

She loved that dog, Ma did. She loved that dog more than anything, and I don't know how Lady did it. I worked hard to make Ma happy, but all the dog had to do to be loved was be herself. Maybe it was her perfect teeth. Sharp white incisors that could tear through a thick steak like paper. Ma brushed those teeth with a human toothbrush and Colgate, and she tied bandannas around Lady's neck each morning and painted her claws pink to match her own, and Lady slept on the other side of Ma's bed, head on the pillow and everything, like a husband.

Mia

(NÉE YA CHAI CHEN, BUNNY, THE HOP)

Lady never did talk much about her childhood. She kept a lot inside, that girl. It's a wonder she didn't have to drag herself along the ground just to get anywhere, with the weight of all those secrets inside her.

Before she arrived at the Hop, business was slow, what with the internet and PornHub and Big Fans. People can find sex work for free, these days. We were old news at the Hop, but we were an institution, and there's value in that. Like movie theaters. Like Cher! Business was slow, but fair. Us Bunnies were sisters, and we kept each other safe. We kept each other happy. If someone hadn't hosted a guest in a while, like Dakota, we helped out. Dakota was having a hard time, and so I convinced one of my regulars to upgrade his appointment to a threesome and invited Dakota along, and we split the profits down the middle. We had a blast, too. Dakota's a firecracker. And the guest had this fantasy about a teenage sleepover, wanted Dakota and me to whack each other with pillows, paint each other's nails, braid each other's hair. I left that date with a manicure, curls, and two grand including tips.

But, yeah, business was slow, no one can contest that. And when Lady turned up at the Hop, business started picking up. The uptick was pretty clearly Lady's doing, and some of the girls didn't like that.

You know why women see other women as competition? Because men put us all in a ring and tell us to fight.

Lady Lane
(NÉE KATE BURNS)

The girls at school hated us, Lacey and me. Maybe because we were kissing their boyfriends long before they were. Maybe because we got paid to do what they did for free. Maybe because we were in control of our stories. Those girls were helpless when it came to their own narratives—rumors that Rachel M fucked Tall Johnny in the disability cubicle, that Jessie hooked up with Joel while she was still dating Teddy from Eastgate, that Brianna wouldn't fuck, but she'd do anal because she valued her virginity and butt stuff doesn't count—but Lacey and I, we generated our stories ourselves. "I taught Ryan Sylvester to eat pussy with a peach and a Sharpie," Lacey told the locker room as we changed for gym. A rumor's not a rumor if it comes straight from the source.

· · ·

It was whatever. The way Lacey and I saw it, we were doing those girls a favor. They never had to experience a bad kiss, one of those tongue-thrusting ones, those lip-gnawing ones, that their boyfriends had seen in porno once and tried to replicate; no, they got the trained kisses, sweet kisses, soft lips, and they got kissed like that because of us. *We don't want your boyfriends*, we tried to tell them. *No one wants your shitty boyfriends.*

And anyway, the Sugar Club was thriving. We were making good money. Before Ma got sick, I'd use half my paycheck on something we needed for the house, detergent or fly spray or cereal, and I'd use the other half on myself. Lacey and I would go to the mall, and we'd walk into stores, chins up, because for the first time in our lives, we had money to spend. We barely noticed the gaze of retail assistants, tracking us through the aisles, keeping tabs and checking for a bulge in our pockets. If we split up, took separate routes around a store, the assistants always followed Lacey, never me. I wondered if she noticed, but if she did, she didn't let it get in the way of her spending. We were high on wealth, and if we couldn't find anything we wanted, we bought whatever anyway. Lip gloss that wanted to make our mouths swell. A keychain that read SLUT. We bought junk we'd never use just for the transaction of it, just to carry the branded bag around for the afternoon. The most important part of every product for us those days was the purchase. Some afternoons, we'd cross paths with the popular girls, and most days we were carrying more bags than them. They'd squint as we strolled past, laden with the fruits of our labor, fresh manicures, makeup as thick as a whole new skin.

We were suddenly watched. Once the kinds of girls who got looked over or not looked at at all, we were newly and abruptly visible. Not only visible but observed, examined, by boys in our classes, strangers on the sidewalks, construction guys, retail assistants, those men who stand in the middle of the mall and try to sweet-talk you into buying some hand lotion made from minerals found in the Dead Sea. The other girls, the rich-pretty ones, they were spectacles by accident or by nature, but Lace and I made ourselves into objects of desire on purpose, tailored our appearances, customized our gestures, speech, expressions; we created ourselves into every man's dream. We bought the expensive hand lotion from the men in the middle of the mall, and they gave us a discount, half off, because that's what men do for the kinds of girls we became.

At first the Sugar Club was a selfish endeavor, but it became more than that. Like a ballerina teaches her dancers to plié, but also teaches discipline and poise. Like a sensei teaches his students to kick, but more importantly strength and courage and balance. Lacey and I taught those boys how to manipulate a nipple, sure, but we taught them more too.

We taught them patience and we taught them pleasure and we taught them how to prioritize the pleasure of another. We taught them how to ask for help, for guidance, to put away their pride. We taught them how to be intimate and slow and tentative and gentle. We taught those boys consent. At a time when boys could only find physical touch through a tackle at their weekly game or a bloody brawl in a parking lot, we taught them how to be close to another without the presence of violence. We taught them to be soft. We helped those boys. Ask me if I regret our business, and I'll say no every time. I liked what we did, and I was good at it.

I still like it. I'm still good at it. It's never been *just* about the money.

Lacey Kahu

I'm not saying Kate had an easy life, no, her childhood was far from perfect, but her ma did keep her sheltered. Safe. She got Kate her own TV set so that when she brought over her manfriends, Kate could spend the night watching a preacher talk about God. When something went down at school, Kate's ma would be banging on the principal's door the very next minute. When they couldn't pay their bills, Ma would make a game of it; their power never got cut off, according to Kate's ma, they were just camping for the week. In some ways, Ma's death was the first bad thing to happen to Kate. Until then, she had someone. Until Ma died, Kate didn't know what it was to be alone.

Lady Lane

(NÉE KATE BURNS)

The summer Ma got sick was hot. So hot we'd both quit bras. The perspiration was permanent that year, and the whole country shone with it. Our fridge doubled as AC. Ma and I left the door open and took turns sticking our heads in the freezer until our sweat grew crisp on our skin. We pressed ice cubes to our rosy cheeks. We soaked our bedsheets in the bath and cocooned ourselves to sleep. It was a race: you had to find unconsciousness before the blankets got to room temperature, which was sweltering.

One evening, it was especially hot. So hot the house smelled of it. Like rotten fruit and cow shit. Ma was running late for a manfriend date, and she asked me to rub her down with fake tan while her pink-licked nails dried. She'd stuck little red diamantes on them to look like cherries.

Aren't they cute? She waggled her hands in my face as I pumped lotion into my palm. *A little more*, she said. *A little more.*

I spread the stuff over her shoulders, her back, her legs, then motioned for her to turn. *Get all the nooks and crannies, bunny*, she said. *Gotta make it look natural. Gotta make it look like I'm naturally golden. Get the girls too*, she said, shimmying her shoulders and letting her big breasts sway. I started on the left, then the right, then the lump, like she'd swallowed a golf ball.

Ma, I said, pressing on it.

Jesus fucking ouch, she said.

What is this, I said.

It's my goddamn titty, she said. *Now get your paws off me.*

Ma, it's a lump, I said. *It's a lump.* I felt for its perimeter. *It's big.*

Lumps and bumps, said Ma. *It all goes to shit when you get to my age, bunny.*

No, Ma, I said. *I think you should have this looked at.*

Oh yeah? With whose money?

We should go to the emergency room.

With whose money?

Shut up, I said. *Get in the car.*

I can't. She scooped the rest of the tanning lotion from my palm and took to rubbing herself down with it. *I have a date tonight.*

The only date you have tonight is with a doctor, I said.

I'll get it checked tomorrow.

Get in the fucking car, Ma, or I swear to god I will cut that thing out of you myself with these nail clippers right here.

Ma rolled her eyes. *There she is,* she said. *My vol-Kate-no.*

I hated the nickname. Ma had used it as an insult ever since I could remember. Whenever I took a stand, put my foot down, she'd make an exploding motion with her hands and match the gesture with a *kaboom! She's dormant until she's not,* Ma would announce to a not-audience, like a circus ringleader introducing the show's next freak. *Once in a blue moon, the true Kate emerges.*

This time, she was too busy beautifying to do the whole bit. She pointed to the near-empty bottle. *Can you at least tan my butt first? What if the doctor's cute?*

. . .

It was incurable, her cancer. *Metastatic,* the doctor told us. He *was* cute, it turned out. Young. He was being gentle with us, too gentle, his voice so soft I knew he was about to break our hearts. *Do you know what that means? Metastatic?*

Sounds like fantastic, said Ma. *I bet it's the best kind of cancer there is.*

Your cancer's incurable. He held Ma's hand as he spoke, and despite all the manfriends, I'd never seen any of her dates hold her hand. It made her, cherry-dotted nails and all, look small. *We can't cure it.*

Thoughts and prayers, Ma said.

• • •

Ma laughed when Americans on TV said *Thoughts and prayers.* When a bomb went off or a plane crashed, when a natural disaster wiped out a whole town or a shooter gunned down his peers, we watched the news with the rest of the world, wide-eyed and afraid. Then, during the aftermath, instead of doing anything, the journalists, politicians, actors, CEOs, they put on their solemnest faces and clasped their hands and instead of sending money, instead of sending help, they sent their *thoughts and prayers to those involved.*

Thoughts and prayers, Ma said to the news.

Thoughts and prayers, she said when she got a demotion for turning up late to work.

Thoughts and prayers, she said when I got a detention.

Thoughts and prayers, we both said, when our water main broke and our house flooded in slow motion.

• • •

We can't cure it, said the doctor. *But we can treat it. Control it. You could live for a number of months.*

What number?

It's hard to say.

Ma frowned. *You're not going to cut them off, are you?* She looked down.

He shook his head. *That wouldn't help at this point*, he said.

Thank god, said Ma. *Because I have to tell you, Doc. Given the choice between my life and my tits—*

Ma, I said. *Can we please listen?*

We're going to do everything we can to keep you comfortable, okay?

Comfortable? You make me sound senile. Like you're going to puff my pillows so I can die with good posture.

The doctor winced. His pity was obvious as food in his teeth, and he wouldn't stop smiling.

Do I have to stay here? If I have to live in a hospital, I'd rather you pulled the plug. You have nice AC though. Don't they, bunny? Nice and cool in here.

Ma, I said. I tried not to cry. I cried.

Come on, bunny, said Ma. *You're fucking up your mascara. Go get us some coffee, will you? It's free, isn't it? The coffee here?*

I left but pressed my ear to the door. Expecting the news to hit her. Expecting her to break down. Instead: *My daughter's a catch,* she whispered to the doctor. *Smartest kid in her whole school. And she's single, you know.*

. . .

For a long time, nothing changed except how often we had to go to the doctor. I kept going to school. Ma kept going to work. We kept going to the grocery store, the park, taking Lady for walks. Death, it turned out, was slow and boring.

Ma felt normal, healthy, she promised, and so after the first medical bill, she suggested we skip her appointments. *Just until I'm actually sick,* she said.

You've got cancer, I told her.

Can you not say that so loud, bunny? she said, looking around the hospital waiting room. *It's embarrassing.*

. . .

Ma's sickness was expensive. The meds, the scans—the doctors charged thousands just to tell us she was still dying and would continue to do so. The Sugar Club wasn't going to cut it. I picked up a weekend job at

Hobbes, the same department store Ma worked at, spritzing rich women with perfume as they passed by.

On the last day of my trial period, my manager squeezed my ass behind the register as I rang up some lady's Chanel No. 5. I was seventeen. When I turned to him, ready to yell, he only tweaked my trembling cheek and said, *Take it as a compliment, sweets.*

I called Ma on my break in search of sympathy, not solution, but she stormed down to the store, face flushed with either humiliation or radiation or some combination of the two.

The radiation gave her a red-hot rash that spread from her heart. Like the muscle was leaking and blood was seeping through her skin. Still, she stalked past me so fast I couldn't even catch her with the cologne in my hand. She walked straight into the manager's office and slammed the door shut behind her, a futile action; we heard every word from the shop floor. *Predator* and *pedophile* and *assault* and *legal action.*

· · ·

The next day I was promoted from scents to cosmetics, where I had a new manager and new responsibilities. It was Ma's old job.

My former manager was fired. He had two kids, one of them my age. She went to my school, was quiet and had hair that curtained her eyes. We'd never had a conversation, but once, when Ma was getting worse and worse and I hadn't done my homework, when I'd been taking back-to-back shifts after school and on weekends just to cover prescriptions and gas for the commute to the hospital each day, she'd shifted her page of math problems over to let me scribble down her answers. When I thanked her, she shrugged.

She was smart, the manager's daughter. Wanted to go to uni to study some kind of science, but she didn't end up going. Instead, just a few months after her father got fired, she dropped out of school and started making drinks at the local Starbucks. I couldn't help but wonder if I had defunded her future.

What if I ruined her life by crying wolf? I said to Ma, when I found out about the girl's new job.

You didn't cry wolf, bunny, is what Ma told me. *That son of a bitch deserved what he got and more for what he did to you.*

But what did he really do to me? Touch me in a place I'd been touched a million times? Call me a pet name? There was no bruise, no injury, no bloody wound to show for it. It's so hard to feel like you're not crying wolf. If I didn't say anything about his touch, would it have existed? He probably forgot it the moment it was over, and if it only existed in my mind, then wasn't it imaginary? Isn't that a wolf?

He deserved it, I said to Ma, *but she didn't deserve it.*

Women are always feeling responsible for the actions of bad men, Ma said.

But she—

She's got nothing to do with you.

Lacey Kahu

Kate's a good person. She is in no way a perfect person, but she's a good person and she's my person. Some people find their soul mate in their partner. Some find their soul mate in a parent. I found mine in Kate at age five when she lent me a shoe.

Lady Lane

(NÉE KATE BURNS)

At school, I didn't like many subjects, but I liked music. I liked the piano. Ma couldn't afford lessons and I barely got five minutes to play in class, so my music teacher, Mrs. Callahan, who wore glasses so thick her eyes were magnified to whole globes behind each lens—the kids called her Goggles—she let me stay after school to practice, to teach myself the keys, to squint at a sheet of music until the symbols started to make sense.

"You can use the piano after school," she told me, "so long as you perform in the talent show. That's the tradeoff." I practiced every day.

Lacey Kahu

She got really into the piano for a while there, but she wasn't really into the piano at all; what she was into was Mrs. Callahan's attention.

Lady Lane

(NÉE KATE BURNS)

Girls like us don't get to have passions," is what Lacey told me when I started canceling my Sugar Club appointments to practice. "Girls like us have to be practical. You really think you're ever gonna make enough money to pay for your ma's treatment by playing the freakin' piano, Kate? No. Focus on the Sugar Club. Business is booming."

But just this once, I didn't want to think about money or my body or the Sugar Club. I wanted to think about me and music and a life I could've had if I didn't have this one. I stayed after school. I played.

I learned Beyoncé and Celine Dion and a Gaga number, because I wasn't about to play any classical bullshit. For the talent show, I'd be playing a Christina Aguilera ballad that I practiced and practiced, pounding at keys until the pads of my fingers bruised blue.

On show night, I wore a dress Lacey stole from a thrift store. It was long, red, sparkling, and it hung from me like drapes, two sizes too big but still beautiful. I shone like something precious. Lacey lined my lips red and she glued fake eyelashes over my real ones, and when I looked in the mirror, the costume felt like a disguise.

"This is stupid," is what Lacey said, looking at me in the mirror. "Girls like us don't—"

And I said, "I don't want to be a girl like us tonight."

The auditorium was full and the spotlight was so bright it made the audience look like a swarm of monsters, hiding in the shadows, waiting to pounce. When my name was announced, I felt famous. Ma kissed me on the nose and reminded me not to smile on account of my teeth. I walked onstage badly. I couldn't remember what to do with my arms.

The stage fright got me, held me tight, too tight, and I sat, center stage, hands over the keys, still. The audience started to laugh. I knew that to avoid thinking about one thing I needed to think about everything else, but I couldn't, I was stuck. I looked out at the auditorium, dark figures, faceless, all watching me, waiting for me to do something, to perform. I couldn't move even when there were shouts of *Get off the stage, bimbo!* Mrs. Callahan marched out from the wings, took me by the elbow, helped me off the stool, let me lean on her as I limped out of the spotlight.

That night, after the show, Ma made us mugs of hot water sweetened with sugar packets from the Hobbes staff room. It was our version of cocoa, and it tasted like home. *You looked like a star up there, bunny,* she said between sips. *Even doing nothing, even just sitting there, everyone in that audience could tell you were special.*

· · ·

When someone looks at you and thinks you're the whole world, and then that person leaves? You realize you existed mostly in their perception of you. You wonder if you even exist at all. Ma died of breast cancer, but I died of my mother's death.

· · ·

Don't you let yourself end up like me, bunny, is what Ma said one night, late, when a manfriend slammed the door so hard the frame splintered and the house shook. I thought she'd stop seeing them once she got sick, but no, she was seeing more manfriends than ever. I looked at her, cheek pink and bloody as meat, red gloss smeared down her chin like a split lip, mascara weeping black beneath her eyes. She stroked the back of my head with her nails, which were neon green and sharpened to a point. I sighed into her touch. There were worse things to be than my ma. When I told her that, she shook her head and took me by the shoulders, hard.

She said, *You've got it all, bunny. Looks, talent, the way you are, you're a star,* she said. *Once we figure out those teeth, you'll be perfect,* she said. *Famous,* she said. But really, teeth aside, I looked like a million other faces, my body like a million other bodies. Sometimes I looked in the mirror and saw this catalogue girl, a paper doll, exactly the shape she's meant to be, and then I smiled and my teeth bucked and I sighed in relief. Feeling, at least, like a self.

Do Paris Hilton, Ma told me. I tied my hair into pigtails and lifted my voice by an octave. She clapped and clapped and said, *Do Michael Jackson,* and I touched the tip of an imaginary fedora and slipped backward on the hardwood. She laughed and laughed and she laughed until she cried and maybe those tears were for me or for herself, but I was just glad to see her smile. *Just as soon as we fix those teeth, we're going to be rich. We're going to have a great big life.*

I don't want to be famous.

You're going to have so much more than this.

I don't need more than this.

There were bruises around her neck. I touched each one softly. I hated when her manfriends hurt her because they never hurt her hard enough that she'd stop inviting them over. I covered the purpled handprint with my own palm and imagined squeezing her throat until I left that kind of mark. Still, I'd never hold Ma's manfriends against her. I, more than anyone, understood the power of desire. I knew what it was to want, to want to be loved so much it hurts.

Fame is love, bunny. Fame's to be loved by the whole world, all at once. Can you imagine how safe you'd be with that many eyes watching you? Fame's the biggest love there is.

....

Mia

(NÉE YA CHAI CHEN, BUNNY, THE HOP)

Some girls turn up to the Hop desperate to be famous, and it's happened before, too. Milly Mason, the porn star? She was a Bunny in the '90s, and she recorded her sessions with guests and sent them to PornHub and quickly became one of the best-known sex stars of our time. Jenny Spice, the Playmate? Hugh Hefner visited the Hop and fell for her in a lineup and invited her to live in his mansion on the spot. She's got her own show now on E! called *Spice Up Your Sex Life*: a marital sex make-over show for middle-aged couples who have forgotten how to fuck. The Hop's a windy, potholed, slow backroad to fame, but it'll get you there, if you really want it. Lady didn't seem to want it, though. She turned up at the Hop with something else in mind.

Lady Lane

(NÉE KATE BURNS)

Ma's view of honest work was twisted, but she stuck by it, steadfast. She'd take a man's wallet from his back pocket with a wink and a smile, and she'd use each of his credit cards until they went bust, but she wouldn't ask the guy for a cent if we were a dollar short on laundry change for the week. *You can't sleaze your way to the top, bunny,* she told me. *Lie as much as you need to, cheat, con, get your tits out of your top and show 'em off, but never sleaze upward. Sleazes kiss asses for a living, bunny, and you can only kiss so many asses before you're left with nothing but shit on your face.*

· · ·

One manfriend, an orthodontist, he took one look at my smile and offered me and Ma all she'd ever wanted. *You know,* he said, running a thumb under my two front teeth, *we have a program set up to help kids like Kate. It's called Route Canal. Free dental care for kids experiencing financial hardship.*

I looked at Ma, eyes wide, dreams coming true.

Financial hardship? Ma said.

She hated charity. She hated giving to charity, and she hated receiving charity. Once, when we walked out of the supermarket, a teenager was set up with a foldout table and a red bucket, collecting donations. *Donate a dollar for child trafficking?* she said as we passed.

Why would I support child trafficking? said Ma. *That's awful.*

I just mean that we could help, is all, said the manfriend, already eyeing his coat at the door. *If you don't want to do it, you don't have to. I was just offering, is all.* He backed up, reversed, closer and closer to being free from Ma's gaze.

We don't want to be your charity case, Ma said. *I'll pay for it. I can pay your full fee.*

The orthodontist tried so hard not to scan our house for evidence to the contrary, the black mold freckling the ceiling, paint peeling off the walls like a sunburn.

I can pay full price, Ma said again. *We can, can't we, bunny, we've got all that money saved up.*

For your treatment, I said. *That's not teeth money. That's cancer money.*

The orthodontist's eyes widened. Ma never told manfriends she was sick because cancer wasn't sexy. *Cancer?* he said.

I'll bring her in tomorrow, is what Ma said. *Give me your business card.*

I don't think I have one on me.

Give me your business card.

He gave her his business card.

We'll be in at nine, Ma said. *Ready to pay full price. Got it?*

The man nodded and finally managed to close the door between him and us.

We can't afford that, I said to Ma.

Sure we can, bunny. She smiled. Her smile was straight, teeth obedient, gums pink. *I'm going to die anyway. You're the one who has to live. Might as well live with a pretty smile.*

That night I waited until Ma went to bed, took her metal nail file and a handful of painkillers, and sat on the edge of the tub with a mirror in one hand and the file in the other. Then I started to saw, back and forth and back again. Enamel rained down like snow. At first, it was a strange feeling, not unlike filing your nails, but then I hit a nerve and the pain was electric. I clenched my eyes, my jaw, and kept going until my front teeth were the same length as the rest of them. My mouth was a bucket of blood. I spit it in the sink and went to bed.

. . .

Ma loved a makeover scene. *She's All That, The Devil Wears Prada, Clueless*—Ma loved any plot point that promised the character a better life, and Ma loved my new teeth. She told me to smile. She told me to keep smiling.

You're going to be a star, bunny. It's just a matter of time, now, she said.

She was sick and getting sicker. I asked for a promotion at Hobbes but was told I'd need a college degree to become a manager, and I was still at high school and college was not on my horizon. I begged Lacey to expand our repertoire of services at school.

"We're not hookers," she said.

Lacey Kahu

Kate wanted to do more so we could charge more. Her ma was sick, and she needed the cash. Her eyes were begging, and I felt bad turning her down. Plus, ever since she fixed up her teeth, the Sugar Club was really thriving. Kate had always been beautiful, but now she looked like a model, like she could walk a catwalk and be exactly where she was meant to be.

Kate never thought of her body as a sacred thing. For us, in those days, sex had nothing to do with love and everything to do with power, and I still believe that. Sex is a transaction, and we just learned about the deal of it all earlier than most girls. We laughed through the virginity speech in health class. We mocked the other girls for believing that the *special someone* in the story existed. We knew, even then, that the *special someone* was fictional as Santa Claus and the Tooth Fairy. The other girls didn't believe in the Easter Bunny anymore, but you could tell from their shiny eyes that they did still believe that some prince would walk into their lives and take their hearts and virginities both.

I don't regret it a bit, our business. Still, I knew we had to draw the line somewhere, and when I tried to explain that to her . . . well, Kate didn't like that. For Kate, sex was a way of getting the things she needed. Companionship, validation, cash; sex would've been transactional for Kate even if she weren't charging for it.

Lady Lane

Lacey and I started researching for the Sugar Club's new services: hand stuff and oral—that's where Lace drew the line. No penetrative sex.

We watched a lot of porn. Regular as our very own religion. We sat on my bed each Sunday, scrolling through misspelled titles, obscure fetishes, leaked celebrity sex tapes. While other kids did their history homework, memorized the dates of the fall of the Roman Empire, the names associated with the Nazi regime, we watched girls suck dick with such vigor they got sick. We took notes on erogenous zones, the earlobe the armpit the back of the knee the nape of the neck. We drew graphs, curves to depict pacing, we calculated the standard deviations between foreplay and ejaculation, we committed the names of obscure moves to memory: the butter churner, the snow angel, the Swiss ball blitz. We watched men coat faces in layers of fake semen, and we found the recipe to make it ourselves. Corn starch, by the way.

We trained our tongues like athletes, worked them around any phallic symbol we could find, and we learned to eat pussy too. I held Lacey's head between my legs as she touched her tongue to different spots. "Here?" I shook my head. "Here?"

"Closer."

"Here?"

"Fuck."

Sometimes kids at school called us lesbians. They thought we were together. We were whatever about it. Maybe we were lesbians or maybe gender didn't make much of a difference to us, or maybe we believed in the power of desire over and above anything as simple as genitalia. We didn't really think much about it; didn't really care. We let them call us lesbians because what we really were was soul mates.

• • •

We ate pussy for $250 apiece. The sales started out slow because, no doubt, those girls thought they were straight, but after our first couple customers, word got out. We could give them what their boyfriends couldn't. We were artists about it. We were masters of our craft. Self-taught sensations. We'd take half the payment up front and the other half upon orgasm.

Lacey fell for one of the customers. Whitney Hughes. Mean and white and thin, she'd been popular from the moment she was born. She'd broken up with Oliver van Ness and was dating someone new, a college guy, she told the whole school. She booked with Lace and told her that the reason for the appointment was that her boyfriend kept assuring her he was making her come, but she didn't really feel anything. Lacey spent a half hour in the closet with Whitney, and when they came out, Whitney was smiling and her eyes were all blurred and spacey and she kept thanking us and giggling. Lacey kissed her cheek goodbye.

"I have a boyfriend," Whitney said.

It's what they all said, afterward, clumsying their way back into wet underwear. They'd say, "I don't like girls."

We assured them of their heterosexuality every time.

Lacey Kahu

Sure, I had crushes, that's natural, but I also understood how to compartmentalize. For me, clients were clients. Kate wasn't good at that. She got overly invested, is what happened. Doctors keep a distance between themselves and their patients. Therapists. Personal trainers. Professionals have to hold their clients at arm's length, and that is exactly not what Kate did.

Lady Lane
(NÉE KATE BURNS)

At school, I didn't have boyfriends, because you don't get paid by boy-friends, but they felt like boyfriends and in my head I called them that, even though Lacey told me that what they really were was regulars. Cli-ents who kept coming back for more; more lessons, more time, they took money from their parents' underwear drawers, secret stashes of change meant for a rainy day, a robbery, they paid me with that petty cash and they didn't seem to feel any guilt about pickpocketing their own.

• • •

One night Oliver van Ness took me to his parents' anniversary gala. He offered two hundred for the night, cash in hand, and I wasn't one to turn down that kind of money. It helped that I still had a crush on him. Sure, he'd told the school he took my virginity behind the gardener's shed, but now he was paying for the misdemeanor, and I'd buy my ma an at-home IV with the cash. In my eyes, we were even. He was for-given. "I'll do it," I said. "But I don't have anything to wear."

• • •

The dress Oliver bought me, I stood on the lid of the toilet to change into it, to keep its hem from ever touching the floor. It was a sheath of emerald satin that felt like being shrouded in wealth. A necklace, gold chain with a green stone that hung so heavy my head lolled forward unless I pulled my shoulders back like a lady. The shoes he got me were too small, but I scrunched my toes and Band-Aided my heels and barely noticed the skin rubbing itself raw all night long. I smiled into the mirror and my smile was straight and white and beautiful and I looked so good. I felt like a fairy tale, and I'd always liked fairy tales. I liked their promise of upward mobility. Ma always explained how bullshit it was that the woman was always a damsel in distress who needed to be saved by a prince. But I wanted to be a damsel. I was distressed.

Oliver's father took my hand lightly, and his mother told me I looked like a movie star. His grandmother kissed my cheek. They gushed. That night Oliver was a magnet, some part of him always touching some part of me. I felt like an accessory, an expensive one, like a Rolex he was showing off to the room. He looked handsome, too; his suit fit like it was made for him, and his eyes sparkled under the glow of the house's many chandeliers. "Are you okay?" he whispered when we arrived. He held my hand tight in his.

"Katherine," is how he introduced me, even though my birth certificate said only "Kate." The long name felt elaborate and ridiculous on me, like wearing a prom dress to a beach barbecue. I understood, though, once I met Christopher and Sebastian and Frederick and Theodore: the rich love to take up as much space as they can afford. A lot.

When Oliver's mother complimented my necklace, I complimented her shoes. When his father asked if I golfed, Oliver rolled his eyes. "Dad," he said. "She doesn't want to hear about your hole-in-one. You don't have to listen to this, honey," he said to me, like we were really in love.

People like this, I learned as soon as I walked into the room that night, liked to be surrounded by people like this. Everyone looked identical, or like slight variations on one another. A mole here, a dimple there, but at the core these people were all the same, and oh, how they loved one another, how they sparkled to be in the company of themselves and themselves. When they conversed, one leaned in and so did the other; when they laughed, both parties tossed their heads back and let the sounds of their joy rise. To be in this mansion was to be in a house of mirrors. One touched the arm of another and the other touched the arm of the one. One removed his jacket, and she would shrug hers off too. To imitate, is what I learned in the first hour of that party. How to act as reflection, as shadow, as twin and double and image. When thanked for coming, I thanked for inviting. When asked a question, I deflected with question. I became whoever I spoke to and I was beloved, at that party, where everyone was in love with themselves.

They said things about how there was no way to become a responsible adult without ever having traveled. They said things about the demise of women, who were abandoning their domestic responsibilities in favor of high-paying careers. They said that homelessness was a choice, and when I asked, "But who would choose to have no home? Why would someone do that?" Oliver's father said, "They do it to make the rest of us uncomfortable, dear."

"That seems right," I said.

At dinner, we ate food I'd never heard of, and I took it easy on the champagne because once Lacey had told me that bubbles made me giggly, and this was not a room of gigglers.

"How did you two meet?" asked Oliver's mother over the soup course. How we met? I thought of the fifty-dollar kiss, of the janitor's shed.

"We're in the same science class," I told her, instead. "We were assigned as lab partners, and he was always making this joke about us having chemistry together. I hope you know you raised a real sweet talker." I smiled up at the room, let my gaze meander the table. I had all of them, my audience. Ma would've been so proud. Oliver kissed my cheek.

"That sounds just like our Oliver," said his father. "And like his old man too. We're romantics, the van Ness men."

After dinner, we sat in the parlor, teacups in hand. The night was winding down, and I was exhausted from the performance, and Oliver suggested that I play the piano for the room. "She's a wonderful pianist," he said. "Self-taught, too."

He was in my music class, Oliver was, and he knew I'd been learning a Katy Perry number for the end-of-semester showcase, slamming away before class, after class, at keys I had no business consorting with.

He led me to the piano and I sat and I played "I Kissed a Girl," and either I'd had just enough champagne or I was in character enough to pull the whole thing off without hitting a bad note.

"That was beautiful," Oliver's grandmother said. "Was that a classic?"

"I've never heard it," said his father. "Did you write that yourself?"

"Yes," I said.

"You should join us in Bali this year, Katherine," said his mother. "We go each winter. We have a house there, right on the oceanfront. Do come with us."

I smiled and nodded and thanked them for the offer and promised to look at flights. When we left, everyone hugged me. They couldn't wait to see me again, in Bali, on the beach. When Oliver kissed my cheek good night, thanked me for coming, called me perfect, I almost expected him to ask me to be his girlfriend, and he would've, if my life were the movie of itself, he would've fallen for me that night, would've asked me to be his, and I almost would've said yes. Thoughts and prayers.

• • •

"Watch yourself, Kate," is what Lacey said when Oliver ignored me the next day at school. "You've got to stop confusing fantasy with reality, or you're going to get yourself in trouble."

But fantasy was my reality. I made money off the make-believe. I was four years old the first time Ma stood me on the corner of Ninth and Main and told me to do Samuel L. Jackson's *Pulp Fiction* monologue while she collected change, and then there was the time we hosted a bake sale at school for Aunt Molly's kidney transplant but I didn't have an Aunt Molly as far as I knew and we raised about a grand for a surgery that would never happen and if I did have a sick Aunt Molly she never got her kidney because we spent that cash on painting our house's walls red. See, I'd been turning the imaginary real my whole life.

Lacey Kahu

Kate never told her ma about the Sugar Club. But she was using our profits to pay Merrill's medical bills, and Merrill must've wondered where the money was coming from. For two people who spent their lives together, Kate and Ma knew very little about each other. Spending time with someone doesn't mean spending time *with* someone.

Lady Lane

(NÉE KATE BURNS)

Our class went off to college, and Lacey picked up a gig at the Purple Panther, a strip club downtown that was the hot spot for bachelor parties and businessmen on lonely lunch hours. I started working full-time at Hobbes, in the cosmetics section, where I pressed packets of lotion—antiaging, skin-smoothing, youth-restoring, we're all trying to grow backward—into any hands I could find. Hardly anyone bought anything, they were all just passing through, and I worked on commission. Lacey made ten times at the Panther what I did at Hobbes.

"I like it," she told me. "I find it kind of validating."

"Stripping?"

"Someone's suddenly judgmental."

But what I was, was jealous. Ma's health was worsening, I could see it in her eyes: all the moisture was gone, she was drying out, the matte of lifelessness, and soon I'd be left with medical bills to pay, a body to cremate, a service to plan. It's cruel, I know, to think about money when your mother's death is imminent, but dying is expensive these days.

"Could I pick up a shift?" I asked Lacey. Ma's new painkillers were more expensive than the over-the-counter stuff she'd been living on. She tried to tell me it was okay—*I'm a tough old bag, I can cope with a little pinch.* But it wasn't a little pinch. When she reached for the TV remote, she yelped.

"A shift at the Panther?"

"Just once a week, maybe, at a low traffic time. Late morning or something, before my shift at Hobbes."

"You want to dance?"

"I need the money."

"Come in with me today," Lacey said. "Come in and meet my boss. She's great. She'll love you. Wear that leopard-print skirt."

"I haven't worn that in years."

"Do you still have it?"

• • •

I wore it. It was too tight, made my ass look like meat packed up and for sale in the grocery store. The Purple Panther was up a set of narrow stairs that separated a dive bar and a hookah joint. It was a single room with a bar and buffet at the back, a stage at the front, walls plum-colored all round. It smelled of cheap bourbon and barf.

Lacey's boss, Fi, was in her mid-fifties and never without a cigarette. The smoke from her mouth was constant, like maybe she was just hot inside. Her hair was white-blond, sparse and spun, cotton candy stuck on the top of her head as if by accident.

"I like your look," is what she said when she saw me. "Show me your tits."

"What?"

She didn't repeat herself. Never repeated herself. I took my shirt over my head.

"Skirt's too tight for you," she said, pointing at the fold of skin at my waist.

"I know."

"Must be really desperate for cash if you can't even afford clothes that fit."

I said nothing.

"We're full frontal," she said. "Means you have to show it all."

"Okay."

"You're okay with that? Some girls think they're okay with it, and then when it comes down to it, they're really not okay with it. Once it comes down to really baring it all, you know."

"I'm not shy."

"You seem it."

"I'm not shy about my body."

"Prove it."

I dropped my skirt. I wasn't wearing underwear.

Fi nodded, unimpressed. "Fine. Why are you here?"

"For a job."

"There are other jobs."

"My mother's dying."

"You can take Monday mornings. Ten through twelve. It's slow, and usually only the creeps are here, but the creeps pay well, and they know the rules so you won't have to deal with any wandering hands."

"What do I wear?"

Fi snorted and smoke puffed from her nostrils. "What you wear isn't really the point, hon."

Fifi Walters

(OWNER, *THE PURPLE PANTHER*)

She went by Bunny at the club, and she was a knockout, don't get me wrong, but my god was she a terrible dancer. Her first few nights she maybe made a couple bucks total. My best girls bring in a couple *grand* a night. I couldn't afford to have a dud out there, and that's what Kate was when she started out, a real dud. I was about ready to give her the sack when she turned things around.

Lady Lane

(NÉE KATE BURNS)

My first dance at the Purple Panther went like this: two men at the club, one sitting in the far corner drinking something brown from a tumbler, the other front and center, like a kid watching cartoons. The song was one I didn't know, and I cursed myself for shrugging when Fi asked for my preferred soundtrack. The stage was lit with little blue spotlights, and I stood in the shadows between them.

"Introducing," the sound guy said over the speaker, "for her very first dance, her stage debut, our brand-new dancer, Bunny!"

I'd expected some kind of training. Employee orientation. Taking Off Your Clothes 101. But Monday rolled around and then it was stage time and I'd barely changed into the cheap lingerie I bought for the performance. It itched, the bad imitation of lace. The hem of the thong chafed my thigh.

The guy at the front fanned himself with dollar bills, leaned back in his chair. I was wearing a trench coat over my underwear.

"Take it off!" he said. I took it off. "There ya go!" he said.

I dropped the coat and walked to the front of the stage. The music was too quiet, the lyrics whispered. The speakers had a scratch in their throat. Mechanical laryngitis. The room smelled like mildew and the air was a little wet, like it had taken a shower a few hours ago. These are all of the things I thought on that stage while I didn't dance.

"Come on, Bunny," said the guy at the front. "Do something."

"What am I meant to do?" I said.

"Dance!" he said. But I couldn't.

The guy at the front gave me a sad smile as he set a single on the foot of the stage and then stood to go hit the buffet. "Sorry," I said, easily heard over the muttering music. The buffet served only meatballs in red sauce and steak sliders and bacon, man food, and the signs were always wrong. They read "meatball's" and "slider's" and I tried to scratch the apostrophes off with my thumbnail, but they were written in permanent marker.

When the song ended, I picked up the dollar, waved goodbye to the almost empty room. "Sorry," I said again, this time to the entire club. The guy sitting at the back watched, watched but never moved, never showed signs of either disappointment or delight at my disaster. The bartender tipped his drink and said, "You'll get 'em next time, champ."

Lacey Kahu

Kate performed every day of her life. Every day, Kate convinced the world she was okay, manipulated teachers into believing that her home life was healthy, lied outright to CPS, but for someone who performed every day of her life, she was a very bad performer as soon as she had to get up on a stage.

See, it's when people know she's performing that she gets squirrely. For Kate, a successful performance means she is the only one who knows she is doing it.

Lady Lane
(NÉE KATE BURNS)

Even though it was midweek, midafternoon, there were more people in the audience at my next Panther shift. The club had a way of creating the illusion of Friday night, no matter the day, the time. Walking out of the Panther after a day shift was like walking out of a matinée showing of a movie; you had to squint in surprise at the sun.

The Panther's door read HOTTEST LADY'S IN TOWN. I told Fi the sign was wrong, and she snorted. "Of course it is," she said. "No one thinks we've actually got the hottest ladies in town."

"I mean grammatically."

"If only you were as good at shaking your ass as you are at punctuation." Tonight was my last chance, she told me from behind her cloud of smoke. "I don't pay girls to stand onstage like fucking mannequins. You gotta move up there, hon."

I nodded. "I can do better."

"If the audience wanted to see a girl acting uncomfortable, they'd go see an Anna Kendrick movie." Fi exhaled, and the smoke stung my eyes. "You gotta show 'em the goods, hon. Got it?"

A group of businessmen crowded two tables, maybe ten, fifteen, plus the same sad guy in the back, still nursing a drink. The eager guy at the front, my only real customer, wasn't there.

Lacey, even though she was off for the day, offered to dance with me. "Just this once," she said. "And I get to keep any tips given directly to me. You can have the stage litter."

I agreed, grateful. This time, I chose a song I knew, some old Britney Spears number.

I ditched the trench, hoping that if I were mostly naked from the beginning, taking the rest of it off wouldn't feel so significant.

"I don't think I can do it," I said to Lacey.

"Why don't you try going into the audience?"

"What?"

"You don't have to stand onstage, you know."

I looked at the men sitting around the table, at the sad man in the back.

"I can go down there instead?"

"Sure. But they'll probably touch you."

I wanted to be touched. If I were touched, it would feel less like a show. More real.

The song started, and Lacey stepped onto the stage. She was so herself up there. It wasn't a performance at all, just her, just Lacey, up there. The men watched, cradling drinks, nodding along to the song. I stepped out onto the floor and began to move around the room, sidling between tables, shifting chairs as I went.

Eventually, I made it to the sad man in the back. He wasn't as unattractive as you'd expect a man who regularly sat at the back of a strip club to be. He had a stupid mustache that looked like one of those novelty ones that comes attached to plastic glasses at the dollar store, and what remained of his hair had so much product combed through it that it looked like someone had raked his head. He wore a too-tight, too-white polo shirt. His eyes, though, were kind.

"Welcome back, sweetheart," he said.

"Thanks," I said.

"I thought we'd never see you again after last week."

"What?" The music was louder tonight. A blessing.

"I thought we'd never see you again."

"Well," I said. "Here I am. Can I dance for you?"

The line tasted rotten.

"I don't know, can you?"

I walked around him, ran my fingers over his chest, shoulders, back. I stood behind him and watched Lacey up onstage as she lowered herself, so slowly, slowly, into the splits. She licked her own thigh. The businessmen roared.

"What do you do for a living?" I whispered, my lips to the man's ear.

"I'm a lawyer."

"Do you enjoy it?"

"I guess."

"Are you married?"

"You ask a lot of questions."

I pressed my chest to the sad man's back, flipped my hair over his shoulder and back again. "Just trying to get to know you." At school, I'd known the boys I kissed for cash. I'd seen Paul Weinstein get bullied on the bus. I'd talked Graham McFarlane out of his lunch money.

Onstage, Lacey rolled out of her full split and spread her legs into a V.

I straddled the sad man's lap. "What're your thoughts on the election?"

"Not so shy today, are you?"

I shifted against his crotch. His crotch shifted against me.

"You're really something," he said. Then he took a handful of cash from his pocket and said, "Can I take you somewhere more private?"

"I'm expensive."

"I just got paid."

"The perfect couple."

"So?" His forehead shone with sweat. "Can I take you to a room, Bunny?"

I let him lead me, the illusion of control that he thought was an illusion that wasn't an illusion. I didn't know where the private rooms were.

• • •

Fi had told me the rules of one-on-one dances, along with everything else. One long paragraph of information, including smoke breaks and song choices and costume changes and drink specials. I had thought I was listening until she finished talking and I had no idea what had been said. Fi didn't repeat herself.

. . .

In stripper movies, the audience usually isn't allowed to touch the dancer, but the dancer is allowed to touch the audience. This, I thought, seemed like a likely rule, but as soon as I shut the door to the private room, the sad man's hands were on my chest.

. . .

Ma and I watched *Magic Mike* often. She liked Channing Tatum, even though she could never get his name right. Chandler Tanning, Tate Channing, Chaney Tater, That Guy with the Ears.

It's Channing Tatum, I told her.

Channing isn't a name, she said. *It's a verb.*

To chan.

. . .

"Have you ever had a private dance before?" I said. There was a poster on the wall behind him. It was titled RULE'S, and the rules were written in red against a black background, difficult to see. I pressed my body against his as I tried to read.

NO TOUCHING THE LADY'S

NO KISSING THE LADY'S

NO REMOVING PANT'S

"I get private dances all the time," the man said, pulling my bra cups down, hands on my breasts. I pushed him into a chair, the only one in the room; only one person was allowed to sit in this exchange. A new song started. A new dancer must have been onstage. I wanted to leave the room and this sad man with the roaming hands. I wanted to go out and take Lacey and drag her out of the club, down the street, into my car, to drive away, start again.

Maybe sensing my hesitation, the sad man pulled out a second handful of cash, began to tuck each bill into the waistband of my thong, one by one. "You're beautiful," he said, and he sounded like he meant it. "My name's Gary," he said, "by the way." And that, the simple gift of his name, was enough. I shifted my hips slowly in time to the music, letting him dress me in money.

"Will you kiss me?" he said. I collected the cash into a wad and put it between my lips, bit down on the stack. I would not kiss him. Instead, I pushed my underwear down and kicked them off the end of my shoe. They landed in his lap. He lifted the fabric to his face.

"I'm voting National," he said, quick to learn the terms of the transaction. "Could I touch you?" He gestured to my crotch.

"No." I pointed at the sign.

"Grammatically incorrect," he said.

"People really struggle with the possessive," I said.

"I'll pay you three hundred."

"For what?"

"To touch you."

I looked at him. Gary. His hair was receding in the shape of a W, and his beard was growing like weeds, patchy and wild. His cheeks were reddened with liquor or lust, and his brow was wet with the sweat of want. I'd done worse.

"I'll use my hand for five hundred," I said. The exact amount of Ma's latest bill. "You keep your paws off me."

He checked his pocket for the extra cash and splayed the notes like a hand of cards to prove the amount. "Deal," he said, reaching for his belt.

. . .

By the time he was done, my wrist ached and I was checking the time. My shift was over, and I had to get to Hobbes. I wiped my fingers on the carpet and stood. He handed over the extra cash. "Pleasure doing business with you," I said, taking the money and stepping back into my underwear, tucking the bills into my waistband.

"The pleasure was really, really all mine," he said. "So, I'll see you back here?"

"Same time next week," I said.

"What's your name?"

"Bunny."

"I mean your real name."

I kissed his cheek, and then I left with over five hundred bucks for two hours of work. I'd take Ma out to dinner, her favorite pizza place, let her order the biggest size, slathered with anchovies and hot peppers, maybe even a side of garlic bread.

. . .

"You didn't get up to any funny business in there, did you?" said Lacey, as I pulled on my jeans backstage. "You know that shit can get us shut down."

"No," I said. "What do you mean? I don't know what you mean."

Lacey Kahu

It was obvious that Kate was offering up more than we were meant to in the private rooms. She'd done it at school while we were running the Sugar Club, and she was doing it again now, and she didn't seem to care that, both times, her actions would have consequences for me.

Don't get me wrong, Kate would've dropped anything, everything, to help me out. She would've given up the world for me; would've died for me.

When my father beat me so bad my eyes swelled until I couldn't see, she stormed my parents' trailer and grabbed all of my shit and we were sleeping, top to toe, in Kate's bed that same night. When the girls at school called me slurs, she yanked full handfuls of blond from their heads and took the detention slip in a blink. Later, when I got deep into the drug scene, Kate was one who kept hold of my hand, the only one trying to drag me back out of that quicksand.

Kate's saved my life more than once, and I know it. She's selfless in the big ways and also so self-absorbed that she can barely see when her actions are hurting the people around her. She's white like that.

She never understood that if someone told the cops she'd been fucking for money at school, she would've been let off with a warning. Or if Fi found out about her jaunts in the private rooms, she would've just picked up a gig at a different club the very next day. She never understood that I would've been locked up for the shit she got bopped on the nose for.

Kate didn't have much, but she had privilege that followed her everywhere she went, and just because neither of us had much, because neither of us had nice things or clothes or cash, she thought we existed in the world as equals.

She's really, really white like that.

Lady Lane

(NÉE KATE BURNS)

The same sad man came to the Panther every Monday. Paid for a private dance with me every time. His name was Gary. He was fifty-four and twice divorced, two kids, an intellectual property lawyer, conservative, very into sailing. He liked proverbs; mistook them for wisdoms and leaned on them in almost every conversation. Sometimes they were boring ones, *That's the way the cookie crumbles* and *The early bird gets the worm*, but sometimes he used ones I'd never heard, *A closed mouth catches no flies*, found from languages other than English, and sometimes, not often, but sometimes, they even made me smile.

I learned these facts about Gary between blow jobs, for which he agreed to pay a thousand a pop. I could've charged more, I'm sure, but I liked Gary. He was nice to me. He paid well. He came back. It was sure money, and I needed it and I was grateful for it. I didn't tell anyone about the oral, and I made him promise not to either. Gary's payments alone were covering Ma's medical costs, and all I had to do was give a single bout of illegal head once a week. Five minutes, tops. Gary didn't hold out well, and Lacey and I had been practicing on Popsicles since primary school.

"Let me take you out," Gary said. I coughed his semen into a handkerchief. He tasted like loose change; swallowing would cost extra.

"Against the rules," I said.

"So's this."

"That's a great point, Gary."

"Come on, just this once. You'll have fun. I'll make sure you have fun."

"I could get fired."

"A cat in mittens won't catch mice."

"What?"

"One date."

He was cute when he pleaded. Like a kid. "Where're you gonna take me?"

"Dinner, to start," he said. "A movie, a play, the opera, whatever you're into." He was falling in love with me. I could see it in his eyes: a softness and a sparkle. He had nice eyes, Gary did. "Come on," he said. "Let me treat you right."

• • •

You know he used to be a stripper, Chafing Tater did, is what Ma told me as we watched *Magic Mike* for the somethingth time. She didn't know I was working at the Panther, or, if she did, this was her way of okaying it. *Used to give private dances for fifty apiece. It's why he dances so good compared to those other clowns. He's had to dance for his life.*

• • •

I said to Gary, "Pay me and I'll do it." I said, "Pay me for the date."

"Oh, come on," said Gary. "You don't like spending time together?"

"I do." I did.

"So why can't it just be a date?"

"I don't have time to date."

"A hundred for the night."

"That's offensive," I said, standing, dressing myself, tossing him his balled-up handkerchief. He tucked it into his pocket. It was an act of love, the way he provided the cloth each time we met, freshly laundered, smelling of lavender.

"Five hundred," he said.

"You pay double that for five minutes of oral."

"No sex," he said. "Nothing like that, I promise. All I want is a date. To eat. To talk. Five hundred. Final offer. I'm not paying more because if I'm only offering you five hundred, then, you're right, you could earn more for a quick hand job, so if you take the five hundred then I know that you actually want to be there. That it's a date you want to be on."

It was sweet. It was flattering. It was important that I didn't catch feelings for Gary. "Tonight?" I said. I was thinking about my car. It had started ticking. *What's that*, Ma had asked, *a timer? You set a countdown to the end of me?* Five hundred would be enough to cover the repairs.

"At seven," he said. "Where do you live, Bunny? I'll pick you up."

"I'll meet you at the pizza place on Eighth." I could bring Ma home the leftovers. "And, Gary?"

"Yeah?"

"It's Kate."

Fifi Walters

(OWNER, *THE PURPLE PANTHER*)

I'm always telling my girls not to date the patrons. Guys are always asking them out. Of course they are. Men confuse lust for love, and they tell my girls they want them, but what those men really want is a version of my girls that only exists on the stage. I've never heard of a relationship that started out here and ended up healthy. No. Those kinds of relationships are destined for failure because the power's off balance from the beginning. The guy thinks he has some kind of proprietary right over the girl's body, and soon enough he decides that his property should be private and he tells my girl to stop stripping. And she usually doesn't want to.

Lady Lane

(NÉE KATE BURNS)

On our date, I ordered triple anchovies, the way Ma liked it, and Gary looked offended. "Boy, you really don't want to kiss me tonight, huh," is what he said. I ate a single slice, picked off every anchovy, not to placate Gary but because I hated them, and took the rest of the pizza to go. I took the free breadsticks too. Gary frowned as I rolled them in a napkin and tucked them into my purse. "You planning on living off breadsticks for the week?" he said. I didn't answer. They'd be too stale to chew after a day or two.

"My mother used to do that," he said. "She used to take the butter packets too. Sometimes she'd tip a restaurant's salt shaker into her coin purse and then at the dinner table at home she'd reach into her wallet and sprinkle it over her pasta."

"Ma used to have us do health retreats," I said, zipping my purse and setting it in my lap. I knew the game well. Poverty Olympics: poorer player wins. "She'd put us on juice fasts so we'd have a reason not to eat for a couple days."

Gary nodded. "Did you do cans?"

"Every Sunday," I told him. "Ma always said only chumps did pickup any day that wasn't Sunday. Sunday's when you've got the Saturday-night Bud Lights all over the streets."

"That's smart," said Gary. "We were the chumps. Got up at six every morning to pick up the cans that didn't make it into the dumpster outside a bar by our house. Only made about a buck a day, but pool the money and we had enough for a box of cereal."

"One morning we made twenty from cans alone," I told him. "After a big rugby game, we circled the stadium at four in the morning to beat the homeless rush. Twenty bucks!"

"So you're stripping for the cash, then?"

"I'm not doing it for free, am I?"

"You just seem too real to be doing it. You seem too . . . I don't know, too smart or something."

"To be stripping?"

"Or exotic dancing or whatever you want to call it."

I frowned. "My best friend's a stripper. You've probably seen her. She's about my height, Maori, tongue piercing." He nodded, sure he had. He was there every day. "She's the most real person I know. She's saving to buy a house. Every girl I've met at the Panther so far is smart. Some are paying for school, you know, some are paying off loans, some trying to get away from abusive boyfriends, some providing for a kid or two, most of them just trying to get by, honestly. Doesn't that make them real? Smart? Isn't that what everyone's doing?"

"Yeah, sure." Gary sat back in his chair. "But everyone else is doing it with clothes on. Not everyone is selling their bodies for a quick buck. I'm just saying, there are other ways to make money. Ways that don't include sexualizing yourself."

"Men are going to sexualize us anyway. Why not profit off it?"

Gary snorted.

"What is it that you do again, Gary?"

"Intellectual property law."

"Right," I said. "Right, so that's helping people sell their ideas, right? They're selling their brains? Their minds?"

"They're selling ideas. They're not selling their brains."

"You think that's so different from what I do? How is it different? I'm not selling my body. I'm selling the right to watch my body dance. An actor isn't selling her body, she's selling the right to watch her act."

Gary crossed his arms and uncrossed them.

"I just mean," I went on, "how is a person showing someone else their ideas, letting someone pay to access those ideas, how is that so different from showing someone your body, letting someone pay to have access to it? It isn't so different from any other work, you know."

"I get what you're saying," he said. "I get it, but selling ideas can't get you pregnant, can't give you diseases."

"Are you happy, Gary?"

"What?"

"Do you come to the club every night because you're such a happy guy?"

"What are you talking about?"

I finished my gin and tonic, sucked the ice clean of any liquor. "Chlamydia's a hell of a lot easier to cure than depression."

He laughed, then. "A drowning man isn't troubled by rain," he said. "You're smart, you know."

"Take me to a movie," I said, feeling empty as a Sunday. It wasn't worth trying to change Gary's politics. He thought Elon Musk was funny and he supported billionaires, was always trying to press Bill Gates's philanthropy on me, was always saying shit like "He donates more than his salary, you know," and I'd look around, up at the ceiling, like I was scanning for a bug, and then I'd whisper to Gary, "Blink once if Bill's making you say this," and Gary would just sigh and slap his thighs in frustration and tell me I'd never understand.

"Take me to a movie," I said to him. "I don't care what we see."

. . .

Every year, on our birthdays, mine or hers, Ma and I would pay to see one movie. One ticket at a senior rate, even though she wasn't, would never be, and one at a children's rate, even when I wasn't. We'd go to the earliest screening, some animated Disney thing with a clear moral message, a bad guy and a good guy, a right and a wrong, then, once it was over, we'd movie-hop. As the day went on, the narratives got more nuanced, the family films gave way to drama, to horrors and romances and thrillers and literary films meant to make us think. We didn't care what we saw; it wasn't important. We didn't come to the movies to be taught a lesson or to be scared, to fall in love or to cry or to think; we came to the movies to escape. We'd skip from cinema to cinema and watch whatever was on until the credits of the last film of the night rolled into darkness and home became inevitable.

We were always the last to leave, picking up any half-eaten popcorn cartons and eating the dregs on the ride home.

· · ·

Our last year together, on the morning of her birthday, I left the house early to buy Ma and me some movie tickets. I danced a quick midmorning shift at the Panther, saw my regulars, gathered enough singles to take Ma out after the movie, somewhere fancy. When I got home, her bedroom door was locked. I knocked. I wouldn't usually, not on any other day, but that day was her birthday and manfriends never came over on birthdays. Birthdays were for family. Birthdays were for us. There was a rustling behind the door. A low voice that shouted, *Fuck off!*

I kept knocking. She barely had the energy to walk around the block, those days, but she'd been seeing more manfriends than ever. I'd learn why a couple months later, but that day I wanted to celebrate, and I wanted to do it just us. *You fuck off,* I said to the manfriend. Then, *Ma, there's a new Megan Fox movie.*

The door swung open. The manfriend was big and naked and dripping with sweat. He took up the entire doorway.

I said fuck off, he said.

You fuck off.

You can join in or you can leave, he said.

Go away, bunny, said Ma's voice. I could picture her, lying there, naked, splayed on her mattress, waiting for this lumberjack to fill her.

Yeah, he said. He was missing a tooth. *Go away, bunny.*

I used both hands to shove his chest. He used just one to punch me square in the nose. It felt like being bowled over by a wave.

. . .

On our first date, Gary took me to see *The Godfather*, which I'd already seen, but the only other option was a new release, some badly written, high-budget action movie starring Vin Diesel and that actress who always talked about how much she liked chicken nuggets in a poorly constructed attempt at being relatable to the public. People had told me I looked like her. I didn't see the similarity. Willa Jordan was her name.

Gary held my hand through the whole film, and by the credits it felt like that was how it was meant to be, my hand in his. It felt as boring and as perfect as returning a book to its place on the shelf, as hanging your coat up after a long day.

He wanted me so much, I could almost mistake it for me wanting him. When he kissed me as the credits rolled, I kissed him back and meant it.

. . .

Gary was plain, but I liked the boredom that came with dating him. It was comfortable. He paid for dinners and movies and gas. I stopped charging him to spend time with me, and I lost my most loyal customer at the Panther, but I was happy. I was maybe even in love. I liked the way he smelled of deodorant and coffee. I liked the way his beard scuffed my cheek with every kiss. I liked how he opened doors before I could even reach for the handle. Was there passion? Well. I'd take being cared for, cared about, over passion any day.

He liked to knit, Gary did, and in the beginning I made fun of him for it, the way he would prop himself up on pillows after sex, take needles and wool from the nightstand, and start to work his fingers. "I feel like I'm fucking my grandma," I told him.

But when he finished a mitten and tugged it tight over my hand and it was a perfect fit, warm, I left it on while I went down on him. He finished the second one the next day, and, just like that, for the first time in my life, I owned mittens. I had warm hands.

When we went out, people stared at us because I was young and he was old and because I was pretty and he was old and because I was a stripper and he was old. But none of that meant anything when Gary and I were together because, when it came down to it, he cared. And that's all a relationship, any relationship, is.

When I introduced him to Ma, he shook her hand and barely stuttered at how sick she looked by then. "You rich?" she asked, her first question.

"I'm Gary," he said, releasing her hand.

"But are you rich?" she asked again.

"Gary, ma'am," is what he said. "G-A-R-Y. Like Larry, or Barry, but with a G."

She snorted and tried a different approach. "What do you do, Gary?"

"I'm dating your daughter, for one."

"Thinks he's cute," Ma said, to me and not him. "Think you're cute," she said, to him.

"Thank you," he said. "I'm a lawyer," he said. "But don't hold it against me."

"Rich," she said. "You're rich then."

"It's a pleasure to meet you," said Gary.

"You had a vasectomy, Gary?"

He choked, cleared his throat. "Excuse me?"

"Bunny doesn't need any babies right now."

"Um."

"Are you handy, at least?"

He shrugged.

"Good with your hands, I mean. We've got a leak. Don't we, bunny? We've got that leak in the kitchen."

Ma and I watched as he tinkered beneath the sink on his hands and knees. "Have you got a wrench?" he asked.

"We look like we're the kinds of girls who'd have a wrench?"

He used his hands to tighten the pipes. Asked for a couple more tools before giving up on asking, on tools, altogether. When Ma and I wanted to hang something on the wall, we used a hairbrush as a hammer. When we had a hinge loose, we used the point of one of Ma's stick-on acrylics to wind the screw tight.

"Are you staring at my ass?" Gary asked, his head still stuck in the cupboard under the sink. We were. He fixed the leak. Ma ruffled his hair when he left. "He's a good boy," she told me. "He's a good boy, that boy."

Lacey Kahu

She met Gary around the same time I met Sunny. He was called Sunny because once you met him, he became your whole world. You couldn't live without him. There were perks to him: free drugs, an immediate reputation, a good set of biceps to keep you safe. Sunny showed up at the Panther and pulled me off the stage and into a private room, and that was the first time I ever did blow. It was like floating. It was like finally being someone other than myself.

So I started dating Sunny and I started doing a lot of blow and then I started doing a lot of dope. Sunny slapped me around, but he always apologized for it, sometimes with a gift, or money, drugs, a tear or two. I moved out of my parents' trailer and lived between trap houses and his apartment downtown and the street.

Why did I do it? I thought I loved him. Drugs'll make you think you love whoever's giving them to you.

Lady Lane

(NÉE KATE BURNS)

Sunny was bad news. Lace got heavy into drugs, and she lost weight and her skin turned gray and her breath started smelling of rot. Like she was going bad inside.

I tried a lot of things, but Lacey didn't want any help. She wanted Sunny and she wanted his drugs, even if it meant homelessness. When I told her she could stay with me and Ma, she only laughed and said, "I'm a grown woman, Kate. I'm not about to live with you and your mother."

"You too good for me now?" I said.

"You want a bump?" she said. Her nose was rubbed raw. She had a new habit of wiping at her nostrils with the back of her hand and checking for blood. She did it quickly, violently; sometimes it looked like she was slapping herself.

"This is bad, Lace."

"What is?"

"This. Everything you're doing."

"What am I doing?"

"Drugs."

"Yes please," she said with a wink.

· · ·

I never messed with drugs. Never had an interest in being out of control. I liked to keep all my cards in my hand even when there were hardly any cards. Even when it was a bad hand, I liked to know what I had and what my next moves could be. That's something I learned from Ma. Lacey's parents, they'd leave the house once a month to cash their unemployment checks and swap the money out for speed on the same trip. Ma, she spent every dollar she earned on us, the house. She always had an emergency fund, and I never had to learn what counted as an emergency.

. . .

Fi had a hard NO DRUG'S ON SITE policy. *I don't want any of my girls frothing and seizing onstage*, she said, *you can do that on your own time.*

I told Fi about the grammatical error in the same breath as I told her I'd heard some of the dancers were getting high backstage. Fi searched our lockers and Lacey lost her job on the spot. When I left the Panther that night, she was waiting outside, high and hysterical. Sunny was there too, but he was on a business call, pacing and talking and cussing loudly.

"Are you fucking kidding me, Kate?" is what Lacey said, picking her fingernails, rocking back and forth on her heels. Her lips were so chapped they bled. Her eyes were yellowed like they needed a wash. She was pretty, Lacey was. She *was*.

"I'm just trying to help."

"Help?" Lacey tried, tried, tried, to light a cigarette. I flicked my lighter for her, but she jerked her head away. I lit a cigarette for myself, and she grabbed it from my mouth. I lit another. "You just lost me my job," she said.

"You have to get clean, Lace. I didn't know what else to do."

"You lost me my fucking job."

"The drugs."

"My job."

We looked at each other.

"What did you think getting me fired was going to do?" Lacey dropped her cigarette and bent to pick it up, her fingers scrabbling against the concrete. She gave up, sighed, and held her hand out for another. I gave her mine. "You thought that if I didn't have a job, I couldn't afford the dope? You know I get that shit for free."

"I just thought—"

"So all you really did was make sure I don't have money to eat. Don't have money for a cab if I need one. A room if I need one."

"A room?" I said. "You're not staying anywhere."

"Oh, you thought that if you got me fired, I might come stay with you and Ma? Is that what it was? You thought we'd move in together like a little sorority? Slumber party?"

"You can, you know."

She could've. Ma loved Lacey for a lot of reasons, but one of them was because Lacey was fat. She delighted in Lacey's body. Was always telling her how gorgeous she looked in her skimpy Panther costumes. *You look perfect, hon*, she told Lacey one night. Lacey was wearing a silver sheath that stuck tight to her skin.

You don't think I look too big? Lacey pulled at the fabric.

You listen to me, Lacey baby. They tell us we're too fat, so we diet. They tell us we're too ugly, so we wear make-up. They tell us we're too slutty, so we close our legs until our wedding nights. What does that make us? Hungry, poor, and horny. That's what. You've gotta learn to be a woman on your own terms instead of theirs, you hear me? You don't owe them any kind of body or beauty or celibacy. You don't owe them shit. The best thing you can do in this world, my girls, is be fat, ugly, and fuck like a goddamn rabbit.

Ma thought Lacey was perfect just the way she was.

• • •

"I don't want to stay with you and your fucking ma, Kate. You don't get to make choices for me. I'm an adult. We're adults now. And you just got me fucking fired from the only job that'd still fucking take me. So thank you. Fucking thank you."

"There are twenty other strip clubs in the city."

"Other clubs?" Lacey laughed, a mean, squinting laugh. "I'm not white, Kate. I'm not skinny. I'm broke. Look at me." I did. I looked. "Look at me," she said. "Look at me."

"I am not you, Kate," she said. "We are not the same."

"I know who you are."

"We have never been the same."

"You're my sister, Lace."

"We're not sisters. You have a house. You have your ma. A bed. Cash. You're white. You're pretty. All you have to do is stand on a stage and the money will come. You have a body that people want. You haven't had it easy, I'm not saying that. I know that. I know that. No one's saying that. But don't you think for a second that we're the same. We are not the same. Our situations are not the same."

I looked at her. I looked down at my costume. We'd had a bachelor party come in that night, and the best man had spilled his bourbon and Coke on me. My stomach, still bare, was sticky with liquor. I touched it. I needed a shower.

Lacey Kahu

It's not that I don't want to talk about it. I've made peace with all that, I have. It's that I couldn't remember those nights if I wanted to. They're gray and swirling in my memory. Nights like storm clouds rolling in.

Lady Lane

(NÉE KATE BURNS)

After she let her go, Fi gave me Lacey's old shift. Nine p.m. through midnight, Thursday through Saturday. It was the big shift. The moneymaker. Those nights brought in dumb-drunk men by the tens, sometimes the hundreds, and I danced the hours away. I was still best in the crowd, still rendered still and solid by the spotlight, but I was good among the audience, and it was easier to collect cash from the floor than up on the stage.

One night I walked in and double-took. A Maori woman, full-figured with curly brown hair, was up there on the stage. But it wasn't Lacey at all. The way this woman moved, too stiff in the hips, she was Lacey's replacement.

That same night, I left the club and Lacey, the real one, was outside, sitting slumped on the sidewalk, head in her hands. I thought she was crying, and I crouched to console her, but when she finally looked up, her shoulders were shaking not from tears but laughter, her face was wide with a grin, her teeth browned, her eyes wild, she laughed and laughed and when I asked if she was okay, she just laughed louder, and when I asked if she wanted to come home with me, she spit in my face and called me a hooker. I gave her everything I made that night and went home.

I tried calling her the next day and every day. Tried texting. But you can't help someone who doesn't want to be helped.

Lacey Kahu

She lost me my job, the only job that would take me, and then, one night, as she finished up dancing my old shift, I ran into her in the Panther parking lot and she gave me her night's tips. Everything she had. She emptied her purse into my hands, said nothing at all, and then drove away. One day, I don't know what happened, the details, but I woke up bruised and sore and I was stretched across the back seat of her car and she'd left a note on the passenger seat saying, "Keys are in the glove box. Please don't steal the car. I'll be back for it before my shift tonight." One night I turned up at her place, her ma's place, with a black eye and a bleeding pussy and she ran a hot bath and lifted me into it and shampooed my matted hair clean and put me to bed in her bed. Both her and Ma were gone when I woke, but on the dining table she'd left a loaf of bread and a jar of peanut butter with a Post-it note reading EAT THIS stuck to its lid. And then there was the day she picked me up from Sunny's place. You can tell your best friend by who's there to drive you home from the worst day of your life.

Lady Lane

(NÉE KATE BURNS)

One night, she called. I'd worked a double at the Panther and Gary was snoring like a steam engine in my ear and my phone was on vibrate on the nightstand and even though Lacey called four times in a row, I slept. When I woke in the morning, it was too late.

Lacey's voice mails were hissed whispers, her voice muffled with her own hand, probably, covering the receiver. *He doesn't want to have it, Kate.* I could see it all in flashback. *I want to have it. I want to keep my baby. But he's not going to let me have it.*

She had spent the night at the hospital with two fractured ribs after Sunny shoved her off their porch steps and booted her in the side, the head, until the neighbors finally caved to her cries and called the cops.

She was in and out of consciousness in the ER, and the nurses couldn't have known better than to ring her emergency contact. Sunny picked her up when she was discharged and carried her home princess-style. Before Sunny came along, I'd been Lacey's emergency contact.

"I need to get out," she whispered when I called her back in the morning. When I picked her up from Sunny's, she limped down the porch steps with a duffel bag. He watched, leaning against the door-frame, bowl of cereal in hand, shouting slurs and thumping the door with his fist.

"You'll come back," he said. "You'll come crawling back."

Lacey clutched her side with one hand, the bag full of her life with the other. I hadn't seen her in a while. I didn't even know she was knocked up. After losing her job at the Panther, she'd hung around downtown for a while, but then she disappeared. I'd called and then given up calling. Texted to no response. I'd told Gary stories upon stories about the Sugar Club and high school and sleepovers and sisterhood, as if I could talk Lacey back into my life.

She looked different now. Sadder, emptier, her eyes shadowed black. I hooked my arm through hers and led her down the last few steps to the car. I helped her ease her body into the passenger seat. She smelled the same, beneath the thick layer of cigarette smoke and sweat and blood; she still smelled, just a little, of home. I drove her away from there as fast as I could.

"I'll get clean. I'm sorry, I'll get help," she said. "For how I've been, I'm sorry."

"Don't."

"I'm sorry," she said.

"Don't," I said. "I love you," I said.

She bled through her jeans and onto the seat of Ma's car. It was a lot of blood for a barely-there baby. Made a pool of red under her ass.

"It was meant to be my choice," is what she kept saying.

Lacey Kahu

Even during her hardest days, Kate let me crash on her couch. That's love. Love is letting a junkie recover from a miscarriage on your futon while your mother's dying in the next room. She was working every day at Hobbes and every night at the Panther, and she was supporting all of us. Gary offered her money, I think, but Kate didn't want his money. What I'm saying is that Kate and Gary started fighting.

Lady Lane

(NÉE KATE BURNS)

One night, a big show at the Panther, a couple hundred, cash in hand. Gary was in the audience, drunk and horny because he got turned on watching other men's eyes on me. When Gary got drunk he got grabby, and usually I didn't mind, sometimes I even liked how desperate his hands seemed for me, but I was tired from a night of grinding on the laps of groomsmen and one of them had forced a finger into my mouth and I couldn't shake the taste of metal no matter how many times I spit. I wanted a shower. I wanted to sleep.

On the way home, Gary kept sliding his hand up my thigh.

"Not tonight," I said.

"What's your problem?"

"I'm tired. I need a shower."

Gary moved his hand higher.

"Not tonight," I said again.

Gary laughed. "You've had strangers' hands on you all night, and now you're telling *me* to stop? I'm your boyfriend." He ran a finger over my underwear.

I slammed on the brakes, swerved the car, his car, off the road, into a ditch. I braced myself tight against the seat, but Gary's head swung forward. His chin smacked the dash, and he cried out. "Are you okay?" I said.

He was checking to make sure his teeth were still there. "What the fuck," he said. I got out and started walking toward Ma's place.

"What the fuck," Gary said again, limping after me, slurring, hand cupped under his chin to collect his own blood. "What the fuck was that, Kate?"

"I said no."

"I'm your boyfriend."

"And I said no." I took off my heels and walked barefoot.

"Are you serious?" Gary shouted, but I didn't turn around. "Don't make this out to be something it's not, Kate. You know this wasn't that."

"Okay," I said.

"So get in the car," he called.

"No," I said. It was a long way back to Ma's place, and it was cold. But the sunrise was red and pink and orange, and it wasn't a bad hike. Felt like walking through art.

Gary Parsons

(LAWYER, PARSONS & PARK)

Does it matter what I say? It seems like you'll believe her side of the story no matter what I say, and I'll be the guy who shows up as nothing more than a punch line. Is that right? I'll tell you one thing, though. I really did love Kate Burns. I did. I loved Kate Burns, but she never loved me.

Lady Lane

(NÉE KATE BURNS)

Ma didn't go through chemo, but she chopped her hair short anyway because it kept getting matted against her pillow with all the time she was spending in bed. A pixie cut, is what she wanted. We used the kitchen scissors and the blank TV screen as a mirror. I eyeballed the length.

Her hair wasn't like mine. Or, it looked like mine, almost exactly the same, but sift the strands through your fingers and the difference was obvious. Her hair was thin, wiry like string. Mine was thick and soft as fur. I always wondered if I got the texture from my father.

I said to her, *Can I ask you something, Ma?*

You just did.

The doctor said you don't have much longer.

He's said that a hundred times. I snipped, and a pat of blond fell to the floor. We both looked down at it. *A broken clock might be right twice a day, bunny, but it's wrong the other thousand minutes.* Ma had never had short hair because men liked long hair. She sighed. *I'm never getting laid again,* she said.

The doctor said you're running out of time.

These aren't questions, bunny.

I don't have any family, I said. *Once you're gone, I'll have no one.*

You'll have Lacey.

Do you know who my dad is? Or do you know any of my grandparents? Are any of them still alive? Do I have anyone out there?

Ma took the scissors from my hand and started chopping, haphazardly, wild. Chunks of hair fell to the floor at random, all different lengths. *Stop*, I said, but she didn't. She cut her hair all the way to her head, twice she nicked her scalp with the blades, twice she yelped before continuing to hack, hack, hack.

. . .

Hobbes didn't have to pay Ma out when they fired her. They couldn't have her working there bald, is what they told her. It was freaking the customers out. A bald lady in cosmetics. Some clause in our contract meant that they could fire us willy-nilly, no further obligation.

They did, in their defense, send a balloon to our house. There was a knock on our door, and by the time we got to it, the delivery person had gone. The balloon was full of helium, and it read OUR CONDOLENCES in golden cursive. Thoughts and prayers.

We inhaled the helium, glug by glug, and took turns prank-calling the Hobbes service desk and laughing and laughing. *Is your refrigerator running?* Ma said in a squeak.

Have you checked on the children? I said.

I'm dying of cancer, she said.

. . .

She kept note of the commercials that promised to help her. A drug that claimed to soothe the burn of radiation. A herbal alternative to chemo. A doctor who thought he'd found the cure for cancer in the blood of the Amazon milk frog of the Maracanã River in Brazil. She didn't seem to want to buy any of the items on the list, just wanted to note them. To want to want them.

Once, I said, *Ma, we could see how much that herbal alternative costs, at least?*

She said, *I'm not paying for a bunch of hippies to give me a hundred-dollar yeast infection.*

Then she doubled over in pain, and I rubbed her back in circles.

. . .

By the end of it, Ma was spending her days crying. I'd never really seen her cry. Not when one of her manfriends started shouting, nor when they started shoving. Not during *The Notebook* or *Titanic* or *Sleepless in Seattle*. Not when we couldn't afford electricity for the month, nor when our dog, Lady, who we'd had for ten years, finally died.

Lady had been lying on the floor, eyes drooping, panting and wheezing, and Ma had said, *It's time.*

I looked at Ma. Ma loved Lady.

Go get the shovel, she said.

What?

Ma sighed and took the wet dish towel from the shoulder of the kitchen sink. She wiped at her day's makeup. She called it *taking off her face*, that smearing of lipstick into a red stain.

She's in pain, bunny, said Ma. *It's the kindest thing we can do.*

Kill her?

That's right.

How is killing her kind?

Death is kind, bunny. It's life that hurts like a bitch.

I got the shovel from the garage and handed it to her and closed my eyes. Just that week, the doctor had told us Ma was deteriorating quickly and he recommended stopping all treatment and just keeping her as comfortable as possible until—

I'd said no. I'd said we had to keep trying. But the doctor insisted and I'd relented and I couldn't help but imagine myself with that shovel, raising it over Ma's head as she lay on the floor, curled like Lady, waiting for the fall.

Ma led Lady outside, and the dog sat, obedient, then lay down. She looked up at Ma.

What if she doesn't want to die, yet? I said.

Death's the one thing you don't get to say no to, bunny, said Ma. *Death's the one thing that has nothing to do with consent.*

Ma lifted the shovel and swung it back down with such strength she could have been healthy. The sound was a dull thunk.

We buried Lady beneath our old apple tree with the very same shovel. I cried, Ma didn't. She plucked an apple from a low-hanging branch and took a bite. *They're ripe,* she said.

I found one that had fallen, picked it up. Right before I bit into its skin, I saw the little brown hole, the rot, the apple infested, being eaten alive from the inside out.

. . .

When the doctors gave Ma just days to live, she didn't cry then, either. She held onto hope for a long time. In *Grey's Anatomy*, she explained, patients often make unexpected recoveries. A kid covered in a thick layer of cement is excavated and lives. A woman with an inoperable tumor is dismantled like a doll and put back together, sans cancer. But doctors in real life were no Meredith Greys. They told Ma she was going to die, and their job was merely to monitor her as it happened.

She didn't cry when they told her she was basically dead, but when we got home from the hospital, she flipped on the television to an infomercial for an electric dog collar. A white poodle galloped around a yard, panting with joy, then the dog stopped suddenly, leaped backward, shook his whole body to erase the electricity, and turned and ran in the other direction. *Call now for a ten percent discount*, the voiceover told us. Ma broke. She howled until she gasped for air. Grief always catches up to you.

. . .

The night she died, I'd made good money out of a bachelor party and I was giddy with cash and I picked up a container of fried rice from the Chinese restaurant that discounted its prices an hour before closing. When I got home, the house was dark and silent, and I knew what'd happened even before I saw the body. No room containing my ma had ever been quiet. But that night, the air was still as a corpse.

Lacey Kahu

I got back to Kate's place that night and she was sitting next to the body. It wasn't Ma. Didn't look a thing like Ma anymore. But Kate was just sitting there, holding her hand like she'd do if Ma was still alive, and she was telling stories. She was like, "Ma, remember when the neighbors put up those Christmas lights?" The stories weren't making sense. Kate wasn't well. She was saying, "Remember when the neighbors put up those lights and we turned them into Shirty Crammers?" What's Shirty Crammers?

Lady Lane
(NÉE KATE BURNS)

Each year, holiday season, the neighbors would put up flashing lights that winked through our windows all night long. The sign read MERRY CHRISTMAS! The *M* flashed red and the *E* flashed blue and the *R* flashed red and the other *R* flashed blue and so on and forever, and it looked just like the cops were outside, always outside, coming for us.

One night, Ma said enough was enough and she and I tiptoed over their yard in our slippers and we spent a long time rearranging the letters, laughing. *I bet we could spell "crap,"* said Ma, but no *P*.

Instead, we spelled TRASHY CRIMMERS.

We spelled STARCHY RIMMERS.

We spelled CHAMMY STIRRERS.

We spelled SHIRTY CRAMMERS.

. . .

The night she died, I sat next to her body for a long time, I think. She was all I had. The only family I had. She was where I belonged. It made sense to hold on to that for as long as I could.

Whenever I'd asked Ma about my father, she'd give me a new answer. Initially, I believed her. *Santa*, is what she told me at eight. *Why do you think he's called Father Christmas?*

I was so smug, at school, on Dad Day, when we were all meant to bring our fathers to school. *Where's yours?* said Rebecca Wiles. *Don't you have a dad?* I just smiled. I didn't need to prove myself to her. Didn't need to laugh in her face, in the face of her stupid plumber of a father, didn't need to sneer and say, *My dad's not here because he's Santa, Rebecca, fuck you.*

When I was ten, in the line for the McDonald's drive-thru, I asked who my father was when Ma ordered a family meal ("meant for three," the sign explained) for the two of us. *That was him,* Ma told me as we drove off with our dinner. She said, *Isn't he nice?* She was talking about the guy who handed over the bag and told us to have a nice night.

At thirteen she told me my father was Jim Carrey. We were watching *The Truman Show* and I said that sometimes my life felt like Truman's.

What the hell does that mean, bunny?

I just sometimes feel like I don't know anything about it. My life.

What do you want to know? I'll tell you anything.

Who's my father?

She was silent for a beat before pointing at the screen. *There he is,* she said, as Jim Carrey crashed into the end of his world.

Sometimes, often, like a habit, I opened every drawer in the house and rifled through the contents. In a movie, the kid would've found letters from her father in there. One for every birthday. I usually found toothpicks, chopsticks, and a condom or two.

. . .

After Ma died, I stopped going to work. Lacey, who was still staying with me, told me that the club might help get my mind off everything, but I couldn't bear the thought of dancing. Of moving. I knew what Ma would say. She'd say, *Don't waste time thinking about shit you can't change.* She'd say, *Get off your ass.* I could hear her in the walls. The house was haunted with her. After Lacey went to bed each night I ducked outside and slept in my car, just to get some peace and quiet.

One day, while Lacey was working the night shift, Gary came to help pack Ma's things. I was asleep in the car, and he knocked on the passenger door and I startled from my daze and cranked the window down and asked him to leave, told him to leave, demanded that he leave, but he wouldn't.

"Let's go," he said. "Inside."

"No."

"Let's go," he said. "We'll go together."

He sat beside me on the shitty couch, the one with permanent dips in the cushions from the weight of us and our ass predecessors. Pre-decassors. Ma and I had spent so many hours on that couch, watching marathons of bad television, classic movies, commercials selling gadgets we'd never buy. Gary took a sweater that had been shed and tossed on the floor. It was hers. He said, "Tell me about this one."

"She got it from the clearance rack at Hobbes. It had a hole in the armpit. When she brought it home, she put it on for me and said, *'It has a hole in the armpit but what does it matter unless I'm flapping and I'm no flapper?'* "

"Tell me about this one." It was her pink beret.

"She bought it the day she got her diagnosis. *I need a hat*, was the first thing she said. She didn't know much about cancer before she got diagnosed with it. Didn't even know much about cancer when she was living with it. She didn't want to research. *It's going to happen whether I know about it or not*, is what she said. She thought cancer meant her hair falling out, so she picked up the hat from a roadside stall. Sung the lyrics to 'Raspberry Beret' at the vendor. Then she told him, *This hat is to cover my cancer.* He gave it to us for free."

"Tell me about this one." We went through all of her stuff like this. Piece by piece. Gary never tired of the stories. He laughed when he was supposed to laugh. When I cried, he let me, for as long as I needed to.

"My wisdom teeth," I told him, when he lifted the gruesome jar off the mantel. The white bones swam in liquid pinkened by blood, mine.

"She kept them?"

"Ma wanted to. She told me I needed all the wisdom I could get."

He set the jar down.

"She'll never see me get married," I said. "She'll never meet my child." He was quiet for a long time. Gary was calculated; it was one of the things I liked best about him, his reaction was always the one he wanted to give. Everything about him was intentional. When a driver pulled in front of him in traffic, he would pause a beat, maybe flash his lights once, before braking to give the car some space. I had never seen anyone in such careful control of the self. *Isn't that scary?* Lacey said when I described him to her. *Feeling like he's always masking his real reactions?* But I didn't feel that way. Your real reaction is just the one you choose to enact.

"Do you *want* to get married?" is what Gary finally said, calm and measured. "Do you *want* children?"

"At some point. When I'm ready. Why?"

"I mean, you're not exactly—"

"What?"

"Fit to be a wife or mother right now?"

Oh. Oh, boy. That was not the right thing to say. See, I knew what Gary thought of me, my job. Society sees women on a sliding scale from human to body, and most people see strippers as a body on a stage to be bought. Gary, at least, saw me as human enough to date me. But he never saw me as human enough to marry or be a mother. I knew that. I knew that from the beginning, but, that night, masochistic and Ma-less, I probed. I said, "Why not?"

"I mean, you're a—"

"A what?"

"I mean you're a stripper."

"You should go," I said.

"Or are you planning on quitting your job?"

"You should go."

"Kate, please."

"Go, and don't ever come back."

He left, and I sat, taking each item from the toss pile, one by one, and adding it to the keep pile. I went into Ma's bedroom and put everything there into a pile too. I emptied her closet, her vanity, and then, in the bottom drawer of her nightstand, a collection of books in a row

with years drawn on their spines. I chose one and opened it. Ma wasn't
the type to keep journals. But the inside wasn't filled with emotional
passages or diary entries. Instead, it had pages and pages of carefully
drawn tables. A list of names, a list of dates, a list of amounts.

Chris, August 10, $200
Mason, August 13, $250
Jack, August 14, $380 (!!!)
Will, August 18, $250

Every manfriend I'd ever met. His name, the date, the amount.
Later, I'd look back and wonder why I was surprised. Or whether I was
surprised. I'd wonder whether maybe I'd known exactly what Ma was
doing all along and just kept the secret from myself.

I flipped to my birthday, April 1993, and then nine months earlier.

Christopher, December 27, $180
Frank, January 1, $410 (!!!)
Jeremy, January 02, $300
John, January 04, $350
Samuel, January 11, $300

I could have been paid for by any number of men. I was a product
of a sale. My worth? Somewhere in the low hundreds.

. . .

Gary called, and he called again and again and again. I blocked his number, and still I heard the ghosts of his phone calls. They woke me up in
the night. I lost track of what was real. I thought I'd known Ma, every
part of her, but she'd kept that secret, that great big secret, from me my
whole life. I barely knew her at all.

Lacey Kahu

I mean, they were keeping the exact same secret from each other. Kate kept the Sugar Club from her ma, and her ma kept her little side business from Kate. Neither wanted the other to know what they were doing to help keep their little family afloat. Neither wanted the other to know their sacrifice. It was stupid, but that might be love.

Anyway, that news, the news that Ma's manfriends weren't friends at all, the news that they'd been customers all along, that hit Kate hard. To tell you the truth, it had been obvious to me that Ma was getting paid for it, and I thought that Kate probably knew it too, and that it was just one of those things we didn't talk about. But the news hit Kate so hard that either she didn't know, or she'd talked herself into not knowing.

Lady Lane
(NÉE KATE BURNS)

I never saw Gary again. That's how relationships end in real life. There's no Empire State Building roof reunion, no running back into one another's arms, no kiss-in-the-rain apology. People love each other and then, in an instant, they don't even know each other. They turn stranger. Disappear from each other's plot completely. Like, Gary who?

• • •

Lacey took me to the salon for the breakup. It was where we went when something was serious. When she got syphilis, we got acrylics and googled symptoms. When she put a down payment on a house, we got our hair blown out. When Ma died, we got Brazilians and let ourselves cry from the pain. When she had to get a restraining order against a customer at the Panther, we had our eyebrows threaded. Good news, bad news, we didn't differentiate. When something changed in our lives, we changed our bodies too.

"Are you sure about it?" Lacey said. We sat side by side in massage chairs, a pair of beauticians rubbing our feet with lotion. "He's a good guy, Kate. He loves you."

"He called me a stripper."

"You are a stripper."

"It's the way he said it," I said. I flipped through the pages of Ma's journal. I kept it with me, always with me, from the moment I found

it, and flipping through it had become a habit. I'd close my eyes, turn
to a page, point at a name. Then I'd try remember that manfriend, that
day. What I'd been doing while she'd been getting paid for sex. As a kid,
I'd thought I was so lucky, meeting Ma's manfriends. Other kids, their
mothers kept their sex lives a secret. Even Lacey didn't know if her
parents still fucked. I'd thought, I'd wrongly thought, that Ma didn't
keep anything from me. I thought I knew her completely. All the way
through.

"You have to let that go," said Lacey. She wasn't talking about Gary
anymore. She pointed at the journal. "That," she said. "Let it go, Kate."

I'd told Lacey about the book and immediately regretted it. She
kept bringing it up. I could see her judging Ma, using it against her, and
I wanted to hit her. I wanted to be the one judging Ma, the one using
it against her.

"Gary told me about this place he went, once," I told Lacey. It was
a cheap salon and the technicians didn't speak much English and the
massage chairs pummeled our backs into submission and we loved it
there. "In Vegas, I think, or somewhere like that. These girls are making millions, Lace. They're millionaires."

"They're strippers?" Lacey picked up a wheel of colors and tried
each one on her index finger.

"It's a brothel."

"Okay," she said. "But you're not a hooker."

"Not yet."

Lacey frowned. The distinction between not-sex work and sex
work, for her, was a matter of morals, it was that which she'd done versus that which she wouldn't. Not ever. The line was blurrier for me, or
maybe it didn't exist. For me, it was that which I'd done and that which
I hadn't. Yet.

"It's called the Hop," I said.

"A little on the nose, don't you think?" Lacey finally decided on a
color, a deep, violent purple. She showed it to her nail tech.

"And get this," I said. "The girls working there? They call themselves Bunnies. Ma called me bunny."

"Because you had goofy teeth, not because you're a prostitute."

"But doesn't it feel like a sign?"

"Why are you bringing that up, anyway?" Lacey said. She leaned back in her chair and adjusted her massage settings. "You're not considering it, are you? You're not seriously considering it?"

The woman doing my pedicure used tweezers to tug a hangnail. "Ouch," I said.

"You have very ugly feet," she said.

Lacey laughed.

"I don't know what you're laughing about," my nail technician said, looking over at Lacey's toes. "You have ugly feet, too." We laughed, then. We laughed so hard the beauticians had to stop working. They huffed and went to help other customers, leaving us to our hysterics, our feet spotted with stray color.

. . .

I sent in my Hop application that same night.

Lacey Kahu

She was clearly hurting. She was self-destructing. She wasn't in her right mind. But what was I meant to do? She needed to get out of that house, away from the memory of Ma, and she needed to find herself. She wanted to know who she was outside of her mother's idea of her. And what was I meant to do? Stop her?

Lady Lane

(NÉE KATE BURNS)

You're not allowed to fly with human remains on commercial airlines. Not a corpse, not a body part, not ashes. The dead are meant to stay where they are.

Ma's funeral went like this: Lacey and I sat in the back row of the church while a cheap rent-a-preacher provided by the funeral home said stuff from the Bible, textbook, read it off like a script for a role he didn't want.

"If anyone would like to say anything about Mrs. Baker, I'd now like to invite you up to share memories." He scanned the empty pews as if there were a full crowd in attendance, a proper service. The church echoed with emptiness.

"Burns," Lacey shouted. "It's Miss Burns."

"If anyone would like to say anything about Mrs. Burns." The preacher paused and gave Lacey a pointed look. "I'd now like to invite you up to share memories."

I got up and told the story about the time Ma and I discovered that *Titanic* is a murder mystery. She had this fight with a manfriend, and when I got home from a shift she was screaming and he was slamming her head against her bedroom door. I got a knife from the kitchen and waved it at him a little and he backed off quick enough. When he was gone and everything was quiet, the door hung loose on its hinges.

I have an idea, is what Ma said.

We took the door to the community pool and dropped it in the water. It floated.

Get on, Ma said. I did. She hoisted herself onto the door beside me. It stayed afloat. *Plenty of room for two*, she said.

So what?

So Rose wanted him to die.

What?

So Titanic *is a murder mystery.*

After my speech, Lacey applauded and I took a bow. The preacher cleared his throat. He did not like the story.

They gave me her ashes in a cardboard box because I couldn't afford to upgrade to the jewelry-chest option or the urn. The box was painted white, and it had a plastic crucifix glued on the top. "Meryl Baker," someone had scrawled in Sharpie, her last name wrong and her first name spelled the Streep way.

· · ·

Just before I left for the airport, I tipped most of Ma into the garden out the front of our house. All but a handful. The last of it, I swallowed with a glass of water.

ACT II

THE HOP

And she frequently forgot,
That her body (all our bodies) is a house of sand.
That it had shattered and is shattering still

—Han Kang, *The White Book*

Lisa Hamilton
(FEATURES EDITOR, *VOGUE*)

What the world knows about Lady Lane's early days at the Hop is minimal. She was a regular Bunny for a while; before she blew up big, she was just another Vegas sex worker—that city's teeming with them—but that's about all we know. The other Bunnies I spoke to for her feature weren't exactly forthcoming. It's like they have some kind of pact: what happens at the Hop stays at the Hop, kind of thing. The other thing we know is that Lady Lane started working at the Hop around the same time as girls started going missing from the streets.

Mia

(NÉE YA CHAI CHEN, BUNNY, THE HOP)

The day she arrived? Of course I remember it. The day she arrived was slow. A lot of our days were, those days, but that day was especially slow. One of those sorts of days you can't imagine it ever getting to night. Nevada summer, hot as a motherfucker, my body lotion kept turning to slime on my skin and no matter how many times I powdered I looked like a swamp monster the very next minute. It was hot. Hot! We were all just sitting in the parlor, talking shit, bored. A couple of the girls had appointments, but I didn't have anything booked for the day and I was just waiting around in case we got a walk-in. The sun was gluing the leather loungers to our bare thighs and our bangs to our foreheads. The radio was playing some electronic music that sounded like a neon sign running out of juice, and Betty wouldn't shut up about her last guest, who'd told her the market was hot for fast food franchises lately and ever since then she'd been gabbing about getting herself a Taco Bell. Calling it an investment. Plus, she was saying, you can make your own specials.

She said, "That's the difference between a successful drive-thru and a dud, darlings."

We fanned our faces with our hands.

"The thing is knowing when to do a two-for-one deal versus when to do a free drink combo. That's an instinct you're born with or not," she told us. "Like today, what special would you do today, Rain?" Rain picked a scab on her knee. "Free drink," said Betty, tapping her forehead, meaning her brain. "Free drink because of the heat, see?"

We were bored. But the day she turned up on our doorstep was the last time I can remember being bored at the Hop.

Rain

(NÉE ASHLEY SMITH, BUNNY, THE HOP)

The only reason I remember the day she arrived is because of the news. The biggest headline that day was something about Hillary Clinton's emails, and the second biggest headline was that twelve hookers had been found dead in dumpsters. Some Bunnies had never worked the streets, but I was waiting to hear names. They only ended up identifying three of the bodies, Prisha Singh, Pauline Davies, Wang Xiu Ying, and when they did, I realized that I didn't know any of my street friends' birth names anyways.

That's how I can remember the day she arrived.

It wasn't. I checked. The back of the billboard read HELL IS REAL and 1–800-CALL-JESUS. A handy reminder for those of us en route to sin.

Back home, Ma and I lived down the road from a church with a sign out front that read LET JESUS ENTER YOU, and every time we drove by it, Ma would shake her head. She'd say, *Not without a condom.*

I was trying not to think about Ma, those early days at the Hop. I was trying not to, but sometimes it seemed like she was more in my head than I was.

· · ·

I was thirsty, I remember that. Thirst was a thing I let myself feel. Thirst was easy. Some feelings are knots of emotion and pith, complicated and heavy, like sadness, like loss, like grief, feel the weight of that, *grief.*

I kept my mind off her by thinking about everything else. Like, highway. Dashboard. Eighty miles an hour. What's that in metric, like 120? The imperial system. Pounds. Ounces. Yards and feet. Toes. That guy who sucked my toe while we had sex. Sex. Sweat. My AC had quit two hours ago, and my face was licked with sweat, drooling down my temple, settling above my lip, and when I wiped at it, new beads took the place of old ones immediately, like they'd been waiting in line, eager for a chance to surface. It was hot. So hot it felt like a trap.

A clanging came from deep in the car's belly. My Corolla was pregnant with something mechanical. I asked it, "Can you be quiet?" but the car clattered its response, and so instead I became louder, it's all relative, sound, suffering, all of it. I lowered my foot on the accelerator and turned up the radio.

· · ·

Ma and I had liked taking road trips. We did it with the windows down and the AC on blast. We liked to feel fast. She'd inhale her way through a pack of cigarettes and I'd puff on pretzel sticks to match. We asked

Lady Lane

(NÉE KATE BURNS)

In some ways, starting at the Hop felt like starting my life over. It felt like a second chance, a chance to be someone new, and it felt right that I had to take two planes and a car to get there—being reborn should take some effort. The flight's hazy in my memory, I popped some of Ma's sleeping pills and passed out right away. The drive, though, it's fresh in my mind.

It was like this: three hundred kilometers of desert, orange and open and flat, like driving on the sun, then there was the Hop. It was this mansion among nothingness. Beautiful and unexpected, a birthmark found during a one-night stand. Coming across it felt intimate. It felt like, *there you are.* Like, *I've been looking all over for you.*

It was easy to find, the Hop was. By the time I got there, its gift shop was billboard famous. Every fifth sign along I-11, slotted between pro-life images of fetuses spiraled in wombs, advertisements for car accident lawyers, some new drug that'll cure your depression, a McDonald's burger, bigger and better than their other ones, then the Hop Gift Shop: CLOTHING OPTIONAL. A girl, arm slung over her breasts, legs spread for drivers, but instead of genitalia, there was a split pomegranate between her thighs, its insides appropriately pink and wet. I wondered how many hopeful truckers had turned in their seats, checked their rearviews, fingers crossed that, for some reason, the uncensored image might be on the back.

the radio questions and let it tell our fortune. *Where are we going?* Ma asked the dash, and I pressed to skip the station, and how we hooted when AC/DC said *highway to hell.* Ma tried again: *Are we going to win the lottery this week?* We landed on a commercial, *Only two dollars ninety-nine!*

. . .

I exited the interstate and things got quiet fast. Without the road noise, the other cars, the signs, the billboards, the world felt still and flat and big. It was not New Zealand. In New Zealand, you existed between mountains. Back home, you were always heading toward something, an end, the edge. Here? I drove. There was a hot haze coming off the tarmac, and I couldn't see the end of the highway—here, I was heading for a vanishing point. The radio dipped into country, then pop, then a religious station with a deejay who kept saying "Hallelujah" in between all the static. It sounded like an exorcism. I killed the sound and drove.

There were these big black birds. They came out of nowhere and started swooping low in the sky, their flight plans following the path of a conductor's hands, they swooped and swooped and swooped. I could almost hear the orchestra they conjured with their wings. Heavy on string. A wailing violin. The birds themselves seemed to be silent. I thought, *If this were a movie, these birds would be some clunky symbolism*, and then I thought, *But this is not a movie.* The birds multiplied. Sometimes they got so close to the windshield I winced.

I hated birds. I still do. Once, as a kid, I tried to pick up a gosling. Tiny, fuzzy, a walking ball of lint. They were waddling in a row at the lake, five of them behind their mother. The last one in line was lagging, weaving drunken zigzags and losing its way. I'd crouched to set it on the right track when its mother turned around. She looked me in the eye and quacked twice, warning shots, then charged. She chased me around the park, wings spread wide, her honking, me howling. Ma held her stomach and laughed and laughed.

You don't mess with a ma's babies, bunny, is what Ma said when the goose finally tired of her tirade. She took her goslings, all five, and drifted off on the water, surrender as sudden as her ire. *We'll do anything for our babies.*

. . .

My phone rang, and I let it. Gary, Lacey, Fi, whoever it was, I was starting anew and I would not be taking the past's calls. I considered tossing the phone out the window, and I would've if I were in a movie, Nicole Kidman on the run, mysterious, shrouded in sexy mystery. I would've lit a cigarette and thrown the phone and watched it shatter in my mirror. But I wasn't Nicole Kidman and I had less than $100 to my name, so I waited for the phone to finish vibrating and switched back to the GPS.

. . .

The owner of the Hop—Daddy—he assured me over one of our many phone calls that my accent would be an advantage. "You've got that exotic factor," is what he told me. "You should play it up," he said. "Wear some Crocodile Dundee shit, you know? One of those hats with the corks."

I didn't correct him on the country. I needed the job, and I got it after sending a portfolio of photographs, portraits, close-ups, nudes, full-body shots, as well as a video of myself engaged in a selection of sexual acts. Daddy called in the middle of the night, oblivious to time zones or uncaring or both. "How soon can you get here?" he said. "I can fast-track your visa. We've got an unexpected vacancy." I didn't like the sound of "unexpected vacancy," but I was nodding anyway. Daddy told me he'd never hired a girl without testing her out first. By *testing her out*, he meant fucking her.

It was three in the morning when I hung up on Daddy, and I got out of bed and packed my bag right then.

• • •

Without Ma, even though I inherited the house, I didn't have a home anymore. I had a run-down, wrong-side-of-town two-bedroom shithole between the city's dump and a patchwork of cow paddocks. I had a toilet that ran without end and rusted pipes and carpet that peeled up at every chance it got and black mold spreading over the ceiling like whispered gossip. It was so quiet in that house without her. Even with the infinite voices of reality television, the Kardashians, *The Bachelor*, *The Real Housewives of Somewhere* blaring in the living room, and the video of a smoker's cough I'd found on the internet and played on a loop, it was so quiet it made me motion sick. Like I was floating, couldn't get my bearings, like being in a suddenly pitch-black space, like missing the last step on the staircase, my whole world vanished in an instant.

Betty

(NÉE JOSHUA BETTS, BUNNY, THE HOP)

Who is Kate Burns? I don't know, darling. I never knew her as Kate. What I do know is the day Lady Lane turned up on our doorstep, everything went to shit.

From day one, she was trouble. Thorn in my side, cloud to my silver lining. Which isn't to say I didn't love her, baby, don't get me wrong, I loved her. I did. But I also loved booze and blow and bearded boys on bikes, by which I mean, you know, I'd always loved things that hurt me. When I was a kid, the boys beat me bloody in the bathrooms for being so feminine, and you know what? I didn't mind it. I wasn't a masochist; I just liked the affirmation—at least I was coming across the way I always saw myself. As a girl. When they called me a faggot, I shrugged. When they called me a girl, I blushed. I was! I was! I was!

Oh, you want me to talk about Lady? Sure, I guess, but know that you're hearing the wrong story, because, baby, I am a hell of a lot more interesting than her.

Lady Lane

(NÉE KATE BURNS)

There was this row of people dressed in white and standing on the corner of the Hop's driveway. I slowed to pass them, to take my turn, and they turned monster.

They yelled through my window. Called me a sinner and held up signs that read KEEP NEVADA BROTHEL-FREE. One of them said, "You're going to hell!" and another one, a child wearing a red baseball cap and a white T-shirt that read NO MORE WHORES, shouted, right at my face, "Slut!"

The word, that one, it was always a slap, but I'd been hit by it a million times. I leaned as far out my window as I could and shouted, "Jesus told me he thinks you're ugly." I didn't know much about the Bible. I didn't even know if Jesus and God were the same person or not, and whenever I asked someone about it, their answer was too slippery to hold. Once I went to a Halloween party dressed as the Holey Ghost because Ma and I didn't have any bedsheets the moths hadn't gotten to.

This woman, maybe the kid's mother, she screamed, "You'll pay for your sins!" And I had to laugh at that, because I wouldn't pay for my sins, I'd get paid for them. I thought about telling the woman that, but then I didn't, I just drove on. They got smaller, smaller in my mirror, but their gazes still felt predator or police, like I was being followed, like I was doing something criminal.

The Corolla gagged and stalled and gave up entirely a hundred meters from the Hop's front door. I cranked the key in the ignition, but there wasn't even a splutter, so I shouldered my backpack. The only parts of me I brought: a toothbrush, a second outfit, underwear, socks, one picture of Ma, me and her on the beach, and the book, hers, the one with the list of manfriends, her sex work log.

I'd started out packing real luggage—trinkets, framed photos, a bunch of Ma's stuff—but looking at it all, barely filling a suitcase, it was depressing. My whole humanity was cabin-sized. I dragged my old pack from the closet instead. I decided on necessities only. I was alone. Why would I want to bring more of myself, sad self, than I needed? It was my chance to start over.

Mia

(NÉE YA CHAI CHEN)

I heard her car, and that's how I knew the new girl'd arrived. This *tha-thump-tha-thump* that sounded like a heartbeat through a stethoscope. I watched her pull up through the peephole. The other Bunnies dispersed, disappeared. They were playing hard to get, but I've always been easy.

She was driving a dump. Loud as anything. Clunking along before it shuddered, went *bang*, and stopped altogether. Her silhouette was all I could see, and the shadow threw up its hands, frustration, anger, and the car door flew wide open like she'd really booted it. She got out.

Here's what Kate looked like: every man's dream. My dream! She was gorgeous, drop-dead, and young, tall as a pole and her legs stopped where her arms started. Her hair was blond and shaggy like a rock star's, and her skin was white but it glowed like she had a fire in her. Her sunglasses were pushed back into her hair and she moved like someone was taking her photograph. I went, "Fuck." I went, "Fuck fuck fuckfuckfuck."

See, beautiful is the best thing for a Bunny to be because it means you don't have to earn people's attention every time, and in this industry, in this world, attention is everything.

When girls like Kate arrived at the Hop, it was the rest of us who took the hit.

Lady Lane

(NÉE KATE BURNS)

There were five white-painted steps leading up to the Hop's wraparound porch. It was decorated with rocking chairs, side tables, hanging baskets filled with pink flowers. A dollhouse. Straight out of a fairy tale. If you didn't know it was a brothel, the place could've been a candy store. No one was sitting outside because it was hot, so hot. I was glad they weren't. I was never good with first impressions, but I was good with other impressions. Ma could do a great John Travolta. I could do a decent Olivia Newton-John. Sometimes we re-enacted the final scene from *Grease*— the one where Sandy transforms her entire self into someone Danny might want to be with. *You're the one that I want*, we sang to each other, shaking our shoulders in time. I loved that scene, thought it was romantic how much Sandy was willing to change to be with John Travolta. Ma clicked her tongue about that. *You don't change who you are for any man, bunny*, she told me. *Especially not a Scientologist.*

. . .

The doorbell was one of those camera ones. I pressed it, practiced my smile, cleared my throat. I was hoping that, despite having barely said a word since leaving the airport, my voice was still in there, somewhere, dormant inside me. No one answered. I knocked, and then there were footsteps.

The girl who answered the door said "Hi!" with such enthusiasm I could hear her exclamation point. "You must be the replacement!" is what she said.

"The replacement?"

"I'm Mia," she said. She was tiny, Asian, gorgeous, barely came up to my shoulder, and looked like she could've been anywhere between ten years old and thirty. Her hair was in pigtails, her mouth painted a pink so pale it looked as if she'd mistaken a stick of chalk for lipstick. Her white dress frilled around the sleeves, and the hem barely reached her crotch. Around her waist was a sash of magenta, which she'd tied into a bow's caricature at the front. I had imagined the brothel to be a little more nuanced, but no, here I was, on the porch of a porn set. Mia sipped from a straw sunk deep in a glass of something frozen and pink. She let go of the drink with one hand to shake mine.

"Kate," I said.

Her palm was wet. It's strange, the things you remember.

"You'll have to come up with something better than that," she said. Smiled. Her teeth were so straight and so white. I closed my mouth.

"Than what?"

"Than Kate."

"My name?"

"You can be anyone here," said Mia. "You're a Bunny now. I had mine picked out before I got here. Mia," she said, pursing her lips around the *M*, a silent kiss, right there in her name. "I like the vowels," she said. "Vowels are sexy. Moans are made of vowels, you know." She paused. "You look like someone," she said, squinting at me as if I was too bright for her eyes, as if there was more to me than me. "You look like someone. Who is it?"

"Someone asked if I was related to Angelina Jolie once?"

"No," she said. "It's not her. Definitely not her." She shook her head. I'd go on to become so familiar with this habit of hers, the way she could rid herself of whichever thought she wanted gone like an Etch A Sketch, this quick toss of the head and she was empty again.

"So then, new Bunny." Her eyes were wide and a shade of blue too sky-like to be biological. She was so feminine I felt like a pile of meat. "Are you coming inside or what?"

When she turned to lead me back into the house, I noticed the powderpuff tail glued to her ass. It shifted, side to side, with every step.

And I remember thinking, I remember calculating, if I turned around right then, got right back on the road, I could've been at LAX in a matter of hours. I could've been home in a day.

Mia

(NÉE YA CHAI CHEN)

Kate looked like she was going to run, and then she pulled this journal out of her pocket and she thumbed through the pages. Once, twice. There was this spark of fear in her eyes and then nothing.

I went, "You okay, hon?"

She smiled, and I'll tell you something, she was beautiful.

Lady Lane

(NÉE KATE BURNS)

I don't usually do the new girl tour," is what Mia said, standing in the Hop's parlor, her voice echoing like she was hooked up to a mic. Everything in the room, like the porch, was pink and white. The floor, white and marble; the walls, striped pastel pink and white. If you licked them, they might taste of peppermint. There was a large desk with a pair of computers, side by side, two keyboards, and a single pink pen with a fuchsia feather attached to the top.

Mia pointed at the empty desk. "But Cheryl's at lunch and she asked if I could show you around, and you want to stay in Cheryl's good books. That's the first lesson I'll teach you, new Bunny. Stay. In. Cheryl's. Good. Books."

Mia talked in fast forward. I watched her tongue perform its gymnastics, and I understood why she did what she did. It was hard not to imagine that tongue, pretty and pink, working its way around the head of a penis.

• • •

There are sex toys in the shape of porn stars' mouths, you know. I've seen them on the internet. Ran a search for a *Merchant of Venice* summary late one night before an English paper was due, and there, on my screen, a barely dressed woman showing me a model of her mouth, inflatable and prelubricated. It was a good imitation of her mouth, too, the plastic pout. The lips, tongue, teeth, fillings and all, men could buy their favorite sex actress's exact face to fuck. I doubt the blow job from the replica ever feels as good as they'd imagined. They never really want the mouth, only want to want the mouth.

. . .

"Are you listening, new Bunny?" is what Mia said.

"Stay in Cheryl's good books," I said.

"Right, so we call Cheryl the Hooker Booker because she makes all our bookings for us, sorts out scheduling and room assignments, and makes sure we get paid. She takes the house's cut, that's fifty percent of every sale, and she deducts your room and board, too. A hundred bucks for every day that you don't put at least a grand on the books. It includes a meal voucher. Hooker Booker, got it?" She pointed to a metal sign on the front desk. HOOKER BOOKER, the sign said. I thought about asking whether the term *hooker* was offensive to those in Mia's profession, but I didn't.

My profession.

Mia went on without waiting for any kind of acknowledgment from me. "Anyway, this is the parlor, it's basically Cheryl's room. It's also where we have parties, special occasions, birthdays, that kind of thing. And it's where we do lineups. Has Daddy told you about those? I'm sure we'll do one today. There's usually at least one a day, even on the slow days. You'll want to figure out your thing first though."

"My thing?"

"Yeah like, your *thing*."

I stared.

"Your thing!" she said, gesturing, wrists rotating in tiny circles. As if it was in the air, the thing, bugging her like gnats in the summer. "Your whole *thing*, you know? Like, who *are* you? Why would anyone want you?"

My face must've done something, because Mia grabbed my hand. "Oh Bunny, I didn't mean it like that. I meant, like, you need a character, you know? A point of difference. Right now you're just kind of . . . blah."

"Blah?"

"Sad, or something. Sad isn't sexy. Are you sad?"

She was still holding my hand. Hers felt too smooth, too unblemished, like plastic. I squeezed, and sure enough, the flesh gave.

"It's basic publicity, Bunny," she said. "You need to develop a character to position yourself in the market, and the market is the Hop. Why should a guest choose you over any of the other girls here? You have to appeal to a certain kind of guy, or to a guy looking for a certain kind of girl. Look at me," she said. I was. I couldn't not. She was magnetic, Mia was, like watching a one-woman show. Her performance was flawless. "I'm doing the cute thing, see? This hair? I bleach it every Sunday to keep my roots from showing. I'm five foot nothing, keep up with my Botox, and see these freckles? They're tattooed on. Hurt like a bitch, but I really think they complete the look. That's my thing. Guys looking for youth, for like, the cute bubbly girl, I'm their pick, right?" Even as she was describing her type, she was enacting it. Her index finger twirling a strand of hair, making a spool of blond. "See? A *thing*."

• • •

There was a television in the parlor, the biggest one I'd ever seen; it covered almost an entire wall and played commercial after commercial. There was no sound accompanying the image, but the advertisements didn't need audio to explain them. A commercial for Pantene or some other big hair brand. Kim Kardashian standing in a crowd of otherwise bald heads; she flipped her hair over her shoulder and it fell like something fluid, rippled, stilled. *Stand out from the crowd*, said Kim's lips. She was looking at the camera, at us. *With Pantene.*

• • •

Pantene, I'd learned back at Hobbes, actually has a twenty-seven percent share of the global shampoo market. Stand out, indeed.

. . .

Mia pointed and said, "What's that?" She was talking about the journal in my hands: Ma's. I'd been thumbing through its pages and the pad of my thumb was raw and bloody with paper cuts and the book's cover was smeared red. I put it away.

"What do you think my *thing* should be?" I asked Mia. "What kind of girl do I seem like to you? Maybe I could be, like, the fun one."

There was a bouquet of flowers on Cheryl's desk, naked ladies. I leaned in to smell them, only to inhale plastic. I'd go on to learn that the logic of the Hop was that performance was always more perfect than the real. Fake flowers couldn't brown. Fake boobs wouldn't droop. And us girls? We were more fantasy than fact too.

Mia frowned. She slurped the last of her drink, and the ice chattered. "No. That's not it. Sorry," is what she said. I liked her already. If I were a guest, at the Hop to get laid, I'd've taken Mia in a heartbeat.

"Let me think," she said, taking a step back, and eyed me head to toe. "You've got that adorable accent, so you've got a jumping-off point. Where's that accent from? England? So you could, like, play up that whole thing, right? Like, you could do the British thing, I'll bet there are guys who are totally into that. Cheerio, old chap. There are guys who are into everything, you've just got to pick your niche. You don't want to go too broad because there's probably already a girl doing that and doing it better than you ever could, no offense, but you don't want to go too narrow, either, or you won't get enough guests. Get it?"

"New Zealand," I said.

"What?"

"I'm from New Zealand."

"Cute," she said with a smile of perfect teeth, straight and white as a suburban fence. "New Zealand. I love that for you. I'm Thai. I've never been to Thailand, though. I was born in Houston. Just outside of it. But my parents are both Thai. Don't tell anyone. The guests prefer it if I call myself Japanese. I guess Japanese is the sexy kind of Asian. Guys who call in, they're always asking Cheryl if the Hop's got any

Japanese girls, and they don't even really mean that. What they mean is that they want a woman who looks the way a white person imagines an Asian person should look. They want our skin so pale we're a shade away from white. When guests like that come in, Cheryl points them to me."

"That's awful," I said.

Mia cocked her head.

"I mean, it's racist," I said. "Of them, the men, not you."

"It's life," she said. "And it's guests, not men. We call them guests. They're not all men. Okay? Got it? Anyways, whatever you're doing now is kind of cute. Maybe you should work with that."

"What do you mean?"

"Whoever this is." She framed my face, Madonna-like. "Whoever this character is? It works for you."

"I'm not being a character. I'm just being myself."

She frowned. "You think a self isn't a character?"

"I just mean that I'm not acting."

"Of course you are, honey." She set her empty glass on Cheryl's desk and started off toward a door at the far end of the foyer. "We all are. Someone will get that," she said about the glass. "The cleaners here are amazing. It's always clean, but you never see anyone cleaning. They're like ghosts."

Rain

(NÉE ASHLEY SMITH)

We watched Mia give her the tour through a crack in the door. Daddy'd finally found a replacement, was the word, and she was a perfect one too. Looked like an angel. Like some real sent-from-heaven, floated-down-to-earth, halo-wearing, hovering-above-the-ground, white-tunic angel. She looked like nothing bad had ever happened to her, and like nothing bad ever could. Like if some gunman saw her on the street, he'd put that weapon down like, *not today.* She was Julia Roberts meets Cameron Diaz. Made for the movies. She hurt me to look at even though she wasn't going to put me at risk. Daddy'd never replace me with a white girl. I told Tiffany she might have something to worry about, though. I told her she'd better get her numbers up or she'd be on the streets by next week.

"Her?" said Betty. "*She's* the girl. *Her?*" But Betty could say what she wanted. We were all thinking the same thing—*We're fucked.*

Lady Lane

(NÉE KATE BURNS)

The room looked like a movie set. Like if a script read "brothel lounge" and it was the set designer's first day on the job. Pink couches lined the walls. There was a bar, a coffee station, a vending machine, all pink. There was an all-white mannequin in the middle of the room, tits like this, and even her pubic hair was plastic. She had her arms thrown up to the sky like a gymnast who'd finished her routine. Her eyes were white and pupil-less. She was looking everywhere because she was looking nowhere.

The room was like the waiting room at a hair salon or a doctor's office or a body shop, but instead of getting my hair blow-dried or my blood taken or an oil change, the service was sex and that's what was being waited for, in here. There were no chairs or mirrors like a salon, no stethoscopes or scales, no clanking of the mechanical. Sex requires only two bodies. Just genitals and a word of consent. I was nervous as hell.

"This is the living room. The lounge. It's where the Bunnies hang out during downtime," said Mia, filling two new glasses with the same pink slush from a Slurpee machine standing in the corner of the lounge. "So, what brings you to the Hop, new Bunny? Scary time to get into sex work. Why now?"

"Scary?"

"The murders," said Mia. She frowned. "You haven't heard about the murders?"

"Murders?"

She pulled up an article on her phone. The headline: "Bodies of Twelve Prostitutes Found Dismantled in Desert Shores Dumpsters." I looked at Mia. She shrugged and said, "It happens."

"Did they find the guy?"

"Which one?" She laughed, but there was a space behind the laughter, an echo. "So, what brings you here, new Bunny? The money? The love? The sex? You want to be wanted? You want to be famous?"

"Money," I said. It wasn't the real answer, but it seemed like the easiest answer. What was I going to do, tell her my life story? Well, back then, no one was interested in my life story. People are only interested in you when other people are interested in you.

"There's plenty of money to be made," is what Mia said.

Into each glass she dropped a plastic straw and an umbrella, pink.

"So, this is the lounge," she said, leaning against the counter. "You're not running away yet. That's a good sign, new Bunny. Some girls turn up and realize, well, I don't know what. The Hop is exactly what you picture when you picture a brothel, isn't it? Maybe it's too"—she tapped her nose—"You know?"

"It *is* a little too . . ." I looked around. The pink. The satin. The leather. TV screens in every corner showing girl after girl after girl.

"Exactly," she said. "But I have a good feeling about you. I think you're gonna stick. So, what's your name going to be, new Bunny? Kate sucks. Katie's more promising. K is a sexy letter, you know, I learned that in a marketing class I took in college. K is sexy, they told us. It's why there are so many K brands. Kodak, Kit Kat, Kroger, Kraft—"

"You went to college?" I said, trying not to sound surprised.

Mia frowned. "You think hookers have to be stupid?"

"You think college makes you smart?"

She laughed. "You're good," she said, lifting her glass in a toast. "I like you."

The drink tasted like lip gloss. I finished it and immediately wanted another. The machine Mia had poured them from was full again. "It's full again," I told her. We were the only two people in the lounge. It seemed like we were the only two people at the Hop.

"Are there other people here?" I said.

"Want another?" she said. I did.

Mia handed me a full glass and touched the lip of hers to mine so lightly there wasn't even a sound.

CSI Miami told me, once, that we toast to ensure the absence of poison in our drink. Clink glasses, and the liquids might splash, mingle, land in the wrong cup.

Mia

(NÉE YA CHAI CHEN)

I liked her from the beginning. When I asked her why she was here, she went, "Money." Just like that. I liked that. I liked her.

A common question from people who have never been sex workers is *Why do you do it?* and they're never satisfied with the truth, which is usually *Money.* They want there to be another reason, something deeper, they want to hear that you were unloved as a child or that you were abused as a teen or that you suffered in some way that pushed you into the industry. They're sadists, all of them. All of them! They feel that there must be damage, and they probe for a bruise like picking peaches at the grocery store. As if money isn't enough of a reason to do anything. As if staying alive isn't enough of an answer.

And so I liked her from the beginning. She seemed real. She stood before the parlor's mannequin, looked it in the eye, took its hand in hers and shook, like *How do you do*, and then she stroked the figure's plastic hair. I knew she was going to be bad for my sales, and I knew she was going to cause some shit, and even though I knew all this from the moment I saw her, I liked her. Kate was cool and she demanded you know it when she walked in a room, but then she'd touch your shoulder like she was your closest friend the very next second, and it had a way of making you feel important. Those are the most dangerous girls. The ones who can chew you up like bubble gum and stretch you out from between their lips and wrap you around their little finger, wad you up and spit you out and leave you to harden on the sidewalk. I felt ugly as old gum at her side. But honestly (honestly!) I felt lucky to have been in her mouth in the first place.

"Are you nervous?" I asked her. "Have you done this before?"

"Loved," I said.

"What?"

"You said 'loved,' that you 'loved' her. Past tense. What happened to her?"

Mia's smile barely shifted. "Love," she said. "I still love her. She's just, you know, it's different when you don't see someone every day. She's not a Bunny anymore. We're like sisters here, us Bunnies, and she used to be one of us."

"She left?" I said.

Mia nodded, then she disappeared. The whole room did.

"It's okay, Lady," she said from the new darkness. The televisions, the lights, it was all gone. Dark. I held my hand to my face, wiggled my fingers, nothing. It was like being in space, or asleep, or dead.

"It's just a reset," Mia said, and she found my wrist in the dark and held it.

"A reset?"

The light was as sudden as the dark. Mia blinked. "Welcome back," she said with a smile.

"What was that?"

"A reset," she said again, then added, "I'm so glad we found your perfect Bunny name. Lady. Let me show you to your room, Lady. I love it!"

"Lady Lane," I said.

"Lady Lane!" She clapped. It was a big part of her repertoire, that little show of applause. "I just love it. Lady Lane! It's perfect."

I wondered if, in her room on a slow night, she still found h giggling, twisting her hair up into pigtails, clapping her h glee. I wondered if, if you did it long enough, you becar mance; the performance became you.

Lady Lane

(NÉE KATE BURNS)

Done it before? It was all I'd ever done. People are always asking, *What made you a sex worker?*, like they're expecting there to be one single event that made this line of work inevitable. I want to know if anyone asks a barista, *What made you a barista?* Or a doctor, *What made you a doctor?* Their answers would probably be just as boring as ours. What made the barista a barista? The sign out front saying HELP WANTED. What made the doctor a doctor? Med school. What made me a hooker? I did. I made me into this. The Panther, the Sugar Club, this was always where my life was headed, ever since Lacey and I sat in the back of Clark's Convenience and found our *Cosmo* quiz hooker names. Mine: Lady Lane.

. . .

"Lady," I said to Mia. "What about calling myself Lady?"

"Oh," she said. "I love it," she said. "And it suits you! Lady. Just Lady? You want a last name? Some girls like to be a little more explicit with their last names. Mercedes Bends, for example."

"Mercedes Bends?"

"Yeah," Mia said. "Lady is better than Mercedes Bends. No offense Mercedes. I loved the girl, but with a name like that, it's no wonder t all the bad seeds." She set our empty glasses on the bar and took d.

Lacey Kahu

It's like I said: Kate had been performing her whole life. Ever since she could speak, her mother made her play roles, dress up in some costume or another for a new scam or their day's get-rich-quick plan. Performing is normal—everyone plays their part during the day—but it's important to have a self to come home to. Kate had been performing as others for so long that the only role she seemed to have no idea how to play was herself.

Lady Lane

(NÉE KATE BURNS)

There was a high-pitched ring.

"What's that?" I said. "Recess?"

"Lineup," said Mia. "You're about to see your first lineup, Lady."

The image that came to mind was prison. Women in orange jump-suits. Confiscated clothing. Mug shots. But when the women appeared, it was as if they were arriving at a party. The party of a man's wildest fantasy. They wore lingerie and stilettos and their hair was so perfect they could've all been in wigs. They were themed, the girls. Each a different genre. One in a cowgirl outfit. The next dressed in leather. A third a cheerleader. Leopard print. Nurse. When they saw me, the girls, they stared.

"Here's Daddy," said Mia, as if I didn't already know. The room shifted when he walked into it.

I already knew she was going to be trouble: the skin, the hair, the accent, laugh, glow, sparkle. She sparkled! The Hop looked like her home from the moment she walked in its door. Me? Not so much. My parents wanted me to be a doctor, and I wanted to make them happy. I went to college, flunked out of bio, lost my scholarship, and had to figure out a way to pay tuition so Pop didn't know how I'd failed him. He ran a 7-Eleven. Mom painted fingernails at a cheap salon. They were the smartest people I knew, and they sold cigarettes and trimmed cuticles just so I could be something. They were always saying that. That they wanted me to *be something*. What does that even mean? I am something!

So I flunked out of bio and started working at a nail salon. I'd helped Mom out as a girl, and I knew my way around a callused heel. The place turned out to be a front. They had a massage parlor in the back, and the massages were of the happy-ending variety. When the owner asked whether I'd be interested in earning a little extra cash, I shook my head, no. When one masseuse didn't show up for her shift, he asked again, and I shook my head, no. I shook my head, no, no, *no*, until I didn't. And then, one day, the day before my semester's tuition was due, I nodded my head, yes.

Some girls fall into sex work, and Lady seemed to want to come across that way, turning up with disheveled hair and a beat-up car like some highway straggler, but she didn't stumble across the Hop, no, she navigated herself here, compass in hand. Lady was made to be a Bunny.

I knew that from the moment I saw her. And then she looked at Daddy. And when she looked at Daddy, I mean, my stomach dropped. People will tell you I was in love with Daddy. I wasn't. I was just comfortable being his favorite, it's a cushy throne to sit on. But when Lady arrived is when I knew it was over for the rest of us.

Betty

(NÉE JOSHUA BETTS)

First impression? So she was cute. So what, darling. We were all cute. She had some kind of accent, which was always a selling point. The Bunnies wouldn't stop staring at her, and I was trying to tell Mia about how a Taco Bell only costs $45K because I was thinking that us Bunnies should buy a couple, as an investment, you know, plus the Hop was in the middle of nowhere and I missed my Cheesy Gordita Crunch so I was trying to do this business pitch that could make us big money, but everyone was more interested in the new girl. Whatever.

Then Daddy arrived and he started kissing cheeks, the way he always did, but when Daddy saw her, Lady, well, it was like the rest of us stopped existing.

Some people are main characters in this world. Daddy's one. Lady's one. It's not until you're around someone, a protagonist of life, that you realize your ears are too big, your voice too quiet, the things you say too jumbled, uncertain. It's not until you're around a star that you realize that you're a supporting character.

And when Daddy and Lady met, it was like a spotlight on the two of them, they were the stars of the show and we were all just the audience, sitting in the dark with tubs of popcorn and cups of soda and open mouths, waiting for something to happen. It was pretty obvious that shit was about to go down, and it was pretty obvious Lady was gonna be bang-smack in the middle of it.

The whole room, all of us Bunnies, we looked at Mia, Daddy, Lady. Mia, Daddy, Lady. Something electric traveling between them. The new girl ran her thumb over her teeth, a nervous thing.

Dakota asked Mia if she was okay, and Mia tried to act all confused, like, why wouldn't she be okay?

Lady Lane
(NÉE KATE BURNS)

Daddy was hot. He had a good head of hair in a soft shade of gray, tanned skin, and a southern accent. In the movie version of my life, he'd be played by Brad Pitt. He was in shape, muscle-clad. Tattoos wound their way up his arm like ivy. There was something about him, some kind of magnetism, some kind of pull, like he was the moon and the Bunnies were the tides. They crowded him, surrounded him.

"Afternoon, Bunnies," he said. His voice was big. He held the whole room in the palm of his hand. They looked up at him with such adoring eyes. He was their celebrity. Their everything. A god.

"And you," he said, and he was talking to me. "You must be my new Bunny. Come here," he said. The other Bunnies parted to let me through, but their looks were freezing and they clung like wet fabric. "Perfect," he said. "You," he said, "are perfect." And if the Bunnies' gazes were cold, then Daddy's scorched. "I've been looking for you for years," he said. He smiled and I melted and I wanted to make him do it again and again. I shook my head to clear the crazy. *He's your boss*, I told me.

"What did you say?" said Mia.

"Nothing," I said.

"I'm Daddy," said Daddy. "Welcome to the Hop."

Ma would've liked him. Would've winked and tossed her hair. Would've beckoned him back to her room. She was always a sucker for the cool guys, drawling, smirking, winking types with tattoos, especially on the bicep, especially on the kind of bicep that looked like it could cause harm.

. . .

Mia did a quick round of intros. Ginger was a Cuban woman of about sixty with a jolt of orange hair and lime green lipstick and a miniature poodle under her arm. Rain was dark-skinned and wearing a lot of leather, her face angular, jaw sharp, hair so dead straight you could cut your finger on its edge. Betty was tall as a pylon and blond and thin, big lips, bigger eyes, a beauty queen, pageant princess, looked like she was made to wear a sash that read MISS SOMEWHERE. Dakota was little and pretty and she hid behind her own self, but she was the only Bunny who smiled at me, and I'd take what I could get, but when I reached out to shake her hand, she flinched like I was about to hit her.

"Two hundred and fifty Bunnies are licensed to work here," Daddy said, interrupting Mia's introductions. "About forty live on-site. I take care of all of them. You're mine, and I take care of what's mine." His voice was low and crunchy. He sounded like autumn. Like warm socks and an armchair. Like hot milky tea sipped in front of a fire. Like I already knew everything about him.

. . .

Ma was always warning me to keep my heart inside. *You're too trusting, bunny,* she said, when I let the mailman in for a glass of water while she was out at work. *Life isn't the movies. Girls disappear every day,* she said. *Women are mugged and attacked and raped and killed. You can't let someone in just because they ask.*

She loved beauty products—especially ones that made her look like someone other than herself. *It's a shell,* Ma liked to tell me as she put on her face. *You know why women wear makeup, bunny? Because makeup's a mask. Keeps them from seeing the real you, keeps them from hurting the real you.* She drew triangles of concealer under my eyes, layered foundation on top of that, two shades too dark. *You need an armor,* she said. *You know why snails have shells? Turtles? Crabs? They're soft inside, bunny. They're soft inside. Just like you.* When she left the room, I wiped my face clean. I wanted to be seen.

. . .

Daddy trailed his fingers down my jaw, hooked a thumb under my chin, used it to turn my head one way and the other. An inspection. I liked it. I'd always loved to be touched—it made me feel real. He exhaled with a deep whistle. "Perfect," he said again, and I felt it.

"Once you're one of us, you're one of us," he said. "We look after our family. Got it?"

I nodded. The Bunnies stood, shoulder to shoulder, a lineup, a skyline.

"Should I?"

"Not this time," said Daddy, tucking a strand of hair behind my ear like it was familiar hair, a familiar ear. "Just watch this time," he said.

"You two lovebirds want to get a room?" Mia called from her place in the line.

Rain
(NÉE ASHLEY SMITH)

I mean, everyone knew Mia had a complicated relationship with Daddy. That was just a fact that everyone knew. We knew that you could usually charge double for anal and we knew that the Hop's bartender got so blacked out by midnight that you could get a beer or two for free and we knew, all of us, that Mia had a complicated relationship with Daddy.

Betty

(NÉE JOSHUA BETTS)

Mia had always been Daddy's contingency, see. She was his favorite unless she wasn't the best seller for the month, his favorite unless there was a tall, cis blond girl on staff, his favorite unless someone like Lady Lane became a Bunny. Mia was Daddy's favorite unless—

Mia

(NÉE YA CHAI CHEN)

I had the same relationship with Daddy as every other Bunny. I'd slept with him when I arrived. I liked him. He kept me safe. He owned the brothel I worked at. He took half of every one of my sales. Sure, it was complicated; can you imagine a relationship like that not being complicated?

Lady Lane

(NÉE KATE BURNS)

The lineup went like this: each Bunny stood in the parlor, a row of girls, like convicts, like schoolchildren, like suspects, like models at a casting, actors for an audition, like picking teams in gym—have you ever thought about all the ways we stand in single file for a supervisor, a watcher, an eye, to help him spot the difference between us, pick us out from a crowd for being something the others aren't?

The guest looked each Bunny over, the way you've seen men do a million times once a woman walks past and he thinks it's safe to stare. But he was unabashed that day, there, at the Hop. He eyed each Bunny, and each Bunny eyed him right back.

He paced, like he was grocery shopping for a particular product, scanning each girl in search of his favorite brand. It was obvious who he wouldn't choose. He had a nose ring and tattoos masking both arms, his neck, and his hair was so greasy it looked wet. He paused in front of Rain, grinned at her, and she raised an eyebrow, unsmiling; he walked on. One girl, white, torn jeans, dreadlocks, a crop top that only covered her breasts halfway, she cocked her head to the side, jutted her chin as if to say *What's up*, and he walked on. Ginger said, "Hey there, sugar," and adjusted her breasts. Mia was not his type but she didn't know it, or she pretended not to, because when he walked past her, she reached out, ran her fingernails down the back of his neck with such light fingers it barely happened.

"Hi, honey," is what she said when he turned to stare. He was sold, took her by the hand. She winked at me as she stepped out of line.

On his way past, the guest stopped. Stared. My matted hair, my scruffy T-shirt. "Who are you?" he said.

Mia said, "No, hon." She said, "Let's go. Let's go have some fun."

The guest followed her and looked back over his shoulder only once.

"See how she did that?" Daddy whispered. His voice was this soft hiss of breath against my ear. "You could do worse than to take notes from Mia. She's our top earner so far this quarter. Been upselling like crazy. Gets a full party out of them almost every time. It's not because she's a salesperson. It's not because she sells herself like some commercial. Mia's good because she's genuine. She wants to give these guys a good time, and they can sense stuff like that. The guys, the guests, they can sense authenticity, and that's what they go for ninety percent of the time. These guys want to feel wanted."

I nodded. "Who doesn't?"

"Exactly," he said. "Who doesn't. Now come here with me, new Bunny. I've got something to show you."

I landed the guy because I always landed the guy. I was good. I'm still good! I mean, this one was nothing fancy and he probably tipped like shit but, but, and it's embarrassing to admit this, but I wanted to show Lady how good I was. Because I *was* good. Back then, I was the best there was. I'd been Bunny of the Year three years running and I had the sashes to prove it, but as we walked past Lady, me and the guest, I noticed him notice her and he paused and she looked at him and he was so entranced by her that he stopped right there. Time went quiet. I looked at Daddy. I looked at the guest. Daddy looked at Lady. The lineup was watching the scene like a tennis match, eyes bouncing from one of us to another. Then the guest asked Lady who she was. He went, "Who are you?" She seemed kind of overwhelmed and Daddy smirked like he'd done something to be proud of and I just ushered the guest away from Lady, but even that didn't stop him turning back to see her one more time. She smiled at the guest, waved, and her smile was whole, like she'd never even thought a bad thing.

Lady Lane
(NÉE KATE BURNS)

Daddy took over the new girl tour. As we walked, he kept his hand on my lower back and I remember thinking, *He feels good.* He did. He felt warm, strong, and he applied pressure in whichever direction he wanted me to turn and I liked being told what to do. And when he looked at me . . . well, I liked the reflection of myself I saw in Daddy's eyes. Ma always looked at me like I was potential wasted. Daddy looked at me like I was potential waiting to happen.

"New Zealand, huh," is what Daddy said. "Lord of the Rings," he said. "Hobbiton. It's meant to be pretty down there. Good hiking."

"I guess."

· · ·

But my New Zealand wasn't pretty, and I never hiked a day in my life except for when our car broke down and I had to book it on foot for three hours to make it to fourth period, just in time for a detention. My New Zealand was trash-lined streets and cows being trucked to slaughter. It was sheep shit and houses with holes in the roof. Homeless people asleep on stoops and roads so potholed they popped our tires once a month. I know what people think New Zealand looks like, like blue lakes and geysers, mountains and oceans and forests and beaches, and I'm sure you can find those postcard scenes somewhere, but that wasn't my New Zealand. People think that the country, maybe by pure geographical distance from the rest of them, somehow exists outside of the world's issues, that it's a little paradise where everyone is happy and healthy and looked after, and maybe people just need to think that there's somewhere in the world like that, that there's an Eden right here on earth, and I don't want to tell them their heaven doesn't exist, so I nodded and I said to Daddy, I said, "Great hiking."

• • •

I met Cheryl, the Hooker Booker. She was middle-aged; looked like somebody's mother. She wore a skirt suit and pantyhose and her hair was coiffed into a hump on her head and her purple lipstick was disobedient, smudged across a tooth. Lancôme's Temptation, was my guess. When I introduced myself, she took down my name, clinical as a computer, and I tried to joke, "Hooker Booker; is that your official title?" But she only asked for the name of an emergency contact.

• • •

"Got any questions?" is what Daddy said as we walked. His body was big beside mine. Heterosexuality is easy to justify when you walk with a man and feel safe. "About anything?"

"Are they allowed to touch?" I said. "In a lineup, I mean?"

"Bunnies, yes. Guests, no. We look after our girls."

"What's the best way to get chosen?"

"You're hungry."

"No, I just mean, all the Bunnies are so, I mean, look at them."

Daddy laughed. "So perfect," he said. And it's exactly what I had been thinking. They were all so different, the goth, the housewife, the dominatrix, the rebel, but they were custom-made for their roles, performing so perfectly they almost seemed real. "We sell fantasies here. Guests come to the Hop to attain the unattainable. We're in the business of making dreams come true."

"For the right price," I said.

"Everything comes at a price."

"Mia says there's a serial killer out there," is what I said, and I tried to sound casual, but my voice, it came out weak and wispy as smoke.

"That's true." Daddy nodded.

"And he's killing hookers?"

"He's killing girls on the streets," he said. "And yeah, it's terrible, it is, but that's not you, Bunny. You're not on the streets. You're at the Hop and you're safe here."

I looked up at him. It was up, too. He was tall. He could've protected me from anyone at all, is what I remember thinking.

"Let's get you on payroll, hey?" is what Daddy said. He pressed his fingertips against my back. "You asked how to get noticed in a lineup, but you just saw Mia do it, didn't you?"

I nodded.

"She was eager. She wanted it. Wanted him. I hate to say it, but there are ways for our guests to get sex from women who don't want it. If they wanted someone unwilling, well, you know." I winced, and Daddy pressed my back harder. He said, "You don't have to worry about any of that here though. Like I said"—he smiled down at me—"you're safe here. I take care of my girls."

• • •

We liked to cut between the interdiction and the climax of the film, Ma and me.

This ship can't sink, the captain says of the *Titanic* before a cut to the final bubbles of submersion.

It's completely safe, they say of Jurassic Park before a raptor tears head from neck.

Rain

(NÉE ASHLEY SMITH)

Would I say I felt safe at the Hop? I mean, it's all relative, right? I've worked as a bartender at a topless dive. I've stripped in dirty basements. I've dealt drugs, the lighter stuff, mostly weed, a little coke. I've worked as a dominatrix in a cell beneath an Irish pub, and I've worked the streets before too. Stood on the corner of Main and Washington, shadiest fucking corner in town, and I eyed up passersby, hoping they'd at best ask my price and at worst ignore me completely. I was out there when the Long Island Killer was on the loose back in 2010, picking up girls who advertised themselves on Craigslist and then disposing of the bodies in burlap sacks. I was out there when girls started going from massage parlors in LA. We even did our own little investigation when three girls suddenly dipped from the Strip without a trace—we tracked their phones and found them all in a trash can behind a boarded-up Toys "R" Us, batteries still fully charged like they'd been dropped in there just a minute ago. We were running on pure adrenaline and turned up to the police station, panting and holding the phones with socks covering our hands because someone had said something about fingerprints. We were afraid of the cops but we thought we were saving lives so we got to the police station and said, "We found their phones." And the cops just said, "Yeah." That's it, just "Yeah." They shrugged, like, what did we want them to do about it?

If you're asking if I felt safer at the Hop than out there, the answer's yes. Out there, I had the cops called on me and I had men grab me and I had my purse nabbed and I had a gun pulled in my general direction and I had it lucky compared to most. The Hop might not've been what most people call *safe*, but it was *safer*, and that's something.

Lady Lane

(NÉE KATE BURNS)

Daddy showed me the bar, the restaurant, the café, the gym. The Hop was a whole city. He pointed at the ob/gyn's office, which every Bunny had to visit each week, and he said, "But you already know that," even though I didn't.

I said, "What do you mean?"

He frowned and said, "Mia did take you to see Dr. Oh, right?"

I didn't want to get Mia in trouble, so I said, "Oh! Yes. She did. Sorry, this is just a lot."

And that, that little white lie, well, you just never know which moments are the ones that change your life forever. But we're not there yet.

Daddy pointed out his quarters, past the tennis courts and the horse paddocks, a house made of mostly glass that reflected light back into the eyes of its viewer. "Off limits," was all he had to say about that.

. . .

There were television screens everywhere at the Hop. They scrolled through commercials, some for the girls at the Hop, some for the outside world. Amy, whose main selling point was that she had the same dimensions as a Barbie doll; Ciara, who was *a veteran of the Hop and the world! Ciara fought for our country and now she's come home to fight for your heart!* Then a car accident lawyer. A drug for ADHD. Then Mia, *our very own Asian persuasion* . . . The screen blinked black at the end of every loop. It read: *The Hop: the girl's of your dreams.*

"It's wrong," is what I told Daddy.

"What is?"

"The apostrophe." I pointed at the screen. "*Girls* is meant to be plural, but the apostrophe makes it either possessive or a contraction. Like: 'the girl is of your dreams.' "

"I don't see anything wrong with it." Daddy looked up. "No one's complained. I don't think it makes a difference."

. . .

His office was the only part of the Hop I'd seen that wasn't white or pink. It was all wooden, a dark mahogany, accented with burgundy leather. On his computer screen, thumbnails showed security footage, high-definition live video of the Hop's grounds. When Daddy saw me staring, he winked. "That's how we keep you safe, darlin'," he said.

There was a cowboy hat sitting on his desk, and he called me darlin', and the rest I could guess. I bet his real name was Dallas or Austin or some other city in Texas. I bet he rode horses growing up. I bet he had a ma who called him baby, and I bet she made pecan pie every Sunday. I bet he wanted to retire on a ranch with a kid or two and a golden retriever and two rocking chairs, side by side on the porch. I bet he'd've pulled me onto his lap when I brought us each a beer to sip alongside the sunset. I bet he'd've called me honey and sweetheart. I bet—

"You're gonna be just fine here, Bunny," is what he said. "You don't have to worry about anything," he said. "Now, tell me, have we got you a name yet?"

"Lady," I said, my voice softer than I wanted it to be. "Is that okay?"

Daddy raised his hands like a surrender. "You're your own boss here, Bunny," he said. "I'm not about to name you. You're a big girl. Call yourself whatever you like."

"Lady," I said again. "Lady Lane."

"Lady Lane." He picked up his hat and set it on his head. "Well, I like it. Suits you."

I adjusted my T-shirt, peeled the cotton away from my lower back. I needed a shower.

"You're probably about ready for a bath," said Daddy.

I frowned, pretty sure I hadn't spoken my want aloud.

"Well, you're sweating like a whore in church, for one thing," he said with another wink. The gesture belonged to him. "Take a look at this," is what he said. He pressed a button on his computer and the thumbnail footage of the Hop's grounds flashed and became thumbnail footage of room interiors.

"What is that?"

"There," he said, pointing at one of the squares on his screen. I recognized the guest's greasy mane. Mia's powderpuff bunny tail. They were standing at the foot of her bed, his arms around her waist, talking.

Daddy said, "She's negotiating." He said, "Remember, no price talk outside of your room. You'll lose us our license for that. Always name your cost once the door to your suite is closed, okay? Now, see how Mia does it? See how she's got him touching her already, like she wants it, like she's giving him a preview of everything he could have?"

"Does she know?"

"What she's doing? Of course she does. Mia's a professional."

"No, I mean, does she know that we're watching."

"See how she's loosening his tie while they talk? See how she's all over him? This is money, Lady. This is gold. You should be taking notes."

"I feel like we shouldn't be watching this."

"This," Daddy said. "This is how we keep you safe, Lady."

Mia had the guest unzip her dress, and she just sort of stared at him as the fabric fell to the floor. Then she lay down flat on her bed. Like *Take me.* Like *I'm yours.* The guest lowered himself over her, and then nothing. Daddy switched the screen back to the ground's security feed. "No freebies," he said with another wink. Then he took a bottle from his pocket and tilted his head back and splashed a storm of clear drops into his eyes. "Glaucoma," he said. Then, "Let me show you to your room. It's a good one. Made sure to give you one of our best suites. See, I have a good feeling about you, Lady. I do. You're gonna be a best seller."

I didn't know if he was being genuine or if this was something he said to every new girl. I was blushing either way. I said, "What makes you think that?"

"Well, the rooster crowed twice this morning."

"The rooster?"

"Exactly. And you know what they say about a rooster crowing twice."

I said nothing.

He said, "I'm fucking with you, Lady. We don't have a rooster. He got eaten by a coyote a couple weeks back." He laughed and set his cowboy hat on my head. "I do have a good feeling about you, though. I have a sixth sense for these things. You're perfect."

Vincent "Daddy" Russo

(FORMER OWNER OF THE HOP)

She was perfect. Did I say that to every new Bunny? Yes, I did. They're usually scared, jittery when they arrive, rabbits, but all they really need is a little encouragement. Tell them they're perfect. Tell them they're stars. That's all a girl ever wants to hear, and if you tell her that, that exact combination of words, she'll believe it. They always do. You think they called me Daddy by accident? I knew how to look after my girls.

But I mean it when I say that Lady turned up with some secret ingredient. Scruffy and badly dressed, underconfident as hell, but the perfect girl to play the underdog in a movie. You know, one of those cheesy, feel-good ones where the girl is special but she doesn't realize it until she gets a decent haircut, takes off her glasses, wears some tight jeans.

That's Lady. Rough enough to be relatable, but undeniably gorgeous. It's a potent blend, that one, and yeah, I knew she had it, *it*, from the minute she arrived on my doorstep. I knew I was going to make that girl a star.

Mia

(NÉE YA CHAI CHEN)

There were a lot of things we didn't know about the Hop, but we knew about the cameras. Daddy introduced them to every new Bunny in orientation. They were security cameras, is what he told the new girls. This is how we keep you safe, he liked to say.

I was jumpy about it when I first arrived because my salon got shut down after an undercover cop came and recorded his session. I wasn't his masseuse, but I could've been, and they put her away in the worst women's prison in Texas. That was eight years ago now, and she's still there. She's still there. The cop, by the way, he let her finish up the massage. He let her make him come, and she's still behind bars. So, yeah, I wasn't happy about the cameras, but Daddy assured me they were there to keep me safe. The Hop's safe, is what he kept saying, and, something about Daddy, something about this place, I believed him.

You might shake your head, might be like, *Stupid bitches*, but there are just a handful of legal brothels in all of America, and no one's talking about regular protocol, no one knows what's normal, it's all kept in the shadows because we're so scared of being shut down. Nevada passes new legislation, and *bam*, we're all sent back to the streets, the strip clubs, the salons. Just like that. Poof! Gone! So we kept quiet and we didn't ask questions and we nodded along with the rules and we stuck to them. And, yeah, I believed Daddy when, during my orientation, he told me those cameras would keep me safe.

What other choice did I have?

Lady Lane

(NÉE KATE BURNS)

Daddy walked me from his office, through the parlor, through a court-yard. The Hop's courtyard was too pretty. Too pruned and perfect. Here's something I learned from working the cosmetics department at Hobbes: the prettiest faces usually have the ugliest insides. A mask is only a mask—there's always something beneath a facade.

There was a bridge over a stream, bushes freckled with roses; I felt like I was walking through the set of a musical. "It's pretty," I said. "It's like a stage. It's like a set for a show."

Daddy nodded. "I see what you mean," he said. "Are you an ac-tress? A dancer? Or a—" He stopped and set his hand on my shoulder. We stood. Daddy pointed. In amid the roots of the roses was a snake, its head strawberry-shaped and tinted pink to match. It turned to look at us.

"Holy shit," said someone, and the someone, it turned out, was me.

Daddy said, "She's just a young one. A rattler."

I said, "It's a snake."

He said, "Yeah, you'll see them around here. Best to steer clear."

"But it's not venomous or anything."

"Sure she is."

"What?"

"She's venomous all right."

"Oh," I said. "Okay."

"Just carefully move around her, okay, Lady?" But I was frozen stuck, watching her watching me watching her. Daddy scooped me into his arms, like a damsel, a princess, and his neck smelled like a man and I had to work hard not to take his earlobe into my mouth and suck. He carried me, slowly, as far on the other side of the path as we could be. The snake's eyes were black, and she watched us all the way.

Dakota

(NÉE JACY ADAMS, BUNNY, THE HOP)

The cameras were a little strange, but everyone else was willing to accept that they were there for safety, and once everyone else accepts something, it's hard not to follow the crowd. I vaguely remember being weirded out by the security feed when I arrived, but every single Bunny I talked to was like, "They're to keep us safe," and, "It's for our own safety," and after awhile I heard those words out of my own mouth. A new Bunny arrived, and she asked about the cameras, and I was like, "Oh, yeah, those cameras keep us safe." It's easy to see how cults happen. People are so convincing.

Lady Lane

(NÉE KATE BURNS)

When we were out of the snake's sight, Daddy said, "Now tell me, Lady." He set me down, but my skin felt engraved with his touch. That's how I felt every time Daddy touched me. Like his fingers lingered on me for hours afterward. And I thought maybe that was what love felt like.

"What exactly made you decide to join us here at the Hop, such a long way from home?" Daddy said. I reached for the journal in my back pocket to check that it was still there. It was still there, and I thumbed its pages, a habit by now, and I said, "Decided it was about time I stopped having sex for free."

He laughed, then, a wide-mouthed, open-throated real laugh. It lasted a long time, the length of a hallway. "I like you," is what he said when we reached a door numbered 33, a lucky number. I liked him too. I liked him already. I had been ready to hate him, ready to write him off as some contemporary pimp, a sleazeball, a creepy old dude with taste too young for his middle-aged tongue and a fetish for power. But that wasn't him. He was kind. Warm. He made me feel like I belonged there, at the Hop, about as far from home as I could've been. He made me feel safe, and I don't know if I'd ever felt that before.

The truth is this: I wanted to kiss him. I wanted him to hold me against his body, and I wanted to feel how it might be to exist in such a sturdy embrace. I was young. I was stupid. So when I thought about wanting to kiss him, I did it. I kissed him. Because that's the kind of shit you do when you're young and stupid.

His mouth tasted of salt, I remember that.

I was embarrassed. "Sorry," I said, stepping back. "Oh my god, I'm sorry."

He smiled and said, "No, you're not, and you shouldn't be."

"It's just, I'm just, well, I've had a rough few weeks. That's not an excuse, but I've, well, I've been feeling lonely, I guess."

"Welcome to being a Bunny, Lady. You'll never be lonely again."

"I like you too," I said. "Is what I meant."

"You're going to be trouble," he said. He took a key from around his neck. "There's something about you," he said, pushing the door open wide and stepping aside so I could go in. "I think I might've underestimated you. You've got trouble in your eyes." I looked back at him. "And an eyelash."

"What?"

"Stay still." He held my eye open with one hand and pressed the forefinger of his other to my eye. It stung. Sure enough, a lash on his fingertip. "See?"

I blinked. "If I blow it away, I get to make a wish," I said.

"That's bullshit," Daddy said. "People make their own wishes come true. You should know that better than anyone."

"Me?"

"Look at you," he said. "You're here, aren't you? Thousands of miles from home. At the best brothel in the country, the world. Fate's a load of horseshit. You're making your own life happen," he said. "What do you think of the room?"

The room. It was about the size of our whole house back home. The bed was bigger than any bed I'd ever seen. A flat-screen television on the wall. Its very own bathroom, tiled, golden tapware. Ma would've flipped. "Wow," I said. "Have you seen this place?"

Ma and I watched *Pretty Woman* maybe once a week. We especially liked the shopping scene, when Julia Roberts goes back into the store where the salespeople were rude to her before, when they thought she was poor, and then she shows them all her shopping bags. We liked to pause on the shocked faces and copy them. Ma and I, hands to open mouths.

She was my acting coach, and she was good at it. *The key,* she told me, when I fucked up a scene, *is to really believe you're the character. Empty yourself of yourself. Forget you even exist.*

Let's do the scene when Julia Roberts shows those ladies who she really is, I'd say to Ma.

She's not showing those ladies who she is, Ma said. *She's showing herself who she is.*

I liked Richard Gere. He looked like hope to me. I looked for him in other men. I looked for him on the street. Ma told me I was buying into the con. *He's a rich narcissist,* is what she told me. *You think he's a good guy because he's willing to date a prostitute? He's an old coot with looming prostate issues and a limp dick. No. She's a good lady for being willing to date him. She's the catch, bunny. She's the star.*

• • •

Daddy returned the key to his neck, and he said, "I think we're gonna be friends, you and me, Lady. I like you. I like you too. And I have a feeling you're about to become the next big thing. You're my new best seller. You're a star. I can see that in a girl, I can tell a girl who sparkles."

I believed him. I felt sparkly. "Thank you," I said.

He took his hat back. "For what?"

"For bringing me here."

He took my chin in his hand. "Bringing you here? No, Lady. You brought yourself here, okay? You're doing this for yourself. And look at you." He framed my face with his hands, winked, and clicked his tongue like he'd taken my photo. "You fit here. You belong here."

I belonged there, is what he told me. I didn't know if I'd ever belonged anywhere. It was exactly what I needed to hear. "Come here," I said, and I stepped back for him to come in. "Come here," I said, and I meant to bed.

He said, "Lady."

And I said, "Daddy."

He said, "You don't have to do this."

And I said, "I don't *have* to do anything." But his body seemed inevitable, and having it seemed urgent. You might judge me, I'd understand, but Ma had died and I was alone and sex was the best way I knew to be with someone.

He said, "Are you sure?"

I said, "Are you?"

And then he kissed me. I pushed him onto the bed. How explicit do you want me to get here? I asked if he had a condom, and he said, "No need," and I assumed he'd had a vasectomy.

Ma was always saying that every man should get a vasectomy upon puberty. *They're reversible*, is what she said about it. *You know what's not reversible? Blood clots. Strokes. Cervical cancer. Breast cancer. All side effects of the birth control I've been taking since I turned twelve.*

I kissed my way up Daddy's body. He looked past me, over my shoulder, at the ceiling. I looked up, and there was a mirror up there, and I laughed. Of course there was a mirror on the ceiling. Of course.

"Men are visual creatures," Daddy explained.

And I said, "What does that make women?"

And then he said, "Come here." And I did.

Mia

(NÉE YA CHAI CHEN)

Do I feel responsible? What kind of question is that? I mean, I guess I was meant to take her to the ob/gyn, Dr. Oh, first thing. But that wasn't my job; I'd never given a new girl tour before, and I didn't realize that Dr. Oh was supposed to be first on the agenda. I'm a hooker, not a tour guide, you know?

Vincent "Daddy" Russo

She was less timid than most girls, I do remember that. Oh, she was scared, you could see that right there on her face, but she wasn't timid. Jumped my bones the minute a bed was in sight. Usually, with new hires, I tested them out at their interview, which meant wearing a condom since I couldn't trust they'd be on birth control or, you know, clean. But I hated condoms and I knew Lady had already visited our resident ob/gyn on her tour of the place and I knew she had the all-clear or Dr. Oh would've called to tell me otherwise, and so, when Lady asked if we needed a condom, I said no. I was glad about it too. Sometimes new Bunnies want to show me how freaky they can be. They want to pull out all the stops, toys and costumes and the dirtiest words they know. Ginger, for example, she was my very first hire at the Hop, and when I tested her out she bit my earlobe clean off and she made it look easy, like biting down on a cocktail sausage, she held up the bottom of my ear and was like, *Oops.* Some girls are wild like that, circus freaks in the sack, but Lady fucked like she was in love. It was . . . it felt like the real deal. She was, and I've always said this, she was a natural. She was going to be huge, and I was going to help her.

Rain
(NÉE ASHLEY SMITH)

It's actually a Hop signature move. The Ginger. Guys with a thing for teeth marks know to ask for a Ginger, and it means we'll bite until you bleed. It's more popular than you'd think.

Lady Lane

(NÉE KATE BURNS)

That first night felt long. Once Daddy left, I took a long nap in my bed, dreamed I was stuck in a loop. That I left the Hop on foot, walking the shoulder of the highway, but as soon as I could no longer see the building behind me, it was visible before me, I walked toward it, past it, saw it shrinking in my rear-view, and then, again, at the exact vanishing point, it appeared once more in the distance.

By the time I woke, it was who knows what time and the Hop was quiet.

· · ·

There were no windows in my room—walls all around. There was a curtain that looked like it might be pulled to reveal a window, but behind it was just more wall. I opened my door for air, but the air was all wrong, I remember that. It was too hot, wet, heavy, like walking into a raincloud. There were stars out, the sky pricked with them, like needlepoint. They were different stars from the ones back home, constellations I'd never met. I drew shapes between them with my finger in the air, tried to force the Southern Cross out of four stars in almost the right position. The moon, though, was the very same one.

· · ·

Ma and I used to watch documentaries when we wanted to do nothing, productively. Ma sided with the conspiracy theorists as a rule. *The flag's not waving*, she cried at the footage. *It was Bush! Avril Lavigne's dead!*

Do you really believe in aliens just because that guy says he saw one? I asked, pausing the film, the man in the tinfoil hat stuck, midstory.

He saw it, bunny.

And that means it's real?

If he saw it, then it is real.

Real in his own head, maybe.

Who's to say that the real doesn't exist in our own heads? She twisted an empty beer can and tossed it in the general direction of the trash can.

• • •

Where was I? Oh yeah. That first night. It was so quiet that every movement, my own, made me wince. I wished Mia were awake. I wished anyone were awake. There was a blinking red light in the corner of the ceiling. I wondered if Daddy ever watched, just for fun, just to keep us safe. I waved, just in case.

See, I'd had a plan: get to the Hop, become a Bunny, and that was it. That was my plan and now I was there and I was a Bunny and the world was wide open in front of me and I didn't have any other big ideas. All I had left to do was exist.

I texted Lacey, I miss you, and turned on the television. The screen was big, clear, and the channels extended into the hundreds. I skipped past political debates and infomercials and landed on a drama. A good-looking man kept turning into a wolf at the most inconvenient times. A first date, a job interview, midflight; the hair on his arms thickened, the down on his face darkened, his ears shifted up, became pointed, canine. Ma would've turned the station over with a snort and some kind of *What'd I tell you, bunny, all men are dogs at heart.* But I stayed for his eyes, a golden yellow, they glowed. It was a marathon, and I watched four episodes before I fell asleep again.

. . .

In my dreams, I was always more Ma than myself. I'd be in her body, speaking in her voice, seeing from her eyes. Manfriends showed up, knocked on the door, I let them in, sent my daughter to her room, took the men by the hand and headed for the bedroom, but that's where things always went dark.

Mia

(NÉE YA CHAI CHEN)

I'm sure everyone's said this, but it's true. It is! She had something. Some *thing*. I'm always telling people that about Lady, and they want me to get more specific, but to get more specific would be to get less accurate. She had *it*.

Betty asked me, "Do you have a crush on her?"

And I went, "No."

And Ginger went, "Don't go getting your heart broken, baby. Especially not over a pancake-ass fake blonde."

I didn't have a crush on Lady, but I could understand why you might. She was so clearly gorgeous and so clearly hurting. She was the spitting image of a damsel in distress, and she played the role like a pro. She was perfect and she was in pain and that's why everyone who met her wanted her. Look at her once and you saw it all, the hurt, the joy, the hope, the drama, looking at her was like looking at a whole life, all at once. Lady was Velcro. Look at her and you couldn't look away. And with girls like that, you can do one of two things: you can be her friend and shadow her on her journey to success, or you can keep your distance and watch her walk the road alone. No matter what, she wins.

I learned that the hard way.

Lady Lane

(NÉE KATE BURNS)

Mia woke me in the morning with a knock that sounded like glitter. Even her knuckles knew their part. I shifted the nightstand that had been acting as deadbolt through the night and opened the door to her standing, smiling, in a white puffy outfit that made me think of lemon meringue pie. She handed me a cup of coffee and pushed past me to perch on the foot of my bed.

"Why was your door blocked?" is what she said. Then, before I could answer, "The Hop's safe, Lady. They look after us here. Daddy's always watching out. Did you sleep?" Her too-red lipstick made her mouth look cartoon.

I looked at her. "There's a serial killer out there, murdering girls like us."

"Not girls like us, no. The Hop's really safe. No one's coming to hurt you here."

The coffee was bad. Mia had a cup of the pink slush she always seemed to be sipping on.

"What is that stuff?" I said.

"This? We call it Pink."

"But what's in it?"

Mia laughed. "You sure are curious." She crossed her legs at the ankle, the spikes of her heels as long as her legs. "You excited for your first day, new Bunny?"

I shrugged.

"Let me help you out with a couple tips," she said. "I don't do this for everyone, you know, but I like you, Lady. There's something about you." It was the second time someone had said that to me since I arrived. Something about me.

"Tip one," said Mia. "Don't fuck with the other Bunnies." Mia had a tic, a quick bite of her lip. Sometimes it happened between syllables, words, sentences, sometimes it punctuated, her very own comma, a brief pause built into her body. "Got it?"

"What does that mean?"

"It means don't steal any regulars. Don't sabotage any lineups. Don't take another girl's sure thing. Look, you're cis, you're white, you're skinny, you're pretty. You're really pretty. You've got a lot going for you, okay? A lot you didn't have to work for. You're going to be fine here. You're going to be successful. So be happy with that and don't fuck with anyone else's sales. Support your sisters, got it?"

"Thank you?"

"Don't be cute." She gestured to the bed, asking me to sit, then took the hairbrush from my nightstand and knelt on the mattress behind me. She started with the ends, brushing quickly but gently.

"I wouldn't even know how to do any of that. Fuck with anyone else's sales, I mean."

"Next rule," said Mia, brushing, brushing. "Don't go clearance, or you'll screw the whole system."

"Don't go clearance," I said.

"Exactly. Don't sink your prices below the mean, or we all have to go cheap to keep up and by the end of the day our pussies will be worth a penny a pop and none of us will make a living."

Don't go clearance. I nodded. "Stop moving," she said. "I'm not saying any of this shit again, so you listen up and you take notes if you need to."

"Don't fuck with other Bunnies' sales and don't go clearance," I said. "I've got it so far."

"Good. Now, tip four."

"Three."

"Whatever," she said. "The last tip I'm gonna give you for free is this one. Make Daddy like you. Get Daddy on your side and make him adore you, and good things will happen. Daddy is the key to everything, really."

I thought of Daddy. Of the day before. "I slept with him," I told Mia.

She paused in her brushing, just briefly, so fleeting it mightn't have happened at all. "He tested you," she said.

"Tested me?"

"He tests out every new Bunny."

Well, that hurt. Because I'd thought, well . . . it doesn't matter. What I said to Mia was, "But I think *I* suggested it to *him*, I mean, I think I instigated it."

"Lady," said Mia. She stroked the back of my hand. "Daddy doesn't date Bunnies, okay? He's serious about boundaries. He tested you out, and he does that with every new girl, but that's all it was."

I shook my head. I felt dirty and weird. I kissed Daddy because I liked Daddy. I slept with him because *I* wanted to. If he was testing me out, if it was regular protocol, surely I would've known?

Mia said, "Anyway, what I was saying was that you should stay on Daddy's good side. He's the ringleader, Lady. The boss man. If you were in a different job, a more, let's say, conventional job, secretary, nurse, you'd do what you could to please your higher-up, right? Your manager, your senior, whatever, you'd stay on their good side, cater to their needs. You'd suck up to them a little because this is a job and jobs are hierarchies, and you, right now, you're at the bottom, new Bunny, and you've got to put in the legwork and you've got to start climbing. Daddy is the fastest way up."

"What's up there?" I said.

"Up where?"

"Why would I want to be at the top?" I said. "I like it down here. Look at my room."

Mia laughed. "You just wait," she said. "Daddy's got powers. He's made celebrities before, Lady. He's taken a girl from the sidewalk and held her hand all the way to the spotlight. He can lead you all the way up there, up to the top, and then step back to let you shine. He can take you all the way up, Daddy can. You get a taste of the next rung of the ladder, and you'll be panting to climb it as high as it goes, just like the rest of us."

I must've been looking nervous, because Mia said, "If you play by the rules, you'll be just fine here, Lady. You just have to play by the rules, is all."

And the question was so obvious, the question I didn't ask: *What happens if you don't play by the rules?* But I knew I'd never get an answer to that.

Mia said, "Listen." She planted a light kiss on my temple, then the other, for balance. She said, "Daddy told me to come by. We're lining up in ten, and he wants you to watch." She paused, cocked her head. "You really do look like someone, you know. I just can't put my finger on who."

"Scarlett Johansson?" I tried, another one I'd sometimes heard.

"No, that's not it," she said.

"What do I wear? For the lineup?"

"You're not for sale yet, Lady. Wear whatever you want for now—we still have to find you a costume." On her way out, she stopped and turned. "Wait," is what she said. "Have you had your physical yet?"

I hadn't.

Mia

(NÉE YA CHAI CHEN)

She hadn't had her physical. She'd slept with Daddy, and she hadn't had her physical. I thought it probably wasn't a huge deal, since Daddy always uses protection with new hires. I was wrong, clearly, but that's what I thought at the time.

Lady Lane

(NÉE KATE BURNS)

The Hop's ob/gyn looked exactly the way a doctor should. She was sixty, maybe seventy, her hair pulled back tight, white coat with a lapel embroidered DR. OH. Her clinic looked like one you'd find in the real world, a clinic open to the public.

"Kate, is that correct?" Dr. Oh was good at ob/gyn voice. She talked like a light breeze.

"Lady."

"Right, Lady." She took a pen from her breast pocket to correct the name. Then she looked up and smiled, and then her face did something else and she said, "Oh. Oh wow. So you're his new Willa."

I said, "His new what?"

But Dr. Oh shook her head. "Nothing," she said. "How are you liking the Hop so far, Lady?"

"I like it fine."

"Great. Could you undress from the waist down? I'll be waiting right outside."

"What do you test for?"

"All STDs. Chlamydia, syphilis, the usual suspects, and pregnancy."

"Pregnancy?"

"Yes, and I'll also get you set up with birth control. All guests use condoms, but condoms can break, fall off, you know, so it's good to have a backup too. Which contraceptive are you currently using?" Dr. Oh paused at the door. "Are you currently using a contraceptive?"

. . .

There was a large painting on the ceiling. The room was a customized clinic, made, like my own room at the Hop, for women to lie in on their backs. The painting was a forest with little pastel rabbits poking their heads out of burrows, from behind trees, over the top of a rock. At first I saw three rabbits, blue and pink and yellow, but the more you looked at the painting, the more rabbits became visible. There might've been a hundred hiding in there.

Olivia Oh, MD

(RESIDENT OB/GYN AT THE HOP)

We tested every new Bunny for chlamydia, gonorrhea, herpes, syphilis, HIV, HPV, and hepatitis, and we ran those tests regularly. We also ran a pregnancy test upon arrival. Just one. That was the law, and that's all we tested for before the girls did their first lineup. Then we provided them with birth control—either pills or an IUD, based on preference.

Lady's bill of health was clear, and her pregnancy test came back negative. For her contraceptive, she chose pills. And that's all I have to say.

Rain

(NÉE ASHLEY SMITH)

Yeah, Daddy fucked his Bunnies. Everyone thinks they're good at sex because everyone else is a liar in the bedroom. I faked orgasms every day, and I told each guest he was the best I'd ever had. Even the ones who jackhammered for five minutes while I thought about what I was going to eat for dinner. "That was amazing," I said, like they all do in the movies. People just can't be critical when it comes to sex, so everyone thinks they're a rock star in the sheets, and Daddy never trusted a résumé, so, yeah, he tested his girls out. He made them get a physical, a full once-over from Dr. Oh, and then he tested them out. Like a job interview, you know? With less paperwork. So, yes, Daddy fucked his Bunnies, but he only fucked them once.

And sure, some girls got attached. Some girls ended up wanting more. But Daddy was usually pretty clear about where the line was. He usually drew the line after sex. That was part of the test too. If you couldn't fuck without developing an emotional dependence, then being a Bunny? Probably not for you.

There was something different about Lady, though. About the way Daddy looked at her. He looked at me a lot, too, you know, I had decent sales figures, and he *really* looked at Mia, his top earner three years running, but even then, he'd never looked at us the way he looked at Lady. Actually, I'd only seen him look at one other girl the way he looked at Lady, and we all know how that went down.

Lady Lane

(NÉE KATE BURNS)

Mia joined us at my costume fitting. She sat beside Daddy, sipping Pink and resting her head on his shoulder. I wasn't jealous. I was trying not to be jealous. He kissed her temple, and she nuzzled into his neck, and I said to myself *He is your boss he is your boss.*

"This isn't a game of dress-up," is what Daddy said. He used his eyedrops, blinked the tears away. "Costume is crucial for your image. For sales. You're your own commercial here. What you choose to wear, it's marketing. It's you." He took the strap of Mia's dress and slipped it off her shoulder. "It's what our guests get to strip off you." Mia slapped Daddy's hand and he caught her fingers and kissed her knuckles, but I was not jealous because he was my boss.

I didn't know if they were all *in love* with Daddy, or if any of them were, but they all loved him, and I got it. Maybe it was that he was the only man on-site. Maybe it was that he promised to care for us. Maybe it was that he was the key to our success. Or maybe it had more to do with the way he touched, like he *had to,* the way he spoke, so close to the ear, the way he smiled as if you, just by being you, were brightening his whole day.

. . .

Mia laughed when I turned to face them in a tiny tulle tutu that made me look like a wedding dessert. She said, "That's awful."

"It's not very you," said Daddy. I looked in the mirror. He was right, it wasn't very me. "A good costume is like good makeup," he said, "it always works best if it's blended into you. If no one can tell you're wearing it."

He said, "Take the skirt off. Let's see it just with the lingerie."

I pushed the skirt from my hips and let it puddle at my feet. I was never shy about nudity. My body was the least embarrassing thing about me. Animal, machine. I had no idea who I was, but my body knew exactly how to be.

"We'd be crazy to hide that body," said Daddy. Despite it all, I blushed. "Let's try something simpler," he said.

There was a rack in the far corner of the room. I started toward it, but Mia stopped me. "We don't touch that rack," she said. "Those costumes are off limits."

"Why?"

Mia looked at Daddy, who looked at me.

"They're old," Daddy said. "Worn. You don't want them."

"They're worn?"

"By Bunnies who aren't here anymore."

"You mean they don't work here anymore?"

Mia nodded. "Right. They don't work here anymore."

"The girl who was here before me, the one whose position I filled, was one of these costumes hers?"

"You sure are curious," said Daddy.

The world went black.

Daddy, in the dark, put a hand around my waist and said, "It's just a reset."

"But what *is* a reset?" I said, only to have the question absorbed by shadows.

My phone lit up with a text from Lacey: How's everything going over there? Have you started saying "howdy" yet?

• • •

The lights came back, and Mia, as if nothing had happened, she said, "I think maybe we should just lean into your natural personality." I was wearing a long red gown and opera gloves.

"Does that happen every day? The reset?"

"Every day, once a day," said Mia, a little bored. "Only when there are no guests here. Daddy doesn't want to freak them out."

"But what is it?"

Mia circled me. I felt stupid, like a girl playing make-believe, trying out every type of woman I could.

"Why don't I just wear my own clothes?" I said.

"You have to be in costume," is what Daddy said. "Your costume is a big part of keeping you safe." He scanned me, top to toe, and I felt like a car, like at any moment he could slap me on the hood and call me a good deal.

"Why?"

"It's part of distancing yourself from the job," he said. "Developing a persona. It's armor, a costume is."

I looked at Daddy. At Mia. "I don't need to distance myself from the job," I said.

We'd exhausted all the options when Daddy finally stood and went to the used costume rack. He pulled out an outfit. White cropped T-shirt and tiny denim shorts. "Try these," he said. I put them on. The shorts were too big, they gaped at the waist. The T-shirt didn't even reach my belly button. I tugged at the hem.

"Oh, wow," Daddy said.

I looked like a bad Britney Spears impression.

Daddy circled me like a shark, eyes all over. "My god, you look just like her."

"Like her?" I said.

Then Mia said, "Oh." She said, "That's who. That's who it is."

And I said, "Who?"

And Mia said, "Willa."

And I said, "Who?"

Mia started to explain, but Daddy set a not-soft palm on her shoulder, and it was like he'd hit an off button and Mia shut her mouth so quickly it was almost like she'd never opened it at all. "This is your look, Lady," Daddy said. "You look great." He cradled my chin in his palm. "Now, look alive, darlin'. You've got your very first lineup tonight."

. . .

Back in my room, my bed was made, my shoes lined up, single file and militaristic, along the foot of my bed. Someone had unpacked my suitcase; my socks and underwear were folded into drawers, everything else hung in a gradient organized by color. The television was on, but silenced.

Mia

(NÉE YA CHAI CHEN)

Could I have sabotaged her at her costume fitting? Sure! Could I have put her in some poufy number that hid her figure and stunted her numbers? Yes! But that's not what we were about at the Hop. We were family there. We were sisters.

And anyway, once I figured out that Lady was Daddy's new Willa, I knew there was nothing I could do to change her destiny at the Hop. He already had his money on her—she was already something special.

Daddy had a set cast list, you see, and whenever one Bunny was out, he looked to fill her spot, and not just with any girl, but with the exact same girl, or as close as he could get to her. We were all just replacements of replacements of replacements there. A movie that'd been remade and remade and remade until no one knew who the original actors were anymore.

White girls had it easier, because Daddy seemed to think he could have twenty identical blond white girls so long as they were in different costumes, but he didn't like having two Black girls at the Hop. Thought it'd confuse the guests. That it was redundant, or something. Daddy thought in stereotypes and white was the only thing that transcended categorization.

I took the place of a Vietnamese girl who'd aged out, and we were both told to call ourselves Japanese. You could tell when Daddy was about to replace you when a girl of your race, or someone from the same continent, or someone that a white person might think was from the same continent as you, whatever, came in for an interview. It meant Daddy was looking for a newer, younger, more virginal you. It meant you'd better start looking at your options.

And, see, the biggest problem with working at the Hop was that once you were out, it was all downhill from there.

....
Lady Lane
(NÉE KATE BURNS)

For my first lineup, Mia did my makeup, layer upon layer. I didn't love wearing makeup and I complained, said, "Do I have to wear so much?"

"It's all part of it," is what she said. She was wearing a cropped T-shirt that read NAMASLAY across the chest. "These men are paying for fantasies. Dream girls don't have zits. Zits belong in reality."

"I don't have any zits."

"You know what I mean." She finished my eyeshadow and kissed each lid. "What color do you want your eyes to be?"

"What?"

She pressed her fingertips to her own eyes and removed her irises. Her natural ones were dark, dark brown. "Blue?" she said, and then she pressed her contacts into my eyes. "Blink," she said, and I did.

"My eyes were already blue," I told her. "What's the point?"

"It's the principle."

Mia folded my hair into a loose braid. She seemed to like me. I liked her too. Or maybe I, like the guests here, only liked to be liked. I said to Mia, "You might be my second ever friend."

She smiled. "Second ever? That's depressing."

"I haven't had much time for friends."

"Well, you're about to have a whole lot of them." Then she said, "Are you freaking out right now?"

I was. I told her about the Sugar Club. "As a kid, I ran a kissing business," I said. "I kissed the boys at school in exchange for cash. I did more than that, too. I pretended to be one kid's girlfriend for a while, and he paid me a grand. We drew the line at sex though. We let them pay for anything but sex."

"So technically you're a half hooker."

"Until today."

Mia smiled. "Until today. Want to know my secret?"

I nodded. She pointed at the ceiling, and I looked up to find my reflection up there. Me, except not, a little off, her eyes a little too blue, her lashes a little too long. The reflected girl was one standard deviation away from Kate. "Her," said Mia. "Pretend you're her."

"I am."

"No," said Mia. "You're down here. She's something different."

I looked up. She was. I waved at her and she waved back, a meeting of two separate people.

"Pretend you're her," said Mia. "And pretend she's in love."

"Pretend she's in love? With who?"

"Every guest. Pretending you're her will help you get distance; pretending she's in love will help you be kind. If you're in love with someone, you're good to them. You give them the benefit of the doubt. You're on their team. It's easy to judge guests at places like this, and some of them will ask for shit that seems weird to you, but if you pretend you're in love with them, you'll be your best self."

"Pretend I'm in love," I said.

"No," said Mia, pointing upward. "Pretend *she's* in love. There's a difference."

Betty
(NÉE JOSHUA BETTS)

Mia immediately loved her. Or, if it wasn't love, it was something. Lust? Enchantment? Fear? It looked a lot like love to me, darling.

Lady Lane
(NÉE KATE BURNS)

My first lineup? Oh, you don't forget something like that. The guy was about thirty and in a wheelchair. Both legs had been amputated, and he had a blanket over his lap. I wished my shorts were longer. I wished I were wearing a bra. The other Bunnies were doing a better job of looking him in the eye than I was. My gaze kept dropping to his legs, or where they would be, the memory of them.

"Hey baby," is what Mia said when he passed her. It was natural, coming from her. It wasn't the *Hey baby* of a construction worker to a skirt-clad passerby or the *Hey baby* of an old man to a teen in a tight dress, no, it was sweet from her mouth, like a kiss blown. I whispered it to myself. *Hey baby,* I whispered, not loud enough for anyone to hear. It sounded stupid. My hands were sweating and I wasn't wearing enough fabric to wipe them on.

The guy stopped in front of me. I looked at the ceiling.

He said, "Hi," and he was talking to me.

I winced, looked at him, then I shook my head, like, *No.* Like, *You will regret this, sir.*

He smirked and nodded, like, *Yes,* like, *I hear your no and I raise you a yes.*

"What's your name?" he said.

I wished I didn't call myself Lady. "Lady."

"That's kind of ridiculous," he said.

I nodded. It was. It suddenly all seemed ridiculous. The Hop, the country, me. "Would you like to go on a date?" the guest said. He was handsome. I felt adolescent. Like I was being asked to dance at prom.

"A date?"

"With me," he said. "Just to be clear."

"You want to go on a date with me?"

"Sure, thanks for asking, let's grab a drink."

I looked down the lineup. The girls were all leaning to see, all looking at me, expressions fixed and judging. Mia, though, she smiled wide and nodded. She mouthed, *Do it.*

Betty
(NÉE JOSHUA BETTS)

She bagged Wheelchair Dave at her first lineup, but we didn't care, since Wheelchair Dave wasn't exactly a get. He was a nice guy, sure. He was handsome, funny, good with his hands. Took his time, if you know what I mean. But Wheelchair Dave had done the rounds at the Hop, darling. The guy didn't like his own seconds.

The Bunnies were talking about her like she was some kind of threat or some kind of prodigy, but I don't know. I didn't get the buzz. So she got picked out of her first lineup, so what? Like I said, Wheelchair Dave always went for fresh meat, and she was about as fresh as they came.

I didn't know her yet, didn't really want to know her, either. She didn't look like anything special to me. I was like, white girl, blond hair, where's she from, anyway? Australia? I wondered if she'd fucked Keith Urban. If she'd fucked Keith Urban, then I would have been impressed. If she'd fucked Nicole Kidman, then I would've worshipped her like the rest of them.

Lady Lane
(NÉE KATE BURNS)

The guest seemed so calm, like la-di-da, like this was so normal. I remember thinking, How can you act like this is normal? See, at the Sugar Club, I'd been kissing other students, kids I saw every day, and at the Panther, the only guy I did anything other than dance with was Gary, and I stopped making him pay the moment sex was on the table. Everything in my life led me to sex work, but I had never actually had sex with a stranger for money.

. . .

Once we took a seat at the bar, the guest said, "Tell me about yourself." He had a nice smile. Good teeth. His hair was buzzed, and there were tally marks tattooed on the side of his head. His eyes were dark brown. He smelled like buttered toast. Like someone's home, but not mine.

"I don't know," I said.

"You don't know what to tell me, or you don't know yourself?"

I shrugged. I was nervous. I'd never been much of a dater. The movies made it look so easy, thinking of things to say, thinking of questions to ask. In a romantic comedy, you could tell which pair of people would end up together by how quick their comebacks.

Like *Notting Hill,* you know? Hugh Grant plays that bookshop owner, spills his orange juice on Julia Roberts, who plays a movie star. *Sorry!* he says. *Do you want to come to my apartment to get cleaned up?*

The two are strangers. *I have soap,* he tells her. *And water. In five minutes we could clean you up and have you back on the streets. In the nonprostitute sense, of course.* Julia Roberts looks down at the stain. *Okay,* she says. She will go to this stranger's apartment; she will use his shower. It's the only obvious solution.

. . .

I was always wishing my life were scripted. That I could read lines off a teleprompter with an endless scroll. The movies only show the main character meeting the love of her life, and maybe that's why one good conversation could send me head over heels. I was always wishing things were more romantic and permanent than they are. Life is embarrassing, but those movie stars are always doing exactly as they should. *Everything happens for a reason,* is what they're always saying. Or *Things will turn out the way they're meant to.* And it must be so easy to believe that when your life is written down for you from beginning to end.

. . .

The screen behind the bar showed Amy, Clara, the car accident lawyer, the ADHD drug, Mia, then: *The Hop: the girls of you're dreams.*

I laughed.

"What?"

I pointed at the screen. "It used to say 'the girl's of your dreams'— girls had an apostrophe, as in the possessive. And now it's 'the girls of you're dreams,' as in a contraction, 'the girls of you are dreams.' It's wrong again."

"You're not very good at this," said the guest. "Do you even work here?"

I smiled.

"You do have a beautiful smile, though," he said. "But you know that. Here, let me start," he said. I took a drink and winced. I'd ordered gin and I hated gin. Still do.

"I'm Dave," he said, lifting his beer.

"Dave."

"That's right."

"That's your real name?"

"It is," he said. "Would you rather I tell you a fake one?"

"I just didn't know if the guests used real names or not."

"You didn't know?"

"You're my first date," I said, too tired to be anything but honest.

"I am?"

"You couldn't tell?"

"I just thought that was part of your bit. The uncomfortable thing,
I mean."

"No, that's all me," I said. "That's some genuine discomfort."

"Your first date, huh?" He frowned. Wondering, I guess, if I said
that to every guest. If it was all an act. He had no way of knowing what
was real. "Well, I'll be," he said, choosing to believe it. What else was
there to do? He said, "What an honor."

• • •

There was a stag's head behind the bar. It didn't look to be mounted on
anything, no platform of wood, and it made it look like the deer had
found his way into the Hop and stuck his head through the plaster, like
his body stood in the other room, on the other side of the wall.

• • •

Dave had been to the Hop so many times he'd lost count. He loved it
there. The fantasy realized. He said, "It's not easy out there for a guy
like me."

"I bet."

"I don't mean the chair," he said. "I'm just an ugly son of a bitch.
You hungry?"

I was. I felt calmer. He was nice. Normal.

"What do you mean by 'out there'?"

"What?"

"You said 'It's not easy out there.' "

"Oh." He shrugged. "In the world."

I smiled. I liked it. Out there as opposed to in here. I liked feeling *in*.

"In the dating world," he said. "It's rough."

"But you're dating. So you're looking for a girlfriend?"

He shrugged. "We're all looking for love, right?" He signaled for the bartender and ordered one side of onion rings and another of fries. "The food's pretty good here," he said. "You'll get to know that."

"I don't think I'm looking for love," I said.

"What're you looking for?"

"I don't know."

"Money?" he said. "That's all I wanted for a while. Cash. Mom worked at a movie theater and Dad left when I was a kid. Grew up with hardly any."

"But then?"

"Marines," he said. "Four years and then—" He gestured to a wheel. "I was ready to get out anyway."

"How'd it happen? Can I ask that? Do people ask that?"

"Car accident," he said. "Can you believe I don't even get a good story out of it?"

"Invent one," I said. "You can be anyone you want to be at the Hop. You were caught in the line of fire."

"Blown off by a landmine," he said.

"Grenade."

"Chopper accident."

"Friendly fire."

"Gangrene."

"Shark attack."

"Performance art."

We went on.

Rain

(NÉE ASHLEY SMITH)

I believe it was her first date, her first lineup, even, that she landed Wheelchair Dave: decent tipper, okay in bed, good with his hands. I was at the bar, on a date with a regular, Paulie, a truck driver with a percussionist's rhythm and a dick like a fucking tree trunk. First time I booked him, Paulie told me that the reason he had trouble with intimacy in the real world was because of his dick being too big, and I was like, *Sure, dude*, but he wasn't kidding. The guy's packing.

So we were at the bar, me and Paulie, and I was slamming vodka shots to try to numb the pain that was to come, and Lady walked in with Wheelchair Dave. She was gorgeous. Drop-dead, but you know that. She looked like a celebrity, like one celebrity in particular, but you know that too. We're not really allowed to talk about it. Daddy had us sign an NDA.

Anyways, Dave was already looking at her like he was in love.

Paulie turned to look, too, but I caught his chin in my hand and pointed his gaze straight at me. Lady was the kind of girl who'd take even your most loyal regulars and call them her own.

The two of them sat a table and started talking. I looked over between shots, two, three, four, and each time I took a peek they'd eased into each other some more. Like a new pair of shoes, you know, they pinch until they don't, and then they mold to your foot, and then they're your favorite pair.

I don't know how long it took me to get comfortable talking to guests, maybe a year, maybe two, and some of them I still feel like a statue around, all stiff and made of stone, just waiting for the date to be over, but Lady was a natural. She seemed to like Dave. To *really* like him. Her face was wide open, like she was giving him everything she had to give.

Lady Lane

(NÉE KATE BURNS)

Back in my room, Dave looked around. He said, "Pretty sparse in here. If I didn't believe you were new before, I'd sure know about it now." But my room had a bed, a couch, table, closet, television, desk, fridge, two nightstands and as many lamps, abstract artwork on the walls, a rug with a floral pattern. I was like, *Sparse?* I'd never had so many things.

"What do the other girls' rooms look like?"

"Decorated," said Dave. "Like them."

"Like them?"

"Decorated to look like them. Mia's has strings of pink lights hanging from the ceiling."

I nodded.

"I guess yours is kind of like you too."

"What?"

"Undecorated, I mean."

"Well," I said. "I'm new."

"I know that," said Dave. "But even the new girls usually have their personas straight before they start taking guests. I knew the last girl, the girl who had this room before you. She was into the whole BDSM thing. Gave me a real hard time. I'm not really into that shit, just for the record, but I liked her. She was louder than you. More, I don't know, something."

"More something?"

Dave shrugged. "She was nice. Always said hello to me," he said. "I only picked her once, but she remembered my name. Always said hi. Always stopped to talk. I'm surprised she didn't tell me she was leaving."

"She didn't?"

"Girls leave suddenly from here," is what Dave said. "That's one thing I've learned. They're here and then they're not. When guys were discharged from the marines, they left overnight, but there was always time for goodbyes. When girls leave from here, it's like they disappear."

I said nothing. I thought of Mercedes Bends, of the used costume rack, of the way Daddy, when he called to offer me the job, had phrased the news of an opening as: *a room has opened up unexpectedly.* I didn't want to disappear.

"What do you think happens to them?" I asked Dave.

He shrugged. "I'm sure they make enough money to live comfortably and then get out of here. They're probably on some island sunbathing and drinking mojitos."

"But why would they leave so suddenly?"

"Maybe they're not allowed to say goodbye," said Dave. "For privacy or something. Guys can get obsessive. That's what some of the girls have told me. Their regulars get attached, too attached, start thinking their Bunny is their real-life girlfriend, or whatever. Maybe you have to make a French exit to keep anyone from following you."

I swallowed, and my saliva tasted of the pink drink everyone sipped on all day every day at the Hop. I wondered if it'd taste like that forever.

"Anyway, I'm surprised they're not making you charge extra." Dave wheeled his chair to the couch. "For being new, I mean."

"They are," I said, without thinking, without meaning to.

"They are?"

"Yeah. I'm more expensive because I'm new." The words happened on their own. My mouth was doing its own talking.

Dave nodded. Levered himself out of his chair and onto the couch. The blanket on his lap fell to the floor, and what was left of his thighs pointed at me. I remember feeling too aware of my own legs. I wished, for just a moment, that I didn't have any.

Why? I don't know, maybe so we could have something in common.

"So, what's your price?" he said.

. . .

Don't go cheap, is what Daddy had told me earlier. We're upmarket here at the Hop, and I want every girl to be earning a comfortable wage. Go cheap, and it cheapens the whole establishment. No sex for under a grand. Got it?

. . .

"For sex?"

"For sex?" Dave laughed. "What else would it be for"

I thought, *Two thousand*, and then I said, "Two thousand." I straddled his lap and found that he had a gun in his belt. I was fresh out of New Zealand, you know, and it was the first time I'd met a gun, and my mouth said "Jesus Christ" before my mind could stop it, and I thought, for a glimpse, that I might throw up.

Dave said, "Everything okay?"

I took Mia's advice: I looked up. Me, her, up there; I winked, and she winked back. I pretended to be her, that girl, someone different, a celebrity, a star. What would Nicole Kidman do if her guest had a gun? I unbuttoned his pants.

"Everything's fine," I said. "It's nothing."

"So, two thousand." Dave whistled. "A hundred percent markup, huh?"

"I don't make the rules," I said, unzipping his fly, trying to forget about the gun, the gun that could kill me, kill anyone, kill. "Don't shoot the messenger," I said, which made me think of Gary, his proclivity for idioms. Don't shoot the messenger. Messenger, IM, chat rooms, Omegle, *You've Got Mail* starring Meg Ryan and Tom Hanks. Tom Hanks.

Castaway. Falling in love with a volleyball. I could've probably fallen in love with a volleyball, I thought. I could've fallen in love with almost anyone, anything, those days, so long as I believed they loved me back. I was trying to think about those things, but in the back of my mind I was all: He has a gun, he has a gun, and "Bodies of Twelve Prostitutes Found Dismantled in Desert Shores Dumpsters."

"Your price will drop if I visit you again, though, won't it?" said Dave. "I won't be paying the new girl tax a second time, will I?"

"That depends, Dave," I said, carefully, *carefully*, setting the gun aside, "on how much fun I have." I looked up at the mirror on the ceiling; pretend like she's in love, Mia had said. I kissed Dave hard. I straddled his lap.

• • •

No unprotected sex, not ever, and no talk of prices until you're in your room with the door closed. Those were the rules Daddy told me. You can only blow him with a condom, Daddy said, and don't do any butt stuff for less than double your asking price for vaginal. Sell him a girlfriend experience, and you'll be rich in no time. Upsell upsell upsell, Lady. You have to close every deal.

• • •

I went slow. I liked Dave. When I imagined my life at the brothel, before I got there, after each interview with Daddy, on the flight over, on the drive from LAX, I imagined the kinds of freaks needing hookers to get laid. Strange kinks and emotional issues. Sociopaths and monsters. But Dave was normal. He was nice, and to tell you the truth, I felt sorry for him. I know how that sounds now, but at the time that's what I was thinking, and you told me to tell you everything.

Anyway, Dave stopped me. He said, "Why are you going easy on me?" I looked down from my perch on his lap. It felt good, having him inside me, I remember that. It felt like having a purpose.

I said, "What?"

"You're taking it slow."

"Giving you your money's worth."

"Is it because of my legs?"

"What?"

He pushed me off him, and his arms were strong. I sat hard on the couch beside him. The fabric itched.

"I don't come here for pity sex," he said. "Believe it or not, I can get that elsewhere. Some girls are really into the amputee thing, you know. Battle scars, and all that. Trauma vultures. They fuck me with sad eyes, those girls. The same eyes you're giving me right now. If I wanted pity, I'd go find one of those girls, but I come here because I don't want the pity. I like how Bunnies treat me like any other customer."

"Okay," I said. "Okay, I get it."

He swung himself over my lap and used his arms as stands. He was fit. Strong. He felt good. It felt good. It felt really good. I think I whispered, "Fuck," and I swear it was involuntary. He smiled.

"There she is," is what Dave said. "I don't need you to go easy on me," he said, but I wasn't listening to Dave anymore. I lifted my legs over his shoulders and he rocked harder. Faster. "Understand?" he said. "Understand?"

I nodded even though I didn't know what I was nodding about. I felt like I shouldn't be allowed to finish. Like, what kind of job pays you for your pleasure? I did, though, we both did, and we were both loud about it, and afterward we sat side by side on the couch, and I said, "Oh boy, I guess I'm a hooker now, huh?"

Dave laughed and I rested my head on his shoulder and he smelled of sweat and man.

"Can I say something?" he said. "Can I just say that you seem, I don't know, these girls are always so good at their parts, their bits, but you don't seem like you're playing a part or doing a bit. You seem real."

"I am real." I looked up at the ceiling, the mirror, myself, and I saw my ma up there.

"It's nice, is all I'm saying. To be with someone who seems real."

"I am real."

. . .

As Ma got sicker and sicker, closer and closer to death, I kept having this dream that I was fading. That my whole body was turning transparent. That people started to see through me. That I was going ghost. I didn't know who I was outside of Ma. I'd never had to exist on my own.

. . .

Dave booked a date for the next week. Another for the week after that.

When Daddy came to my room that night on his rounds, there was a dog at his side and a booking sheet in his hand. He leaned on my door-frame and whistled. "I sure know how to pick 'em," he said. "Booking a regular on your first time. You're a natural, Lady." A natural.

"Who's this?" I said, crouching to scratch the dog's ears. A German shepherd, shiny coat, wet nose. The dog nuzzled into my chest.

"This is Rabbit," he said. "She's my right-hand woman."

"Rabbit," I said. "Nice to meet you, ma'am." I shook her hand and then stood. "Hey, Daddy?" I said. "Thanks for bringing me here. I had a lot of fun today." I did.

He smiled. My god, he had a great smile.

"I got you something," he said. "It's not much, but." He took a plaque from the back pocket of his jeans. A golden plate with the name, my name, LADY, engraved in black. "Wanted to make you feel more at home," he said.

I took the nameplate and held it up to my door. "Will you help me?" I said.

"I'll see to it," he said.

"Thank you."

"You already said that."

"I meant it."

He reached for my hand and held it in his. And I thought, *I will not fall in love with Daddy.* I thought, *It would be very bad to fall in love with Daddy.*

"Do you want to come in?" I said.

But no. Daddy just said, "Good night, Lady." He kissed my forehead and he said, "Sweet dreams."

Rain

(NÉE ASHLEY SMITH)

It's like I said: Daddy fucked his Bunnies, but he only fucked them once.

Dakota

(NÉE JACY ADAMS)

Right, he tested every Bunny once, but other than that, Daddy didn't sleep with his Bunnies. Except for Willa. Rumor had it, Daddy slept with Willa more than once. It never bothered me; I've always liked girls better, I've always felt safer around women. It's not that I've been any kind of assaulted, either. I grew up sheltered. I was adopted by a rich white Catholic couple who lived in a mansion in Burlington, Vermont. They sent me to a private boarding school, and it was there that I started seeing girls, rather than boys; penises just never really did it for me. And yeah, that didn't go down well with my adoptive parents. They told me I was headed straight for Hades, and kicked me to the curb with a suitcase of clothes and a gold-leafed King James. I got on a train to New York that same day, and my seatmate happened to be a dominatrix from Brooklyn. I'd never heard of BDSM, but I'd been going to church my whole life, so the notion of punishment for pleasure came easily. I dommed for three years, spitting in men's mouths, urinating on their faces; I never loved the work, but I liked the outfits. A lot of leather, a lot of lace, heels that near doubled your height. Then I learned about the Hop. Word on the street was that girls were making triple at the legal brothels what we were making in the dungeon. So I packed my car and drove across the country. I asked my first guest if he wanted me to spit on him, and he looked at me like I was insane.

He said, "Could we maybe just talk?" That was a nice change.

Lady Lane

(NÉE KATE BURNS)

I expected to feel something after my first guest. Some kind of change. But no, I felt the same. The truth was, having sex with Dave for money felt no different than having sex for free. It was every bit as intimate, every bit as real, and, to be honest, probably better than most one-night stands I'd had.

My room was quiet. The night was long. I wasn't tired. I watched myself on the ceiling. I looked so much like Ma. I'd never really thought about it before, how much I looked like her, until she died and I started seeing her everywhere, in my own reflection in windows, mirrors, glass. She was everywhere. She was everywhere I was. I wondered if Ma would be proud or disappointed in my new self. "Ma?" I asked. "What do you think, Ma?" I asked.

• • •

When Ma gave me the sex talk, it went like this. *Have sex when you want, bunny, give him the milk, but don't go giving away the cow for free.*

I don't think that's how it goes, Ma.

The cow doesn't miss her milk, but if she gives the farmer her whole self, he'll fatten her up and kill her for meat.

There was a fishbowl full of condoms in my childhood bedroom. Sitting on my nightstand like a faithful little pet. *You don't want to end up like me, bunny*, is what Ma told me about contraception. *You don't want to regret not giving your girls a better life.*

. . .

Here's a fact I missed from the story, from before she fell sick: Ma got knocked up when I was about six. I remember the time in blinks. The way she cried, her head hung between her legs on the toilet, underwear in a slump at her feet, little stick gripped tight in hand, she waved it at me, the proof of her pregnancy. *What am I meant to do with this*, she wept. *What am I meant to do with this?* I thought she meant the stick, and I took it from her and I threw it in the trash. Like, problem solved.

I'd wake to the sound of her sickness. She'd gag into the toilet bowl and I'd climb out of bed. We spent each morning before school, before work, holding each other on the cold bathroom tile. I knew she was pregnant without her having to tell me. I'd seen movies, TV shows, and I'd read a couple books, and I knew that a vomiting man meant death or disease and a vomiting woman meant babies.

. . .

She grew in gasps. Suddenly she was one size, and then suddenly she was another. It wasn't like getting fatter, that slow growth of girth and gut, no, there was no gentle accumulation. Her pregnancy grew like implants. Like some surgeon was botching a stomach job once a week. I was always surprised at her new shape.

Her feet inflated. Her cheeks filled. Her eyes sank back. Her hair thickened. Her breasts swelled. Like an amateur artist had created a woman in my mother's image, like her enough for anyone to tell who she was supposed to be, but every feature, every part of her, just slightly off, just a little not-Ma.

The night she went into labor, she woke me with her howls. *You stay here, bunny*, she said, as she hoisted her body into the back seat of a manfriend's car. *You watch over the house. I'll be back.*

With my little sister?

That's right, bunny. With your sister.

When she got home, she'd deflated, not all the way, but most of it. She looked vacated in her eyes, too. She wasn't carrying my baby sister. She was empty-handed, not even her purse clutched to her chest.

Where is she? I asked.

Who? said Ma. And I knew not to ask a second time. And I knew not to ask ever again.

· · ·

The Hop quietened down around midnight, and I hung up my costume, rubbed my face clean, pulled off my shirt, my shorts, my underwear, and then I noticed, in the crotch, little specks of red. Of blood. I looked at the blister pack of birth control on my bathroom counter. Three days at the Hop, three pills taken, blood in my underwear. I looked up at the mirror on the ceiling.

Bell Hobbes

(NÉE MAYBELLINE BURNS, SISTER OF KATE BURNS)

How long have I known about my sister? I found out who she was by accident. Meg and Morty, my adoptive parents, they told me who I was from the beginning—as in, I knew I wasn't theirs in the same way as Brit, my adoptive sister, was theirs.

They told me my biological mother already had one kid she could barely support, and Meg and Morty had been mourning Brit's twin, who was stillborn. Finding me was fate, they liked to tell me. The switch happened at the hospital. My mother birthed me, named me Maybelline after the cosmetic company, a parting fuck-you, and then she handed me off. Sometimes I imagine how she might've kissed my tiny forehead, right between the eyes, and said, "You deserve more than I could ever have given you." Sometimes I imagine that she hurled me across the room like a rugby player, wanting only to fling me as far from herself as possible.

I knew I was adopted, but that's about all I knew. And, I mean, the Hobbeses were a great family, they were rich, they let Brit and I do whatever we wanted, and our house had two pools plus a hot tub—why would I have wanted anything different?

I found out about the Burnses when we had to do our family trees at school and I googled my own name, my full name, my birth name. *Maybelline Burns*. Buried beneath a pile of complaints about allergic reactions to lipsticks was a news article from the morning of my birth. It read, "The first baby born on Waitangi Day this year was Maybelline

Burns, daughter of Merrill Burns and sister of Kate Burns, Maybelline, at 6 lbs exactly, was born at 12:04 a.m., three weeks premature. 'Much easier than my first,' Burns said, when asked about her birth. 'Slipped out like an old tampon.' "

There was a photo of Merrill above the article, a baby cradled in her arms. The baby was me. The mother was a younger iteration of our cleaning lady. The woman who came over every Saturday morning, hair whitened with cheap bleach and eyes yellowing like an old photograph, the one who always smelled of cigarettes and tacky perfume, whose nails were plastic and various shades of neon and sharpened to a point. Merrill. My mother. My *real* mother.

Every Saturday morning she knocked on the door, and sometimes I answered it and let her in, always being extra nice because Meg and Morty taught us you can tell someone's true character by how they act around poor people. So I'd ask her how she was and I'd make her a cup of tea and I'd tell her about school and I'd always clean my room a little before she arrived. To be nice.

The day after I found the article about her, Brit and I had been drinking the parents' oldest bottle from the wine cellar. We knew they'd be mad, but the parents didn't like confrontation so we'd never face consequences. We'd never faced a consequence. At the bottom of the bottle, I told Brit about my mother, my biological mother, our cleaning lady, and just as I was finishing the story, Merrill opened Brit's bedroom door.

"Your parents aren't home but I'm headed out," she told us. She didn't know I knew. I wondered if she took the job to be closer to me. I wondered if she ever picked up my pillow as she made my bed, held it to her chest, imagined what if. "You girls be good," she said. I watched her, wanting her eyes to linger on me. Wanting something. Recognition. Acknowledgment. She closed the door behind her.

As a kid, I'd played a game. I searched for myself in the people around me in an attempt to find my real mum. Everyone looked like my mother if I squinted long enough. The woman buying coffee at the front of the line, how her cowlick fountained from the same spot on her scalp as mine. She could've been my mother. The old man with the newspaper, see how his pinkie finger curled inward, shy, like mine. He could've been my mother. The baby yawning over his father's shoulder, the way his nose was biased to the left. That baby could've been my mother too. Three people, maybe siblings, maybe friends so close they'd grown into each other like climbing plants, entangled and become one over time, see how they stood, heads ducked just so, almost the exact way I stood, they too could've been my mother. It was comforting, having a mother everywhere I went. It's probably why people believe in God.

Anyway, Brit was the one to suggest it that night, wasn't she? That we follow Merrill to see where she lived? The details are blurry. This was a few years ago, now. One of us suggested following Merrill home just to, I don't know, to see where I came from, I guess. So we followed Merrill that night, Brit driving, me shotgun. We drove for a long time. Out of the city, the outskirts of the city, then out into the country.

"Where does this bitch live?" said Brit.

"Can you not call my mother a bitch."

"Meg's your mother."

"You know what I mean."

We pulled up to a tiny weatherboard house that looked like it had been white a long, long time before. There was trash in the yard. The mailbox was comatose in the gutter. I felt sick. Brit held my hand tight in hers. I had never wanted to be her real sister more.

Merrill parked diagonally across the driveway, didn't bother to lock her car, wrestled with the front door for a while before giving up and kicking it open. Once inside, she didn't turn on any lights.

"Is she just sitting in the dark?" said Brit.

"Maybe she went straight to bed."

"Should we check?"

"No."

"Come on. Aren't you curious?"

"Brit, no."

"We'll take a one-minute peek, and then we'll get back in the car and I'll take us home."

"Ten seconds," I said.

"Five," said Brit. We crouch-ran the length of the pocked path to the front door. Brit tried to look through the peephole. I peered through the window. There was a fire burning. Merrill and a younger version of her—Kate, it must have been—were curled together on the hearth, laughing, their faces lit by the flames. They looked like they belonged to each other.

Did I knock? No. No, I didn't. We left, and I never reached out to Kate. She didn't know I existed.

ACT III

....

THE RISE

It occurs to me that I must not know altogether what I am, ei-ther, and that others know certain things about me better than I do, though I think I ought to know all there is to know and I proceed as if I do.

—Lydia Davis, "A Friend of Mine"

Mia

(NÉE YA CHAI CHEN)

A week in, and Lady started picking up guests quicker than most. She was good. Popular, sure, but she didn't upsell, which was where the real money was. You could make your millions at the Hop, but you really had to make double that, since half of every deal went to the house. I was still the best-selling Bunny. I had regulars who spent whole weeks with me and barely spared a look at anyone else. I was good at what I did, and I knew how to keep guests loyal, but Lady had that thing. The thing that made men look, and once they looked, they couldn't look away. She didn't seem to know about it. Or she acted like she didn't. Lady didn't seem to know who she was, and when everything went down, I think the only person surprised by it was Lady herself.

Lady Lane

(NÉE KATE BURNS)

My next clients were, in this order:

A nervous young couple who wanted to shake up their sex life. They kissed each other in front of me. I kissed each of them in turn. They were gentle. Quiet. He watched his wife the whole time, kept asking her if she was okay.

A twentysomething in a Nirvana T-shirt wanting to lose his virginity. He told me about his fears. Insecurities. He'd never been kissed. He had an online girlfriend who wouldn't talk to him on the phone. He knew he was being catfished, but without her, he would go days, weeks, without a conversation. He came in under a minute but hung out for the rest of the day. We ordered burgers to my room and watched anime. He said he wanted to take me to Applebee's next time, for two-dollar margaritas.

A guy with so many earrings that our sex sounded like a concert. It was his first time at a brothel, he wanted me to know. It was his first time paying for it, he wanted me to know.

I drank coffee with an old man and listened to his complaints about technology. It was the end of privacy as we knew it, he explained. His daughter had bought him an iPhone so they could keep in better touch, and he didn't want to be ungrateful for the gift, so he kept it in a PO box at a faraway post office so that it couldn't watch him or know where he lived.

One guy brought a prop, an inflatable dragon that he sat in the corner of my room to watch us. He was careful with the dragon. He kissed the tip of her nose.

One guy with autism who wanted to do a test date before he tried it out in real life. He opened every single door for me and pulled out my chair at the bar and he was going to be just fine out there.

A young guy requested both me and Ginger, and he wanted us to fight in front of him and Ginger taught me to make it look like she'd punched me by clapping my hands and turning my head at the same time as she threw her fist, and this guy, he loved it, he cheered.

One guy whispered that he loved me right before he came, and I believed him.

. . .

The thing that surprised me most about the Hop in the beginning was how much I liked almost every guest. When they left, I'd feel lonely, like that sudden emptiness that comes with dropping a beloved at the airport, or a best friend closing the door behind themselves after a sleepover.

. . .

Each night I debriefed with Mia, who was such a fast friend I barely remember how it happened. Her friendship was easy as blinking, natural. When we were done for the day, we talked back to bad TV. When a *Bachelor* contestant said she wasn't there to make friends, Mia said, *How original*, and we threw handfuls of microwave popcorn across the room. When a Chopped chef used the ice cream machine, we told him, *There's not enough time*, and there wasn't. He served the judges a cold, sweet soup and we said, *We told you so*.

Our favorite show was the same werewolf drama I'd seen on my first night at the Hop. *We're Wolves*, it was called, unfortunately. Every episode was the exact same: this guy would mutate at an inconvenient time and then have to try to cover his tracks. It was terrible, predictable, we loved it. We guessed where he'd transform at the beginning of each episode. "Barber!" I said.

"Movie theater!" she said.

He went wolf at a museum, which meant Mia won. Museum was more movie theater than barber.

During commercials, we talked. This was how Ma and I did it too. Our relationship was built from blocks, each one the exact size of an ad break.

"You're doing better than most newbies, you know," is what Mia said, as a car accident lawyer told us to call him. "You must be good. What's your move?"

"My move?"

"Mine's telling them how much I want them. Telling them I need them. That I just *have* to have them. It's nothing groundbreaking, but it works almost every time."

"I don't really have a move," I said.

Mia frowned. "Right," she said. That day, her T-shirt read BUT FIRST, COFFEE. I'd never seen Mia drink coffee, never seen her drink anything other than Pink. I got it; Pink was good. "You know we're not in competition with each other, don't you, Lady?" she said. "You know we're family, right?"

"Sure."

"The girls, all of us, we share what's working for us, we talk about guests, we help each other. Okay?"

I didn't understand what she was getting at. I hadn't been mean to anyone.

"You're just picking up guests quickly, is all. We share, around here. We're a community."

I looked up, and I was up there, on my own ceiling. Always looking back at me. "Dave told me something," I said. "He told me I seemed real."

Mia rolled her eyes. "If that isn't the most man thing I've ever heard. Once I dated this guy who told me I should stop wearing makeup. I'd been setting my alarm for an hour before his, just to get up and put on my face. He liked natural girls better, is what he told me one night when I was wearing a bright red lip, so I turned off my alarm. I woke up the next morning, and he was lying there staring at me. He was horrified. He goes, 'I didn't mean like that.' "

"You're beautiful all the time."

She was. She was barefaced right at that moment. Her eyes were their natural brown. Her hair was loose and wet from a shower. When she was on, Mia was dazzling, a whole circus right before your eyes. But when she was done with appointments for the day, she turned soft, young, she laughed with her whole body, and when she touched you, it felt like love.

"Well shit, Lady," she said. "Maybe this is how you keep picking up guests. You look at them like this. Keep looking at them like this, and you won't just have regulars, you'll have stalkers."

I didn't know what she was talking about. "I'm just nice to them," I said. "That's all. And anyway, look at my numbers compared to yours. I'm no you."

"You could be," said Mia. She took a tube of lipstick from her bra and uncapped the lid. She drew her signature sherbet shade on her lips, two coats, three, then she kissed me. I swear she tasted of candy. "You can be anyone, here," she said, pressing the tube into my palm. When she left for the night, I looked up at the ceiling, at the version of me who lived up there, and she was less me than usual. More makeup, hair done—she looked like Ma. It was so lonely there without her.

Lacey Kahu

She was different, the first time I called. Something had shifted. She was different, but she seemed happy.

"Lace," is how she answered the phone. "Hi, Lace."

I said, "Kate, hi, how are you?"

"Lady."

"What?"

"Lady. I go by Lady here."

"Lady? Like your dog?"

"My hooker name, remember? From *Cosmo*? Lady Lane."

There was something in her voice, something new. I said, "Are you okay?"

Instead of answering, she asked about the Panther. Asked how things were going. It was clear that we should've been talking about Kate. I mean Lady. She had just started working at a brothel, you know, we had a lot to cover, but sometimes Lady didn't want to talk; she wanted to avoid her own life. So I told her about my newest regular. A guy with an eye patch who liked to fling it onto the stage, and after every dance, I'd have to return it, like, *Here you go, Steve.*

She laughed at that one. And I went, "You okay now, Lady?"

And she said she was.

I said, "It's okay to miss her, you know. It'll get easier."

And then she said good night.

Lady Lane

(NÉE KATE BURNS)

One guest, a man, plain, wearing plaid, he wanted me to lie still and snore lightly, as if in a deep sleep. He wanted me to wake about two minutes into the act, and I was meant to thrash about. Flail. And if it wasn't too much trouble, he said, he'd like me to scream.

"What's it about?" I asked him afterward. He was satisfied with my performance and requested another appointment for the following week.

"About?"

"The sleeping thing. The kink."

The man scratched his stubble, laughed uncomfortably.

"I'm not trying to shame you for it," I said. "I'm sorry. You don't have to answer."

He told me a story about his grandfather, who would shuffle into his room in the night. By the end of the story, he was crying, big heaving sobs like he was dragging all that emotion up from the deepest parts of him.

"I'm so sorry that happened to you," I said, holding his head in my hands.

"You know," he said, "it's not even the act—I mean, it was bad, what he did, it was, but that was twenty years ago now. It's like it stuck to me, though, grew on me or something, like he passed it on or like it's hereditary, you know. He gave it to me like a bad gift or a curse or something. It's with me all the time. It's who I am. I can't, you know,

I can't . . . perform unless it feels like—" He paused. "Like she doesn't want it."

I didn't know what to say. What I was thinking was: *Some people don't feel the need to take their trauma out on others.* But I think I just went, "Oh."

"But lots of people fantasize about rape," he said. "Right? It doesn't make me a . . . it doesn't make me a monster, right?"

I said nothing. I didn't know the answer. Fantasizing about raping someone *did* seem monstrous to me.

He said, "They think I'm a monster."

"Who?"

He gestured to the whole world, and tears welled in his eyes.

"Oh," I said.

He cried and he cried.

• • •

Afterward, I asked the parlor full of Bunnies, "Have you ever had a guest with a rape fantasy?"

Rain was giving Dakota a massage and Betty was making herself a drink and Mia was reading a book and Ginger was scratching her little poodle, Noodles, behind the ears.

Betty snorted. "Only every day," she said.

"How do you deal with it?"

"Deal with it?" said Betty. "We're in the service industry, darling, and the service is fulfilling fantasies. You deal with a rape fantasist by fulfilling the fantasy."

"Doesn't it make you feel—I don't know."

"Would you rather they acted on it out in the real world?" Betty opened a tiny umbrella into her cocktail.

Betty

(NÉE JOSHUA BETTS)

Rape fantasists? Sure, darling, but they were usually the good guys. If they weren't some kind of good, why would they pay a grand a pop for a bad imitation of their fantasy when they could make the real thing happen out in the wild for free, something that happens every single day? No. Those were the responsible guys, see? They were trying to do the right thing. We got pedophiles too, you know. Those ones wanted you to dress up like a little kid and talk in a higher pitch and drink a cup of milk while they tried to seduce you. That one was harder for me to come to terms with, the pedos. My first week I had a guy ask me to wear a diaper and call him Dad and I had to excuse myself to go hurl in the sink before the session. He made me suck a lollipop while he touched me. Wanted me to giggle like a girl when he put it in.

He asked me how old I was. Said, "How old are you, sweetheart?"

I said, "Fourteen?"

He shook his head.

"Ten?"

No.

"Five?"

"You just turned three, I think," is what he said with a smile. I gagged, darling, I did. But the logic's the same, isn't it? The alternative to them being brave enough to bring that fantasy to the Hop is them acting on it in life. These guys aren't monsters. They've got a monstrousness to them, and they're choosing not to act on it, and that makes them quite the opposite, don't you think?

Lady Lane

(NÉE KATE BURNS)

Daddy wouldn't give me the time of day. I told myself I just wanted to be on good terms with him, but, well . . . I don't know what I was looking for. I was looking for something, someone. A place to belong. A person to belong to. I was looking for him.

. . .

The Hop's pool was a sparkling blue, and it was a hundred degrees out, and I had the afternoon off. I sat on the edge and dangled my legs. The water was cold and chlorinated and it distorted my feet, turned them into mutated versions of themselves. A sign read: NO LIFE GUARD ON DUTY. SWIM AT YOU'RE OWN RISK.

"You getting in?"

I turned around, and there was Daddy, leaning on the gate. He had a toothpick in his mouth and a Stetson on his head and he looked straight out of something Clint Eastwood directed. He was hot.

"No."

"No?"

I kicked my legs. The water was cold. I told him, "There's a spelling mistake on that sign, you know." I was insufferable, I know that now.

"Damn, you really like spelling."

"It says 'Swim at you are own risk.' "

Daddy laughed. "Who cares?" he said. I did. Did I?

"I can't really swim," I told him.

Daddy took off his hat and set it on the gatepost. He unlaced his boots and tossed them in a pile. He unbuckled his belt.

I said, "What are you doing?"

"Come on," he said.

"I can't," I said.

Daddy took off his shirt and revealed boxers beneath his jeans. "Come on," he said.

It was hard to tell how deep the water was.

"I won't let you drown," Daddy said. He took the hem of my shirt and I lifted my arms and he added my clothes to the pile.

"Jump," he said, once I was down to my underwear.

"No."

"Jump," he said.

I curled my toes over the pool's edge. Daddy took my hand in his. "I'll jump with you," he said. "Three, two." He jumped before he got to one and he dragged me with him and we fell in a tangle into the water. The water was so cold it snatched my breath, and when I surfaced, I was gasping.

"It's okay," is what Daddy was saying. "It's okay, it's okay." His arms were around my waist and he held my body tight against his. "Lady," he said. "Lady," he said. "You can touch the ground."

And he was right. I stood, and the water barely even reached my shoulders. I felt stupid.

"Not so scary," Daddy said.

"You can let me go," I said. But he didn't and I could feel his erection against my leg and he bit my earlobe and I closed my eyes.

"I have to go," he said.

I didn't want him to. I said, "Don't go."

"I have to go."

Betty
(NÉE JOSHUA BETTS)

I know a snake when I see a snake, and Lady? She was a snake. She turned up, started hoarding guests like crazy, barely talked to a Bunny that wasn't Mia, didn't seem to give a single fuck about friendship, and started schmoozing Daddy off the bat. Mia was always telling me to give her the benefit of the doubt, but I've never trusted the Aussies, darling. The whole country's full of snakes.

Lady Lane

(NÉE KATE BURNS)

Honestly, I wasn't really thinking about friendship during my first few weeks at the Hop. Ma had just died, Gary and I had just split, and I'd just left Lacey alone halfway across the world to move to Nevada and start working as a hooker. I was going through some stuff, you know? It was a lot. I was tired. Still, Mia was always telling me I had to try harder with the other girls, and I heard her but I didn't know how to begin. For me, back then, with Ma, with men, my relationships were built on finding out what a person wanted from me and making them pay for it. For a long time I sat in the parlor and watched the televisions while they hung out, as if a friendship could be built on nothing but physical proximity.

. . .

One day, maybe a week or two in, the Hop's screens started showing a commercial featuring me, and I had no idea how they got the footage. I was in costume, smiling, laughing, there was a voiceover, a sultry timbre, an American accent that said, "Introducing the Hop's newest Bunny, Lady! All the way from New Zealand, Lady is a wonder from down under. Eager to please and waiting for someone just like you." At the end of the video, I looked straight into the camera.

Mia's commercial was different. It seemed as if she'd filmed it especially. She walked toward the camera, moved her hips, shimmied her shoulders. "Mia is the Hop's own Asian persuasion and Bunny of the Year three years running. There's nothing this Bunny won't do to bring all of your wildest fantasies to life." She blew a kiss.

"Did you record your own commercials?" I asked the parlor, which was full of Bunnies in costume. A bachelor party was due to arrive in ten minutes, and we were all waiting for the lineup bell. They turned to look at me.

Finally Rain said, "I filmed mine the day I got here." Then she started acting it out, talking around a cigarette, which rested between her teeth, lilac lipstick marking its shaft. She never lit it, didn't smoke, as far as I knew. It was all just part of the act. Her commercial came on after Mia's, and Rain took the cigarette and pretended to exhale in perfect time with her screen self. "Rain's a depraved girl with a bad attitude," she lip-synched. "Let her do naughty things to you"—she paused, winked—"If you dare."

The Bunnies applauded.

"I didn't record mine," I said, after the room quieted down.

"Obviously you did," said Betty.

The other Bunnies didn't love me, and I got it. I was breaking records, Mia told me one night; I was pulling guests too quickly, establishing regulars, I was taking money they had been earning, could still be earning if only it weren't for me. She told me not to worry too much, that the girls would come around. "We're sisters," Mia told me. "The Hop's a sisterhood, and when it comes down to it, Bunnies show up for Bunnies."

Betty pointed to the screen, and I was up there again. We were on a loop. "If you didn't record it, how're you up there right now?"

"I mean I didn't know about it," I said. "I didn't know I was being recorded. I didn't know."

Betty
(NÉE JOSHUA BETTS)

She played dumb. She was all, *I don't understand*, and *What's going on*, and I can't stand that bullshit, darling. I'm allergic to faux-stupid. Lady knew exactly what she was up to, that damsel act, wooing Mia, collecting guests faster than any Bunny I'd seen before. And her relationship with Daddy? I'd like to see her try to talk her way out of that one.

Lady Lane

(NÉE KATE BURNS)

Every night Daddy stopped by, and every night I invited him in, and every night he said no. I could tell he wanted me, there was that familiar hunger in his eyes, but something was holding him back.

"Come in," I said one night, after a long day of guests.

"I can't," he said.

"You can," I said, "you just won't."

"No," he said. "I won't."

I sat on the floor, on my side of the door. "Please," I said. "Sit." He sat on my welcome mat. "There," I said. "Is this allowed?"

"This is allowed," he said.

"Do you want me?" I said. Honesty, and all.

"I do," said Daddy. "Very much."

"Then why?"

"Things get complicated," said Daddy. "I'm your boss," he said.

"But I like you," I said.

"I like you too," he said.

"Can we be friends?" I said. "Is that allowed?"

"That is allowed," he said. "Friends."

"Friends!" I said. "Like Rachel and Joey!"

"They hooked up," said Daddy.

"But they shouldn't have," we both said, at exactly the same time. He laughed.

"Tell me something about yourself," I said.

"Like what?"

I shrugged. "Anything. Friends tell friends things about themselves."

"You want to know why I got into the brothel business?" he said. "My mother worked the streets when I was a kid. She worked the Strip in Vegas. Whenever she went to work, I'd take a steak out of the freezer to thaw for when she got home. We never ate them, the steaks, they weren't for eating. See, meat reduces swelling. When she got home, I'd be waiting with a cold steak to press to her wounds. I got into brothels to keep women like my mom safe." He looked at me. "Is that something enough for you?"

I showed Daddy the journal, which was in my back pocket, where it lived. "This is my ma's," I said. "Was. She's dead," I said. My throat ached. I would not cry. Daddy leaned across the doorway to tuck a strand of hair behind my ear. "She had sex for money," I said. "A different guy every night. I didn't know she was getting paid for it until I found this journal when I was packing up her things. It's her records. The names, dates, amounts, they go back to my birthday."

I was crying.

"Lady," Daddy said, "Look at you." He held my hand and looked me in the eye so hard it was like he wanted me to combust. He said, "Who your father is, is irrelevant. How you came about doesn't matter. The fact that you don't know, I mean, we don't know how the pyramids came about, how the stars came about, how our world came about. The fact that you don't know makes you a space of infinite possibility. You're perfect," is what he said.

• • •

Whenever Ma told me we'd be rich one day, I'd be famous one day, we'd live in Hollywood and wear Chanel and stroll among the stars, I believed her. Believing's easy. Tinker Bell thought she needed to be believed in to stay alive, but what she really needed was for people to *tell* her they believed in her. Whether they really believed in her or not, we'll never know. So I told Ma I knew she'd make us rich and I told her I knew she'd get us out of our tumbledown life and I told her that I, too, wanted to be famous, a star. What I really believed? That's my business. What you believe to be real is one of the only things you get to keep as your own.

. . .

Daddy took my hand and pressed a kiss to my knuckles. One hand, then the next. "I'm going to make you into something, Lady," he said. And when he said, "I'm going to make you the next big thing," he sounded just like Ma, and I chose to believe him.

Mia

(NÉE YA CHAI CHEN)

Lady told me there was nothing going on between her and Daddy, and I believed her. I chose to believe her.

"We just talk," she said.

"What do you mean, 'just' talk?" I said.

"I mean, we're not having sex."

"Sex?" I said. "Sex is how you get to know a body. That's easy. Talking's how you get to know a person. That's what'll get you in trouble."

Lady looked at me.

"I'm just saying, be careful, okay? We're Daddy's profit, first and foremost, okay? That's what we are to him."

····························

Dakota
(NÉE JACY ADAMS)

It's easy to convince yourself that the people in control of you care about you. Politicians, CEOs, God. But the relationship is usually predator and prey. Have you seen how a cat will play with a mouse with such soft paws before eating him alive?

Lady Lane

(NÉE KATE BURNS)

One guest, a man, middle-aged and mundane. He was wearing a suit and tie. I looked at his shoes. Ma was always telling me to look at a man's shoes. *That men know how to wear a suit and they know how to trim their beards, but the shoes, everyone forgets about the shoes and that's how you can tell who the man really is,* Ma liked to tell me.

The man introduced himself with a soft Italian accent, and his teeth looked pressure washed, and his shoes were polished and tied with a double knot. *You can't trust a man with tidy shoes,* is what Ma was always saying. *Who has so much time to spend on their feet?*

"Are your teeth real?" I said.

"What?"

"Your teeth."

"Of course they're real." He gnashed them together, and the sound was a cheap plastic wind-up toy.

"I mean, I know they're real, but are they yours?"

"They're in my mouth, aren't they?"

I took him back to my room, and he agreed to pay two grand to choke me. He was good at it, well practiced, he knew to squeeze the sides of the throat rather than crushing the windpipe.

"Can you tell me you're dying," he said, his voice still so soft, buttery.

"That I'm dying?"

"Tell me I'm killing you."

"You're killing me?"

"Make me believe it."

"Ouch, sir, you're murdering me."

"That's really not good," he said. "Make me believe it."

"Make *me* believe it," I said.

The man squeezed my throat so hard that a gurgling noise came out.

He left a five-hundred-dollar tip and I thought, damn, if only Ma were here to see this.

• • •

As I washed myself off, soaped between my legs, I noticed a smear of blood on my fingers. I noticed it, then I washed it away. It's so easy to keep a secret from yourself.

Mia

(NÉE YA CHAI CHEN)

By the time she'd been at the Hop three weeks, if Lady was in a lineup, the rest of us didn't have much of a chance. I saw the other girls swapping glances, and I saw their resentment growing, but there was nothing to be gained through jealousy. When I told them that, Ginger said, "It's not about envy, honey, it's about etiquette."

But it was envy, and envy is a pointless emotion; it's an ugly expression to wear. Back in school, I was jealous of the way white girls got to build themselves from the ground up. They got to be a blankness, an emptiness, and fill their personality with whatever they wanted, the cheerleader, the goth, the loner, the geek, but I was Asian and that's how the other kids saw me and that's what I had to work with.

But jealousy is all-consuming, it is the only thing you can be while you're feeling it, and for years I was silent and furious. A corner kid. No one knew my name, and the kids who did couldn't pronounce it. I watched, observed the social system silently from the outside, until one day, one girl, a popular girl called Kaelynn, we were in the cafeteria and I unwrapped my tuna rice bowl and she told me my lunch smelled like pussy. Then I went, "Your pussy smells like tuna?" And people laughed! And I made friends!

The thing about jealousy is that you do it to yourself, and it never hurts the people you're jealous of. Jealousy is an act of self-harm.

Lady Lane

(NÉE KATE BURNS)

It wasn't that I didn't want to be friends with the Bunnies, it was that I wasn't at the Hop to make friends—I was there to make a living. A life. Plus, I hadn't made a friend since I gave Lacey a shoe when we started school, and I didn't know how to make friends with women. I was intimidated. I was afraid of them. I was just more comfortable around men. When I told Mia that, she rolled her eyes. She said, "Don't be one of those." I still don't know what she meant. One of what?

Betty

More comfortable around men? It doesn't make sense, like, statistically, to be more comfortable around men. Had she ever read the news? Women don't kill people. There was a reason that every single suspect the cops were pulling for the Desert Shores Killer case was a cis white guy; they were going by statistics. When Lady said she was more comfortable around men, what she meant was that she was more comfortable being uncomfortable. Some girls just love playing the victim.

Mia told me I was being a bitch and that I just had to give her time, and maybe I was and maybe I did, but before Lady got to the Hop we were a community, a sisterhood, and if we were taking too many appointments away from the other girls, we'd skip a lineup or two. But Lady was there at every one of them. Blue eyes blinking big, tongue slowly licking her lower lip. She took each man by the hand and walked him right by the rest of us.

"You're rich," said Mia. "What do you care?"

I was, too. My husband was a pilot, and we had a mansion in Vegas and a condo in Palm Springs and a lake house on Tahoe and a villa in the South of France. I wore Dior and carried a Louis and my lipstick was Chanel and I drove a Jag, but it wasn't always that way, for me.

Before I got to the Hop, I worked underground. Literally and figuratively. The brothel, called Under Where, was in the basement of a mattress store, and if anyone asked what I did for a living, I told them I was on unemployment. The basement was dirty; a punctured pipe dripped once every two seconds, just frequent enough to score a man's thrusts.

I didn't have health care and I didn't have dental. I didn't have car insurance and I lived in my car and I had a pet raccoon called Bandit who got rabid and I had to put him down myself, by running over his neck one night in the dark. Another night I got a nasty pain in my gut and I thought it was from a long day of bargain-bin appointments and I tried to sleep it off, stretched out over the back seat, a bag of frozen peas pressed to my stomach and a fever coming on.

"Maybe you should go to the hospital," a colleague suggested the next day when I turned up to work in the middle of summer wearing layers upon layers of jackets and sweat.

"Who's paying?" I said.

But then I passed out and some thoughtless bastard called an ambulance and I had to get an emergency splenectomy. I was unconscious and had no say in the matter but if I did, I would've chosen to die. I couldn't afford all of that.

When I woke up, Madame Pauline was at my bedside. She kissed my wet forehead and told me not to return to the brothel. "You frightened the customers," she whispered in my ear, and then left.

But I had a loyal customer in Mr. Waldorf, who came on odd days, Monday through Friday, and paid me a couple hundred to tickle his dick with my acrylics, easy. He told me stories while I worked. About his family, his childhood dog, growing up Mormon, he was good with narrative and polite and he tipped in secret so Madame Pauline couldn't take a cut.

I gave him a call as soon as I was discharged.

"I can still see you privately," I told him, after explaining my dismissal from Under Where. "I can come to your place."

"I was just thinking about you," he said. "Why don't you come over for a drink." He gave me his address and I was there in ten and he poured me a martini and then another, another, dirtier and dirtier, and then, instead of going home, I never did. I liked him. I still do. He's kind to me and generous with his time and he treats me like I'm smart. He told me I could recover at his place for as long as I needed, and he told me he'd look after me, emotionally, financially, but I told him I wanted to work. He understood. The deal was that he wouldn't let me go back to working underground. Too dangerous, he said. So, he introduced me to Daddy and the Bunnies and the Hop, which he frequented, and you know what, they say money can't buy happiness, darling, but here's what it can buy: a roof over your head, a surgery, your life.

We got married two months later, Alexander and I, in a beautiful beachfront wedding.

We're still married. I love him. Do you have any idea how hard it is to find someone who respects us enough to marry us? I'm the luckiest girl in the world.

Lady Lane
(NÉE KATE BURNS)

Daddy and I met at the threshold and talked. We did it every night, sat across the doorframe from each other. We touched. Held hands, caressed cheeks, he ran his fingers through my hair and I rested my hand on his knee and he rubbed my feet with strong thumbs and I brushed my thumb over his lips and he kissed my knuckles one by one, but that was all we ever did. Nothing more. He refused to cross the line.

He told me about his mother and I told him about mine. I hadn't really talked about Ma's death since it happened, and I felt comfortable doing it with Daddy. He got it. He got me.

I told him how Ma wanted me to be famous.

"But you do want that, don't you?" he said.

I shrugged.

"Of course you do," he said. Smiled. "Every girl wants to be famous."

I told him how, on the months Ma and I couldn't afford the power bill, we lit the fire and had campouts.

. . .

It's fine, Ma would say, when the lights shut off. *We're fine*, she'd say as we emptied the fridge in order of perishability. *Everything's fine, bunny,* she'd say, as the house slowly descended into cold. *We're just fine, bunny,* she'd say, as we built a fire from the neighbor's stacked wood.

Girl Scouts, Ma called us, and she fastened a safety pin to the lapel of my pajamas. *You earned the Good Bunny Badge,* she said. We sat too close to the flames to keep from shivering, to keep one another from remembering why we were camping out. The pin would warm, then it would start to burn. I didn't take it off. I loved my Good Bunny Badge. We slept in front of the fireplace, head to toe, toe to head. In the morning, when we woke, the fire would be out, or the last pathetic ember might be stuttering its goodbye, and I'd change into my clothes for the day, and I'd run the pad of my thumb over the thin red line left on my breast by the pin.

• • •

I told Daddy about how, when the people from the church down the street came to our door, they said, *Have you been introduced to our Lord and Savior, Jesus Christ?*

Ma said, *Yeah, we met at the office Christmas party. Cheeky bastard touched my arse.*

• • •

I told him about how Ma was good at knowing the lines to every movie and bad at knowing the lyrics to any song. She sang along to the Beatles: *Yeah, you got that something / I think you'll understand / When I say that something / I want to hold your ham.*

It's hand, I told her.

I hear ham, she said.

Why would someone say "I want to hold your ham"?

Because it's his turn.

To hold the ham?
To hold the ham.

. . .

We laughed, Daddy and I. And it felt good for someone else to know Ma, her stories, our stories. It felt, some nights, like bringing her back to life for a minute. Daddy, me, the memory of Ma, we almost felt like a family.

Vincent "Daddy" Russo

I hired her as a Willa Jordan replacement, but she became more than that. She was more interesting than Willa. Deeper. Willa had the makings of a star, but Lady had the makings of an icon. We would talk most nights, and talking, with Lady, it was easy as water, flowing and cool. She had that quality. Celebrity in her DNA. The more I learned about her the more I thought she could really *be* someone. If you're asking me whether I ever had a romantic relationship with Lady Lane, the answer's no. She was a promising project, a prodigy, even, but she was still a prostitute.

Lady Lane

(NÉE KATE BURNS)

Something I haven't really talked about is the food. The Hop had three restaurants. One was the Bunny Bar, where you drank a beer or an ice-packed cocktail and ate French fries dunked in ranch or chicken tenders crunchy with panko. One was the coffee shop, Bunny Brew, where there was every kind of sandwich you could imagine—Reubens, meatball subs, a grilled cheese with caramelized onions and pine nut pesto. One was the Bunny Bistro, where the menu was full of movie foods—oysters, caviar, pâté, filet mignon, shaved truffles, Parmesan. I'd never eaten foods with such flavor. Growing up, we ate ramen or rice or rye cereal, and no matter what Ma and I were calling dinner that night, it always tasted like loose change to me.

Daddy would turn up at my door with two silver trays covered in domes, and he'd whisk off the lids like my very own magic show, and I think he liked to see how excited I was by a poached duck egg or a scallop ceviche. It was the first time I'd been able to taste, really taste, without the sour note of a budget lodged in my throat.

Mia

(NÉE YA CHAI CHEN)

I went to Lady's room one night, to hang out, watch a movie, chat, and saw her sitting in her doorway facing Daddy, who was sitting on her doormat. They were sharing a whole branzino and holding hands and looking at each other with such, I don't know, such something. Something tangible and electric. Daddy didn't fuck his Bunnies more than once because he thought it'd be crossing a line to do so. But seeing him sitting there with Lady like that? Worse lines had already been crossed. I watched them for a long time. Was I jealous? If I was, I wasn't sure of which one.

I didn't tell the other Bunnies what I'd seen. Lady needed all the help making friends she could get.

Lady Lane

(NÉE KATE BURNS)

My fourth week, and we were all sitting in the parlor, waiting for a lineup. Rain was showing us a prototype for her new dildo line. It was hideous, veiny and pink, and it flashed Technicolor in time with its vibration pattern. She was going to make millions from it, she thought, but Ginger was saying that the real money wasn't in dildos anymore, no, because girls were finally learning that toys didn't have to look like dicks to get them off, and the real money was in vibrators designed for function, not phallus.

The two were debating when Dakota came in crying. She was wearing sweatpants and a Miller Lite hoodie. It was the first time I'd seen a Bunny out of costume. Even Mia seemed to wear hers through the night.

"Have you seen her?" Dakota said, wiping her nose with her sleeve.

"Who?"

"The new girl," said Dakota. "She's me."

"She's you?" I said.

"Oh god," said Mia.

"Do you have any appointments scheduled?" said Rain.

"One," said Dakota. "Tomorrow. And Daddy asked me to meet with him afterward. I'm fucked."

"Why are you fucked?" I said.

"Daddy brought in a replacement," said Mia.

"She's basically white," said Dakota. Dakota was Native American. She sometimes wore a feather in her hair, and her costume made her look like Pocahontas, but she didn't seem to mind feeling like a token. It was what kept her safe at the Hop, or it's what *had* kept her safe until now.

Dakota
(NÉE JACY ADAMS)

Most of the Hop's guests were white men, and if they were looking to hire a Native American escort, what they really wanted was someone who looked the way they thought a Native escort should look, which meant Pocahontas. And Daddy had found a new Pocahontas, which meant I was out.

I told the Bunnies, "My sales aren't even that bad. I bet he's punishing me for getting the flu last month."

Lady was like, "Daddy wouldn't do that."

Lady Lane
(NÉE KATE BURNS)

The other girls turned to look at me. "What?" I said. "Daddy wouldn't do that, would he?" I believed in him.

Mia ran her fingers through Dakota's hair, which was long and dark and braided in some places. Betty took her hand. Everyone was quiet. Sad. Mourning a loss that hadn't happened yet. It seemed ridiculous to me. I said, "Well, what if this new girl can't replace you?"

"What?"

"She's your replacement because she looks the way you look right now, right? But what if you didn't look like that anymore?"

Dakota sniffed and ignored me and everyone took to whispering their condolences and it was clear that, in their sisterhood, I was a distant cousin, a newcomer, an unwelcome guest at the family table, but Mia had told me to make an effort and I wanted to. I wanted to be their friend. Their sister. I'd never had a sister.

"Let's cut your hair," I said. "Let's cut it all off. No one here has short hair."

"Daddy doesn't hire Bunnies with short hair, Lady," Mia said softly. "Men don't like short hair."

"But Dakota's already hired," I said. "And who says this is for men?"

Betty shrugged. "It's not a bad idea, darling."

"We get like one woman guest a day here if we're lucky," said Dakota.

"A guest a day isn't bad," said Mia. "Plus, you've got your regulars."

Dakota looked at Mia, then at me. She mimed cutting her hair between her fingers. She'd been chewing her lip, and the blood swelled on her skin like a bud coming to bloom.

Rain

(NÉE ASHLEY SMITH)

So, Lady cut Dakota's hair. I wasn't excited about it, I'll say that much. Dakota and I, well, we had *something*. I don't want to call it a relationship, because we'd never called it that. But I did sleep in her bed each night and she did bring me orange juice each morning, pulp strained out through a pair of her pantyhose. It might not've been your usual relationship, but if someone removing the bits from your juice isn't love, what is?

Dakota

(NÉE JACY ADAMS)

Rain and I were hired at the Hop around the same time. We both had dominatrix pasts, and that's a job that tends to toughen the skin. Emotional calluses, you know? We were hardened. Our first conversation went something like, "What are you looking at?"

"Huh? Nothing. What are you looking at?"

"I'm not looking at you, if that's what you think."

"Well, I'm definitely not looking at you."

It was insufferable. We went around and around like that. A cat-and-mouse routine. The truth was, we were both looking at each other.

Lady Lane

(NÉE KATE BURNS)

The other Bunnies sat around us, Dakota and me. They sat in a circle like we were gladiators in the ring or about to fight in a pool of Jell-O. I hummed as I trimmed, and the girls joined in. We did "Rich Girl"—the Hall & Oates version. Then Dakota told us about one of her clients, a cowboy, who liked to play Colonization in the bedroom. He liked to tie Dakota's hands behind her back and stick a rag in her mouth and he called her "Navajo" and he liked it when she chanted, but she didn't know any traditional Indigenous chants because she was adopted and she grew up in Vermont and so she just rapped Eminem's "Lose Yourself" in an accent. Rain gave us a demonstration. *Palms are sweaty, knees weak, arms are heavy, there's vomit on his sweater already, mom's spaghetti.* It was so funny, it was so sad and funny and sad. We laughed until we cried.

When I was done, Dakota's hair stuck out and up, but she pulled it off, she looked younger, lighter, like something magic.

"Thank you," she said. The Bunnies applauded. I shrugged. Rain handed me her terrifying dildo. It was her latest prototype, and she had fixed the short-circuiting issue, she assured me, pressing the thing into my palm.

"I want you to have it," she said. "Try it out." I'd be the first woman to try the Monster, she told me like it was an honor. I pinched it by the shaft.

"This haircut could save my life," Dakota said.

Ginger tweaked my cheek and said, "Attagirl, honey."

Mia winked at me.

Rain hugged me hard, and they were being dramatic, sure, but it felt good to have helped.

Rain

(NÉE ASHLEY SMITH)

She looked beautiful, but I'm not sure that Dakota could've ever not looked beautiful. More importantly, she was safe. Lady hoarded guests, and she didn't seem to give much of a fuck about us Bunnies up until that day, and, you know, she might've just thought she was giving a haircut, but really she was saving a life. She saved Dakota with that haircut. And that made her okay with me.

Lady Lane

(NÉE KATE BURNS)

One guest, a man, he had a stutter and he kept apologizing, kept apologizing, apologizing.

"It's okay," I told him. "It's fine."

"It's worse when I'm nervous." He was sweating diamonds on his shirt. I reached for its hem and took it over his head. I got a washcloth from the bathroom and ran it under the faucet and pressed the towel to his skin.

"Feels good," he said.

"Can I ask you something? How long have you had it? Or were you born that way?"

He closed his eyes, took a long, slow breath. He said, " 'You do not do, you do not do any more, black shoe in which I have lived like a foot for thirty years, poor and white, barely daring to breathe . . .' " He did the whole thing without a single stammer.

"Plath," he said. "Poems bring me back. Plath. Plath specifically. My father used to read poetry to me before bed."

"Doesn't she write about, like, death?"

"Dad was a weird guy. This"—he gestured to his mouth, as if the stutter was somewhere in there, like it was his tongue short-circuiting—"It started when he died."

"How'd he die?"

But he couldn't make it through the next sentence. He pulled a book out of his bag—Plath—and I rested my head on his shoulder and we took turns reading to each other. He stayed two hours.

Betty

(NÉE JOSHUA BETTS)

Lady was like booze in that way. You hate her, you get used to her, and then, one day, you accidentally like her. A couple nights after Dakota's haircut, I knocked on Lady's door and gave her a glass of champagne.

She invited me in and thanked me. "What's it for?" she said.

"Congratulations, darling," I told her. "On becoming my friend." We toasted. As I was leaving, Daddy turned up.

Lady Lane
(NÉE KATE BURNS)

Betty left and Daddy arrived and he said, "Cute little trim you gave Dakota the other day." He leaned on my doorframe. He was drinking bourbon or something equally as brown from a tumbler. Rabbit was at his side, sitting obediently. I scratched her ears and she licked my wrist.

"Looks good on her. I don't usually hire short-haired girls. Men don't love it."

"That's a pretty big generalization."

"Her sales have picked up. You did good."

"Thanks," I said. "I used to cut my ma's—" I paused. Daddy waited. And then I said, "Wait, how did you know I was the one who cut Dakota's hair?"

Daddy only winked.

I said, "Do you want to come in?"

And he almost did, that night. I saw it in his eyes.

Vincent "Daddy" Russo

I almost did that night. I almost went in. But I had rules for a reason, and I'd broken them once before and that ended badly and I made a pact with myself. No more breaking rules. No exceptions. Lady was a Bunny and I was her boss and that's all we could be to each other while she was at the Hop. But I had big plans for that girl. I'd made stars before, and I could do it again. It was all just a matter of timing.

Mia

(NÉE YA CHAI CHEN)

I was Daddy's favorite until Willa Jordan arrived. I was making the big bucks and upselling like crazy, sometimes I barely made it back to the Hop for a night before being picked up for another girlfriend experience. I was having a blast. I had one regular VIP who liked to take me out on his yacht for weeks at a time with him and his wife. We sailed around Hawaii, stopping at little islands, exploring the beaches. They taught me to dive and we dove for shellfish and crabs and grilled them on the boat's deck and ate them with white wine under the stars. Paid vacations, you know? Can you believe some people feel sorry for us?

Those days, when I did make it back to the Hop, Daddy came to my room with a kiss for my cheek and a gift for my neck. Gold, silver, diamonds, he knew how to purchase jewelry, Daddy did, and back in those days, in the pre-Willa days, I was wearing a new pendant every morning.

Then Willa arrived and things changed. Daddy stopped coming to my room, started going to hers, and he stopped looking at me, I mean *really* looking, and he started looking at her, I mean *really* looking. And I might've loved Daddy, or something like that, until Daddy fell in love with Willa. I got jealous. Of course I did! I'm human, you know. I didn't like Willa. I didn't like her accent; I didn't like her pretty blond hair or her blue eyes or how she moved like a movie star. I was grateful when Daddy made her famous. I was happy when Willa left the Hop. It's immature, I know; I'm better than that, now.

And Lady wasn't Willa, either. She looked like her, sure, but she was nothing like her. And she kept asking me *Who's Willa, who's Willa, who is Willa.* But I couldn't say because Daddy made us sign an NDA. I hated keeping it from her. I wanted her to know all of me.

. . .

One day, maybe her fourth or fifth week at the Hop, a guest picked Lady and me, both of us, out of a lineup. He wanted a threesome, and he was willing to pay big.

"Are you okay with this?" I asked her, and she shrugged like it was nothing. That hurt. It wasn't nothing for me.

Lady Lane

(NÉE KATE BURNS)

I had my sights set on Daddy. I wasn't thinking about Mia like that. I could see that she was beautiful and I could see that she was kind and sweet and she cared about me, I knew all of that. But I'd never thought of her in that way. She was my friend. My best friend at the whole place. In the whole country. Even if I were thinking of her in that way, I wouldn't have jeopardized our friendship for anything.

So, yeah, when the guest picked us out of a lineup, I nodded. "Sure," I said. "No problem," I said. And Mia, maybe for just a glimpse, looked a little hurt.

"Are *you* okay with it?" I asked her, and she nodded, performance back on, mask in place.

Mia

(NÉE YA CHAI CHEN)

The guy asked Lady and me to kiss. We did. Her breath was spiked with spearmint. Then he asked me to bite her lip. I did. She moaned, and the sound seemed real. Then he asked her to take my shirt off. She did, slowly, gently. He told her to touch my chest and I yelped at the cold and she laughed and breathed into her palms to warm them and this guy was touching himself in the corner the whole time, but I barely noticed him after a while. The whole time, the whole hour, Lady and I were both looking up, up at the ceiling, the mirror, with every new move, every new piece of clothing shed, every kiss, we looked up, up, up.

Lady Lane

(NÉE KATE BURNS)

It was, I don't know. It was a lot. I felt a lot. I felt so many things all at once, an emotional stew, and I kept looking up at the mirror and reminding myself of Mia's advice: pretend you're her, that girl up there, to give yourself some distance. But every time I looked up, I saw Mia and I saw me and I saw us and, here's the real kicker, we looked so good together.

It didn't take long before I forgot there was a guest in the room at all. Mia kissed her way down my body and I could barely breathe and then she settled between my legs and started with her mouth and, I mean, holy shit. Holy *shit*. I wrapped myself around her and pulled her close. I have no idea how long we spent in that room.

Mia

(NÉE YA CHAI CHEN)

I guess the guest left at some point. When Lady and I finished, we looked around and he was gone. "He's gone?" I said, and we just laughed. Then she turned on the TV and we watched an episode of the bad werewolf show we'd been keeping up with.

"Do you think he'll turn into a wolf at an inopportune time on today's episode?" I asked her.

"No way," she said. "Not a chance."

"On a hike," I said.

"On a college campus," she said.

It was being in bed with your best friend.

Lady Lane
(NÉE KATE BURNS)

It was my fifth week at the Hop when, one morning, Daddy turned up at my door before I woke. His knock was in my dream as one of Ma's manfriends turned violent, beating my bedroom door down with his fist. But it wasn't a manfriend and Ma was dead and here I was, at the most famous brothel in America, a hooker, Lady.

I woke up nauseated. I remember that. The overwhelming wave that surges, the dry mouth, tickle in the back of the throat. I thought it was because of the dream, memories resurfacing in the form of sickness. I chugged a glass of water and opened the door. Rabbit ran past me and jumped on the foot of my bed, curled up, and fell asleep.

Daddy looked me up and down, the way he did, and he said, "Morning, sleepyhead." He gave me a cup of coffee, black, and said, "Didn't know how you took it. Cream, sugar, I played it safe."

"Just like this is fine," I said. But what I was thinking was that he looked handsome, so handsome with his hair ruffled with sleep, and that he, this handsome man, was bringing me coffee. Coffee in the morning, like a real couple, like two people in love. I said, "Come in?"

"No, no, I'm just doing the rounds," he said. "But I wanted to offer you an opportunity."

"An opportunity?"

"I can't remember a new Bunny landing as many guests in her first month as you did. Not in a long time."

"Since Willa," I said. "Mia said I broke Willa's record."

Daddy smiled a tight smile and said, "You did such a good job with Dave. Man's been coming here for years and hasn't ever rebooked with the same girl. He likes to play the field, the dog."

"Thanks," I said. "I liked him."

Daddy laughed. "Sure you did," he said. "I've got a VIP coming in later this week and he wants to skip the lineup for privacy's sake, just wants a one-on-one, and he asked me to pick the girl."

"And you're picking me?"

"I believe in rewarding good behavior."

Good behavior. Like I was a kid getting stickers for doing my chores.

He said, "You rebooked on your first sale. Not every girl can do that. You keep this up and you'll be one of the top Bunnies in no time. Maybe you'll even be Bunny of the Year. Keep it up, Lady, and I'll see what I can do for you."

"Do they pay more?" I said. "VIPs?"

"They pay whatever you tell them to pay, Lady. You're your own boss."

"Except you're my boss."

"Exactly," he said. "Now, I'll need you to sign a nondisclosure, okay? To keep you safe."

"To keep me safe or to keep me a secret?"

"They're one and the same, aren't they?"

I shrugged and Daddy headed for the door. "You're doing good, Lady," he said.

"I like it here," I told him, and it was the truth. I did.

He ran a hand down my doorframe. I thought about kissing him.

"Maybe you should think about decorating some," he said. "It looks like you just moved in."

"I did just move in."

"Why don't you head to the store for some cushions? You could order them online? Amazon brings packages right to your door, you know? Delivers in two days."

"Do you work for them?"

He laughed. "You're funny, Lady. Why don't you get some cush-ions? Make your guests feel more at home."

"Daddy," I said. "Who's Willa?"

Daddy frowned.

"People keep saying I'm your new Willa. Who is she? Who *was* she?"

"You've got to stop worrying about so many things, Lady," is what Daddy said. "You're going to stress that pretty head of yours." He kissed me on the forehead gently, and I felt smaller than myself. The lights went out—a reset, but Daddy held me close. "Let me take care of you, okay?" To be taken care of. Has anyone ever wanted anything but that?

I'm not sure that I was in love, but I was something. Enamored, maybe.

"I'll take care of you, okay?" Daddy said. "Come on, Rabbit." He whistled and the dog jumped off my bed and followed him away, to-ward his office.

When he left, the nausea returned. I ran to the bathroom and threw up once, twice.

A woman throwing up in a movie always meant pregnancy, but I'd been taking my birth control like clockwork, every morning, 8:00 a.m., I had an alarm and everything. A virus. I decided it was a virus. I checked my stomach in the mirror and it was flat as a board. A virus. I ran a search for Willa and the Hop, but the only results that came back were Willa Jordan interviews and film trailers. Willa Jordan was a famous movie star. She was not a hooker and she was not, I was certain, the Willa everyone kept comparing me to.

It sounds stupid now, I know that. But if someone tells you that you look like Cindy, you don't assume Crawford.

Mia

(NÉE YA CHAI CHEN)

No one knew about Willa Jordan's time at the Hop. Daddy made sure of that. The day she left, so did all evidence of her being a Bunny. I was always kind of waiting for the news to break, for people to find out, the tabloids, a scandal, but it never happened. Daddy was good at cleaning up a crime scene. He was a magician like that: could make almost anything disappear like, poof! Could I have broken Willa's Bunny news myself? Sure, for thousands of dollars probably, but that's what I'm saying. I would never betray a Bunny, not even Willa Jordan. We're sisters here, at the Hop. We have to be. There are people out there who want us dead, and there's safety in numbers, you know.

Rain

(NÉE ASHLEY SMITH)

The day everything changed, Dakota and I were in bed, scrolling through our phones. We were at that comfortable stage in our relationship, or not-relationship, or whatever it was. I loved being around her, beside her, even just to do things I could've done alone. Checking Instagram, doing my makeup, waxing my legs. I wanted her to be there for all of it. That might be what love is. We were in bed and Dakota said, "Fuck." And when I asked what was wrong, she just turned her screen. They'd found another ten bodies. All sex workers. All from around the Las Vegas area. The first time, the bodies had been found scattered in dumpsters, but this new lot was found out in the open. Dismantled limbs in the streets. This guy wasn't even trying to hide.

"Any names?" I said. There weren't. There wouldn't be. The world doesn't think of us as people; the world sees hookers as bodies even before they're dead.

Dakota was shaking. Pale. She'd never worked the streets before. I held her and said, "We're safe here, baby." I kissed her hand.

"I have the lowest sales," she said. "I can barely cover room and board. I've had the lowest sales for weeks."

I shook my head. "Ginger."

Dakota laughed, but it was not a happy laugh. There was no joy there. "You know he's not getting rid of Ginger."

I called in sick that day. Told Daddy I had a cold and told him Dakota would pick up my appointments.

Betty

(NÉE JOSHUA BETTS)

That morning, you know the one I'm talking about, darling, the one that started the avalanche. That morning the cops had found ten of us, dead and disassembled and strewn on the streets. They never found the girls' names, so all they ever were, officially, legally, was just a mess of unidentified arms and legs. The Bunnies gathered in the parlor and when the bell rang, none of us lined up. How could we? Most of us had worked illegally before, you know. It could've been us.

Rain said, "What do we do?" She'd phoned in sick that day and she did look sick, or sad, or something. She looked like she'd been crying, and she was holding Dakota's hand. I poured myself a drink. This life's too difficult to get through it sober, darling, don't you think?

"But we're safe here," said Lady. "Right?"

No one answered. It was just like her to think of her own safety.

"Ten," said Dakota. She counted Bunnies in the parlor. Ten.

Daddy arrived and said, "Why's no one lined up?"

Lady Lane
(NÉE KATE BURNS)

Daddy told us not to worry. He kept saying, "You're safe here." He hugged every Bunny, and I was the only Bunny who hugged him back.

"Surely there's something we can do, Daddy," Mia said. "Can't you hire more girls?"

Daddy said something about diminishing returns, and I looked at him, like, seriously? Diminishing returns? People were dying.

"Can we donate money, or something?" Dakota said. "To their families?"

Daddy frowned at her. "I mean," he said, "you can do whatever you want with your money, but I didn't think you'd have enough to spare."

Everyone knew Dakota's sales were low, higher than only Ginger's, but the way Daddy said it—Dakota was crushed. I'd never known him to be cruel. I looked at him, really looked at him, and he looked like a stranger to me. Like a stranger I didn't want to know.

"But, Daddy," I said, didn't know what else to say.

The screens, all around us, they kept playing commercials, products and products and products. Girls were dying out there, and we were being sold shampoo.

"Lady," said Daddy. "Your VIP is on his way."

The Bunnies glared. I didn't want to do it. It was the first time I hadn't wanted to see a guest, but I really, really didn't. I wanted to help my friends mourn. I wanted to be with my family.

Mia

(NÉE YA CHAI CHEN)

Lady looked at Daddy like, *Who are you?* And I was glad she got to see the real him before it was too late. When you meet Daddy, you're meeting the guy he wants you to think he is. You're meeting the Hop's owner. The salesman. The marketing, publicity, advertising. You're meeting a PR stunt personified and he's easy to love, that version of Daddy. He's easy to love because he tells you that you're perfect, a star, a bestseller, and then he puts you up for sale because what you really are to him, all you are to him, is another product on his shelf. Lady might've thought she loved him, but what she really loved was how he made her feel. Those are two completely different things, and one removes all agency from the self.

Dakota

(NÉE JACY ADAMS)

When Daddy said we were safe there, he meant we were *only safe* while we were *there*.

Rain
(NÉE ASHLEY SMITH)

Lady's VIP turned up, and she had three other appointments booked for the day too. Mia had a regular coming in later. I'd given both of my guests to Dakota. No one else had anything on the books. We looked at Lady like, *This is your chance to do something.* And that day, for the first time, she did.

She said, "Dakota, are you busy?" Dakota shook her head, and Lady said, "Dakota can have him. Dakota can have my VIP."

I could've made out with Lady right then, but instead I put an arm around her shoulder. Mia took her hand.

Dakota said, "Are you sure, Lady?"

Betty kissed Lady's cheek.

"I'm sure," Lady said. "He's all yours, Dakota."

Ginger patted Lady's shoulder. Ginger was our mother, all of us. She was a rock. Her sales had been at the bottom for a couple years, but Daddy never gave her the boot. Daddy wasn't loyal, but it seemed like he felt some kind of loyalty to Ginger—maybe he felt like she was *his* mother, too.

It was Ginger who taught us family. She taught us that you don't become a Bunny the day Daddy hires you, and you don't become a Bunny the day you host your first guest. You become a Bunny the day you become our sister, and just like that, Lady became one of us.

Vincent "Daddy" Russo

The Hop was a business. You can demonize me, villainize me, you can call me a sellout, whatever, but the Hop was a business and profit was the bottom line and, yeah, I had to get rid of girls who weren't earning. Say what you want, but I built that place with my bare hands, and I saved more lives than I ruined.

What I mean is that I didn't feel bad for saying no. When Lady tried to give her VIP to Dakota, I said no. I did. VIPs come in expecting top-shelf treatment, and Dakota wasn't top shelf, she was a niche market product for guys with a Sacagawea fetish. That's not an insult, it's just a fact.

Lady Lane
(NÉE KATE BURNS)

I told Daddy I didn't want to do it. The VIP. "I don't want to," I said. "I can't."

He hardened. He used his eyedrops. He looked back at me. He said nothing, just stared, silent. The room seemed to grow, and I felt tiny and childish and afraid under his gaze. He didn't say that I didn't have a choice. He didn't have to.

Dakota said, "Keep your VIP, Lady. It's fine."

I looked at Mia.

"Go, Lady," she said. "Do it."

So I went. I went back to my room, threw up in the toilet, because the nausea was constant by then; I touched up my lipstick and answered the door when the VIP knocked.

Liam Carson

(ACTOR, *WE'RE WOLVES*, ETC.)

I do not have anything to say about my time at the Hop. You can direct any further questions to my publicity team.

Lady Lane

(NÉE KATE BURNS)

I recognized him immediately. He was an actor; you know him. I knew him, but he looked different in person, without the wolfy sideburns they made him wear for the show, without the ears sprouting from his scalp. He had been in other stuff, too. Movies. Pulpy and poorly written, but easy to watch. Like reality television for men. Throw enough punches, fast cars, and D-cups in the script, and you've got a big-screen win on your hands. That's what Ma was always saying about those Vin Diesel movies. *I could write the next big action flick myself,* Ma said, when we left the latest *Fast & Furious* movie with armfuls of everyone's leftover popcorn cartons. People never toss their trash at the movies. Put any human being in a room dark enough, and they'll forgo all basic etiquette. We turn animal in the dark, all of us.

Get me a Vin Diesel and some skinny blond with fake tits. Put them in a truck. Let's say she's hitchhiking because her boyfriend got punchy and he pulls over to pick her up. She's real mean to him, to Vin, in the beginning. Thinks he might be a creep. But it turns out he's looking for something.

What? I said, more invested in her movie than I'd ever been in *Tokyo Drift. What's he looking for, Ma?*

His little brother's gone missing. He's looking for his little brother, a naughty little shit who's into doing drugs. No, wait, into dealing drugs. He deals. Vin Diesel thinks the little brother's gotten himself into some shit,

and now he's going looking for him. Skinny blond tits agrees to help find
him in exchange for a ride to wherever he's going.

And then what?

You got a million bucks?

What?

I'm not giving the story away for free, bunny. You call yourself Par-
amount and pay me a million bucks upfront, and I'll tell the rest of the
story.

I never heard what happened to Vin Diesel and Skinny Blond Tits,
but I liked to invent my own endings to the story depending on my
mood. If I was happy, daydreaming before drifting off to sleep, Vin
and Tits found the little brother and got married. If I was sad, because
I couldn't go on a field trip or because it was college application season,
Vin and Tits found the little brother's corpse and Vin Diesel died from a
broken heart. If I was mad, at Ma or at Lacey or at some client who got
handsy in the janitor's closet, Vin and Tits got in a fight and he pushed
her out of the passenger seat and watched her body roll along the highway in his rearview mirror.

. . .

He was getting older, the VIP, I'll call him X for the sake of the NDA.
He looked much older than he looked in the werewolf show Mia and I
liked to watch.

"Hi," I said, when I opened the door.

X looked around, nervous as a rabbit, and ducked into the room
without being invited.

"I'm Lady," I said.

"Sure. Can you take a look out there? Make sure no one saw me?"

"Oh, yeah," I said. "There're a hundred photographers out here."

The fear in his eyes.

"I'm fucking with you," I said.

"I'm X," he said.

"I know."

"You're familiar with my work."

I said nothing.

"Well, shall we get started?" he said, shrugging off a jacket that must've been more for disguise than warmth. It was still blazing hot out there. "Your boss told me you're the best of the best."

"He did?"

"Sure." He nodded. Then frowned. "Damn," he said. "You look like my girlfriend."

"I get that a lot. People telling me I look like someone. I think I must just have one those faces."

"No. No. It's not like that. You look just like her. The outfit and everything. It's actually kind of freaky."

"Freaky?"

"Freaky," he said, leaning in to squint at me. "You could be sisters."

"Who is she?"

"Willa. Willa Jordan."

Willa Jordan. She was the first female Bond. She won an Oscar for playing a young Audrey Hepburn in the movie of her life. Ma and I watched her soap *California Girls* every night at 5:00 p.m., our very own happy hour, and Ma had told me once that I looked a little like her but was twice the actress she was. *She has better teeth, though*, is what Ma said.

I thought of Daddy and Mia and the way the Bunnies kept saying, *She looks just like Willa*, and *Daddy's new Willa*, and *Willa's replacement*. Willa wasn't a common name, is what I was thinking.

"Did she used to work here?" I said. I was sure I was wrong, but I had to ask. "Was Willa Jordan ever a Bunny?"

X frowned. "No one's meant to know about that."

Willa Jordan, Oscar-winning Willa Jordan. Willa Jordan from the movies. A Bunny. A hooker. "Willa Jordan was a Bunny?" I said. "*Willa Jordan was a Bunny?*"

"Yeah." He nodded. Grimaced. "It's a secret, okay? Can you just, I mean, can you keep a secret? She'll kill me."

"Why would she keep it a secret?"

"Because," he said. "She's, like, a serious movie star."

"Hookers can't be serious movie stars?"

X snorted.

"Is that what you think?" I said. I felt myself getting angry. Over-reacting. I knew I needed to calm down, take a breath, perform, but my mind was on the murders, the lives, the Bunnies, my sisters. "How can you be dating Willa Jordan, a hooker turned movie star, and still believe that hookers can't be movie stars?"

X shifted, uncomfortable. "You did sign an NDA, right? You can't tell anyone about Willa, and you can't tell anyone I was here. No one can know I was here. I would die."

But he wouldn't die. Women were dying out there every day, but this man would not die. I looked at him and I tried to breathe. *Empty yourself,* Ma would say. *Become the character,* she would say. But I couldn't. I couldn't feel like Lady Lane or like Daddy's new Willa or like this man's wildest fantasy, because all I felt was a low rumble of fury. At him and at Willa Jordan and at the world. People were dying. Girls were dying. Sex workers were dying, and all this guy cared about was no one finding out that he'd visited one. My gut was hot. My throat ached. "Why do you keep it a secret?" I said. "Your visits here. Why do you hide them?"

"I mean, it's obvious, isn't it?"

"Because you're in a relationship?"

"No. That's not it, I mean, Willa and I, we're not monogamous, you know."

"So why would you care?"

"I'm not a pays-for-sex kind of guy. No offense or anything. My fans wouldn't like it."

"It's legal, you know. Here, in Nevada."

"Legal, sure," he said. "Sure it's legal, but it's not exactly . . . you know."

"I'm not sure that I do know." *Breathe,* Ma would say.

"I mean, there are connotations."

"Connotations?" *Empty yourself,* Ma would say.

"Implications."

"Implications?" *Become your character,* Ma would say. But in that moment, I was all self. And all I was, was angry.

"You know what I mean. You're playing dumb." He scratched his stubble. "You know? I'm X. I don't pay for sex."

"Except you do, and you are."

"Right."

I'm not sure that I can explain what happened next. Something happened in me. Something switched. *Vol-Kate-no,* is the way Ma would've explained it, the way everything came up at once. The women dying at the hands of an angry man, their bodies so dismantled their identities were never discovered. Their identities, so difficult to discover because the women were working illegally. The laws that made these women illegal, these women wanting to work to survive. The only thing they had to sell was sex and for that they became criminals, punishable, imprisonable. Gary, who thought strippers could not be mothers. Sunny, who kicked Lacey so hard her baby died inside her. Oliver van Ness, who wouldn't date me in public because to him I was more genital than girlfriend. These men who thought of us as bodies long before we were dead, and because of this, and because the law thought hookers weren't worth protecting, because of all of this, maybe it didn't even feel like murder when that serial killer took apart each new girl; she was already nothing but body to him.

And then the VIP said, "No offense." *No offense.* He said, "It's nothing personal."

Well, of course it was personal.

That's when I started talking. Angry and loud. I said, "You know, maybe, *maybe,* if people thought that guys like you did things like this, then there wouldn't be so much stigma around it." I said, "Maybe then, it wouldn't be such a big deal. Maybe then it would be more socially acceptable, and if it were more socially acceptable, then maybe it would be made legal in this country, and then maybe it would be made legal in the world, and then maybe there wouldn't be so many girls working the streets and getting attacked and raped and murdered. And maybe, you know, maybe you're a little responsible for that," I said. "Maybe you killed those girls whose bodies were found in a dumpster. No offense."

You know what he did? That son of a bitch. He laughed. He raised his hands like, *Whoa, down girl,* and he said, "I didn't really come here for a lecture, babe." Then he said, "Your boss said you were a professional. Unless this is part of your little bit, in which case I might be into it. I mean, is it? Is this your thing?"

But I wasn't done. I was far from done. I was, I don't even know the word, I felt animal, monster. I said, "Those women are dead because of men like you. Men who have the power to change things, to save lives, men who could do something about it and don't. Men who protect themselves instead. Men who make girls like us sign nondisclosure agreements because, why? Because you're embarrassed? Of us? I'm embarrassed of you."

And that's when X unzipped his fly and took his dick out of his jeans.

I barely saw it. Everything was hazy, blurred. "It's fucked up," I said, kept saying, couldn't stop saying. "You're fucked up. It's so fucked up. People are dying. Girls are dying. You're killing people, and you don't even care."

Which is when X's breathing got heavy. He reached for my chest. I slapped his hands away. Then I slapped his face, once, twice, I think. "Your *girlfriend* is one of us," I said. I was pummeling him by then. My fists on his chest. "You *love* one of us, and you still want us dead? You'd still rather protect your little ego? Your image is more important to you than a life?"

X held my fists, hard, and said, "Get on your knees." I didn't.

His semen hit my stomach. He groaned and grunted, bovine and primeval. He came in this never-ending gush and closed his eyes and smiled. I went to the bathroom and fell to the floor and hurled into the sink. This neon-pink vomit. I looked up, at myself, my reflection, and wiped my mouth. Everything was falling apart. I was.

He knocked on the door and said, "How much do I owe you?"

He thought we'd had an appointment. He'd *enjoyed* himself.

I told him to get out. I think I said, "Get the fuck out."

He said, "Can I make another appointment?"

Can you believe that?

Rain

(NÉE ASHLEY SMITH)

There will always be assholes. Baristas will tell you, restaurant servers will tell you, retail workers will tell you, sometimes customers are assholes and that's just a truth of client-facing work. Working the streets, most everyone was an asshole. Most every guy I met tried to screw me when it came to payment, and I got hit more times than I can count. One guy trashed my room and pissed on my carpet and another beat me so bloody the grout between the bathroom tiles was stained pink forever.

Don't get me wrong; there are good guys picking up girls on the streets, too. Before Daddy hired me, I was dealing and stripping in LA, doing some house calls on the side here and there. I met a guy at my club. A nice guy. A neurosurgeon. They don't have much time to date. He asked me to come back to his place, and I tucked my switchblade into my bra and took his hand. I didn't need the knife. He was kind. He made me a martini, and we made out on his couch. It was three in the morning but when he heard my stomach growl, he put on a Frank Sinatra record and cooked spaghetti from scratch and twirled me under his arm in the kitchen. We ate on his balcony, looking out over the city, and then we sat in his hot tub and he massaged my shoulders. I fell asleep in the water and woke up in his bed. This could've so easily been the start of one of the bad stories, the worst ones, roofies, rape, but no, this guy was good; I found him asleep on the floor beside the bed, fully clothed, using my purse as a pillow. I whispered him awake and told him to join me. We didn't leave that bed for twenty-four hours after that. He ordered delivery and I called into work and he brushed my teeth with his toothbrush. It took twenty-four hours for him to learn everything about me and he seemed to like all of it. He seemed to like *me*. Then he said, "You know, I just realized, I don't know what you want from life. What do you want to be when you grow up? Are you studying?"

"Studying?"

"I mean, why are you stripping? Student loans?"

I wanted to lie. I usually did. I usually told people I was studying to be an accountant because no one ever asks follow-up questions of accountants and I had that boring, boring word ready to go, but then I looked at this guy, this kind, sweet, smokin' hot guy, like Jamie Foxx in *Law Abiding Citizen* hot, and I liked him. I liked how he asked questions with his eyebrows instead of his words, I liked how he touched me while he talked, unconsciously, accidental, and I liked how he used his hands while he explained his work, as if he were sewing the stitches right there in front of me. I liked him. I didn't want to lie to him. I said, "I'm not studying," and I said, "I like my work. This is what I want from life. I *am* grown up."

He stopped touching me then. He said, "*This* is what you want from life?" He sat for a long time. Eventually, he said, "I like you, Ashley," and then he said, "But I don't think we're . . . compatible."

I said, "Compatible."

And he said, "I'm a surgeon."

I dressed myself for the first time in two days and went to leave, and before I did, he tapped me on the shoulder, like maybe he'd had a change of heart, but instead he gave me money. A whole wad of cash. And he said, "Sorry we got our wires crossed."

I kept the $500 and used it to buy myself a new pair of shoes. Daddy called me a couple days later. He had a vacancy, a Haitian girl had just been let go, and he thought I'd make a perfect replacement.

·················

Mia

(NÉE YA CHAI CHEN)

On the outside, girls get conned out of thousands, they get attacked, assaulted, murdered. At the Hop, I was hit only twice, and one of the times I consented to it. Don't get me wrong, some of our guests were gross, but we were allowed to turn down anyone we didn't like, and we had a panic button on the side of our nightstands, and if we wanted someone blacklisted, Daddy wouldn't ever let them back in the door. He *did* keep us safe.

So Lady had her first bad guest; it was always going to happen. When I was working in the salon, we had this lady with a gangrenous foot come in once a week for a pedicure. She smelled of old meat and her foot felt like a carcass, but that's the service industry for you. Lady had her first gangrenous foot in the form of a guest, and when I arrived at her room to get the VIP gossip, she was crying. I held her and I told her it'd be okay.

"He wouldn't stop," she said. A sob caught in her throat.

"It's okay," I said.

"He wouldn't stop touching himself," she said, wiping at her face. "It's stupid," she said. "I don't know why I'm so . . . It's stupid. I'm sorry."

But it wasn't stupid. It's impossible to tell what'll stick with you. It's impossible to know what'll hurt the most but the hurt is valid regardless of cause. Feelings might not always be logical, but they are always real.

. . .

Lady was trembling, her whole body alive and shaking. I took her foot in my hands and started kneading. I'd learned, back at the salon, how to massage tension out of the toes. "Tell me the whole story," I said. "I'm here," I said.

"He came on me," she said, then she laughed a little. "That's it, that's all it was."

"Okay."

"No, Mia," said Lady. "He came *on me*. On *me*."

And this is what I'd warned her about, and what we'd all warned her about. A persona is a costume, an extra layer, and if you're playing a part, then the jizz never lands on *you*.

Betty
(NÉE JOSHUA BETTS)

Liam Carson is a son of a bitch. He'd been a Hop regular for years, and after Willa left, he became my client. Had a thing for tall white girls. I was glad that Lady took him instead. He paid well, but some guests aren't worth any amount of money.

Lady Lane

(NÉE KATE BURNS)

Mia was sitting cross-legged on my bed, rubbing my feet, pressing her thumb hard into the heart of each toe. I was exhausted from the VIP encounter, and my body felt rubbery and used. But with her there, with Mia there, things felt easier.

"One bad guest," is what she said. "It was one bad guest." She told me a story about a woman with rotten feet. "Think of all your good guests. Think of Dave!"

I lay back on my pillows.

"You like it here, don't you, Lady?" Mia said. "I mean, not today, obviously, but do you like it here? On every other day?"

"I do," I said, "on every other day."

"Do you ever want anything more?"

"Than this?" I looked around. "I've never really thought about it."

"This is going to sound stupid," said Mia.

"Tell me."

"It's my secret dream to open a place of my own. I know it's impossible with all the regulations and everything, I know it's a pipe dream, but it's a dream."

"I love that dream," I told her.

"I want my brothel to accept health insurance. For veterans or people with disabilities, people with mental health stuff, you know? Like, sex as a form of therapy."

A wave of nausea surged and swelled, and I ran to the bathroom to throw up a waterfall of Pink. I rested my forehead on the cold of the toilet seat.

Mia said, "You could've just said you didn't like the idea."

"Shut up."

Mia flushed my barf and tied my hair into a bun, wiped the corners of my mouth with a warm washcloth. "You're not knocked up, are you?" she said. She cupped her palm and filled it with water from the tap and tipped it into my mouth. The lights went out.

"People say this house is haunted, you know," Mia said into the dark. "It used to be a hysteria clinic." The lights came back on and Mia said, "People say this house is haunted by the ghosts of girls past. Ones who were treated here. Ones who had to stay here for months on end, being treated with orgasm after orgasm until their muscles tore and their clits couldn't feel anymore. Diagnosed with an illness that doesn't even exist."

I said, "Do you believe it? Do you think the Hop's haunted?"

Mia frowned. "No, I don't. Not by ghosts, at least. We're mostly safe here. It's on the outside that we're in danger. It's not the house that's haunted, it's the industry. Our whole profession's haunted."

"By what?"

"By the world." Mia rubbed my temples. "By those protestors outside. Religious nuts. Cops who throw us in jail for making a living. Customers who never pay up. Abusive pimps. The government, the law, Daddy. The world wants us dead."

I swallowed another surge of bile.

"Do you think people can be haunted?" I said.

"I think," she said. "I think that's called being possessed."

"I think I'm possessed," I told her.

"By who?"

"I sometimes feel like I have a lot of people inside me."

Mia said, "Then you're in the right line of work." She winked like she was joking, but there wasn't a smile on her face. I threw up again, nothing but bile, retched into the toilet bowl.

"Seriously," said Mia. "We should get you a pregnancy test."

I thought about the possibility of a baby. I thought about the way it sometimes felt like Ma existed inside me, a part of me. I thought about Kate, myself, and about Lady, also myself, and about which one lived inside the other. Gary had told me I wasn't fit to be a mother. Ma had said I didn't need babies. Sunny had kicked Lacey's baby dead. Ma had taken her pregnant belly to the hospital and come home with nothing at all.

"I'm not pregnant," I said.

ACT IV

THE SCANDAL

I'm nobody! Who are you?
Are you—nobody—too?
Then there's a pair of us!
Don't tell! they'd advertise—you know!

Emily Dickinson, "I'm Nobody! Who are you?"

Willa Jordan

(NÉE HANNAH SNITCH, ACTRESS, *LADY BOND*, *CALIFORNIA GIRLS*, ETC.)

We're always being told not to search ourselves. *You'll regret it*, they're always saying. *You can't be loved by everyone.* But I always have been. Had been. Loved by everyone.

It's not that I haven't had my fair share of internet trauma. You saw that picture of me in a bikini in Hawaii after I'd just eaten a burger. The headlines were all "Is Willa Jordan Expecting?" and "Willa Jordan: Curvy in Kauai" and "Willa Jordan Weight Gain," and it might sound superficial, but my body's my body and I have to live inside it and I hate the way the whole world feels as if they have the right to comment on it, the way the media feels some kind of ownership over it and tells my stories without knowing anything about me at all.

And there was the other time too, of course. The time my nudes were leaked. That was a whole different thing. It was 2011 and I was a C-lister at best, and one day I was in commercials and music videos and playing a side character on a soap opera, and the next day my naked body was everywhere, all over the internet. Suddenly, everyone wanted an interview, a photo shoot, a statement. The world saw my asshole, and it launched my career.

Lisa Hamilton

(FEATURES EDITOR, *VOGUE*)

Willa Jordan was gorgeous and charismatic and a decent actor. She was all of those things before her nudes leaked. Her character on *California Girls* was beloved even though her airtime was minimal and she had that celebrity glow written into her DNA and she walked around like she was famous long before anyone knew her name. Which is all to say that Willa Jordan might've made it even if those pictures didn't go viral back in 2011. But they did. And when they did, the whole world was alive with Willa gossip. People couldn't stop talking about her.

Willa's *California Girls* character was a high schooler, and she was too old to be playing the role, but you know how it goes in Hollywood. Here, girls play high schoolers until they're thirty, and from then on they play mothers. So there's this photo of Willa Jordan, and at that point the public knew her as a preppy schoolgirl who wore Mary Janes and pigtails in *California Girls*. People described her as a tease, jailbait. And suddenly there was this leaked photo of her on her hands and knees on this red silk backdrop. She's facing away from the camera, in the photograph, looking back over her shoulder. Her rear end is in close-up, and she's got this heart-shaped mole on her lower back that people were just infatuated with. She's beautiful, barely legal, and biting her lip. The world knows that photo, even now; it's imprinted on a whole generation of memories. It's iconic. Willa Jordan was a C-lister, but that photo made her a household name overnight.

It's complicated, though, because it was a total invasion of her privacy, a nonconsensual disaster, but it really did make her a star. What do you do when the source of your success is also your deepest trauma?

Lacey Kahu

Everyone heard about Willa Jordan's nude leak back in 2011. I remember the boys at school all pulling up the pictures on their phones and moaning at them. I remember Lady, who was Kate back then, she snatched their phones out of their hands and said, "You're part of the problem."

Lady Lane
(NÉE KATE BURNS)

September 12, 2016. That date's tattooed on my brain; it was the day that changed my life. It was the day after the VIP appointment and I was still a little shaken from it and Daddy turned up at my door. I threw up, my morning routine by that point, opened the door, and took the cup of black coffee from him. Everything was normal, I was normal, my life was still my life.

Daddy pointed at my coffee and said, "Drink that." He said, "You're going to want to be awake for this."

"For what?"

And then he said, "You're in the news."

Lacey Kahu

Next thing you know, Lady was in the news. They were calling her a Willa Jordan lookalike, and I guess I never saw the resemblance before, but could I see it in the video that was suddenly all over the internet. It was shot from up high, looking down on Lady and Liam Carson, that guy from the bad werewolf show, and he was jacking off while Lady talked and talked. She was giving this big speech about sex work and girls dying and men not respecting hookers, really good stuff, really important stuff, and then Liam Carson came on Lady's stomach. As soon as I saw it, I called her.

Lady Lane

(NÉE KATE BURNS)

Lacey called and she was like, "Do you need me there? I'll come right now. I'll get on a plane today."

And I think I was in shock. I was like, "Why?"

Betty

(NÉE JOSHUA BETTS)

I mean, it wasn't ideal, darling, but it also wasn't the end of the world. Don't get me wrong, it didn't say much for the security of our security footage at the Hop, and it didn't do much for our promise to keep each visit discreet. But still. Lady looked gorgeous in the video, and it wasn't like it was really porn, darling. She was fully clothed! Or, you know, mostly. I'd done things in my room I'd never want the world knowing about, let alone seeing, and all she was doing in the video was talking and honestly, it was a good speech. Compelling. She was impassioned and emotional and articulate and if one of my sex tapes was going to be leaked, I'd want it to be that one. She looked good and she sounded smart. Things could have been worse, is all I'm saying. Things could always be worse, it's just hard to see that sometimes. It's easy to point to a crack in your own sidewalk and call it the end of the world.

Mia

(NÉE YA CHAI CHEN)

Lady seemed like she was maybe in shock, and I didn't know what I could do to help. Something I didn't want to bring up with her was this: there was a serial killer out there targeting sex workers, and now, overnight, she'd become the face of the industry. I didn't say any of this to her, and she didn't seem to have thought of it herself.

I went to Daddy and I said, "Daddy, you need to keep her safe."

And he said, "From what?"

Daddy didn't have to be thinking about the serial killer all the time because the killer was never going to come for him.

······················

Dakota

(NÉE JACY ADAMS)

The truth of it was that Lady was always going to be safe. Mia was running around like a chicken with its head cut off because she was worried the Desert Shores Killer would see Lady's face plastered everywhere and decide to hunt her next. But count the number of white hookers that guy killed. See, he was only killing girls the world wouldn't miss. Which meant Lady was never in trouble. I would've been in trouble, Rain would've, Ginger, Betty, even Mia, we all would've been easy targets if we'd been outed, but Lady, she became a celebrity. And that's about all you need to know about how the world works, isn't it?

The first I knew of Lady Lane was that leaked sex tape. It wasn't even really a sex tape. I mean, it was a video of Liam Carson masturbating while Lady Lane gave this soliloquy about sex work. The tape might've gone viral because it was this surreal phenomenon showing Liam Carson, Hollywood's favorite unproblematic boyfriend, at a brothel with this prostitute who looked almost exactly like his girlfriend, Hollywood's favorite unproblematic actress, Willa Jordan, but the speech is what really stuck. Everyone knows that speech. Everyone knows it to this day. If Lady Lane had just been engaging in sex in the video, the news would've blown up and died down, the way things do with a celebrity scandal, but that speech started a conversation and the conversation lasted.

Willa Jordan

(NÉE HANNAH SNITCH)

I saw the leaked Lady Lane tape along with the rest of the world. Did I know that Liam was still visiting the Hop? No. Was I surprised that he was? Also no. It's where I met him. Before my days of being famous actress, Willa Jordan, I was a bestselling Bunny, and Liam came in one day, a VIP, one of my first guests at the Hop.

Back then, I'd recognized him immediately. Yellow eyes and hair that hung low on his forehead like an awning. I knew him from *We're Wolves*, which was brand-new at the time, but already destined for failure. It wasn't a good concept and he wasn't a good actor, I knew that even before I was one. He did have great eyes, though.

"I'm Willa," I said.

Liam said, "Sure. Can you take a look out there? Make sure no one saw me?"

He was obnoxious.

"I'm Liam," he said, once we were behind closed doors.

"I know."

"You're familiar with my work."

It wasn't a question. I said nothing.

Liam liked it hard and fast and he liked for me to face the wall and when he came, he growled, canine, and I cringed. He was still inside me when I said, "What, are you turning wolf or something?"

"Shut up," he said. And he was different postcoitus. Softer. More human.

"By the way, I hate your show," I said.

"By the way, me too," he said. He made another appointment for the next day.

. . .

I never loved Liam. Not really. Liam was cute and stupid and safe. Safe because there was no way I could ever fall for someone who believed the moon landing was faked and who thought that there was a possibility— *Admit that it's a possibility, Wills*, he said—that the world leaders might be lizards. He'd seen a video on YouTube. Liam was safe because he wasn't real, not to me, and so when I had a love interest in a new film, I could let myself fall head over heels, nothing holding me back. He was safe because he was fine with being my accessory and because I wrote his speeches, his interviews, his social media posts. I used him to curate my own image from the outside. He was an ideal boyfriend in no way, but he was an ideal boyfriend for me. Until that Monday morning. Until that tape leaked—which is when he became a liability.

Liam Carson was a twat, but back then he was a perfect boyfriend for Willa because he was a bit stupid and a pushover and he did anything we asked of him. He'd been acting since he was a kid, so he was used to being told what to do. Liam was basically all product by the time he met Willa, and he liked her enough to make their relationship viable to the public. So they started dating. It gets blurry at that point. Were they *really* dating? I mean, yeah. They went on dates. They slept together. They went on vacation together. Liam loved Willa, I think, and Willa might've loved Liam too, in a way. Their relationship was made for the public, but a lot of it happened in private. It worked. Except the one thing he couldn't seem to quit was the Hop. He went back monthly in some half-assed disguise and made the Bunnies sign an NDA, but Liam's not smart enough to keep a secret from the whole world. It was a miracle, really, that the scandal didn't come out until it did. But then, inevitably, there he was, jacking off to a Willa Jordan lookalike all over the internet.

Willa Jordan

(NÉE HANNAH SNITCH)

I woke up that Monday morning, the morning of Liam's leak, took my phone from my nightstand, left my Do Not Disturb mode on, because it's important to ease into the day like a bath, my therapist is always saying. I breathed along to my Breathe app. In a Meyers interview last year, I said, "Sometimes I feel like, without Breathe, I'd just suffocate and die." The audience loved that one. They laughed. I wrote it myself, well, Breathe.com wrote the bones, but I made it my own.

I was trying to write a film, too, a romantic comedy about a sex worker who falls in love with a guest. It wasn't *Pretty Woman*. It sounded like *Pretty Woman* in theory, vaguely, but it wasn't *Pretty Woman*. I was three pages in, and it was good stuff. That Monday morning, I sat down at the typewriter and stood back up. You shouldn't force yourself to write. People can tell when you're writing without inspiration because it reads like sandpaper.

Instead, I read my daily affirmations aloud, the way my spirit coach was always telling me to. "I am worthy of love and my love is worthy," and "Happiness is a choice and I am making it today," and then I let my bunnies, Coco and Chanel, out of their cages and I kissed their little noses and they hopped off to breakfast. I listened to my yoga instructor's voice tell me to *BE PRESENT* and then to *SMILE AT THE SUN*, and then I googled myself, the way I always did, every morning, because the people loved me, *loved* me, and who doesn't enjoy a little confidence boost in the morning, but then, there it was, right there on my home page: the video of my boyfriend jerking off to my doppel-gänger. I zoomed in. I zoomed out. I turned off my phone and the screen went black and, in doing so, it stopped telling me to *BREATHE*, and I did, for too long, long enough that a pain started to thrum, deep in my chest, and when I finally remembered to inhale, it came out as a gasp. By now I'd convinced myself that what I had seen, just a handful of breaths ago, wasn't real, and I turned my phone back on. Let the noti-fications roll in. There were thirty-five missed calls. The texts reached the hundreds. Other apps vibrated at me, too. My phone wouldn't stop trembling, or was it my hand, no it was my phone, it was both.

A new call, my publicist, and, instead of answering, instead of in-haling *two-three*, exhaling *two-three* the way my therapist would tell me to do, instead I lifted my phone over my head, tensed my arm (I was a good softballer back in school), and threw the phone, hard, across the room. It hit the painting that hung so proudly opposite my bed, took up the whole wall. It broke through the thin canvas and left a gaping hole in Aphrodite's stomach.

I used my second phone to call Liam, and when he picked up I said, "Liam."

He said, "Willa."

"Have you seen?"

"Yes."

"Are you okay?" I said.

"Am I?" he said. He sounded gluey. He was just-woke-up-Liam and I know it's a cliché, the mussed hair, the night-grown stubble, but he was so stupid-cute in the morning, like a kid, for just a second he forgot how to be Liam Carson, star of *We're Wolves*, and he was so human, his voice gruff and untrained, his laugh too scratchy to sound good on-screen.

"I'm okay," he said. He was cool about it. Way too cool about it. I heard him walk to the kitchen, pour coffee into a bowl. A bowl, because he'd been to France one single time.

"Are you going to ask if I'm okay?" I said.

He said, "If you're okay?"

Liam did this thing where he would take a sip and then store whichever liquid he was drinking, water, low-cal beer, vodka, today it was
coffee, in his cheeks like a chipmunk for a second or two before swallowing. It was no big deal. Just big enough to ruin my life. And even
though I couldn't see him, I knew he was doing it. I breathed, *in two-
three*, *out two-three*.

I said, "I mean, you're meant to be my boyfriend and you jacked off
to my doppelgänger at a brothel, my old brothel, where I worked, a fact
we've been trying to keep hidden for years, and now the footage is going
viral." I said, "Do you think I'm okay?"

"It's not such a big deal," said Liam. "It'll blow over."

"Blow over," I said. To be a man in Hollywood is a very different
experience from being a woman in Hollywood. Men make a mistake,
go quiet for a week, release an apology statement, and then bounce back
with a new movie screened to full theaters. But the public holds grudges
against women. Britney Spears, Anne Hathaway, Lindsey Lohan, when
it comes to women, the world refuses to let things go. It means that we
can't fuck up. Not ever. And this, Liam's Hop visit, it was a monumental
fuckup.

"Everything blows over," he said. "And all publicity is good publicity, right? Call Angela? Or Paula?" My agent, my publicist, respectively.
"It'll be okay, Wills," Liam said. "You know your girls will find a way
to spin it. This'll probably end up being good for your career. Casting
directors might take you more seriously, or something?"

What Liam didn't understand was that the leaked video was going
to affect me more than it ever did him. "You think people are going to
take me more seriously now they've seen my boyfriend's dick?"

"Call Angela."

I hung up, but the phone rang again. It was Angela. She said, "I've
been calling for hours, where the hell have you been? We need to get
on top of this, Willa. We need to get on top of it two hours ago."

"Angela?" I said.

"No it's the fucking Grinch who stole Christmas. When can we
meet?"

I said, "I'm not leaving the house today."

"You bet your ass you're not. I'll be over in ten to action plan."

Last time, when my nudes took over the internet, it had launched me from soap star to serious celebrity. And yeah, that photo might've made me, but that doesn't mean it didn't hurt. It did. Still does. I said, "Ange, am I going to be okay?"

And she said, "Don't call me that, you bitch."

. . .

I'd known Angela since high school. We met in drama class when we were assigned as partners on a dialogue project. She was a terrible actress, Ange was, couldn't remember a single line, even after we'd rehearsed the five-minute scene between Romeo and Juliet for a week straight. We would sit in the basement of the school's theater, smoking weed and eating pre-popped popcorn forced out of the vending machine by a clever contraption comprising a wire clothes hanger and a glob of Silly Putty. We rehearsed back and forth to no avail. Angela couldn't recall a single sentence.

Eventually we decided that I would play both parts, one side of my face painted as Romeo, the other, Juliet, while Angela played the part of the background. Her job was to stand behind me, foliage dripping from her arms; she would be the garden. We got A's for the project because I was, *am*, talented, and because Angela knew it. Knows it.

We were in Sydney, where we boarded at a private high school downtown and Angela went by Ange. "Is it short for Angela?" I asked her, one of those days in the basement.

I liked the way my voice sounded down there, the way the bare concrete walls contained it, kept it held and safe. I liked the steady drip-drip of the leaky pipe, the way it kept pace, taught me rhythm, meter, cadence. The blank walls—I could project some imaginary castle or whichever other setting onto them, a backdrop. It was my first rehearsal space.

"Yeah," she said. "But Angela makes me sound like some grown businesswoman with insurance and a perm, and if I ever become her, just fucking shoot me, okay?"

But she'd been going by Angela, not Ange, since she got to LA, and I didn't acknowledge the name change and I didn't shoot her either. Instead, I hired her. Angela was a shitty actress, but she was a fantastic agent.

. . .

"Listen, don't post a fucking thing, okay?" she was saying. "Don't do a fucking thing, don't breathe a fucking breath until I get there. I'll call Paula. I'll bring coffee. You hear that? I said I'll bring coffee. Don't even go down to your local fucking Starbucks. Willa, you hear me? We need to get on top of this before you can be seen."

"I hear you."

"You're in hiber-fucking-nation from now on, got it?"

"Hiber-fucking-nation. Got it."

"Got it?"

"Got it."

"I'll be there in fifteen." Which meant twelve. She's a fantastic agent.

"Should we, like, donate some money to homeless children or something?"

But she'd already hung up, and I was talking to the drone of a call gone dead. I put the phone on silent because I knew that as soon as the line was free, it'd ring. It'd ring ring ring all day. All day every day for weeks. I salvaged my cell from the floor, but it was so smashed that the screen looked like a web, and instead I opened my laptop. Searched myself and scrolled. Willa Jordan. I'd won an Oscar, a fucking *Oscar*, and still, the first image that came up in a Willa Jordan search was of my stupid boyfriend's penis. I made it to the fifteenth page of Google before there was finally a photo of me, arm in arm with Liam on a red carpet, him in a Gucci suit, kissing my cheek, golden statue cradled in my arms like it was our firstborn.

. . .

When I was a kid, I saw a man outside the movies. I was headed to a *Dirty Dancing* matinee, a rerun, and he was sitting beside the theater, busking, a puppet show—his hand wore a sock with two googly eyes stuck to its toe and the man's fingers moving inside like the sock had a mouth and was speaking gummy. The sock said, "Hello there," when I walked by. It said, "Hey, you!" and I stopped. I looked at the man, whose teeth were mostly missing, skin accordioned with age.

"What's your name?" said the sock. The man's mouth was still.

"Hannah," I said, because it was, back then.

"Hi, Hannah," said the sock. "I've known many Annas but only once a Hannah and I like Hannahs so much better, don't you?" The man picked up a sandwich and took a bite and chewed but the sock kept talking. "The Hannah I knew was a hand model. The most beautiful woman I've ever seen. She loved cats. Had four and fed twenty others. She drew a beauty mark above her lip every day, hoping it might eventually get stuck. She liked to bake, cakes, muffins, but was terrible at it. Burned everything she ever made, but I ate it all anyway and stored the charred bits in my cheeks and spit them out when she turned away. Hannah. She had these hands. The longest fingers, like stems or like streams. My Hannah's hands were insured for a million bucks apiece and I got to hold those hands for two weeks. Just two weeks I got to kiss those hands. And by the second week, I thought I was going to put a ring on Hannah's million-dollar hands, even though the only kind of ring I could afford would bring down their value by thousands. But then."

I was crouched on the footpath. "What happened to her?"

The sock said nothing.

"What happened to her?"

"What happened to who?" said the sock. Then the man laughed, laughed until he wheezed, choked, doubled over, and I ran into the theater and the whole movie, it could've been any movie, I stared at the screen but saw only the sock, holey and woolen and talking. The man who laughed through the gaps in his teeth. *Who*, he had said, *what happened to who?*

I'd wanted to act ever since.

But women start acting by modeling. You have to look good silent before they let you speak. So after graduating, I sent my headshots to every modeling agency I could find, and this scrappy little LA label got back to me and they said they liked my look. I'd been waiting my whole life to hear those words. I asked when I could start, and they said they'd fast-track my visa and they got me over here within the month.

The agency was in a basement under a nail salon and the door was stuck closed, so you had to contort your way through a side window to get in. I wasn't deterred. My first agent, whose name was Leslie, who turned out to be a man, middle-aged, sideburns, bad tobacco habit, the whole sleazy deal, he looked me up and down and spit into a jar and went, "You do nudity?"

And, you know, I'd seen *Titanic* and I'd seen *Basic Instinct* and I saw myself as a Kate Winslet or a Sharon Stone and so I said, "Yeah, I do nudity."

And then Leslie said, "Well there's a topless bar in South Park looking for C-cups." He looked at my chest and then at me. "That sound about right?"

I wanted to cry. Went to walk out the door and the door was stuck because it was, and then Leslie goes, "Wait up, kid." He goes, "Scorsese frequents the place, Cowboy Joe's, and he's been known to pick up extras from behind the bar."

. . .

At Cowboy Joe's we wore Stetsons and stilettos and nothing much else, and when Shania Twain came on, we had to stop what we were doing, pouring drinks, rolling cutlery, bussing, and we had to look a patron, any patron, in the eye, and we had to say, "Let's go, girls." If it was someone's birthday, we had to lasso them up and dance on their laps, and if someone asked for a Mustang Sally, we had to let them put their face between our breasts and shimmy. It was humiliating, the job, but the nudity was the least humiliating part of it. And, well, Scorsese didn't come in a single time, but Daddy did. Daddy did.

Daddy came into Cowboy Joe's alone, ordered a beer and a bucket of wings, and sat.

Men came to Joe's to watch the girls, but they hardly ever came alone, and the ones who did were creeps, but Daddy wasn't a creep, he was hot and tall and sweet to the servers, and to me he said, "Who're you?" When I went to answer, he said, "No. Who d'you want to be?"

So I'd gone with him to the Hop and I'd posed for the photo. *The* photo. I'd crawled over a sheet of scarlet satin. I'd looked back over my shoulder. I bit my lip and winked and smiled. It was the photo he used for my commercial, and I thought it had disappeared from the Hop when I did. But then, one day, the day after I'd done a Buzzfeed interview about wanting to take on bigger, more serious roles, there it was. The photo, my Hop photo, all over the internet.

I knew Daddy leaked it, even at the time, but I never confronted him about it. What was I meant to do? Accuse him of getting me everything I'd ever wanted?

• • •

Angela knocked. When I opened the door, she said, "You look like a fucking troll doll, darling. You know you don't have to stop blow drying just because the world's seen Liam's dick?"

She handed me a Starbucks and a brown paper bag. It was a doughnut, which I couldn't eat, but I liked smelling them and sometimes I picked the sprinkles off, one by one, and called it breakfast. I wasn't naturally thin, but the world thought I was, and it was important for the world to think you were naturally thin because if they knew you weren't, then they'd know you were dieting all day, every day, and dieting was frowned upon. Antifeminist.

Angela said, "How many times have I told you that as soon as you're in the news, you have to look nonstop fabulous?"

"Many."

She pushed past me, marched down the hall, through my bedroom, to my bathroom, started the shower, cranked it to scalding. "Even in your own home, darling, I mean it. What if Jason came up here and took a picture of you right now? He could sell it to the press for thousands." She grabbed at the hem of my pajama top. Tugged. I kept my arms at my sides.

"Jason wouldn't do that."

"Doormen are still men, Wills."

"Can you stop being paranoid?"

"Can you stop being an idiot? This is my job. I'm doing my job. Go get in the shower. Wash your skanky hair. Put on some makeup, for Christ's sake. I have a plan, but I'm not telling you about it unless you look like a human being."

She wrenched my arms up, pulled my shirt off.

"I do look like a human being."

Angela said, "No you look like Shrek's scrotum." She dragged my shorts down and pushed me toward the shower. "Go."

The water was good, so hot on my skin I hissed, but I didn't turn it down, I got used to it. I'd always been adaptable, able to get used to almost anything. Playing a vampire the previous summer, when I guest-starred on Liam's show, I sat in hair and makeup for four hours each day while they whitened my skin, glued pointed tips to each tooth, lengthened my lashes, reddened my eyes. I didn't move a fucking muscle. The first ten minutes were torture, but stay still long enough and you turn statue. Limbs forget they are. Bones set. Skin solidifies. Even your blood stills. My costume team said I was the easiest actress they'd ever worked with.

. . .

Daddy had landed me my first role, a side character on *California Girls*, and I spent three seasons showing up intermittently to say a line or two, but I wasn't known. Not then. But when the photo of my asshole went viral, Ange's phone started ringing. Since, I'd starred in an indie film about Aboriginal oppression that won big at the awards and a risqué porn-lite with a Franco brother that critics hated so much they couldn't quit talking about it. My career grew like a living thing after that image leaked, and I had to start turning away roles. I started saying no to television because I was a "film face," said my publicist. I said a very public no to a *Casablanca* remake that wanted me to play Ilsa for less than half the salary of the actor playing Rick, and the people loved the feminism of it all. I played the love interest in a cheesy romcom, then starred in a serious drama about a woman who spirals into insanity as she mourns the loss of her mother, and after that, the critical acclaim, the awards, the applause, I landed the role of Lady Bond. The high-budget, gender-bending action movie got the whole world talking. Women applauded. Men were furious: *Are they just going to remake every good movie with girls now?* Everyone had an opinion. I didn't care because, you know, opinions, like assholes . . . Whatever. My name was known by the world.

• • •

"We release a statement." That was their big plan. "We release an apology, written by you, post it all over social, and schedule an interview with the *New York Times*," said Angela, stirring six zero-calorie sweeteners into her coffee. She took a sip, winced, and added another two sachets. "We get on top of it, fast. We take the lead. What do you think?"

I picked a sprinkle from my doughnut and let it melt into nothing on my tongue. "It's boring."

"It's brilliant," said Paula. "It's brilliant, darling. It's simple. Quick. An instant solution to all of our problems. Get on the bike." She pointed at my Peloton, and I climbed aboard. Ange and Paula sat at the breakfast bar and halved the doughnut. I started pedaling, hard.

"The world has seen my boyfriend's dick," I panted. "The world has seen my boyfriend jack off to another woman at my old brothel, and you want me to post a 'sorry' on Instagram? And that's it?"

"People will love it. We'll spin it like: strong woman takes control of her narrative. It's brilliant. It's perfect. Let us do our jobs, Wills. You focus on yourself. I'll get Celine in here today, get her to ease all your tension. The full works. Massage, facial, nails, all of it. You'll feel so much better, darling. I'll get a photographer in here tomorrow. We need some pictures of you and Liam holding hands, looking solemn, sad, a united front. I'm thinking Manuel should take them, would that be okay?"

She turned on *E! News*, and they were talking about me. "What will Willa Jordan's next move be?" Ryan Seacrest, with his serial killer smile. Ryan Seacrest has probably buried a body.

• • •

The difference between my leak and Liam's leak was that when I was naked on the internet, I was the one in danger, and when Liam was naked on the internet, I was still the one in danger. The journalists would be on the story immediately, and they'd research Liam's past at the brothel, the Hop, and I was part of that past. And if they uncovered my story, my time as a Bunny, well, you can imagine. I needed a better plan than a posted apology. I knew that.

Rebecca Vernan
(REPORTER, *PEOPLE* MAGAZINE)

Willa Jordan's team released a statement. Something about respecting her privacy at this time. Liam Carson's team released an apology. But Lady was a mystery. Everyone wanted to talk to Lady Lane. Everyone wanted an interview, a statement, a story. But the owner of the Hop, I forget his name, he put the whole place on lockdown. We camped outside the joint, in the parking lot, a whole crowd of us just waiting to get a glimpse of the girl who looked so much like Willa Jordan, Liam Carson's mistress, the one whose speech was all over the world. But she gave us nothing. We didn't even see her shadow.

Rain

(NÉE ASHLEY SMITH)

Lady was everywhere. She was in every single tabloid, every news outlet, all over social media. People were making memes about her. Every
time we turned on the TV or radio, someone was talking about her
speech. Every single guest calling for an appointment was asking for
Lady, and every walk-in was disappointed not to find her in a lineup.
She couldn't make it to lineups anymore. She had back-to-back bookings. She blew up overnight—everyone wanted to meet the girl who
got jizzed on by Liam Carson. What they maybe didn't realize was that,
for Lady, that experience was an assault.

Betty
(NÉE JOSHUA BETTS)

It happened soon enough after the #metoo movement and the "grab 'em by the pussy" stuff for Lady's video to become big news. The debate over what constituted assault was at its climax, darling, and not the good kind. Walmart changed their name to #WalmartToo for the month, which was a lot to unpack. Kroger tried to start #metoomonth, but Halloween kind of has a monopoly over October. Facebook changed their logo to teal, the color of, I guess, sexual assault? Thank god for the conglomerates, darling. Saving the world one hashtag at a time.

Lady Lane
(NÉE KATE BURNS)

My name was trending. Both of my names. Kate Burns was the top search on Twitter and #ladythetramp had gone viral. The original video had a thousand clicks, then ten thousand, a hundred thousand, a million, just like that. People were making different versions, too. Edits. Ones in black and white and ones that tried to zoom in to get a better look at me, at him. There were ones with voiceovers and ones that had a series of crass grunts superimposed over my speech when X ejaculated and one that even animated X to turn wolf partway through.

I looked pretty, in the video. Mia told me to look for silver linings, and that is what I came up with. I looked good. I looked less like me and more like Ma. I looked undeniably like a hooker, my boobs bigger than my T-shirt, heels so high my legs looked taller than me.

I scrolled through the videos, watching each one, watching the numbers of views tick up, up, up. Ginger sent emails to PornHub, YouPorn, Reddit, 4Chan, any website with a copy of the video. She sent a letter of complaint threatening to take legal action if the footage were not removed. The video stayed. It grew.

Google me a month prior, and you would've found nothing. No trace. Good luck finding my Facebook page among the millions of Kate Burnses. Type my name into any engine these days, and it will come back with too many hits to count, all of them about me. Google Kate Burns now, and I'm the main one. I am *the* Kate Burns. But I'm not really. The news articles, the journalists, the bloggers, the Instagrammers, the public, they all get me so wrong, even still, even now—they don't know me at all. Fame isn't being known by the world, it's being misknown by the world. Back in those days, I'd never felt more multiple. They all thought they knew me, but they all knew a different version of me, and, really, *really*, no one knew me at all.

Every article told some variation of the same story:

The news:

Sources say that Liam Carson's mystery prostitute is Kate Burns, 23, from rural New Zealand. The Willa Jordan lookalike is now known as Lady Lane at her place of work, the Hop, a legal brothel in Nevada. Previously a dancer at Auckland strip club the Purple Panther, Kate Burns became a Bunny only recently, but she is already bringing in the bigwigs, including Willa Jordan's beau, Mr. Carson.

The tabloids:

We're *Wolves* hottie Liam Carson caught red-handed at Nevada's most fa-mous brothel. Naughty Liam might be more dog than wolf after all. What will Willa say?

The more progressive media tried to liberal-up the language, and still fucked it up:

A reminder that sex workers have enough trauma to deal with without you blaming them for breaking up Willa and Liam, too. Let's leave them alone.

"That's the stuff that gets me," said Mia, when she finished reading the article aloud. "It's not the hooker stuff or the whore stuff. Call me a fucking streetwalker strumpet slut, for all I care."

We lay back on my bed and watched ourselves watch ourselves from above.

"Those feminists who call themselves inclusive and then tell us that in order to be in our industry, we must've been through some kind of trauma."

I said, "I think they're just trying to be—"

"I know what they're trying to be," said Mia. "Eight in ten women have been assaulted in this country, Lady. Eighty percent of women. Can you imagine if they all became sex workers?"

I yawned. I was tired. Fame is tiring. I felt like I was in a million pieces. I said, "Do you think it'll die down?"

Mia held my face in her hands, held the pieces of me together.

. . .

We reached out to Willa Jordan, Liam Carson, and Kate Burns for comment, was how every article ended.

They had, too. Reached out. Cheryl was fielding calls, and Daddy doubled down on security at the gate. Cops were stationed outside, standing around the Hop's courtyard like garden gnomes. Guests were being escorted in one by one, vetted at the door, and none of the girls wanted to be picked from the lineup, no one wanted to miss out on the drama.

Lisa Hamilton

(FEATURES EDITOR, *VOGUE*)

The only statement we could get was one from the owner of the Hop, Vincent Russo, otherwise known as Daddy. He said, "We are working as hard as we can to find the source of the security footage leak. We can assure our guests that this privacy breach will not happen again. Lady Lane will not be offering a statement at this time; however, she is still taking appointments, as are our other Bunnies. It's business as usual here at the Hop. Call 1800-800-6969 to schedule a session today."

Rebecca Vernan

(REPORTER, *PEOPLE* MAGAZINE)

The only statement the owner would give was basically a sales pitch, a commercial, and so, yeah, it didn't take long for people to start speculating that he was the one who leaked the tape as some batshit crazy publicity stunt.

Lady Lane

(NÉE KATE BURNS)

Someone wanted to write my autobiography. Someone else wanted me to do a tell-all on *Oprah*. For every day I didn't tell the story myself, the world told it on my behalf. I wished Ma were around. I wanted to ask her: *Is this what you wanted?* Despite having been watched by the whole world, I felt invisible. I felt written over by everyone else's stories of me.

I was sitting in the parlor with the other Bunnies; we were drinking Pink and scrolling through news stories, reading the odd line aloud, when Betty pointed at one of the TV screens.

"Your commercial hasn't always been like that, has it, Lady?" is what she said. All of us Bunnies sat and waited for the loop to finish, for my ad to come back around, and when it did, I saw what Betty was talking about. The commercial used the security footage of me, talking, talking, and X, his face blurred, touching himself. Even the tagline was different; now it said: *Lady Lane: THE HOP'S VERY OWN WILLA JORDAN LOOKALIKE.*

We watched the loop a couple more times. Dakota eventually said what we were all thinking. "He wouldn't have leaked it on purpose, right? Not while there's a serial killer out there targeting us."

Vincent "Daddy" Russo

Was the leak good for business? Yes. Does that mean I leaked the footage? No. No, I'm not confessing to anything, let's make sure we get that straight.

Lady Lane

(NÉE KATE BURNS)

Liam Carson arrived in the night in a beat-up Jeep and an actual disguise, this time. A beard that looked real and spectacles instead of sunglasses and a pair of old Levi's, with a wifebeater and tattoos up his arms that hadn't been there at our appointment.

Daddy met him at the gate and brought him to my room himself. The two of them sat on the foot of my bed. Daddy said, "Obviously it's not ideal that your name is public, Lady."

I looked at him.

He went on, "I mean, some guy out there is killing hookers, and now you're the most famous hooker there is."

I looked at him.

"But I think we can work with it," Daddy was saying. "I think we can keep you safe even with the world knowing your real name."

"You think," I said.

"I'd rather you didn't speak to any reporters," said Liam. "It'd be best if you kept quiet about the whole thing."

"Best for who?" Daddy said. "Lady's the one who's been ambushed here. She should be able to do what she wants."

"What I want to know is how that footage was leaked," said Liam. "It's obviously your footage."

"I have the best security system on the market," said Daddy. "I can't help that we were hacked."

"Here's the deal," said Liam. "If you both keep your mouths shut to the media, I won't press charges. Otherwise you'll be hearing from my lawyers."

"*You* owe *her*, son," Daddy said to Liam. "You owe her big-time. Ever considered paying for her silence?" He was a good negotiator, Daddy was. He'd make a great hooker.

"I'm not paying," said Liam. "I didn't do anything wrong."

"Well then," said Daddy, dusting his hands. "We've got some interviews to schedule."

Once Liam left, Daddy turned to me, rested his hand on my hand. "You should see your bookings sheet," he said. "You've got a waitlist as long as your legs. This is going to be good for you, Lady. Your sales, your profits. It could be really good for us."

I looked at him.

"What?" he said. "You're not going to kiss me again, are you?"

I said, "Did you leak it?"

"What?"

"The tape. The security footage. Did you leak it?"

Daddy's hand tensed over mine. He squinted. His jaw pulsed, slow and rhythmic. "I'm here to keep you safe," he said. "You know that, don't you? You know that all I care about is your safety, don't you?"

"It's just that, I saw my new commercial. It calls me a Willa Jordan lookalike now, and the change happened so quickly after the leak."

"Obviously we have to take advantage of it," is what Daddy said. "*Vogue* wants an interview with you. And *People* magazine. I've got calls coming in left, right, and center. They want you on *Good Morning America*. We'd be crazy not to turn this into profit."

"What if that guy comes after me? The killer?"

"The Hop is the safest place for you to be. I think we can keep you safe *and* make the most of this financially."

"You think," I said.

"What?"

"You *think* you can keep me safe."

"Right," said Daddy.

I shook off his hand. "What if I don't want any of this?" I said. "What if I just want to go back to my life. What if I want to keep working, seeing guests, just let this whole thing pass?"

He said, "Well, it's your life, Lady. I'm not about to tell you what to do. But you're an expensive asset right now. What with all the extra security measures and having to pay Cheryl overtime to manage the media calls. You're expensive, and I wouldn't want to have to let another Bunny go to keep affording your extra costs. You know it's not safe for girls on the streets these days."

I looked at him. He looked at me.

I said, "Is that a threat?"

He said, "No, of course not." He stroked my hair and said, "You're going to be great, Lady. We're going to make you a star."

People tell you who you are to them; all you have to do is listen.

ACT V

THE FAME

If I didn't define myself for myself, I would be crunched into other people's fantasies for me and eaten alive.

Audre Lorde, "Learning from the 60s"

Bell Hobbes

(NÉE MAYBELLINE BURNS)

The day my biological sister's video leaked, my adoptive sister, Brit, called and said, "Let's get matching tattoos." She was working on shaking her rich-girl image, which meant a nose ring, a pink streak in her hair, a skateboard, a Big Fans account, for which she was charging $50 per subscriber, such a high rate that she could barely hold onto a single fan, but that didn't matter, she didn't want to be a porn star, she just didn't want to be herself. And now, a tattoo. It was seven on a Saturday morning, and Brit was ringing to say she'd made us an appointment at the Ink Rink, the only parlor in town that didn't card so long as you paid in cash.

I was like, "What?"

And she was like, "Tattoos. Tattoos! I'm thinking left boob, right over the heart."

"But the parents—"

"Won't know," she said.

"Let's just go for a walk. We could go to the mall. Get matching T-shirts instead."

Brit was always like, *You're such a plank, Bell.* That's what Brit was always saying to me. It meant that I was wooden or stiff, I think, a virgin, which was the worst thing for girls to be. Brit thought it was feminist to be sexually liberated, but you know what's not feminist: chlamydia. It was whatever. I would've preferred Bell the Plank than Brit the Slut any day of the week.

"Matching T-shirts," Brit snorted. "Tweedledee and Tweedledum. Come on. Think about it! Tattoos. We'd be real sisters."

She was always talking about being *real sisters*. A *real sister* would skip class with her. A *real sister* would slip out of the house in the night to go to some college party down the street. A *real sister* would get matching tattoos.

"I don't think that's how biology works."

"How would you know?" Brit was sipping coffee. I could hear each swallow through the phone. Brit didn't even like coffee, but she drank it every day because she was working on her image, always, always working on her image. If I checked her Insta right now, she would've already posted her morning latte, posed beside a muffin, no, an acai bowl she'd never eat, and a book she'd never read. No hashtags, obviously, because hashtags are for boomers. "We haven't been to a science class all year," she said.

She wasn't wrong. Our attendance was down, way down, but that was all part of it, all part of Brit's big scheme to be some kind of different. She didn't want her parents' life. Her life. It was inauthentic, is what she told me. She was looking for some kind of deeper truth. So we'd been hanging out at universities.

"Hear me out," she'd said on our first university day, when I asked why we were loitering in the commons. "Who hangs out at uni?"

"Us?"

"Hot professors and hot uni students." She pointed at a man with a briefcase and then a girl carrying a guitar, singing and playing as she walked, barefoot. "This is the perfect hunting ground," she said, "these are our people. Progressive, liberal people with the right opinions." A man with a megaphone said something about prison abolition and everyone else in the building ignored him. "See?" Brit said. "This is where we meet our future husbands." We were sixteen. "Or wives," she said. It was a Tuesday, 2:00 p.m. We went home alone, or not alone. Together.

"We'll both get a BH for Bell Hobbes and Brit Hobbes," Brit said, about the tattoos. "It'll bind us."

"We live in the same house. Isn't that binding enough?"

Brit swung my bedroom door back on its hinges, mug of coffee nursed in one hand. "You're so fucking boring," she said into the phone, despite being within an arm's length of me. "Do something exciting for once. Do something the parents will disapprove of, for *once*." She took a tube of lip gloss from my vanity and leaned into the mirror to apply it. "They seriously won't know. We'll get them right above the nipple. You won't even see it in a bikini." She said all this as she glossed her lips so none of her consonants landed, but she could have hummed the sentence and I'd still be able to understand. I did know her through and through. Like real sisters.

Brit kissed the glass of the mirror and left a murky pout behind. "Come on," she said.

We looked nothing alike. Brit's hair was alive with volume, while mine sulked around my face like drapes. Brit's eyes shone, so green they were almost yellow, while mine were a weepy blue. Brit had a real body, the body of an actress, boobs, an ass, her clothes had things to cling to, not me, a walking toothpick and just as exciting to look at. Brit hated her fancy life, and I was mostly just grateful to have a home. No one could tell we were sisters because we weren't. "Come on, Bell. Please. It's like a blood oath. We'll make promises. To be together forever."

"Okay," I said, mostly because arguing with Brit was futile. Once she wanted something, she got it, and if she wanted something for me, then I got it, too. "Okay, fine. We'll get tattoos."

"Yes!" Brit said, squeezing my fingers. "See, *this* is something real sisters would do."

The word *real* and the word *sister*. Her intention was good, I knew that. Maybe a tic left over from our childhood days, when Meg would make sure to call us both her daughters. When Morty would come home from work and greet the whole room, me included, with *Family, I'm home!* But it only ever felt like what it was: a poorly disguised therapist's method for making me feel included. Real families don't have to label their biological connection to one another. Real sisters don't say things like *real sisters*. They just are.

Brittany Hobbes

(ADOPTIVE SISTER TO MAYBELLINE BURNS, STUDENT, FENBROOK HIGH)

I hated her, as a kid. Growing up, the parents' top priority was making Bell feel wanted, and how do you think that made me feel? I get it, I'm lucky. I had one of those princess beds and I had a plastic kitchen that could really cook, and every year, every single year, they threw me a birthday party with catering. That's lucky, right?

But it wasn't like Bell had it hard either. The parents brought her home from the hospital as a newborn. Sure, she had a poor mother, but she never experienced the consequences of that poverty. She'd been a Hobbes her whole life, and yeah, maybe I resented that she got all the Hobbes perks and an interesting adoption story to boot. Sue me.

When we were younger, I took it out on her, all that misplaced anger. Do I feel bad about it now? Yes. Can I change the past? No. And anyway, it's not like I ever hurt her. Not really. I just played a few little pranks to demonstrate all the ways in which she wasn't a "real" Hobbes. Each year we'd get identical Christmas sweaters, the whole family, with HOBBES stitched on the back like it was our team, and I would find a way to ruin Bell's, unspool its wool or cut the necessary letters to leave it saying only HO. Or the time, after Meg got Bell and me matching Rachels at the salon, I snuck into her bedroom and recut her hair in the night, gave her a set of jagged bangs that not even Meg's designer stylist could fix. Or, when I got my period, long before Bell got hers, I used to leave used tampons out on our shared bathroom counter. The message: *See how we don't bleed the same.*

But things changed between Bell and me when we started intermediate school. On the first day, one of the boys, one of the ones who always sat at the back of the bus, he called Bell an orphan. "Hey Brit," he called from his throne at the back when we got on. "Ditch the orphan and come sit with me."

Bell Hobbes

(NÉE MAYBELLINE BURNS)

It was Charlie Jones who called me an orphan that day. Weedy little jerk. He called me an orphan, and then Brit was like, "What did you just call her?"

And Charlie was like, "Sorry, does she prefer bastard? Stray?"

Brit marched down the bus and punched Charlie Jones square in the nose, and the crack was one out of the movies. There was silence and then whistling and whooping and people stood to high-five her, to pat her on the back. When the applause died down, she came back to where I was sitting, our seat, and she tucked her hand into mine and we stayed that way the whole ride to our new school. We might not've been biological sisters, but we were sisters.

• • •

The tattoo parlor was dirty and the artist looked like he lived in a sewer, but his hands were steady and Brit was insistent, so I sat in the chair and closed my eyes.

That's when Brit went, "Holy shit."

I jumped, and the tattoo artist was like, "Yeah, you're going to need to not do that."

And I was like, "Sorry."

And Brit was like, "Check this out."

And that's when she showed me the video. My sister, my *biological sister*, Kate Burns, and Liam Carson, the guy from the wolf show. Willa Jordan's boyfriend.

I sat up, and the tattoo artist was like, "Yeah, you're going to need to not do that."

"That's my sister," I said.

"No, that's the chick from the new James Bond," the tattoo artist said.

"That's not your sister," said Brit. "I'm your sister."

Lacey Kahu

When her ma got pregnant, back when we were kids, Lady and I had been so excited about having a new sibling. We started collecting dropped toys from the street, stray baby socks, names we liked. Lady wanted to call her Shania as in Twain. I wanted to call her Celine as in Dion. For a minute there, we had interests like normal girls wanting to play house. We were always talking about dressing the baby, feeding her, being big sisters, showing her the ropes.

Then there was just nothing. Ma came home from the hospital empty-handed, and Lady didn't want to talk about it. It was like I'd hallucinated the whole thing.

Bell Hobbes
(NÉE MAYBELLINE BURNS)

On maybe our hundredth viewing of the leaked video, back home, icing our chests, Brit was like, "She looks just like you."

And I was like, "No, she doesn't," even though the first time she showed me the clip, at the tattoo parlor, I did a double take.

I said, "Do you think I should reach out?"

Brit was like, "It's not like you even know her."

But I felt like I did. For a while, I made the drive out to the Burnses' place every day, obsessive, obsessed, like a show I couldn't quit. I sat in my car and watched Kate and Merrill live their lives until my windows fogged up and I couldn't watch them anymore. They weren't even interesting; they were boring, usually. They loved TV and sat in front of it for hours and hours on end, but they talked the whole time, chatted and laughed their way through entire movies, whole seasons of shows. I wondered if they ever really ended up watching anything at all. I did know them.

I stopped going over there after Merrill died, though. Kate looked so sad, so sad that I was tempted to run up the path and knock on the door and hug her and tell her, "I'm your family." But I wasn't and I couldn't be, so I stopped going.

• • •

Bored of watching the clip on repeat, Brit went to the uni to scout out a new love interest while I read every article I could find about Kate, or

Lady, or Liam Carson, or Willa Jordan. The whole world was covering it. Serious outlets, newspapers, gossip blogs, YouTubers, and every social media user had something to say. I was reading a *Cosmo* article that called my sister's speech "empowering," when Matt knocked on the door.

Matt, my boyfriend, he didn't know about Kate or Merrill. He knew I was adopted and assumed I didn't want to talk about it, so we didn't. We spent most of our time kissing. He was an okay kisser.

When I answered the door, he was like, "Hey," but I didn't want to let him in. I was doing research. I was watching the video. I knew my sister's speech by heart by now.

I was like, "Hey."

"Can I come in?"

I must've hesitated because he was like, "Is something wrong?"

I let him in, and he kissed me.

"What's up?" he said.

"Oh . . ." I waved my phone. "Nothing," I said. But he must've caught a glimpse of my screen, which was open to the video of Kate and Liam Carson, and Matt was like, "Holy shit, are you watching porn? That's so hot."

"No," I tried to say, but he was already kissing me, pushing me back, back toward the couch. He pushed me down onto the cushions and then reached for the hem of my shirt.

I let him lift it over my head. It was a new development for us, the undressing, and not long ago I would've crossed my arms, armor, whenever he tried to move things along. But with enough *come on, Bell*s and *just your shirt*s and *why not*s, I'd relented the week before, and now here I was, topless and shivering. The house was too big for it to ever be warm inside.

Matt took the state of my nipples to be a result of stimulation and not temperature, and I let him keep thinking that, because boys' egos are fragile, and it's important to let them think they're in control, was what Brit always said.

Matt was like, "You want me," and he unclasped my bra.

I nodded. My new tattoo ached.

"So let's do it then."

"Do what?"

"Don't make me spell it out, Bell."

"Spell what out?"

You're a plank, Bell, is what Brit always said, and I knew I was and I knew Matt wouldn't wait around forever. I knew I should just get it over with. Brit was always saying, *Just get it over with.* And, *It's not a big deal.* And, *You'll like it, it's fun!* But there was a reason it was called losing your virginity. I didn't want to lose anything.

"You're so beautiful," Matt said. He was always saying that kind of shit. Boys think a compliment doubles as lube, but they're wrong. Offer up an adjective, and girls'll want to keep it forever. What if he doesn't think I'm beautiful without makeup, without clothes, without virginity?

I was like, "Shut up."

"You are," he said. "Look at you." He took out his phone and snapped a photo before I could cover myself. He smiled at his screen and turned it to show me.

"It's blurry," I said. "You can't even see me."

"So let me take a better one."

"No!"

"Come on, babe. Pose for me." He held his phone sideways and started shooting. I laughed and kept myself covered. He was like, "Work it, girl. Come on, if we're not going to do it, at least give me something to work with at home." And that made me smile. He was a good talker. Funny. Smart. I dropped my arms, lay back on the couch, and arched my back, and Matt was like, "Yes, babe. That's so hot."

And I felt it. I did. I felt like Kate, like Lady, my sister, in the video. I felt sexy, like her, like I could excite this man just by being. I unclasped my bra for the second time. "Switch it to video," I said.

"What do you mean?" he said. His voice had a rattle to it, like something had been shaken loose. He reached for his crotch. I watched. He didn't bother with his belt, just palmed the denim, camera still pointed at me.

"I want to make a video," I said. I unbuckled his belt. His breathing was heavy and rasping. "Are you recording?" I said. He nodded. I dragged his jeans all the way down. He was hard. Then I took the phone from him and set it up, up high on a shelf, angled downward, just like Kate's video, and then I said to Matt, "I want you to touch yourself."

"What?" His face was red, and there was a line of sweat over his lip.

"I want you to touch yourself while you watch me."

He reached for himself.

"Keep going," I said. I ran a finger across my chest, down my stomach, fingered my waistband.

He wheezed.

I smiled. I recited, "You know, maybe, maybe, if people thought that guys like you did things like this, then there wouldn't be so much stigma around it—"

"What are you talking about?"

I went on, "Maybe then, it wouldn't be such a big deal. Maybe then it would be more socially acceptable, and if it were more socially acceptable, then maybe it would be made legal in this country, and then maybe it would be made legal in the world, and then maybe—"

He came.

I took the phone and shut off the recording. The video was under two minutes long.

"Sorry," he said. "That was fast. I'm not usually—"

I was like, "It's fine," and sent the video to myself. He zipped his fly. Then I said, "Brit'll probably be home soon." I wanted him gone. I said, "You should—"

"Yeah," he said. "I should." He laughed, and I wished he wouldn't. Wished I could say *Shut up shut up shut up.* Had his laugh always sounded so chipmunk? He looked smaller. He looked like a boy. I could suddenly imagine him as a kid, could imagine him crying for his mother in the night. I felt powerful.

He was like, "Are you okay?"

I ushered him to the door and said, "Are you?"

"That was . . . ," he said.

"I'll see you, Matt."

I closed the door and dressed myself and felt a pain in my chest. I'd forgotten about my tattoo—the little BH, black with a shadow of irritated red. It was itchy and raised like it had been embroidered. There were little droplets of dried blood at its edges. Matt hadn't noticed it.

I pressed the flesh and winced. Pus seeped from around each letter. My body was rejecting its new brand. It was saying, *You are not a Hobbes.*

I watched the video, my video, of Matt touching himself while he watched me recite Kate's speech. I really did look just like her. My sister. My *real* sister. I took Meg's car and drove, a drive I'd driven so many times, to the place that could've been home.

Brittany Hobbes

Bell got weird about going to her biological family's house. For a while there, she was going most days to watch her mother and her sister through their window. I knew she wanted to know them. She wanted to know where she came from, but, to be honest, I was afraid. I was afraid that she'd knock on their door one day and her mother would invite her in and hug her and she'd never want to leave. She wasn't my blood sister, but she was more family to me than the parents ever were.

When Lady Lane's tape leaked, I freaked out, because even though Bell didn't really visit their place after Merrill died, I knew she was comforted by knowing where Kate was, under an hour away in light traffic. But now Kate, Lady Lane, she was halfway across the world.

Bell Hobbes

(NÉE MAYBELLINE BURNS)

When I pulled up to their house, there was a sign out front. New. I could make out what it said from down the road: For Sale. The car had barely stopped before I jumped out and ran to the window, cupped my hands to the glass and peered inside. The place was empty and dark. Of course it was. Kate was in America, Nevada, a place called the Hop. I knew that from the leaked video and the articles. My tattoo burned on my chest, itched, it didn't want to be there. And suddenly it was very clear to me. That I needed to meet my sister. My real family. I needed to go to the Hop.

I ran a quick Google search and found a phone number. I called, but someone named Cheryl said, "A biological sister that Lady doesn't know about yet?" Her accent sounded just like a cowgirl from the movies. "Sure, honey," she said, "sure you are." I heard her whisper, "Fucking con artist," before hanging up on me.

Lady Lane
(NÉE KATE BURNS)

Cheryl managed my books, spacing my appointments far enough apart that I could interview between seeing guests. Daddy set up interviews with every major outlet.

I told him I didn't want to do them, and he told me I would do them, so I did them. After his threat, what choice did I have? I couldn't let him send a Bunny to the streets because of me. He wrote my script, and I stuck to it as best I could.

"I love my job," I said into microphones. "I love it here, at the Hop. I feel safe here."

· · ·

In one interview, the reporter asked, "What do you want the future of sex work to look like?"

Well, Daddy hadn't provided me with an answer for that question, so I said, "Obviously sex work should be legalized everywhere. It's the only way to keep sex workers safe. The victims of the Desert Shores Killer probably would still be alive today if sex workers were able to operate in safe, legal environments."

"And what do you have to say to people who suggest that legalizing sex work will just encourage young women to sell their bodies?"

I lifted my hands, wiggled my fingers, said, "Does it look like I've sold my body?" I said, "I've had guests who have served in the military and lost their legs. I've had guests who sleeved their arms in factories. I've had guests whose bodies are failing them, who've had to opt out of surgery because of America's health care system. Does it look like *I've* sold my body?"

"You know what I mean," said the reporter.

"Do I? Or do you just consider sex work to be selling the body because you think a woman's value is tied to her virginity?"

After the reporter left, Daddy said, "I told you not to go off script."

I looked at him. I said, "We hadn't written an answer to that question."

"Next time, say you don't feel comfortable speaking to that subject."

"Was my answer wrong?" I said.

"Stick to the script," said Daddy.

. . .

A few days later, Betty showed me photos she'd found. Hundreds and hundreds of people on the streets all around the country, protesting to decriminalize sex work. Everyone carrying homemade signs that read DOES IT LOOK LIKE I'VE SOLD MY BODY?

That did make me feel good. I didn't like the world talking about me, but I did like that I'd got the world talking.

Willa Jordan

(NÉE HANNAH SNITCH)

Daddy didn't want sex work to be more broadly legalized because he'd lose his monopoly. You ever wonder why Daddy cared about his girls so much? He didn't. All powerful people really care about is power, and power is relative, and in order to have that power, they require there be those without it. Daddy was one of those people. He got a kick out of playing god. He liked to toss girls to the streets for underselling because he liked for his Bunnies to be afraid of him. He liked taking girls like me, like Lady, and making us stars because he liked knowing he could. What we wanted didn't matter. Daddy landed me the role on *California Girls* and then leaked my Hop commercial to get me off *California Girls* and into more serious roles, and he didn't do that because he wanted the best for me, no, if he wanted the best for me he would've found a way to help me consensually, without having to splash my nudes over the whole world and humiliate me in the process. That was him making his mark, that was him pissing all over me and saying *She's mine.* And it did make me a star, but really *Daddy* made me a star. He liked that I owed him my entire career. It was a debt I could never repay. I smelled like his piss, and that smell would never wash off.

And he was doing the exact same thing with this new girl, this Lady. He was letting her interview with all of these big outlets, and he wouldn't have let that happen if he weren't trying to make her a star. The *leak* wouldn't have happened if he weren't trying to make her a star. I watched the video a hundred times through, and after a while

I kind of even forgot that Liam was in it. Lady was magnetic, and her speech, well, I cried a couple times. It was a really good speech. And that's what gave me the idea, a big, scary idea, but if I pulled it off, it would be a good idea.

I wanted to make a movie.

....

Lady Lane
(NÉE KATE BURNS)

I had a list of men who were waiting around for a cancellation, some who were content with waiting three months before their appointment, just to ensure they saw me. I was wanted. I was desired. But it wasn't me they wanted, not really, they were coming for a Willa Jordan lookalike. They were coming to fuck the girl who got jizzed on by Liam Carson. Even the women outside the Hop, standing out there with signs saying my name in glitter, LADY LANE, my fans, had no idea who they were idolizing. Fame means everyone knowing your name and no one knowing you at all.

One guest, a middle-aged man wearing skinny jeans, he'd come all the way from California, he told me, to get humiliated by Willa Jordan. He was wearing a collar and I held his leash and walked him around the Hop and when we got back to my room he wanted me to step on his neck with my bare foot. He said, "Can you say her line?"

"What line?"

"The one from the end of the new Lady Bond? I'll do the guy's line, and then you do her line. Okay?"

"Sure."

"You fight like a girl."

"A girl who can kick your ass."

"No, it's, '*This* girl can kick your ass.' "

"No, it isn't."

He stopped touching himself and frowned at me.

"Sorry," I said. "*This* girl can kick your ass."

. . .

The video's views climbed and climbed, and just as they started to plateau, Liam Carson released an apology statement: a screenshot of the notes app on his phone. Some bogus explanation including a made-up sex addiction. So, the note said, I fucked up. Something that a lot of you don't know about me is that I am a sex addict, and when Willa is away on production, I suffer from withdrawals that have a negative impact on my health, both mentally and physically. Willa knows of my condition and we have talked about it at length. She has accepted my apology, and I promise, to her and to all of you, to continue working on myself, and to do better. I feel so lucky to be with someone like Willa, and every day I thank god that she sees me for who I want to be, rather than who I am, which is a flawed human being who, just like everyone else, makes mistakes. I am so sorry to any fans disappointed by my behavior. Please know that no one is as disappointed in me as I am.

The world loved the statement. This is how you make an apology, the internet said. They left clapping emojis and fire emojis and heart-eye emojis.

Wait a second, someone posted on Twitter. Liam Carson's apology might be successful when it comes to the personal, but it completely evades all larger political conversation.

Another statement from Liam's publicity team ironed that crease out in under a day. They donated $100,000 to Sex Workers United, and Liam posted a note on his social saying: While I support sex worker rights and believe that all sex workers should be afforded personal safety and security under the law, I am ashamed of my patronization of the Hop and hiring Kate Burns, or Lady Lane, to engage in sexual relations with me, and I will not be returning to the establishment.

Even though he'd denounced us, our phones started ringing off the hook. All publicity is good publicity if you're thinking only of profits and never of people. Cheryl couldn't keep up.

Dakota
(NÉE JACY ADAMS)

Daddy was happy. He was whistling his way around the grounds. Sales were booming since the leak. The whole world was talking about the Hop and Lady and sex work. He bought Lady all of this stuff, stuff she never asked for. These new costumes, outfits custom-made for her, and I loved Lady, I did, but it was hard not to resent her. She couldn't make it to lineups anymore because she was fully booked for months. Cheryl started offering the men on Lady's waitlist the rest of us Bunnies as contingencies. She offered us up at a discounted rate. Ginger complained. She said she'd never gone clearance, and she wasn't about to start now.

I took whatever cash I could get, discount or not. I still hadn't had an appointment in weeks.

Lady Lane

(NÉE KATE BURNS)

Daddy started bringing me gifts. Thongs that fit like skin and bras that accounted for my one slightly smaller breast. He bought me other things, too, a pair of earrings, little heart pendants with pink stones freckling the silver. A vase filled with so many red roses that, after a couple days, my floor looked like a crime scene, puddled with petals. A bike with a basket. A leather jacket embroidered LB for Lady Bunny. I didn't want it. Didn't want any of it.

He said, "We need to figure out our next move, Lady." He said, "I think we could get you a show on MTV, that might be a good place to start, how does that sound to you?"

How did it sound to me? I never wanted to be on MTV.

One night he knocked on my door and handed me a bottle of champagne, two glass flutes, and a punnet of strawberries. "Romantic," I said, letting the door back on its hinges.

"We're celebrating," he said.

"What?"

"You."

"We're celebrating me?"

"You've got a hundred guests on the books."

"A hundred?" I wondered how many manfriends Ma had hosted in her life, how many names were written down in her books.

Daddy popped the cork and sipped the overflow and filled the flutes and passed one to me, clicked the lip of his glass against mine. "You're making good money," he said. I nodded. I was, it was true. "And you're about to be a star," he said. "To Lady," he said, taking a sip.

"To Lady," I said. I didn't drink.

·············

Mia

(NÉE YA CHAI CHEN)

Lady was doing all of these interviews. When the first one aired, on *Good Morning America*, I went to her room with popcorn and candy.

She'd done the interview by correspondence, and her room, the bed, where we were sitting right at that moment, was in the background. It was a weird feeling. Lady's face appeared on the screen, and I clapped and whooped and kissed Lady's cheek. She blushed. I loved that blush.

Lady went, "We don't have to watch this."

And I went, "Are you fucking crazy? It's your first big interview! Of course we're watching it." I put my arm around her, and she rested her head on my shoulder, but something was up. She felt too stiff, or something. Too rigid.

The interviewer said, "So, Lady Lane, tell us, how did you become a sex worker?"

"I've been doing it my whole life," said Lady. "I love my work. I love connecting with guests and making people feel good, both in their minds and their bodies. I find my job really rewarding, and since I started at the Hop, I've felt more safe and supported in the industry than ever before."

I squeezed her arm. "You're doing amazing," I said. "You're perfect."

Lady looked like she was going to cry.

"Do you have anything to say about the Desert Shores Killer?" the interviewer said. "Do you think these horrific events would stop if sex work were to be more broadly legalized?"

Lady shifted, not the body beside me, but the face on the screen, her jaw tensed, just slightly, so slightly you wouldn't notice it unless you really knew her, really loved her. "I don't know," she said.

"You don't know?" I said, turned to her, the real Lady, the one beside me.

"You don't know?" said the interviewer.

Lady, the one beside me, chewed her lip.

"I don't feel comfortable speaking to that subject," said the Lady on-screen.

I turned the TV off and faced her. "You don't feel comfortable speaking to that subject? You don't feel comfortable saying that sex work should be legalized?"

Lady Lane
(NÉE KATE BURNS)

Mia left. She didn't kiss me, didn't hug me, wouldn't touch me. "Mia," I said, and she turned, giving me a chance to explain. But what was I meant to do? Tell her about Daddy's threat? I knew that Mia, given the choice between speaking out about the realities of sex work and saving her own life, she'd choose the industry in a heartbeat. Me? I chose Mia back then, and I'd choose Mia every time.

• • •

I had a booking with a VIP, a CEO, a billionaire, you know him. He wanted to take me on a weekend-long date, and I begged Daddy to let me stay at the Hop.

I said, "Please, Daddy, I can't go." I needed to make things right with Mia.

"These are important connections to make, Lady," Daddy said. "Get your head in the game."

The CEO took me to Vegas. The city looked like it was having a mid-life crisis. Wearing too much cologne and too much jewelry and staying up too late to sleep with strangers, finish the bottle, cut another line, dance until its buildings had blisters, until its streets were bruised and bleeding out. It was night when the CEO and I arrived, but the lights were so bright I cupped my hands to my eyes and blinked.

He wanted me to sit at his side, quietly, no, *silently*, while he played blackjack. People raised their phones at us, and at first I assumed they were taking his photo—he was famous, after all—until one woman asked him to step out of the frame. She wanted my picture, and mine alone.

One woman came up to me and asked if she could give me a hug. And I said, "Oh, I'm not her. I'm not Willa Jordan."

And she said, "No, you're the one from the tape, right?"

"Oh," I said.

She hugged me and said, "Does it look like I sold my body?"

I said, "No?"

She laughed and said, "No, that's your line. You said that."

A lot of people recognized me. I signed so many chests, my only pen ran out of ink. Some people thanked me. Some called me a slut. The CEO and I walked down the Strip hand in hand, paparazzi in tow, past all of these women standing in a line. I asked the guest what the women were doing, and he raised an eyebrow at me, like *Are you stupid?*

They were hookers. They wore tall heels and thick makeup and cheap nylon dresses that clung to their bodies like lovers. I knew I should've been feeling grateful or something, that I should've been thanking someone—Ma, God, Daddy, my lucky stars—for giving me the gift of the Hop, but all I could think about was where those girls bought their clothing. Whether, just down the street, sandwiched between a 7-Eleven and a liquor store, there was a Hookers "R" Us, racks packed with tacky sequins and thongs with tassels that swayed at the slightest movement.

"Hey," said one of the women, tall, dark-skinned, gold-glittered eyelids. "Willa," she said. "Willa Jordan."

The woman had scabs on her face, welts framing her mouth, a bruise on her cheek, and her eyes were red with bloodshot. "Willa," she said. "It's me. It's Mercedes."

The CEO tugged my hand.

"Mercedes?" I said.

"Remember me?" said the woman. "Remember me from the Hop, Willa?"

I said, "Mercedes Bends, right?"

"Mercedes Bends." The woman laughed. "I forgot about that shit. Funny. Funny shit. How are you, Willa? How's everything? How's the Hop?"

The CEO pulled on my wrist, hard. He said, "Let's go."

"You take care of my regulars," said Mercedes as the CEO dragged me down the street. "You take care of that room, Willa, because I'll be back. I'll be back for it and I'll be back to Bunnying in no time. I was made to be a Bunny, you know. Daddy was always telling me I was made to be a Bunny." We were barely in earshot anymore, but Mercedes was still going. "I'm a natural," she shouted. "Daddy's always telling me that. Daddy says I'm a natural. Daddy thinks I'm perfect."

The hookers tossed business cards into the air like confetti. Up ahead, a Black woman in tall heels and a tiny dress was facedown on the hood of a police car, surrounded by cops. One held her hands behind her back. Another shoved her face against the car.

"What did I do?" she said over and over.

The other women backed away.

"Why're you only arresting me?" the woman said, her cheek hard against the hood.

"Should we do something?" I said. The CEO ignored me.

"Tell me why you're only arresting me, Officers," said the woman. "Because I know you know I'm not the only one."

The officers didn't respond. The woman began to cry. Her face glowed blue and then red and then blue and then red.

• • •

The CEO checked us into separate rooms at the Bellagio. He didn't want me, it turned out. He just wanted to be seen with me.

Mia

(NÉE YA CHAI CHEN)

We were all sitting in the parlor, us clearance Bunnies and Lady, who was back from her VIP date, who I was trying not to look at, I was still so hurt, so betrayed by her. She kept trying to catch my eye, and I kept turning away. That's when Rain came in, crying, sobbing really—looking just terrible. When I asked her what was up, she went, "She's gone."

"She's gone?" I said.

"Dakota's gone."

Rain

(NÉE ASHLEY SMITH)

I got back from an overnight at a VIP's house. It was this white guy with an exoticism thing, which is always, you know, I was born in Michigan, but he kept saying, "I'm so happy to be sitting across from such a beautiful African woman," and when I offered to get us a round of drinks, he said, "You're such a strong, independent African woman," and was it offensive? Yes. But the whole time I imagined going home to Dakota and telling her the story and watching her face light up, the way she'd rock back and forth, clapping, laughing, tears pooling in her eyes.

So, when I got back to the Hop, I went straight to Dakota's room. I'd stolen this cute little gnome from the guest's bookshelf to give her. Dakota loved gnomes. Collected them. I wrapped it in a bow and took it to her room, but when I opened the door, it was empty. Cleared out. Her stuff was gone, her smell was gone, she was gone. Just like that. Gone.

Lady Lane
(NÉE KATE BURNS)

We were all sitting in the parlor, and Mia was refusing to look at me, she had tears in her eyes and her mascara was bleeding and I itched to wipe the smudges on her cheeks, but she wouldn't let herself within an arm's length of me, when Rain came running in and told us Dakota was gone. Everyone stood to hug her, and I said, "She's gone? Where?"

They stared. Sometimes I still felt so new at the Hop. Even almost two months in.

"Daddy let her go," is what Betty said.

"Let her go?"

"Kicked her out," said Rain.

I couldn't believe it. I had stuck to his stupid script, and for what? What I realized, then, was that his ultimatum to me was a false one. He was going to do whatever the fuck he wanted, whether I agreed to his terms or not. His threats weren't empty, but they weren't honest either, and they had nothing to do with me.

Daddy arrived, and we all turned on him.

"Daddy," said Rain, charging up to him, her cheeks a furious red. "Where's Dakota?"

"Dakota and Ginger had to leave," said Daddy. The lights went out, and everyone was quiet. The resets had a way of pressing pause on any scene. The Hop broke for a moment.

When the lights came back on, Mia was holding Rain around the waist and Betty had an extra supporting hand on her shoulder. They were holding her, but really they were holding her back. She wanted to fight.

"Where'd they go, Daddy?" I said. "Where is Dakota? Where's Ginger?"

Daddy shrugged. "That's up to them," he said. "They're big girls. They can do what they want."

"You sent them to the streets?" I said.

Mia

(NÉE YA CHAI CHEN)

Us Bunnies, we looked after each other. Hell, no one else was looking after us. The world wanted us dead, our country wanted us outlawed, and Daddy wanted our money, but we were sisters and we were a community and a family and soul mates, us Bunnies. We showed up for each other. When Daddy sent someone to the streets, it was an attack on the whole family.

Betty

(NÉE JOSHUA BETTS)

We looked out for each other, sure, but there was only so much we could do. Daddy was in charge, and he never let us forget it. As a kid, in high school, I worked at a tech store. The manager made us do team-building exercises every week, fall into our colleague's waiting arms and hold hands and lean back and share fun facts about ourselves, and then, once a quarter, he'd compare our sales figures across the board and fire the bottom two earners. I'm not sure that community can really exist where hierarchy does too.

Vincent "Daddy" Russo

People act like I sent these girls to the slaughter. I didn't. I fired them from their jobs for underperforming. That's what I did. That's business. They knew the risks on the streets, and if they didn't want to take those risks, they should've got themselves grocery store jobs instead.

Mia

We were still all sitting there in the parlor when Willa Jordan turned up. And we were all kind of just like, *Girl, not now.*

Betty
(NÉE JOSHUA BETTS)

She walked through the front door like it was totally normal for her to be there. She's pretty, Willa Jordan is. Boring, but pretty.

Willa Jordan

(NÉE HANNAH SNITCH)

The Hop looked just the same as the last time I was there. Four years ago, when I arrived fresh from a shift at Cowboy Joe's with a Steve Irwin accent and the name Hannah Snitch. Daddy had showed me the grounds (that fountain, those gardens) and told me he could sense something, *something special*, about me. Knew I was going to be a big deal. I'd been suspicious, certain he said it to every new Bunny that walked through his big pink door, but I believed him because I wanted to.

He was always telling me I was a natural, Daddy was, but nothing about what I was doing felt natural. I learned how to make men love me, learned how to be loved. Be beloved. When a man wanted to be dommed, I changed into leather and cracked my whip. When a man wanted to be coddled, I tucked my head into his neck and let him talk my ear off. Once a guy wanted to me to stomp on him in my scariest stilettos, and I strapped the shoes to my feet and climbed aboard and I didn't stop until he was bloody all over from the special acupuncture session. I did it, but it never came naturally, not to me. I wanted to be an actress.

I didn't love being a Bunny, but I was good at it because I was a good actress. It took me two months to become Daddy's best seller. To become Daddy's favorite. He came to my room each night, mug of hot cocoa in hand, paternal, romantic, dropped two marshmallows into my drink and sat, sipped a dark lager as we talked business, to begin, but our conversations had a way of wandering, meandering into the meaningful.

The sorts of conversations that left you feeling full and sleepy. When Daddy left each night, I missed him. I wondered more than once if what I felt for him was love.

. . .

When I walked into the parlor that day, not long after Lady's tape leaked, the Bunnies all turned to stare, cold, but Daddy smiled. He smiled like he'd known I was coming.

"Willa," he said. He rubbed the stubble on his chin and grinned. Stood. Walked toward me, tall as a tree, and held out a hand to shake. "Willa Jordan," he said. "Well, I'll be."

Betty
(NÉE JOSHUA BETTS)

Willa ignored Daddy and the rest of us and she pointed at Lady and said, "I want to talk to you." I thought she was going to beat Lady up. Slap her for taking her man, you know. I was a little disappointed when that's not how it played out. I liked Lady fine by then, but the girl probably could've used a slap around the ears.

Lady Lane
(NÉE KATE BURNS)

Willa Jordan looked at me, and she said, "You." She said, "I want to talk to you."

She looked less like me in person. Up close she was glowier, shinier, she looked richer and cleaner and more famous. Light seemed to move with her, around her, compliment her at every turn. "Lady," she said. "Right? Lady Lane."

"Yes," I said.

"I'm Willa," she said.

"I know," I said.

"I'm sorry about Liam," she said. "He's such a brat."

"A brat," I said. I was stupid. Blank. I didn't know what was happening, but I knew that everything seemed to be happening at once. I looked at Mia, kept looking at Mia, but she still couldn't meet my eye.

"I have a proposal for you," Willa said, and then she told us about her idea for a movie. She wanted to make a movie about the Hop. The ins and outs of sex work. She wanted my story, specifically, from the beginning. When I asked why me, she said, "You're what everyone thinks of when they think of sex work right now. Thanks to that tape, you're the face of the industry."

I could feel the other girls' stares. I looked at Daddy.

The Bunnies waited, waited for me to do something, all of them except Mia, who poured herself a cup of Pink. I would've done anything to get her back on my team.

"You want to make a movie?" I said to Willa. "You want me to be in a movie?"

"It's more like a documentary. It's a polyvocal script," she said. "Jumping around between different women in the sex work industry. I always wanted to make a movie, but I was just kind of playing around with the idea until, well, now feels like the right time. I figure that the best way to get on top of this little hiccup in my image, your tape with Liam, is to confront it face on, right? My agent wanted me to release an apology statement, but that was a Band-Aid and not a solution. Have you seen the internet? It's brutal. People are animals on that machine. They would've found out about my Hop days eventually, and then I'd have an even bigger issue on my hands. So," she shrugged, "I decided I'm going to own it. My past. I'm going to make it into art. It's the only way. I have to tell the world myself, about myself, from my own mouth, I have to say it so they don't say it in the wrong way. I'm going to make my past into something beautiful. Take control of the narrative."

"Take control of the narrative."

"That's right."

"And you want me to be in it?"

"I want you to *be* it," said Willa. "It'll make you a star."

She went on, "It'll be low-budget and scrappy. Rough. I want to make it over the next few weeks. And I do mean weeks. I've got to get on top of the story first. I want to tell the whole thing. It's already script gold. A handsome brothel owner falls in love with one of his hookers and turns her into a celebrity. An up-and-comer tries to fill the void left by said celebrity and gets famous in the process. The leaks, mine and yours. How entangled we all are. The Hop will be our set—look at it, it was made to be in the movies. I want the real authentic Hop to shine through. It'll be good for your sales, Daddy. I know your sales are down. Porn's everywhere, and there are all of those online escort services now, and you've got to be competing with the internet. Right? I bet that Big Fans site has taken a bunch of your traffic. Seems like everyone's a porn star these days and brothels are becoming irrelevant. I mean, aside from Lady, who—well, I'm assuming your sales are up, because of me, mostly, no offense—but I'll bet the rest of your sales are down, Daddy. Big time. Am I wrong? But set a movie here, *my movie*, Willa Jordan's director debut? Her tell-all exposé? The story, the scandal, of her life. People will watch it all over the world. People will be lined up out your door, all the way to the highway. You'll never have a quiet day again."

Daddy looked at me. Then at Willa. "You'll only paint the Hop in a positive light," said Daddy. "No twisting things around."

"Fine," said Willa.

Daddy said, "And I want veto rights. You paint the Hop in a good light, you only interview my best sellers—Lady, Mia, Betty—and you run every single word by me before you wrap."

Willa nodded. "Deal." They shook hands.

The Bunnies looked at me.

Mia

(NÉE YA CHAI CHEN)

Lady said, "I won't do it."

I looked at her then.

Daddy blinked. "You *will* do it."

"No," said Lady. "No, I won't do it."

Willa took her by the shoulders. "I get that you're scared, honey," she said. "It must be really scary having your name out there, being associated with sex work when sex workers are dying every day. You must be scared. But we will keep you safe. I promise, okay?"

"No," said Lady. "No."

Everyone stared.

Willa said, "I'm putting my life on the line too, Lady. I'm outing myself as a sex worker too. I know that's scary but think about how many lives we could be saving. This movie, we're going to bring all of this to light. We're going to be honest and real and we're going to help people understand the industry. We're going to tell our stories."

I took Lady's hand, then. Squeezed her fingers. She needed me more than I needed to be angry. Lady squeezed back. "I'll do it on one condition," she said. "I'll only do the movie if Daddy promises to bring Dakota and Ginger back."

"Lady," said Daddy.

"Daddy," she said. She looked calm, sounded cool, but her hand was wet and clammy with sweat. I wanted to jump her bones right there in the parlor. Instead, I kissed her cheek.

She said again, "I'll do the movie if you bring Dakota and Ginger back."

Rain started to sob.

Betty

Morale was high around the Hop for a while after that. Dakota was coming back, Ginger was coming back, and some of us were about to be in Willa Jordan's movie. Lady was going to be the star of the show, of course she was; Willa Jordan was casting, and Willa Jordan was white, pretty, straight, and cis, and if she couldn't cast herself as the lead, she'd cast her lookalike instead. Willa had this big dream. She wanted the film to change the way the world thought about sex work but even by the greatest stretch of her imagination she couldn't put anyone other than a white girl in the spotlight.

Still, things were looking up, and the rest of us finally got our sales back to almost normal, what with Lady being so booked. Everyone had something to be happy about. A bachelor party came in and booked a full house, which meant every Bunny working that night would be in the parlor with the guests, milling around, chatting, drinking just like a house party back in the real world. I loved parties, darling, and the Hop knew how to throw a party.

Rain

(NÉE ASHLEY SMITH)

The Hop's parties had a way of turning into orgies. It's what was expected from a room full of hookers and twelve drunk guys about to see their friend get hitched, but the guys who came in that night were older. It was a second marriage, and the rest of them were wifed up with a couple of kids each, and they weren't really interested in sex so much as being at the most famous brothel in the world for a night. So we set up a poker table in the parlor and played deep into the night. The men were too drunk to be any good and Lady and Mia were only interested in looking at each other and Betty's bluff face is a telling pout and I was the only one hungry enough for the money to try at all. I came out of that game with a couple grand to give to Dakota, and that's not a bad night. Daddy broke up the party around two a.m. Lady was meant to do an interview the next day.

Lisa Hamilton

(FEATURES EDITOR, *VOGUE*)

The news got out. The girl from the leaked Liam Carson tape, Lady Lane, was going to star in Willa Jordan's directorial debut. It was a huge story. I got a call from Willa, who I knew from a number of features I'd done on her over the years, interviews about her rise to fame, about her own leaked photographs, and, most recently, about the James Bond remake she was cast in as the lead. She called me and said, "I want a cover story about my movie." She wasn't playing around.

Lady Lane
(NÉE KATE BURNS)

I did Willa's *Vogue* interview, and I answered the questions honestly, ignoring Daddy's script. I had the power now. I was the one in control.

When Lisa Hamilton asked why I got into sex work, I said, "I like it." I scratched Noodles's ears. I'd found him asleep outside Ginger's room the day after Daddy fired her, and when I picked him up, he growled and bared his teeth, but he'd slowly warmed up to me, and now he spent each day trembling in the crook of my arm. I'd taken to whispering in his ear. "Your ma will be home soon," I told him, and I wondered whether, to him, it sounded like a prayer.

When Lisa Hamilton asked what my family thought of my career, I said, "I don't have a family."

When she asked what was next for me, I shrugged and said, "This movie, I guess."

Lisa Hamilton

(FEATURES EDITOR, *VOGUE*)

She was giving me nothing. Nothing.

Willa Jordan

(NÉE HANNAH SNITCH)

Lady was so dead set on keeping her life a secret, but celebrities don't get to have secret lives. I tried to tell her that. I took her aside at the *Vogue* interview, and I was like, "Lady, listen, if you're going to be famous, you're going to have to try harder. You're going to have to give Lisa something to work with."

And Lady just said, "I don't want to be famous." She said, "I want to be a sex worker. I'm just doing this for my friends."

Well, Lisa loved that line.

Lisa Hamilton

(FEATURES EDITOR, *VOGUE*)

That was *the* line. We had it right on the cover. *I don't want to be famous.* As soon as Lady gave us that quote, I scrapped my whole idea for the photo shoot. At first, I'd had this vision of her in a low-cut, full-skirt white Marilyn Monroe—style dress. Balenciaga had made a shorter, sexier, more contemporary version of it for the upcoming season, and I'd thought it'd be perfect for the Lady Lane shoot. I wanted to stand her over a vent, wind blowing, a red lip, the whole deal. The only difference between the famous Marilyn shot and Lady's would be a pair of crystal bunny ears I'd commissioned from Swarovski, this jewel-studded headband with rabbit ears poking up, both of them covered in pink diamonds. It was incredible. I had the whole shoot imagined before I even met Lady, but when she said that line, *I don't want to be famous,* I reimagined all of it on the spot. She had to be naked. Vogue had never done a nude cover before.

Lady Lane

(NÉE KATE BURNS)

Vogue wanted me to be naked on the cover. I didn't mind. I'd always been comfortable in my bare body. It's how I felt my most real. In editing, they ended up winding a quote around me, over my chest and around my pelvis, so that I was wearing the line *I don't want to be famous* like lingerie. The only thing I wore in that shoot was a pair of diamond bunny ears, and Lisa, the interviewer, she let me take them home. I love those ears.

Willa Jordan

(NÉE HANNAH SNITCH)

At the end of the shoot, the photographer was looking through his shots, which were incredible, and he went, "Oh, and congratulations, by the way."

And Lady said, "Thanks, I guess. It's been so surreal."

And the photographer said, "So it's your first, then, I'm guessing?"

And Lady said, "My first photo shoot, yeah."

And the photographer laughed. He said, "No, I meant, your first kid."

Lisa Hamilton

(FEATURES EDITOR, *VOGUE*)

He showed Lady the photos he'd taken of her body, and sure enough, there was this little raised, rounded bump that made a slight shadow on her lower abdomen. She was pregnant. And I already had a good story based on her quote, the premise that she didn't want to be famous but would do what it took to save her industry, but this, her pregnancy, it changed things. The new story became this: an average woman, this small-town sex worker from rural New Zealand who didn't ever want to be seen, to be known, but now here was her body, betraying all of her secrets on the cover of *Vogue*. It was gold. No, it was platinum. That year, Kendall Jenner was the face of our September issue, but no one remembers that cover. People remember Lady Lane's cover.

·······························

Lady Lane
(NÉE KATE BURNS)

I think I laughed. I was like, "I'm not pregnant."

Willa Jordan

(NÉE HANNAH SNITCH)

She said that there was no way she could be pregnant. She said something about bloating and then another thing about a stomach virus, but that photo wasn't lying. She was knocked up, and I was ecstatic about it. I'd found the perfect ending to my movie.

Lady Lane
(NÉE KATE BURNS)

I couldn't believe it, so I decided not to. I went back to the Hop. I put myself to bed.

Mia knocked, and I invited her in. She said, "How was the shoot?"

I said, "Good."

And she said, "I'm proud of you." I think it was the first time anyone had ever said that to me. Maybe the first time anyone had ever been proud of me.

"Are you okay?" Mia said, looking at me, *looking* at me. I'd spent most of my life feeling like I was missing something. Ma, Daddy, they told me how I was going to be something, but Mia made me feel like I was enough just the way I was. She made me feel whole. People are always saying that you should be looking for your other half, but who wants to feel partial? If you ask me, you should be looking for someone who makes you feel whole all by yourself.

Mia said, "You know, you don't have to do any of this, right?"

But I did have to. I did have to because I wanted the world to think differently, and I wanted to help make changes. I did have to because people were holding signs that read DOES IT LOOK LIKE I'VE SOLD MY BODY? I did have to because I wanted to make the world better for girls like Mia and like Dakota and like myself. I did have to because I'd never been honest with myself, and now, finally, I wanted to tell the truth. Because if I was pregnant, hypothetically, unlikely, but *if* I was pregnant, I wanted my kid to know my whole story, no secrets, I wanted

her to know all of me in the way that I never knew all of Ma. I wanted
the world to be better for her, and I could help make that happen.

Daddy turned up, knocked lightly, and said, "Can we talk?"

Noodles looked up from his nap just long enough to snarl. Good dog.

"I'm busy," I told Daddy. I wasn't afraid anymore.

Mia snorted. Daddy looked like he wanted to throw something,
like he wanted to hurt me, but what could he do? I was responsible
for ninety percent of his sales at that point, and without me, he was
nothing. Bankrupt. He turned and walked away and Mia kissed me
and I kissed her back and she ran her hand down my arm, across my
stomach, and I felt a little flip in my gut, a flutter, and that's when I
knew. Or, I had known, but I was so good at keeping secrets, especially
from myself. My whole life I'd been avoiding thinking about the things
I didn't want to know. Ma's work, Lacey's addiction, the sister Ma promised but never brought home. Secrets are isolating. The size of a secret
is an arm's length, and that's how far it keeps you from the people you
love.

"Wait," I said to Mia, and she stopped in her tracks. I said, "I need
to tell you something."

Mia

(NÉE YA CHAI CHEN)

Lady turned the TV up to full volume and then, in a whisper, she said, "I think I'm pregnant." I froze. I was like, *how*? The Hop's so strict about birth control. But then I remembered the day she'd arrived. The way she'd slept with Daddy before I'd taken her for her physical with Dr. Oh.

I looked up at the red light on the ceiling. I said, "Are we happy about it?"

And she nodded, smiled this real, true smile. She *was* happy.

Then I said, "Do you know whose it is?"

And she said, "Mine."

Lady Lane

(NÉE KATE BURNS)

I didn't want to know who the father was. It could've been anyone. I didn't care. It wasn't relevant. Not to me. I said, "I don't want to know."

And Mia said, "But, listen, when Daddy tested you out, he——"

I said, "Daddy's had a vasectomy."

She said, "Did he tell you that?"

I thought back, but I could barely recall that day. So much had happened since then. I tried to remember, but then I realized that, honestly, I didn't really care.

"I don't think he has," said Mia. "And you hadn't had your physical."

I said, "It doesn't matter." I said, "She's mine." And then I said, "And I think I want to keep her, I mean, I know I do, I mean, I'm going to keep her, raise her, and so, you know, just, if you don't want any of this to happen"—I gestured between her body and mine—"Now would be a good time to back out. I'm giving you an out. No hard feelings."

But Mia, she climbed onto my lap and wrapped her arms around my neck and kissed me and she said, "You're going to be an amazing mother." She kissed her way down my neck, my chest, my ribs, to my stomach. She whispered, "You've got the most amazing mother."

Olivia Oh, MD

(RESIDENT OB/GYN AT THE HOP)

Lady Lane came in and told me she thought she was pregnant. She was right. She was about ten weeks in, which was exactly the amount of time she'd been at the Hop. When I asked her who the father could have been, whether she thought it was a guest or a partner from before her time at the Hop, she just shrugged.

Mia was there, with Lady, and she said, "Lady doesn't want to know."

I explained that we could do a paternity test, but Lady said, "I don't want one." She said, "What does it matter whose it is? Gary's, Daddy's, a guest's, this isn't their kid. This is my kid."

Then she took Mia's hand and looked at her. She said, "She's *our* kid, if you want her to be," and the way they looked at each other, well, they were very clearly in love, is all I have to say about that.

Lady Lane

(NÉE KATE BURNS)

One guest, a woman, Ma's age, she'd paid a premium to get an appointment with me and I was having trouble focusing because Willa wanted to start filming the next day and I was jittery. The guest was telling me that she'd always suspected she might be gay, but was raised religious, got married to a man she liked, sure, but definitely didn't love, had kids, got old. She was shy and embarrassed and she looked like she was in pain. She said, "Sorry, I'm blabbing. I'm nervous."

"I've always had a thing for Willa Jordan," she said, when I asked what she wanted from our time together. "Those are the kinds of crushes I let myself have because it seems like other women, straight women, they let themselves have those kinds of crushes. On celebrities, I mean, because they're not real people, you know? It's not really like a gay crush because it's a crush on an idea more than a person. And ever since I saw *California Girls* I've had a crush on Willa Jordan, and then I saw that video of you, you know the one, and some things resurfaced and, well, you really do look just like her, and I thought, What do I have to lose? I mean, really, what do I have to lose?"

I asked her again what she would like from our time together, and she laughed. "Maybe I should just go," she said. "I'm sorry, this was stupid." She stood and winced.

I said, "Are you okay?"

"I'm fine," she said. "I've got this . . . I'm sick," she said. "It's nothing."

"What do you mean?"

"I've got this tumor," she said. "And I kind of thought, I thought that before I died I might as well, you know, try this out. I might as well see what it's like to be, you know, with a, you know."

"You're dying?"

"The tumor. I fundraised all this money for the surgery. And then I woke up, and the doctors told me they didn't manage to get it all. I'd need another operation, and even then they weren't sure that they could get it all out. I couldn't afford all of that, but I could afford to do something."

"And you chose this," I said. "You chose to see me."

She picked at a hangnail. Her blush was deep and spreading across her chest. "I'm going to go," she said.

"Wait," I said. "Stay. Will you please stay?"

She paused.

"I'm nervous too," I said.

"You're nervous?"

I nodded.

"Why're you nervous?"

"Honestly," I said. "I'm better with men than I am with women. I know men. Women . . . women make me nervous."

"Women make *me* nervous," she said.

"Can I hug you?"

She nodded. I held her. She smelled of spring.

"I can't believe I just told you all of that," she said. "I've never told anyone that, and I just told you, a total stranger. Can you, I mean, do you have, like, doctor-patient confidentiality?" She laughed. "Of course you don't. Stupid."

"I can offer you collateral, though," I said. "I'll tell you something no one knows about me."

She stepped out of our hug, but I pulled her back in, aware of that little red dot on the ceiling, of Daddy, who was always, always watching.

"I'm pregnant," I whispered in her ear.

"You are?"

She knelt and kissed my stomach, and her touch was soft and sweet and I swallowed and swallowed to keep from sobbing. She reached for my fly and looked up and said, "May I?"

I smiled down at her. I wanted her to. I wanted her. I stepped out of my costume.

She gestured to my underwear. "May I?"

I nodded and she pulled them down, and for someone who had spent her life denying her own sexuality, she was good with her tongue, had the right ratio of quick to slow, soft to not.

When she left, she kissed each of my cheeks and thanked me. "And," she said, turning back before disappearing forever, "for what it's worth, you'll be good at it." She pointed to my stomach. "At that, I mean."

Willa Jordan

(NÉE HANNAH SNITCH)

We started filming. I wanted the finished project to be a documentary made up of individual interviews with Lady, myself, Daddy, and the other Bunnies, as well as some reconstructed footage, like Lady driving to the Hop, arriving, walking up to the front door. I wanted footage of her meeting Mia, getting the tour. I wanted footage of them skipping Lady's first ob-gyn visit, I wanted all of it spliced between these short little interview snippets, so it became a really full, whole story.

Lady Lane
(NÉE KATE BURNS)

The night before filming started, Mia sat on the floor of my room, painting my toenails pink. "I'm so scared," I told her.

"I mean, maybe you shouldn't be doing this movie," is what Mia said as she painted. "Are we sure this is a good idea? What about the baby?"

I slapped a hand over her mouth and turned the TV up. Daddy couldn't know. I didn't know what he was capable of and I didn't want to find out. Not yet. Not now. Once the room was loud enough for us to go unheard, I said, "What about the baby?"

"You've kind of got a lot on your plate."

"This is going to sound stupid," I said. Mia blew on my big toe to dry the paint. I said, "But I think this movie might be fate."

"Fate?"

"Fate. Like, I'm meant to do it. Like, I was born for it."

"Fate." Mia took a sip of her Pink and offered it to me, and just the sight of it, I caught the vomit in my mouth and swallowed. The morning sickness still hadn't subsided.

"You okay?" she said.

I ran to the bathroom and threw up in the sink.

"I'm worried about you," is what Mia said. "We need to take care of you. You're the most important part of all of this."

"Ma wanted me be an actor," I told Mia. I told her about Ma's acting lessons. About the day she took me to the mall in the city and told me to sit outside the automatic door and play homeless. She teased my hair big and rubbed my face with coffee grounds until it looked like I'd never taken a shower even once. I cried and held a plastic grocery bag out for change. I sat behind a cardboard sign that had ANYTHING HELPS. GOD BLESS written on it in crayon. A number of people stopped, dropped coins at my feet. One mother even gave me a twenty. I kept at it for a few hours while Ma trawled the parking lot for cans to add to our collection. I only stopped when a woman, maybe Ma's age, came around the corner shouting that I was on her turf. She was missing most of her teeth, and she was wrapped in a Thomas the Tank Engine blanket, and she smelled like rotten meat. She had her own sign in one hand (ANYTHING HELP'S. GOD BLESS) and a puppy in the other, its fur sparse and ugly but its belly full and round. I packed up and went back to the car, and Ma was sitting in the driver's seat smoking a cigarette. She checked the time. *Done already?* She thought each of my roles should take a full working day. *That's real method acting*, she said. I gave her the bag, and I'd made about a hundred bucks in just a couple hours and Ma looked at me like I was the real deal. *You're made for this*, is what she told me.

. . .

"See? Fate," I said to Mia.

"I always thought fate would be . . ."

"What?"

"Less pukey," Mia said. "You know, you don't have to be everything your ma wanted you to be. Maybe she wanted you to be something you weren't, so that she could be something she wasn't. Maybe she wanted you to be famous for her. That was *her* want. But you're allowed to want things for yourself."

I used my hand towel to clean the sink and looked around for another to wipe my mouth, but I was out. "Fuck."

"I'll go get one from my—"

"No. Don't go." I took her hand, and she didn't wince even though there might've been barf between my fingers.

....

Mia

(NÉE YA CHAI CHEN)

She absolutely had puke on her hands, but when you feel about someone the way I felt about her, when you're *really* in love with someone, you love all of them. Even their puke.

She said, "Don't go." So I didn't.

Lady Lane

(NÉE KATE BURNS)

Mia took my hands and ran them under the faucet, rubbed soap up to my wrists, and when they were dripping wet and clean, she frowned at them, then at my dirty hand towel, then she took off her T-shirt (GOD'S FAVORITE) and ran it under the water. She wasn't wearing a bra. I thought about breastfeeding. About work. Could I still work while I breastfed? Did I have enough money saved up to take maternity leave? Did I have enough money to support a brand-new life? And what if I couldn't breastfeed? What if I had the same breast cancer gene as Ma? Are you allowed to feed a baby from a cancerous breast? To shake the thoughts, I played my usual game—avoid thinking about one thing by thinking about everything else. Breasts. Nipples. I thought about the guest who wanted to suck my nipple and bleat like a goat, and then I thought about how a group of goats was called a trip, and then I thought about how a baby goat was called a kid, and there we were again. My scariest thoughts must've been hollow, because boy did they have a way of rising to the surface.

"Hey," said Mia.

"Hey," I said.

"Do you want to talk about it?"

"What?"

"Whatever's going on up there?" She knocked on my head.

"I'm really scared," I said. "Not of the movie. Of the baby." And it felt good to say it. It felt good to share the burden of fear.

Mia wrung out her shirt and pointed to the bed and told me to lie down. Then she pressed the damp fabric to my forehead, and all of those bad thoughts vanished, just like that.

"Thank you," I said.

"Now talk," she said.

"Ma died of breast cancer," I said.

"Right," said Mia. "I remember."

"I was just thinking, maybe this is dumb, I guess, but I was thinking, what if I have the gene? Am I allowed to breastfeed? And how am I meant to work while I'm lactating? What if I get breast milk on a guest? And what if I pass the cancer gene along to the baby? And what if she dies because of me? What if I kill her?"

Mia kissed my shoulders as I blabbed, then she said, "We'll figure it out." Just like that. *We'll figure it out.*

I closed my eyes. I was exhausted. I was so, so tired.

"I'll read you a bedtime story," Mia said. But I didn't have any books, and I told her just to turn on the TV, but she said that was not the same thing.

Then she said, "I have an idea." She went back into my bathroom and returned with a shampoo bottle. She sat on the foot of my bed and rubbed my feet and started to read, first in English, about lathering and rinsing and repeating, and then, when she ran out of English, she read it all again in French.

And for that night, everything slowed down enough for me to catch my breath.

I wanted to get the reconstructed footage shot first, because I knew Daddy could pull the plug at any minute, kick us off the property and leave us without a set. The Hop *was* this film, and we needed it. Without it, we had nothing. So, we dove right into the deep end.

Lady Lane

(NÉE KATE BURNS)

They made me look so much like myself that I didn't look like me at all anymore. The hairstylists and makeup artists, they were skilled in re-creation. Or translation. From reality to realism. The movie version of me had eyes like mine but made bigger by clever eyeliner and mascara tricks. The movie version of me had a mouth like mine but redder, skin like mine but so layered thick with product that I looked as if I'd been sculpted from clay or wax.

We were filming the Hop scenes first because Willa had told the whole crew she wanted to get out of Daddy's way as quickly as possible. She said, "We don't want to limit his business," but I'm pretty sure what she really meant was that Daddy could pull the plug on this whole project at any minute.

Willa Jordan
(NÉE HANNAH SNITCH)

The other reason I wanted to film the reconstructed footage first was because Lady was going to start showing, and I didn't know how Daddy was going to react to that news.

Lady Lane

(NÉE KATE BURNS)

I wasn't showing yet. That image, the *Vogue* one, was some trick of the light, some weird prophetic photography, but in person, you really couldn't tell I was going to be a mother.

Mia kept saying, "You're going to be a great mom." But I wasn't so sure.

Ma was always telling me, *I know I can't give you much.* She wasn't wrong. She couldn't send me on the field trips the rest of the class went on. How they'd board a bus, shuffle off to a museum, zoo, gallery, or beach once a term, get back giggly and excited and knowledgeable about some new thing they wouldn't quit talking about until the next trip I stayed behind from, too. Ma couldn't give me a connection at her company who could hook me up with a managerial role straight out of high school, like Oliver van Ness or Whitney Hughes, who were mediocre students at best, barely an extracurricular on their transcripts, but nonetheless employed into cushy white-collar work the day after graduation. No, Ma couldn't offer any nepotism. On a lot of nights, Ma couldn't offer me dinner. She couldn't give me a dress for my prom, or a pair of shoes to run cross-country. She couldn't give me piano lessons when I showed promise, and she couldn't come to parent night at school because she was busy entertaining a manfriend for a couple hundred bucks to pay off the last of our mortgage.

She couldn't give me much, Ma couldn't, but she could've given me what I really wanted. I wanted her to love me. To be proud of me. I wanted Ma to see me. And she could've given me that. She had a perfect set of eyes. *Twenty-twenty vision*, she was always boasting, whenever she got her eyes tested for a renewed driver's license. *You know why it's called twenty-twenty, bunny? Because I can see like a twenty-year-old. This eye?* She pointed. *Can't even drink in America. And this one?* She pointed. *Can't legally rent a car.*

What she saw in place of me, Kate, was a daughter she was failing to care for. She saw not my smile, but the way my teeth wonked because we couldn't afford braces. If I brought home a good report card, she only saw that she could never send me to college. I tried going the other way, too. It's how Lacey got noticed by her parents, after all. "Do something bad," Lace told me when I mentioned my want for Ma's attention. "Fuck something up. That always works for me."

It was true. The day Lacey got caught stealing tampons from the pharmacy, the day we were escorted back to her parents' place by a couple of cops, her father opened the door and whacked her right around the ears, once, twice; he barely acknowledged the cops, his eyes were so trained on Lacey. The next day, at school, she had a pair of black eyes and finger-shaped bruises up her arms. She'd had a whole night of parental attention.

But when I got suspended at sixteen because Danny Kipp told a teacher I'd charged him two hundred quid for touching my you-know-what, the narc, my ma just shook her head sadly and said, *I know it's my fault, bunny. Can't help teaching you all my bad habits.* She took me to the clinic for condoms and a free HIV screening, and while I was being tested she ran home for an appointment with a manfriend. She didn't come back until the night; the clinic's doors had long since closed, locked, and I was sitting on the bench outside, sharing a cigarette with a homeless guy who kept dozing off mid-sentence.

Instead of seeing me, her kid, the one who loved her unconditionally, instead of seeing everything I was, she saw what I couldn't be, and she thought she was the reason for that. When I asked for piano lessons, thinking I could make her proud, she picked up more manfriends than ever, maybe hoping to save for music school, although she never admitted to it because if she admitted to it she would have opened up the possibility for failure and Ma didn't like to fail, didn't want me to see her as a failure, and when I told her that I didn't need to go to music school, I meant it, because I cared about music, I did, but really, really, when it came down to it at the end of the day, all I wanted was for Ma to be happy.

She couldn't give me much, Ma couldn't, but I barely needed anything at all.

. . .

If she could've seen me now, making more money than I knew what to do with, my name in the news and a *Vogue* cover and a movie in the works, I wondered if she'd be proud of me. Wondered if she'd watch me act from the wings. If she'd quote my lines back to me like one of her shows.

Mia

(NÉE YA CHAI CHEN)

With Lady being cast in Willa's movie, she couldn't do many of her appointments, and so we all got our sales numbers back up. Higher than ever, actually. And I was glad to be seeing guests regularly again, but I also wanted to watch Lady film. She liked for me to be on the sidelines, she looked at me when she was feeling overwhelmed. She told me I felt like air.

Lady Lane

(NÉE KATE BURNS)

She did. Mia was oxygen. She helped me breathe.

Betty
(NÉE JOSHUA BETTS)

We were all sitting in the parlor, waiting for a lineup that was due in a few minutes, when Rain came in with Dakota. They were holding hands, and Rain couldn't keep her eyes off the girl. "You're back," Rain kept saying. "You're back. You're safe. You're mine." Doesn't it just make you sick, darling? Love?

When I said, "Where's Ginger?" no one had any answers.

....

Dakota
(NÉE JACY ADAMS)

Daddy had come to my room and told me to be out within the hour, or security would put me out themselves. I didn't know he'd done the same thing to Ginger that very day. If I'd known, we could've kept each other safe. But Daddy's power came from doing things in the night, keeping us all in the dark, literally, figuratively; he liked his Bunnies best with blindfolds on. And so I didn't know. I didn't know. And since I didn't know, I couldn't keep her safe.

Lady Lane

(NÉE KATE BURNS)

I knocked on the door to the Hop. Knocked on the door to the Hop. Knocked on the door. Knock, knock. I knocked on the door to the Hop. Knocked on the door. I knocked. I knocked.

"Cut!" Willa was always calling. "Cut, cut, cut." Then some kind of instruction. "Knock harder," or "Look more nervous," or "Why don't you try calling out, ask if anyone's there or something. More real, Lady. Make it more real." Most of the documentary was going to be made up of direct interviews, but Willa wanted some reconstructed footage in there too, and for that, I had to act. I had to act as my past self, as Kate, as whoever I was the day I arrived at the Hop. I'd changed a lot since then, since the day I arrived, poor and alone and unpregnant.

"Cut!" Willa called again. "You're bad at this," she said. I was. I was frustrating her, I knew that, but I had never been good with an audience.

Then I heard someone calling my name, and I turned and there was Dakota. She ran up and hugged me. "Rain told me you did it," she said, squeezing so tight I thought the baby might pop right out of me then and there. "Thank you," she said. "Thank you, thank you."

When she stepped back, she was crying, and Willa looked at her cameraman and said, "Did you get that, Dennis?" The guy gave a thumbs-up. "Okay," said Willa. "New idea. Instead of reconstructing footage, how about we just construct it. Lady, do you have any guests booked in the foreseeable future?"

But I wasn't listening to Willa. I looked around, and I asked Dakota, "Where's Ginger?"

Willa Jordan

(NÉE HANNAH SNITCH)

Lady was a bad actress, but she was a devastating presence. What I mean is that in order to get anything worthwhile, we had to capture her living authentically. We had to film her scenes as they happened to her in real life, in real time. So we started recording everything, all of it, a constant eye on her; more like surveillance than cinema.

Lady Lane

(NÉE KATE BURNS)

After the first day of filming, I noticed the blood. Daddy promised me he was still looking for Ginger and that he'd bring her back so long as I kept working and filming, that was the deal, but, that night, when I changed out of my costume, everything was wet and red. There was so much blood, heavier than any period I'd ever had, more blood than when I'd filed my teeth down to size, it was the most blood I'd ever seen, pooled in my underwear like a disaster. I called Mia, and Mia called Dr. Oh.

Olivia Oh, MD

(RESIDENT OB/GYN AT THE HOP)

She had a weak placenta. The baby was fine, but Lady needed to stop working. I told her she shouldn't be seeing guests, and that she shouldn't be in this movie they were making. I prescribed bed rest: she needed to stay horizontal if that baby was going to make it.

It wasn't even a decision for Lady. She just nodded. She knew what she wanted.

ACT VI

THE END

That bitch in the mirror like yeah, I'm in love.

Lizzo, "Soulmate"

Bell Hobbes

(NÉE MAYBELLINE BURNS)

It was a long bus ride from LAX to Carson City. Three hundred kilometers of desert, orange and open and flat, like driving on the sun. From there, I sat at a gas station on the outskirts of town, eating red licorice and asking strangers where they were headed. It wasn't safe, I knew it wasn't safe, but I'd come too far not to make it all the way to Kate, Lady, and it didn't take long, anyway, just an hour or so, to find someone en route to the Hop.

The parents had called. Brit had called. They knew I'd flown to LA, because the charge was on the emergency credit card, but I wouldn't tell them where I was headed. I didn't want them following me. This was a thing I had to do alone.

I hitched a ride with a trucker. He had a thick beard and a beer belly and breath that reeked of tobacco and processed meat. When I hoisted myself into the passenger seat, he held out a bag of jerky. He was like, "Hungry?" and I held up my Twizzlers in response.

"They'll kill you," he said, forcing a whole handful of meat into his mouth and chewing loudly. "Why you headed to the Hop anyways? You don't look like their usual clientele."

"I'm a Bunny," I said. "A new one." I didn't know why I was saying it, just trying the word on for size, maybe.

"You're a Bunny?" He looked at me, and I wished he wouldn't. His truck swerved to the right, and I held the corners of my seat. "How old're you, like fifteen?"

I was seventeen. "Nineteen," I said.

"Like hell," he said. "I got a fifteen-year-old back home, and she looks just like you. A lot like you."

"I look young for my age," I said with a shrug. "Which is a positive in the profession, you know. Men like young-looking girls."

"Not me," the trucker said. He shook his head so hard little beads of meat flew. "Not me, sweetheart. I like 'em older. Always had a thing for older ladies." He looked over. "No offense, though, honey. You're pretty enough. You're very pretty. Might even make an exception for you, you know." He winked and then laughed and then choked.

I closed my eyes and pretended to sleep the rest of the way.

Lady Lane

(NÉE KATE BURNS)

I told Willa about my placenta and Dr. Oh's bed-rest prescription. I was lying in bed, and Willa was sitting at my feet, and the cameraman was there, his lens pointed at us.

"What're we going to do?" said Willa.

But I knew what I was going to do. I was going to do everything I could to keep the baby safe. "Cast someone else," I said. "Everyone else here has more interesting stories than I do, anyway."

"You're the face of sex work," said Willa. "None of the other Bunnies have been on the cover of *Vogue*."

"I never asked to be," I said, but I'd been sent a copy of the cover, and it was something. That photograph, my naked body, the bunny ears, the slight curve of my belly, it was the first time I'd ever really recognized myself. Still, I said to Willa, "I never wanted to be."

And we were like that, stuck in a stalemate, a face-off, when there was a knock at the door. Loud and angry. Like the whole door was about to break down. I knew what'd happened before it happened. I looked up at the blinking red dot on my ceiling.

When Willa opened the door, he stormed right past her, ignoring his threshold rule, ignoring her entirely. He stood over me and said, "You're fucking *pregnant?*" I looked up at the blinking red light. *This is how we keep you safe,* is what Daddy had said about the cameras.

Vincent "Daddy" Russo

Lady had potential, but that's all she had. If she'd just listened to me, if she'd just done what I said, she'd be famous by now. The next Willa Jordan. A star. And instead, what was she? Pregnant. She was pregnant. She was of no use to me pregnant. I said, "So you're taking care of it, right?"

Lady Lane

(NÉE KATE BURNS)

By "taking care of it," he meant getting rid of it. "No," I said. "No, I'm having it."

"Well, then you're out," said Daddy.

"I'm out?"

"Dr. Oh said you can't do the movie, and you can't see guests, right?" said Daddy. "That's what you just told Willa."

I looked at the cameraman. Willa had gone, to give us a minute alone, but her cameraman's lens was still pointed at me.

Daddy said, "If you can't do either of those things, you're not really of any use to me, Lady. It's time to go."

Thoughts and prayers.

"You're firing me," I said.

"You're out," he said. "Pack your things. I want you out of the room by the end of the week."

"What're you going to do?" I said. "My appointments still make up the majority of your sales. You don't have a replacement."

I'd thought I had enough power, by then, to be invincible. Untouchable. But no one's untouchable to a man. They've always touched whoever the hell they want.

Bell Hobbes

(NÉE MAYBELLINE BURNS)

I knocked on the door to the Hop, this big, ridiculous pink door, and a woman opened it. She was mother-aged, normal-looking, and she was like, "Do you have an appointment?"

I was like, "Uh, no."

And she was like, "We're fully booked."

But I'd made it all that way and I was desperate, so I said the only thing I could think of. "I'm applying to be a Bunny."

The woman let me in. "I'm Cheryl," she said, and handed me an application.

Obviously, I didn't want to be a Bunny. I was a virgin. I was Bell the Plank, but the only way into this place without an appointment seemed to be by being a Bunny yourself. So I took the application, and I started to fill it out. Name, age, employment history.

"I'll need to take your photograph," the woman said as I filled in an imaginary emergency contact. I didn't have an emergency contact anymore; what would Brit or Meg or Morty do? Fly halfway around the world to come to my aid? It's called an emergency because it's emergent. I had no one to save me here. I wrote down random digits and hoped they sounded like an American phone number.

"My photograph?" I said.

"For Daddy, to see if you'd make a good fit."

"Daddy?"

"Who's this?" said a voice, a masculine voice, and there was a man, old, maybe fifty, or something, standing in the doorway to the parlor. He was big and strong, a cartoon of a man. Daddy, I assumed.

"Daddy, this is Maybelline," said Cheryl. "She's filling out an application."

The man, Daddy, he walked toward me with his hands in a frame shape, like I was a photo he was taking. "Maybelline," he said. "Is that your Bunny name?"

"She got the job?" said Cheryl. "She hasn't even finished filling out her—"

"She got the job," said Daddy, taking the application out of Cheryl's outstretched hand and folding it into a square, tucking it into his pocket. "I have an unexpected vacancy, and you are going to make the perfect"—he laughed—"Like, *really* perfect replacement. Wow." He paced around me, in a circle, touching parts of me with his fingertips, my hair, my jaw, my shoulder. "I'm not one for fate, but . . . wow. It's uncanny," he said. "Where are you from, Maybelline?"

"New Zealand," I said.

"New Zealand!" he said. "Amazing. How did you hear about the Hop?"

"I—" I looked at Cheryl, who, when I'd called and mentioned being Lady's sister, had called me, and I quote, a "fucking con artist," and so instead I said, "I saw the leaked Lady Lane tape." Which wasn't exactly a lie.

"What a coincidence," he said. "She's the one you'll be replacing."

"Replacing?" I said. "She's leaving?"

"She's leaving," he said.

"Has she already gone?" I said.

He frowned. "Why?"

Willa Jordan

(NÉE HANNAH SNITCH)

It was a disaster. Without Lady, my movie was nothing.

I called Daddy from my hotel's bar. My vodka was watered down. I knocked back the glass and ordered another in the time it took Daddy to pick up. The bartender looked at me in the way that meant he had recognized me. "Hey," he said. "Are you—"

"No," I said. I was usually personable with fans. It was important to my image. I was the down-to-earth celebrity. The actress you could get a beer with. I brought chicken nuggets to a movie premiere, once. *Willa Jordan*, people said, *she's just like us!* But I didn't have time to sign coasters or take pictures tonight. Daddy picked up.

"Willa Jordan," he said by way of greeting.

"Are you fucking serious, Daddy?" I said to him. "Fired? We've already started filming her."

My second vodka was stronger. The world treats you better when they think they know who you are.

"She can't do the movie anyway, Wills. And she can't see guests anymore, either. What other choice did I have?"

"You could try being a decent human being? You just kicked a pregnant woman to the streets."

"The Hop is a business," Daddy said. "It's my responsibility to keep the business running. Plus," he said, "I already found a replacement. Maybe my new girl can be in your little movie instead."

. . .

At the Hop, I didn't have much competition when it came to my type—I was the only thin, white Bunny at the time. It was a smaller institution then. A baby brothel. A sex start-up.

When Daddy arrived at my door with champagne and my first Bunny of the Month plaque, I popped the bottle and took a swig as he unbuttoned my jeans and knelt. I tasted, he said, like strawberries. I knew it was bullshit. I'd tasted pussy. But, drunk with power and bubbles and his tongue, I chose to believe him. He came back the next night. The next night. The next. Strawberries became our thing. I woke to punnets beside my bed. He bought me berry-themed lingerie, and on my birthday, my cake was pink and fruity. We fed each other bite for bite, like the movies, and sometimes he drizzled them in chocolate and once he put one inside me and it got lost in there. He laughed. I screamed and hurled the rest of the box at him. He laughed harder, and that only made me madder. I hit him, I think. Then he took my face in his hands, kissed me, and said, "Your face is just as red, right now." I looked up, the mirror on the ceiling, he was right. I was rosy with rage, my lips still red with juice. We spent the night taking turns putting our fingers inside me, trying to maneuver the stray berry out by the stem. When I told him I loved him, I wasn't lying. He didn't say it back.

The next morning I woke to an empty bed, and he had me shipped off to an audition within the week. See, Daddy doesn't see his Bunnies as his equals, and loving one of us as a partner would mean having to see us as people, not products. So I was barely at the brothel for six months before he sent me off to work in Hollywood. He got me an audition for a new soap, *California Girls*, and came into the city with me. He knew the director, shook his hand, nodded his head, and next thing you know, the role was mine.

My first day on set, the director took an immediate liking to me. "Daddy's girl," he called me. He stopped by my trailer just to talk industry, and he always brought me a glazed donut in the morning. He "didn't like his actresses to get caught up in the diet culture of Hollywood," he told me, handing over a jam-injected Krispy Kreme. I liked how real he was compared to everyone else. How he took me seriously despite my lack of credits. The first thing he'd asked me was whether I related to my role, not what he'd seen me in before, which was the question everyone else in LA liked to ask, even before a *How are you?* or a *What's your name?*

The other actresses on the show watched me with what I thought was jealousy, though he suggested it was envy.

After filming the first-season finale, he invited me back to his place for drinks. When I declined, since I'd promised to eat a celebratory dinner with Ange, he nodded and smiled and said, *I understand.*

But then, when the day was wrapped, as I wiped the heavy layers of makeup from my face, he opened my trailer door. No doughnut in hand, this time. Before I could turn to face him, he unbelted his jeans. He never touched me. Instead, I watched him jerk off in the reflection of my vanity. When he came, it covered the back of my head. I was eighteen and he was fiftysomething. I never told anyone, and I filmed two more seasons of the show. When he brought on a new girl, started bringing her doughnuts, I kept an eye on the young actress, a look she might have confused with jealousy.

Next thing you know, Daddy's leaked my Hop photograph, the one of my ass, and I'm off *California Girls* and into bigger, more serious roles. In Hollywood, men rule, and even as they're helping you, they're using you, manipulating you. To powerful men, women will always be more product than person. They make us into whichever object best suits their needs. You get used to it; you get desensitized, you start letting them have their way.

• • •

The bartender delivered a third vodka, unordered by me, and pointed to a guy down the end of the bar. I shook my head.

"Okay," I said to Daddy. "I'll meet your new girl." But I wasn't about to let Daddy control my movie. I wasn't about to let Daddy control any part of my life ever again. I tucked a fifty under my glass and stood.

"You too good for a drink, Willa Jordan?" said the vodka-orderer.

"I don't take drinks from strangers."

"Strangers?" he said. "I've seen everything you've ever been in."

Back in my room, I took the footage we had of Lady and I trimmed it down on my computer, ordered it, edited it. It was two minutes long, including the reconstructed material of Lady arriving at the Hop and then the real material of her hugging Dakota and her pregnancy announcement. It was a trailer. It was rough, choppy, amateur, but you could tell from even those two minutes of film that this story had heart.

Lady Lane

(NÉE KATE BURNS)

It was getting late. I was throwing things in my backpack, and Mia was taking them back out again. She was crying. I was crying.

"We'll figure something out," I said to Mia, putting Ma's journal in the bag. "We'll figure it out." But I don't know if I believed myself. I was pregnant. I couldn't work. I couldn't film. I was famous and fired and pregnant and meant to be on bed rest. The collection of situations I'd found myself in did not look good on paper, but I barely cared, couldn't find a way to care about anything beyond keeping the baby safe. It was a new animal, this version of me. Unknown to me, but not unfamiliar. What she felt like, more than anyone, was my ma. Ma, who kept me safe even when it was the frustrating decision, difficult decision, wrong decision.

Mia took the journal back out of the bag and said, "I'll take care of you, I'll take care of you," but what was she going to do?

I was going to have to fly home, to New Zealand, I was sure of that. I called Lacey to tell her I was pregnant and coming home, and she whooped, happy, as Mia howled. Lacey said, "Took you long enough. Come home right now."

Mia said, "This is her home."

And it can make you feel divided, having the self belong to so many places, but it can make you feel big too—that there is enough of you to belong to more than one.

I rubbed Mia's back. She kept saying, "I'll come up with a plan, I'll save this, I can fix this, I just need to think of a plan."

"It's okay," I said. "I'll be okay, I swear."

"We'll both leave," said Mia. "We'll go to New Zealand together. We'll become sheep farmers. We'll buy overalls."

"We're not becoming sheep farmers."

"We'll open our own brothel," said Mia. "We'll figure out how to open a brothel, and we'll do it. We'll get married so you can stay in the country and we'll open a brothel, my dream brothel, with health insurance, remember?"

I kissed her mouth closed. "It's okay," I said. "We'll figure it out."

Mia kissed me back, was still kissing me when she arrived. The new girl. My replacement.

Bell Hobbes
(NÉE MAYBELLINE BURNS)

She looked just like me. Lady Lane did. She was in bed, when Daddy
and I arrived at her door and she looked like bed is where she should
have been. In the video, she was tall, all legs and boobs and skin and her
voice was clear and everything about her shone with fame. Here, in her
room, she was pale and small. Her hair languished around her face
and her eyes were red and sad. She looked like me. I was like, "Hi?"

Daddy did introductions. "This is the replacement," is what he said
about me.

A bell rang, and Daddy looked back over his shoulder. "I have to
go," Daddy said. "Lineup. Mia, would you finish giving Maybelline
here the tour?"

When he left, I turned to Lady. "I'm Bell," I said.

Lady Lane

(NÉE KATE BURNS)

She was a littler, younger, cuter version of me, standing in the doorway. I looked up at the ceiling, at the me up there, and we exchanged a look. An are-you-seeing-what-I'm-seeing look.

"What the fuck," is, I think, what I said.

Mia said, "Holy shit."

"Sorry," said Bell. "But you don't happen to be, I mean, obviously you are, but, I mean, you're Kate Burns, aren't you? Or Lady, I mean? Lady Lane?"

I said nothing. She talked like me. She moved her hands like me. I looked back up at the ceiling, where I was. The real me. Or Ma. Or, not the young version standing in my doorway. Nausea rose, and I swallowed to keep the sick down. There were so many versions of me, I was starting to feel infinite.

"I'm sorry, I don't want to freak you out," said Bell. "The last thing I want to do is freak you out. But I think I'm your sister. Your biological sister, I mean. I think we have, or, I guess it's past tense, I think we *had* the same mother. Merrill Burns? She was my mother, biologically. Technically. I never really knew her. She gave me up at the hospital to my parents, the Hobbeses, you might know them, I think, your mother worked for them, after all. For us, I guess. Maybe you did too, actually, for a while, at Hobbes, the department store, back home in Auckland. Anyway, I just, I don't want to freak you out."

I looked at her, at Bell. I remembered Ma's pregnancy, the way she had left for the hospital promising a sister and then returned empty-handed, and I'd said, *Where is she?*

Ma had said, *Who?*

My sister, my mother's daughter, me.

"Hi," I said. "Hello."

"Hi," she said. "Hello."

"I'll give you two a minute," said Mia, standing, but I didn't want her to go. I pulled her hand until she sat back down, right there beside me, where she belonged.

"How are you here right now?" I said to Bell. I gestured for her to come in, to sit down. She hovered slightly above my mattress. Like she was afraid she might catch a disease from it. "It's clean," I said. She blushed and stayed perched on the perimeter. She looked rich because she was rich. "Why are you here, Bell?" I said.

"I tried to call. I saw your tape, and I went to your house, your old house, in Auckland, I mean, but you were gone and the house was for sale and I tried to call, I really did try to call, but that woman—Cheryl, is it? She was really adamant about protecting your privacy. Even when I told her I was your sister."

"So you came here?"

"So I came here."

"And Cheryl let you come see me?"

"Not exactly," said Bell. "I applied for a job," she said. "I got here today, I hitchhiked in from Carson City, and Daddy hired me on the spot."

"You hitchhiked," I said. "That's really dangerous."

Bell said, "But Daddy said you're leaving the Hop?"

"He kicked me out," I said.

"He kicked you out?"

Mia choked back a sob.

"I'm pregnant," I said.

"You're . . ."

"Pregnant," I said.

"So he's kicking you out?"

"He's kicking me out," I said. "He's, Daddy is, well, you shouldn't trust Daddy, okay? If you take one piece of advice from me, make it that."

"What do you mean?" said Bell. "I'm not staying. I came here because you were here. I don't want to be a Bunny. God, no. I'm a virgin. Plus, I have to finish high school. I have to graduate. I'm applying to college, you know, I can't, I never meant to, I mean, I don't think I could . . . no offense."

"Wait," I said. "High school? How old are you?" I tried to do the calculation in my head, but my thoughts were spinning, twirling, abstract and ungraspable.

"Seventeen," said Bell.

"Seventeen," I said. "Underage." I looked at Mia, who looked back at me. We had the same idea.

Mia said, "Have you signed your contract?"

Bell nodded. She took a piece of paper out of her pocket and handed it to me. It said her name, the date, and the date she was born, her *real* age: seventeen. The contract was signed twice, once by Bell and once by Daddy. "Why?" she said.

I said, "You're seventeen?"

"I am," said Bell.

"She's seventeen," Mia told me.

"She is," I said.

Which is when Willa arrived, tipsy and teetering, and said something along the lines of "What the fuck is happening right now?"

Willa Jordan

(NÉE HANNAH SNITCH)

I turned up, and Daddy had managed to find Lady's literal twin. Like, Lady and I looked like we could be related. Our faces were alike, and they moved in eerily similar ways. We had some of the same mannerisms, and maybe, at a slight distance, you might confuse us for one another, but you could tell us apart without much trouble, and no one we really knew would ever mistake us for one another. But this girl, this new girl, Bell—she really *was* Lady. And I realized that Lady could do all of the interviews, the talking, from bed, and Bell could do all of Lady's parts in the reconstructed footage. That was really the only plan I had. The rest of the movie was going to be candid caught footage.

I said, "Holy shit," and then I said to Dennis, "Are you filming?" He was.

"Willa, listen," Mia said. "We have an idea."

They'd come up with an alternate ending for the movie and for, I guess, Lady's life.

Mia said, "What if we had a way to bring Daddy down?"

And I was all in. I was done with Daddy, and who doesn't love a takedown?

Lady Lane

(NÉE KATE BURNS)

Willa showed us her trailer, and it wasn't good. I mean, it was great, but it wasn't well done. She was bad at editing, and the sound didn't quite match our mouths' movements, our characters spoke before we did, but the result was something homemade and more real than it would've been if it were perfect. It looked rushed and urgent, and that was an authentic feeling. We *were* rushed. This *was* urgent. I had fewer than two days before I had to be out of the Hop. We had two days to tell a story, finish a movie, and show it to the whole world. Willa told me her plan. She was going to release the film online, snippet by snippet, as she filmed it. She'd upload each segment to a Big Fans page and people would have to subscribe to watch.

"But it's not pornographic," I said. "Big Fans is for porn."

"Doesn't matter," said Willa. "They'll just flag it as pornographic content anywhere else," she said. "YouTube, Facebook, Instagram, Tik-Tok. But if we upload it to a porn-streaming site, there's not much they can do. What're they going to do? Flag it for not being pornographic enough?"

Lisa Hamilton

(FEATURES EDITOR, *VOGUE*)

It was a new kind of movie and an old kind of movie all at once. It was porn meets the box office. It was Lovelace's *Deep Throat* with a political agenda. It was *Playboy* if only Hef were a feminist. It was camgirling with a plot, an Instagram Live meets breaking news. It was uncensored reality TV with a low budget and no prize at the end, but higher stakes than any old season of *The Bachelor*.

Mia

(NÉE YA CHAI CHEN)

Willa wanted to release the footage as it happened, in almost real time. She wanted to record constantly, 24/7, and then trim the footage down and put it online. It was almost performance, almost reality, a strange combination of the real and the not, and she wanted to start on the spot. It felt right. It felt like taking Daddy's power from him—that always-watching-eye—and using it for ourselves. The end of the movie, Willa Jordan said, would be our Daddy takedown. The whole world would see him fall, is what she promised. And we liked that idea. We all did.

So Lady lay in her bed and Willa asked her to tell her story from the beginning, the very beginning. Lady started with her own birth. She basically had one day, her last day at the Hop, to tell it all. She said, "I'll start from the beginning: I was named after the baby born just before me at Fenbrook Hospital. That's what Ma always told me."

Lisa Hamilton

(FEATURES EDITOR, *VOGUE*)

People caught on quickly. *Vogue* posted about it, and then everyone posted about it; the internet moves like that—online gossip spreads faster than an STI. We shared the link to Willa Jordan's Big Fans page, which was the platform she used to upload each episode of the story, and then, in moments, the link was everywhere. People joined by the thousands. They paid a couple of dollars to access the page, and the page had a couple of million subscribers all sitting there, watching, waiting to see how Lady's story unfolded.

The few minutes of tension between segments was a nostalgic one. Something akin to the pause between TV episodes, before Netflix and binge-culture, sometimes having to wait a week for the next installment. The anticipation only made Lady's story more interesting. Growth happens in that in-between, and the silences between Willa's latest segment and the next were full of conversation in the real world. Twitter was aflame with the hashtag #thehop. Important conversations about sex work and the legalization of it and women's bodies and privacy, all these big important things were on everyone's lips, but when Willa uploaded a new chapter of the story, it was like the whole world went silent just to watch.

Lacey Kahu

Lady told all of it. She told of her schemes with Ma, of the manfriends, the cancer, Hobbes. She explained the Sugar Club and the Purple Panther. She was unfiltered and unflinching. It was like hearing my story told back to me. I tuned in with the rest of the world. People tried to call me. Whitney Hughes and Oliver van Ness and Gary, all those bottom-feeding scavengers, they came crawling back and begged me for answers. They wanted to know if Lady was going to out them. I laughed in their faces. Or, you know, in their ears. Lady was doing so much more than getting her personal revenge. She was fighting back for the whole industry. For something that was all about her, it wasn't really about her at all.

Bell Hobbes
(NÉE MAYBELLINE BURNS)

Well, it was my story, too, wasn't it? It was the story of my life—the one I could've lived. It was the story I was never meant to know. The story of the life that Ma never wanted me to have. But I'll tell you something: that life didn't sound so bad to me.

Willa Jordan

(NÉE HANNAH SNITCH)

Lady sat in her bed, propped up against pillows, this little white poodle in her lap, and she talked. Mia rubbed her feet just outside the frame and listened. Bell listened. I listened. Lady was easy to listen to—she talked well. She storied well. She got so invested in her own memories, you could almost see the scenes playing out in her pupils. People were obsessed. There were more people subscribed to the Big Fans page than had gone to see my new Bond film on opening weekend. The page crashed from traffic every time I uploaded a new segment, and then Twitter crashed from the discourse following the segment. For just a minute there, for one single day, we ran the internet.

Everyone was waiting for the grand finale, and that was the part of our plan I was most worried about. Lady's stories were easy—they'd already happened. The grand finale of Ma was her death. The grand finale of Gary was a breakup. But the grand finale of Lady's time at the Hop? The whole world was desperate to know, and they'd learn how it went in real time, along with the rest of us. I breathed along to my Breathe app just to make sure I was still doing it. A couple of Bunnies joined in and we exhaled in time. It felt good, that we were all in this together.

Lady Lane

(NÉE KATE BURNS)

Ma loved a good takedown. She loved *Heathers*, when Winona Ryder kissed the mean girl on the cheek and said, *There's a new sheriff in town.* She loved it when Katniss and Peeta split the poisonous berries to break the system and bring down the Hunger Games. She loved it, in *Gone Girl*, when Rosamund Pike turned out to be the one in charge of her own disappearance. I think Ma thought that our life, too, probably had a plot twist waiting for us.

I'd learned a lot of good from Ma. I'd learned my worth, and that I had talent, and that I did not need a man in my life. She fed me, clothed me, and, and I really believe this, she loved me. But she kept a lot from me, too, her work, her pregnancy, herself. You can't really know someone unless they let you.

I didn't want what Ma wanted. I didn't want the big love of fame. I wanted to let myself be known, loved, a little love, a quiet love.

Willa Jordan

(NÉE HANNAH SNITCH)

The best thing about Daddy watching the Hop so closely, his constant surveillance of his Bunnies, was that he was too preoccupied to see any of our Big Fans content. He was so obsessed with controlling his world that he barely took notice of the outside world at all. What he could see, on his security feed, was Lady sitting in bed, and the rest of us sitting around her, like she was telling us a story or bidding us an elaborate goodbye. He didn't know she was talking to the whole world. And he didn't know what was coming to him. And it was. It was coming.

Bell Hobbes

(NÉE MAYBELLINE BUNS)

The takedown was a three-part plan. They sent me in first. I knocked on Daddy's office door, and when he opened it, he was all smiles and all sleaze. He ran a thumb down the side of my face, and my instinct was to bite it right off. I didn't, even though it would've made a great scene. Instead, I smiled right back at him. My drama teacher was always saying that the most important part of acting was to fully believe your role. Become the character. I leaned into Daddy's touch. Behind him, on his computer screen, a grid of thumbnails, each playing a different scene. I saw Lady's bedroom, there, with her in the bed and the other Bunnies crowded around her.

"What's that?" I said.

"That's how we keep you safe," said Daddy.

I bit the insides of my cheeks until they bled.

Daddy said, "So, your tour's over? How'd you like the grounds, new Bunny?"

I said, "It's gorgeous here. I love it. Thank you so much for hiring me."

He said, "Don't thank me. You're perfect. You're exactly the replacement I was looking for. I should be thanking you."

I glanced at Willa and her camera guy, who were right around the corner. She shot me a thumbs-up, and just like that, we had a confession. Daddy'd hired an underage girl, and we had the evidence on tape.

Willa Jordan

(NÉE HANNAH SNITCH)

The plan was innocent, really. We didn't want to lie or manipulate any of the facts. We just wanted the world to see Daddy. Who he really was.

I knocked on his door, and he opened it and did his usual Daddy thing, held my cheek, turned my head left and then right, an inspection, an examination. "You're still perfect, you know," he told me.

"I know," I said. He laughed, and his laugh—well, you can't blame me for falling for Daddy back in the day. He did have something.

"When can I film you?" I said.

"Film me?"

"For your interview?"

"I'm going to be in the movie?"

"Sure," I said. "You should say your part. Talk about how you keep your girls safe and how you abide by all regulations. Make sure everyone knows you're running an aboveground place. Don't you think?"

Daddy nodded. "That makes sense."

"Do you want to change first?"

Daddy was wearing a Stetson and a flannel, his uniform. "Probably," he said. "Should I put on a suit?"

"Unless you want the whole world seeing who you really are."

He laughed. "You know I've got nothing to hide, Wills."

"Oh, come on, Daddy," I said. I put my hand on his leg and worked my way up his thigh. His eyes clouded over, and I loved that familiar buzz of power. "You have a few skeletons in your closet. It's what makes you interesting."

He swallowed hard. His Adam's apple looked like it might choke him. I kissed his neck and said, "Leaking those photos was the best thing you could've done for me. You might bend the rules, Daddy, but you look after your girls."

Daddy caught my chin in his hand and looked me dead in the eye. He said, "Damn right I do."

And that was enough of a confession for me. We weren't trying to prove anything to the cops—we just needed to prove it to everyone else. So I stood, dusted off my lap, and said, "Well, best be going."

I left him sitting there with his chin on the floor. I didn't like being a Bunny, because I had other dreams, but man did it feel good to render a man speechless.

———————————
·······························

Lady Lane

(NÉE KATE BURNS)

I pressed my panic button, and Daddy came running.

"What?" he said.

"I just wanted to say goodbye," I said. "I'm leaving." I pointed at my packed bags.

"Well," said Daddy. "Good luck with everything." He turned to go.

Mia was at my bedside. Noodles was on my lap. Betty and Rain and Dakota and a handful of other Bunnies were there too. There was a hole in the room where Ginger was meant to be. She still hadn't been found. The other person missing was Willa's cameraman. Daddy couldn't know he was being seen, so instead of using Dennis and his big camera, Willa was recording the interaction on her phone, uploading the footage in real time to Big Fans Live. The whole world, for the first time, was watching him, instead.

"Kicking a pregnant woman to the curb," I said, and Daddy turned back. "A real classy move."

"You can see why I have to let you go, though, can't you?"

"Because I can't work."

"Right."

"Because I'm pregnant."

"Right."

Daddy was already halfway out the door when I said, "Daddy? The baby, *this* baby—it's yours, you know."

He didn't even turn around. Didn't even look back. I was no longer the body he needed me to be. And despite everything, despite myself and the way I felt about Daddy, despite Daddy, and despite all of it, it hurt. Mia squeezed my hand. She'd been outside the frame during filming, but it suddenly felt wrong that she wasn't in the picture. Mia, who loved me, all of me, entirely. I pulled her up to sit beside me, and she did. She kissed the tears from my cheeks.

———
·················

Mia
(NÉE YA CHAI CHEN)

She was crying, and I lost my shit. I don't get angry, not often, not really, but seeing Lady in bed, holding her belly, watching Daddy walk away from her, tears rolling down her face, well . . .

Lady Lane

(NÉE KATE BURNS)

Mia said, "Daddy!" And Daddy turned around. Willa went wide-eyed—
this wasn't part of the plan. The whole world was seeing this live.

Then Mia said to Daddy, who was standing right outside my room,
"We're people, you know." Daddy frowned, and Mia went on. "We're
people. You've been kicking girls out of the Hop for years, blacklisting
them so they can't get legal work ever again. You've been killing us,
girls like us, even while you say you're protecting us, but what you're
really doing is controlling us, using us, abusing us, and disposing of
us. You don't keep us safe, Daddy. You keep us scared. And we don't
want that anymore."

Daddy's jaw tensed. "So what? What's the big plan? Are you gonna
call the cops? What will you tell them, huh, Mia? You going to tell
them that I fire employees for underperforming? That's not an offense.
You going to tell them I let girls go for not meeting their quota? That's
business, Mia, not a crime."

"Bell is seventeen years old and you hired her. That's a crime."

Daddy's smile faltered, just a little. "So you're turning me in for
hiring underage girls?" he said. "Is that it? She hasn't even taken a
client."

"And we know you were the one who leaked Lady's security footage. And Willa Jordan's back in 2011."

Daddy smirked. "I see. And do you have proof?"

"No," said Mia. "We don't. But we also don't need it."

"I'm pretty sure the cops are going to want some evidence."

"We're not going to the cops," said Mia. "We're just going."

"Going?"

"Going."

"Going where?"

"It doesn't matter," said Mia. "What matters is that we're leaving you. All of us. And without us, all you are is a guy in a big pink house."

Daddy looked at the room full of Bunnies, and he didn't have a single ally left in the place. He shrugged. Said, "I can get more Bunnies in a heartbeat." Then he walked away.

"Good luck with that," is what Mia said to his retreating back. I loved her in that moment. I love her in every moment.

Mia
(NÉE YA CHAI CHEN)

Lady grabbed my face and kissed me. Willa got that on camera, too.

Lisa Hamilton

(FEATURES EDITOR, *VOGUE*)

The internet exploded. It was all anyone could talk about.

Lady Lane

(NÉE KATE BURNS)

I took my bag, the only bag I had, and I walked, or waddle-limped, to the parlor to say my goodbyes. Mia, in that heated moment, had told Daddy all his girls were leaving him, but I knew that couldn't happen. I didn't want it to happen. Those girls were safer at the Hop than they'd ever be out in the world, and I wasn't about to take anyone's safety from them.

Noodles followed me, trotting at my heels. He'd become my shadow, and I hated him, yappy little shit, but he was mine. Until we found Ginger, he was mine. I scooped him into my arms and he snarled, then sniffed me, then settled. There was an ache in my throat and a knot of muscle in my gut. Leaving was the wrong thing, I knew that. I loved my job and I loved my sisters, but the Hop was Daddy's house, and I couldn't live under his rules anymore.

The parlor was full. Every Bunny working that day was there, and they all had their bags packed too. I started to cry. The hormones, and all.

I said, "What the hell are you all doing?"

Mia said, "I told you, we're leaving."

"Everyone?"

"Everyone's seen Willa's footage. No one wants to work for Daddy anymore."

Betty took my backpack and slung it over her shoulder. "You shouldn't be lifting in your"—she eyed my stomach—"condition."

Rain and Dakota were holding hands. Rain said, "You thought we'd let you leave without us?"

I said, "We don't have work out there."

Betty said, "We could buy a Taco Bell."

Willa said, "We've made enough cash on Big Fans to last everyone for a while."

I said, "We don't have a plan."

Dakota said, "Speak for yourself. Rain and I are getting hitched."

Rain

(NÉE ASHLEY SMITH)

For some girls, leaving the Hop was an easy decision. Lady had to. Mia had to for Lady. Betty had a backup plan in her husband. Dakota and I, it was riskier for us, we didn't have the support the other girls had, but we did have each other, and we never had any kind of security in Daddy, anyways, and Willa Jordan promised that the Big Fans profits would be split between all of us Bunnies, and we figured that would tide us over until we could figure something else out.

I was still panicking. I didn't want us to end up working the streets, or homeless, or dead. I said, "Maybe we should just let the others leave. Maybe we should stay. We're safe here."

Dakota looked at me. "When was the last time you felt safe here?"

"You know what I mean. We need a plan."

And Dakota said, "Marry me. How's that for a plan?"

Dakota
(NÉE JACY ADAMS)

Love was enough of a plan for the both of us. So we left.

Lady Lane

(NÉE KATE BURNS)

I looked at the Bunnies. This room full of women wearing tiny costumes and heavy makeup and scared eyes. I said, "This is stupid."

Mia put her hand in my back pocket. "It only works if we all leave," she said.

"I don't want to leave," I said. "I like this job."

"None of us are leaving the job," said Mia. "We're leaving the Hop."

I said, "Girls are dying out there."

Dakota said, "Daddy could throw us out on our asses at any time."

Rain said, "Maybe it's better to be the ones in control of leaving."

Betty said, "Daddy isn't what makes the Hop safe, darling. We're what makes the Hop safe. And we're taking this show on the road."

I said, "We're all leaving?"

Mia said, "We're all leaving."

I didn't want to leave, but sometimes you have to do things you don't want to do in order to get the things you need.

Bell Hobbes
(NÉE MAYBELLINE BURNS)

It was . . . I don't know. I'll never forget the feeling in that room. Have you ever been backstage, about to perform, looking out into the darkness, squinting in the hopes of seeing what's out there? It was that. But there was safety there, too. It was finally spotting your family sitting front row. It was this room of support and security and sisters. I held my sister's hand, and she turned to me and smiled. She said, "And what about you, little one?"

I had to go home. I said, "I have to go home."

Lady looked around the room. "Well, we have to make a new one."

Willa Jordan

(NÉE HANNAH SNITCH)

The last shot is the one everyone remembers. It's the Bunnies, maybe thirty of them—all costumed up, made up, lined up, their suitcases trundling behind them as they walk out of the Hop, through the parking lot, and down the street, through the desert, off toward the horizon.

Lady Lane
(NÉE KATE BURNS)

It was a lineup in motion. We walked. We weren't walking away from the industry, but we were walking away from the Hop, and Daddy, and the danger he put us in. We were walking away, but we were walking toward, too. Toward what, we didn't know, but something. Toward something better. Toward something new.

....

Epilogue

LISA HAMILTON: Despite never showing at the movies, *The Hop* was a booming success. Lady Lane's face was everywhere for a while. She gave some great speeches about sex worker rights and the issues with the industry and how people think of it. She was a spokesperson for a minute, but then she sort of faded, slunk out of the spotlight, and I think she liked it better that way.

LADY LANE: My face was everywhere. They kept calling me the face of sex work and I was, but I shouldn't have been. The world was happy for me to be the face of the industry because of the kind of face I have. A white face. A thin face. But I wasn't representative of the industry. Most sex workers don't look anything like me. When people ask why I stepped out of that spotlight? It was never meant to be mine.

WILLA JORDAN: People loved *The Hop*, and I won awards for it, got a lot of acclaim, and that's all fine, but the real thrill, for me, was when Daddy found out what we'd been doing. He must've called me and hung up a thousand times. We never actually spoke—I guess he couldn't find the words to fit the betrayal. I know that feeling.

MIA: Daddy couldn't find anyone to work for him. Of course he couldn't; he'd told the whole world exactly who he was. So us Bunnies bought the Hop's grounds with the Big Fans profits, and we've applied to take over the business. We want it Bunny-operated. We want our bodies to be our own.

LACEY KAHU: I came to Nevada to be with Lady for the birth, and I'm staying for the Hop. I'll make more at the Hop than I ever made at the Panther, and I still don't have to do sex, Lady promised me. She said she'd be fine without me if I wanted to go back home, but, you know what, I like it here.

BETTY: My husband and I spent a few weeks in Cabo after all of that. I couldn't do the drama, darling. But I did like seeing myself on a screen. Have you seen me? I'm a star, aren't I? The movie might've been Lady's story, but it was her supporting cast who made her shine.

DAKOTA: Rain and I got married, but we haven't taken our honeymoon yet. She's . . . well, she's trying to save the world first.

RAIN: We still haven't found Ginger. No one knew her birth name, and we have no idea if she had any family out in the world. We had an oasis at the Hop because we were working legally, safely, and we had security systems. We were privileged as fuck. Most sex workers in the world don't have a panic button on their nightstand, and those girls are in danger of being murdered every day. When we open the new Hop, we're getting as many of those girls off the streets as we can.

LADY LANE: We're planning to hire a bunch of girls from the city, but there're only so many beds. There are twenty-one legal brothels in the United States and about two million sex workers. Does that seem right to you?

DADDY: Me? I'm opening up a new shop. The Cat House. Hottest girls in town. Call 1800-600-6000 for an appointment today.

LADY LANE: Daddy's new spot, the Cat House, got its approval before we got licensed to run the Hop. That's business for you. Mia thought we should go to the police with our evidence and shut him down, but the reality is, even a Daddy-run brothel is safer than the streets.

BELL HOBBES: I went back to New Zealand to finish high school, graduated, and now I'm at university, studying law. I'm specializing in sex worker rights and my thesis is on the Desert Shores Killer case. I'll still visit Lady every summer, and Mia, the rest of the Bunnies, and my niece, of course. She's the love of my life.

LADY LANE: Isn't she the best thing you've ever seen? Her name? Well, Mia and I named her the same way Ma named me, after the baby born before her at the hospital. Her name is Kate. Kate Ginger Burns. You can't make this shit up.

Acknowledgments

This book is the product of a thousand conversations. Conversations over cups of coffee, bottles of wine, steak dinners, pancake breakfasts, shots of whiskey taken quickly in the corners of strip clubs, walks in the desert, cigarettes on stoops, bedroom tours, weed-pulling, wall-painting, manicures, pedicures, long phone calls, middle-of-the-night texts, glitching Zooms, and letters through the mail; this story is a puzzle of stories told to me by women in the sex work industry, women who want to share their worlds, and who want to make their worlds better. Without these women, this book would not exist, and all of my gratitude belongs to them.

My sincerest thanks to my editor, Terry Karten, for asking all of the important questions, and for letting me find the answers myself.

To Susan Golomb, for taking me under your wing, thank you. Thanks, too, to the rest of my people at Writers House, who really know how to go to bat.

To my team at Harper, thank you for standing behind my stories. Thank you for helping them out into the world.

To my film agents, Addison Duffy and Jasmine Lake at UTA, for imagining my worlds anew.

To my teachers, Lindsey Drager, Paisley Rekdal, Michael Mejia, Sharon Solwitz, Brian Leung, and as always (and always and always) Roxane Gay.

To my pod: Jess and Matty and Nick and Corley and Jamie, thank you for making these hard years some of my best yet. To the rest of my U of U colleagues, thank you for reading with such smart eyes. And to Allie, thank you for your sisterhood, your friendship, for sharing your best bottles and wisest words. I will never not be in awe of your heart.

To my friends: Sand, Soph, Stace, Moz, Kels, Noah, Charlie, thank you for being my people.

To Bret, who I feel so lucky to be loved by, and so lucky to love.

To my grandparents, Diane and Sidney, the best cheerleaders, even from halfway around the world.

To my brothers, Nick and Andrew, for making me crazy and making me smarter, thank you for being my family.

To Dad, for being a rock, a moral compass, and my favorite Sunday phone call.

And to Mum, who I will never stop needing, and who I know will never stop being there.

Resources

If you are a sex worker needing support, or if you want to support sex worker rights and help make changes to the industry, these are some organizations who work toward visibility, destigmatization, policy changes, and legal and medical aid for sex workers:

- SWAN: www.swan.net

- The Sex Workers Project: www.swp.urbanjustice.org

- DecrimNOW: www.decrimnow.org.uk

- HIPS: www.hips.org

- COYOTE: www.coyoteri.org

- Global Network of Sex Work Projects: www.nswp.org

- NZPC: www.nzpc.org.nz

About the Author

DIANA CLARKE, who is from New Zealand, holds an MFA from Purdue University, where Roxane Gay was her thesis adviser, and is in the doctoral program at the University of Utah. Her work has been published in, among other outlets, *Glimmer Train*, the *Rumpus*, *Black Warrior Review*, the *Master's Review*, and *Hobart*. Her debut novel was *Thin Girls*. *The Hop* is her second novel.